"We have to ge

"I will." Patrick w........ .... Jennie's son along toward the truck. "Stay here." Patrick unclipped the leash from his dog, Tucker, and dropped it to the ground. Then he clicked his tongue again.

Tucker moved with him, keeping beside Patrick's leg in a perfect "heel" where he tracked with every footstep Patrick made.

They were partners. Each one watching the other's back.

The gunman shoved Nate toward the truck.

The boy cried out, a sound that rang across the mountainside as clear as the night sky. Patrick took two more steps and brought his gun up just as another man emerged from the house.

"Hey!" Jennie screamed down at the valley. "Hey, I'm right here! Come and get me!"

He nearly faltered.

"Mom!" The boy screamed for her, the sound of it so full of fear that it hurt to hear.

A gunshot rang out, whizzing above Patrick's head.

He hit the dirt, and Jennie screamed.

Lisa Phillips
and
Carol J. Post

Duty to Protect

Previously published as *Desert Rescue* and *Trailing a Killer*

LOVE INSPIRED
INSPIRATIONAL ROMANCE

LOVE INSPIRED®
INSPIRATIONAL ROMANCE

ISBN-13: 978-1-335-46294-7

Duty to Protect

Copyright © 2022 by Harlequin Enterprises ULC

Desert Rescue
First published in 2021. This edition published in 2022.
Copyright © 2021 by Lisa Phillips

Trailing a Killer
First published in 2021. This edition published in 2022.
Copyright © 2021 by Carol J. Post

Recycling programs for this product may not exist in your area.

For questions and comments about the quality of this book, please contact us at CustomerService@Harlequin.com.

Love Inspired
22 Adelaide St. West, 41st Floor
Toronto, Ontario M5H 4E3, Canada
www.LoveInspired.com

Printed in U.S.A.

CONTENTS

Lisa Phillips is a British-born, tea-drinking, guitar-playing wife and mom of two. She and her husband lead worship together at their local church. Lisa pens high-stakes stories of mayhem and disaster where you can find made-for-each-other love that always ends in a happily-ever-after. She understands that faith is a work in progress more exciting than any story she can dream up. You can find out more about her books at authorlisaphillips.com.

Books by Lisa Phillips

Love Inspired Suspense

Secret Service Agents

Security Detail
Homefront Defenders
Yuletide Suspect
Witness in Hiding
Defense Breach
Murder Mix-Up

Visit the Author Profile page at
LoveInspired.com for more titles.

DESERT RESCUE

Lisa Phillips

Behold, I will do a new thing; now it shall spring forth; shall ye not know it? I will even make a way in the wilderness, and rivers in the desert.
—*Isaiah* 43:19

To all the dog lovers out there, this one's for you.

ONE

"Come on." Jennie Wilson held tight to her son's hand as they crept down the back steps of the house.

A house where they had been held for hours. Nearly a whole day, if she'd correctly tracked the rise and subsequent fall of the sun.

"Run, Nate. Stay right by me."

His smaller hand gripped hers, fingers tight. Nate was nine years old. It had been just the two of them since she'd found out she was pregnant and the father had split town like he didn't care at all. Since her father had died of a heart attack when Nate was two.

Nate and Jennie.

They didn't need anyone else. Or, at least, they hadn't until yesterday, when gunmen took them from their home after dinner and escorted them here. Left in an empty room, not tied up. The door unlocked. They'd sat there all night and then all day while those two men yelled threats and waved guns around.

She was done waiting for rescue that might not even come. She'd seen those two men out the window, standing in front of the house, talking. Jennie had tugged Nate down the stairs to the back door so they could make a run for it.

Nate stumbled. He inhaled sharply, and she stopped to catch him. But he hadn't gone down, just planted one knee in the ground at the bottom of the stairs and launched back up like he hadn't stumbled. She could've hugged him. The kid wanted to get out of here as badly as she did.

Over his shoulder Jennie spotted a man at the back door, looking out. He was a huge, dark figure, silhouetted by the light inside. But she could see the gun in his hand.

"Come on." Her words were a harsh whisper in the dead of the New Mexico desert night.

The house was set into the side of the mountain, hidden from the town's view. Terrain around them was dust and sagebrush. Shrubs. The occasional growth of sand shinnery oak, which was nothing more than a bush.

There was nowhere to go.

God, keep us hidden. She didn't want their escape to be in vain. Only God could hide them from these men.

"Hey!" The gunman's growl rang out.

Jennie tugged on her son's hand, but in his tennis shoes he was faster than her. They raced together down an incline, what amounted to the yard of this abandoned house. Would she rather be dead than a hostage? Now was too late to ask herself that. The damage was done.

She'd taken the only chance they'd had for escape and made a run for it. Banked on the fact that they hadn't tied her up and that it might mean they weren't willing to hurt her and Nate.

Did I make a horrible mistake?

"Mom."

She saw a white fence rail. "Climb over."

Her son hopped over it. He'd always been independent and never seemed to mind being alone. She hoped tonight didn't change that.

She launched herself at it but the sole of her boot slipped and she felt her shin slide over the wood. Jennie hissed out a breath. She forced the pain away and climbed regardless, the same way she took care of her son even when she had a migraine. Or got up and went to work in the barn, where she fired her pottery, when she was beyond exhausted. The way she saved one twenty-dollar bill every month for Christmas those times things were tight.

Because she was a mom, and that was what moms did.

He waited for her on the other side. She dropped down.

Behind her, she heard the man roar as he raced down the yard. Another man exited the house, his face shadowed against the yellow light from inside.

"Go." Jennie grabbed his hand.

Nate's was already there, fingers curling around hers. So much trust.

They disappeared together into the dark of night. Above them an ocean of stars she'd always loved. This land. The places her mother had walked, and the things she'd showed Jennie before she'd died.

The God she had introduced Jennie to.

Help us.

Those men would catch up. She and Nate needed a hiding place, but there was nothing out here. Mountains stretched up to the right, as though they could touch the night sky above through sheer force of will. To the left, her town sat at the bottom of the valley. Between, there was only desert.

No houses. Not even a tree.

Cold air seeped into her jeans and the thin sweater she wore over her T-shirt. Nate was in his pajamas, as he'd been just out of the bath when the men had burst in. She'd made them wait so he could get shoes and she could tug her boots on.

A gunshot rang out, over to her left.

Too far aside to have been someone intending to shoot them. Were they trying to force her to stop by frightening her? She couldn't let that happen.

"Come on." She was babbling and repeating herself.

"I'm going as fast as I can." His words were breathy.

"I know." Jennie tried to tamp down the fear.

Her shin cried out with every step, shooting fire up her leg, and she thought she might be bleeding. She wanted to tell him she was sorry. So sorry.

She'd worked so hard to keep Nate from the life she had lived as a child. Surrounded by the worst of humanity, people who bought illegal substances and sold those drugs to whomever would buy them.

Now the past had finally caught up to her.

Her leg nearly gave out. She had to stop soon, or she would simply collapse. They needed a place to hide.

Jennie pulled in a long breath and tried to think.

Another shot rang out, far to her right.

She flinched and let out a squeak. Her son whimpered, and she thought he might be crying. Her heart broke, hearing that sound.

Jennie stumbled. She caught herself before she landed on her injured shin and saw the shinnery oak beside her. *Nate.*

She grasped him in a hug and rolled, ducked behind the bush. *God, hide us.*

"Where'd they go?"

Nate sucked in a breath. She tugged him closer, wrapping her arms snugly around his little body. He tucked himself against her. Knees pulled up, hands grasping the sleeves of her sweater. She would thank God every day for the rest of their lives that she had him sleep in fleece-lined sweats and a long-sleeved shirt in winter even though he complained he got sweaty at night.

If they even survived this.

A male voice said, "I don't see them."

Jennie hugged her son and just breathed.

"Go back to the house. Get two flashlights and call it in."

"You wanna tell the boss we lost them? He'll kill us."

"Then don't call in. Fetch the lights and get back out here. I'll need help bringing them to the house after we knock 'em out and hog-tie 'em."

Nate sniffed, tight against her chest.

Jennie touched her lips to the side of his cheek. He was cold. Hungry.

"Fine."

She heard the one leave. That left the other—the one who wanted to tie them up—close by. Jennie figured they'd reached this far by just going for it. They could do that again.

Move and risk him hearing her, or stay and risk him finding them?

Nate squeezed her arm. She figured that meant she should loosen her grip on him. He shifted a fraction but didn't go anywhere. Best kidnapping buddy ever. She'd loved him fiercely since the day she'd learned she was pregnant. Now she thought she loved him even more.

A twig snapped.

They both gasped, tiny noises that sounded like a hundred twenty decibels in the night.

The man moved off, circling around.

When she thought he was far enough away, Jennie tapped her son's back. He shifted off her lap so she could get her feet under her and crouch. Ready to spring into action and defend him to the death.

And she would die.

This man had a gun. Whether he intended to kill her or recapture her didn't matter. She would come out of this only one way if she challenged him.

The moonlight illuminated enough that she could see. A night like this, she knew if they stayed out it would be as bright as daylight with only natural radiance once their eyes adjusted. The minute the other guy showed up with flashlights, all that would be gone.

The man was moving away.

They could head in the other direction, crest the side of this mountain and get to the road. Head back toward town. Flag down a motorist, praying it wouldn't be one of these guys.

Nate squeezed her hand.

She tugged on his.

They moved together, racing up the hill at an angle. Around a bush. She prayed they wouldn't twist an ankle in some creature's hole as they ran and ran, every step farther from that man and his gun.

On the far side of the mountain, the terrain fell away. Jennie gasped. They angled left, taking some animal's worn path.

And then Jennie's foot slipped. The sand slid out from under her, and she fell. Out of instinct, she let go of Nate's hand before she dragged him down, too.

Jennie tumbled end-over-end down the mountain to the tune of her son's heart-shattering cry.

"Mom!"

That had been a child's cry. State police officer Patrick Sanders glanced across the open desert at the base of a mountain.

Had he found what he was looking for?

Tucker sniffed, nose turned to the breeze.

Patrick's K-9 partner, an Airedale terrier he'd gotten from a shelter as a puppy and trained, scented the wind. His body stiffened and he leaned forward. As an air-scent dog, Tucker didn't need a trail to follow. He could catch the scent he was looking for on the wind, or in this case, the winter breeze rolling over the mountain, and search a general area.

Patrick's mountains, the place he'd grown up. Until right before his high school graduation when his mom had packed them up and fled town. They'd lost their home and everything they'd had there.

Including the girl Patrick had loved.

He didn't want to think about her, or what her father had said to him. Patrick shook his head. *Too bad.* He wouldn't get what he wanted. There was no way to not think about her, because Jennie Wilson was the woman he was out here looking for.

He heard another cry. Stifled by something; it was hard to hear as it drifted across so much open terrain.

He and his K-9 had been dispatched to find Jennie and her son Nathan. A friend had reported them missing yesterday, and the sheriff wasted no time at all calling for a search and rescue team from state police.

It figured a girl like her had grown up and gotten married—even if she'd kept her maiden name—and she'd had a child. She had been beautiful in high school, both a good and bad thing. He'd been too young to deal with feelings of that magnitude. Turned out, she was the only woman he'd ever loved.

Was it the son who had called out? It had sounded like a child.

The danger was now. He didn't need to get mired in a past that was nothing but a bittersweet memory to keep him warm on this chilly night. It was January and a cold wind blew through the desert, making thirty-eight degrees feel like twenty-eight. He shivered beneath the collar of his jacket while Tucker trotted ahead on a mission.

The dog had caught a scent and was closing in. The curly fluff on his body shifted as he moved.

Patrick let the Airedale's coat grow out a little in the winter. Not that Tucker worried much about extreme temperatures. He loved ninety degrees as much as he loved snow. Patrick had also never met a dog so happy to be given a task.

As a terrier, it was about the challenge. Tucker had proved to be both prey driven—like fetching a ball—or food driven—like a nice piece of chicken, or even a raw carrot sometimes—when he felt like it. Life was to be lived on his terms, which kept Patrick on his toes, needing to be as in sync with the dog as possible. Sometimes all Tucker wanted as a reward was a second of praise for a job well done and he was good.

Life with Tucker was like a constant conversation.

Right now the dog had to find Jennie and the boy so

Patrick could transport them to safety. Then he intended to get out of town again. Back to his life in Albuquerque and studying for the sergeant's exam.

Tucker tugged harder on the leash, a signal the scent was stronger. He was closing in. Patrick's night of searching for the missing woman and her child would soon be over.

Tucker rounded a sagebrush and sat.

"Good boy. Yes, you are." Patrick let the leash slacken a little. He circled his dog and found her, lying on the ground.

"Jennie."

She stirred. Her eyes flashed open and she cried out.

"No, no." Right now he was just a dark figure leaning over her. "State police. I'm a K-9 officer." Most people softened when confronted with a police dog in a search and rescue situation. "I'm Officer Sanders."

He would get into the rest of it later. After she recognized him.

"Sanders?"

He helped her sit up. "Easy." He crouched, and Tucker leaned over to sniff without breaking his sit.

"This is Tucker. He's a search and rescue dog, here to find you and your son, Nathan."

She gasped. "Nate. I let go of him when I fell. Those men…" She scrambled to her feet, nearly knocking him over. "They're probably still up there. How far did I fall?"

She spun around.

Patrick said, "Sheriff Johns called us here to help find you both. It's our job." He motioned to his dog and figured he'd be reassuring. "Finding people is Tucker's favorite thing to do. He loves kids."

"Patrick."

"Yes, Jennie. It's me." Did she have a concussion? Maybe he should call for a helicopter to fly her to the hospital, but she wasn't swaying or slurring her words.

"You're really here."

He nodded.

"We need to find Nate."

"I have a T-shirt from your house. Tucker can get the scent and find your son."

She blinked. "He's—"

Patrick finished for her. "Nine years old and up there with armed men, right? In danger." He grasped her elbow. "So let's go."

The quicker he got them both to safety, the quicker he'd be able to leave town again.

For good this time.

She stood, seemingly steady enough on her feet. Determined to get to her child. He grabbed the evidence bag from the side pocket of his cargo pants and let his dog smell the contents.

"Tucker, find."

TWO

Tucker set off. The long leash snapped tight and Patrick followed at a brisk pace.

Jennie had to hustle to keep up. Her legs didn't want to move that fast, but she forced them to stick with the harsh pace. *Nate.* Jennie prayed with every step as they climbed up the side of the mountain.

She was so tired. Her head throbbed, and she could feel the sticky wet on her leg. But did that matter, when her son was out there somewhere? He was either alone on the mountain in the dark, or he'd been caught. Dragged back to that house. Or taken somewhere else at gunpoint.

And now this man in front of her showed up? Of all the people in the world, the love of her life—or so she'd thought at one point—was the responding police officer.

Nate.

Patrick might be here, but her son was all that mattered.

Your son.

Did he not know? How was it even possible that Patrick seemed to have no clue Nate was his son?

He'd talked to her father before he left.

The boy Rick Sanders, whom she'd known in high

school, was no more. This was a man, Patrick Sanders the police officer. His youthful features had matured into handsome ones, catching her attention now far more than ever. Or she'd hit her head. Yet she couldn't help but notice he looked…strong.

Jennie had been relying on herself, and God's strength, since the day he'd left town. She didn't need a man in her life now. No, what she needed was Officer Sanders and his K-9 with the vest that read Search and Rescue.

Tucker sniffed the air as he battled his way up the steep trail. Every step the animal took was like a competitive athlete going after that gold medal while he dragged Patrick along. The dog's shaggy coat looked warmer than her thin sweater and he was focused in a way that made her think he was on an adventure. The animal seemed to love his job.

She'd been about to explain exactly who Nate was before Patrick had cut her off, reminding her that finding Nate was the priority here. Was he being purposely obtuse?

He was right, though. They had to find Nate. He was probably so scared.

That had nothing to do with the fact Patrick clearly hadn't wanted to be there for her when she'd found out she was pregnant. In fact, he'd left town without even talking to her. Telling her father that he wasn't interested in being part of her life anymore. Her dad, the criminal, had vowed to stick with her through it while the best guy she'd ever known had deserted her.

Talk about a slap in the face.

As soon as this job was done, he would no doubt

leave all over again. He'd moved on to bigger and better things, this town nothing but a memory.

The thought of him having a new family slashed through her worse than any knife.

She looked for a ring on his left hand, but he wore gloves. Maybe he had a wife. A family. He wouldn't need Nate, or Jennie, in his life. Another woman wouldn't want an old girlfriend and her son showing up.

A whimper worked its way up her throat. Maybe it was better if she let him go on believing Nate wasn't his, and then he would just leave. Life would go back to normal. That might not be fair to him, but it would certainly be easier for her. Why did doing the right thing always have to be so hard?

"Come on, Jennie." He sounded irritated.

She started to reply, but her foot caught on something and she went down. Her injury smarted and she cried out in pain.

"Tuck!" Patrick barked the dog's name as a command.

She looked up. The dog stopped and turned, looking about as impatient as Patrick. She clambered to her feet, Patrick there holding her elbow.

"Quickly but carefully, okay?"

She nodded.

"We'll find your son."

The words cut through her. *Nate.* It didn't matter if Patrick had no interest in him. The two of them were a team, and they would get through this.

He looked down at her, then knelt. "You're bleeding."

She winced as he shifted her pant leg. "It's fine. We need to get Nate back."

He stood. "You're sure?"

She nodded, and man and dog set off again. In the

moonlight, she saw the outline of his gun and shuddered, even though he was a cop.

She looked up at the hill beside them, the steep incline. She groaned. "How far did I roll?"

Surely, the house where they'd been held was just over this ridge. She would get Nate back, give him the biggest hug ever and promise nothing bad would happen to him again. That wasn't realistic, but it didn't mean she wouldn't believe every word she said.

As the dog climbed the hill, practically dragging Patrick behind him, Jennie followed. She kept her gaze on the back of Patrick's jacket.

Walking away. Her going after him. The same way she'd done so many times in high school—the girl with the criminal father and a crush on the football captain, the golden boy. So her life had basically been a giant cliché, which occasionally she thought was amusing. When she wasn't angry at him for leaving her alone and pregnant.

He'd known what her father had been like, and yet Patrick hadn't even told her himself that he didn't care about the baby. He'd left it to her father to give her that message.

Clearly, Patrick's only concern here was getting this assignment done as fast as possible. Hot anger roiled in her empty stomach. But it was better than fear. Fear left a person powerless. Anger was like taking back control. Though, that wasn't more than an illusion, whereas fear was *very* real right now.

God, help me find Nate. Help him not be scared. Don't let him get hurt.

It wasn't Nate's fault that the land they lived on was useful to bad men. Drug traffickers. Neither was it his fault that Jennie had refused to allow them to cross her land. She didn't want armed bad guys anywhere near her son. Thinking they could do whatever they wanted when it was *her* property. She had a right to keep her son safe.

First, she'd called the sheriff. He'd driven out half a dozen times and had even spoken with men on her land. They'd told him they were merely lost. The last time, she'd called the Drug Enforcement Agency.

She was still waiting for a callback.

And then this happened?

Being taken from their house and held at gunpoint was a clear message. *Let us do what we want. Or else.*

She needed to get Nate back before she lost everything good in her life.

Tucker had the scent. He could smell the boy on the wind, and knew he was close by. Now it was just a case of the dog tracking it to the source, where the scent would be strongest. How he could tell the difference between her son Nate's smell in the air, or what was likely embedded in Jennie's clothing, Patrick didn't know. A canine's capacity to differentiate scents was fascinating.

And not something he needed to be distracted by right now. Though that would be better than the full force of being here with Jennie.

Never mind that he'd dreamed of her a million times over the years. He'd even thought about contacting her a few—thousand—times.

He didn't need to lose focus when Tucker was on the long line, working. Still, it was part of Patrick's makeup as a cop to ensure the victim present with him was all right.

"How are you doing back there?" He glanced over his shoulder.

She had on jeans, cowgirl boots and a thin sweater that probably wasn't doing much to ward off the cold.

"I'm…" She hugged herself. "I'll be good when we get to Nate." She glanced up the hill again.

She was bleeding. Might have even hit her head. She'd said something about falling, but she still wasn't slurring her words, so she likely didn't have a concussion.

He'd hear all about what happened in the hospital, when she got medical attention. Safe. Sound. Her and her son.

Why did helping them seem different than what he did for any other person he'd ever helped as a cop?

Patrick didn't have the time to think about it too much. He pulled off his jacket and tucked it around her shoulders, which allowed her to pick up her pace to match the dog's.

By his side now, she said, "I thought dogs weren't supposed to pull on the leash."

"When he's working, it's all about tension. If I let it slacken, he'll lose focus."

"And this is what you do? Rescue people."

Patrick said, "Sometimes. We also go into situations where there may be bad guys hiding, and Tucker will find and flush them out. Recently we did a training course set up like a disaster zone. Tucker is certified to go in when there's been an earthquake or a building collapse. He can be sure-footed even when the terrain is unstable and still find his man."

"Must be nice," she muttered.

"We will find Nate." He glanced up at the top of the hill. Close now. Both of them were breathless. He was sweating, despite giving away his jacket. Most people preferred to be distracted. "We were specifically requested by Sheriff Johns because he knows what Tucker and I can do. And because I know the terrain."

She said nothing.

He acknowledged to himself that the terrain here was definitely proving unstable. And he wasn't talking about the mountain.

Too many of his memories were associated with the town at the bottom of the ridge. Mistakes. Things both of them would probably rather forget. After all, they'd built lives. Separate ones, after vowing they would never part.

He blew out a breath.

Tucker's head snapped to the side.

Patrick watched as the dog picked up on something then let out a low growl.

"What is it?" Jennie whispered.

"I don't know." But he had a free hand poised to reach for his gun nonetheless.

"God, keep him safe."

She whispered the words, and he knew they weren't for him. It seemed too intimate for him to be part of her private prayers. Did she believe now? Good for her that she had faith to fall back on at a time like this.

He'd left his faith behind a long time ago. Right around the time he'd been torn from her life, unable to come back. Not that she'd wanted him anymore. All they'd had? She'd tossed it aside the second things got hard. No longer interested. So he'd walked away from everything.

It had been the most painful experience of his life.

"He's all alone." Her soft voice carried to him on the breeze. But reassuring her could only go so far. He had to find her son. It was the only thing that would truly give her peace right now.

Tucker crested the ridge.

Patrick clicked his tongue and got the dog's attention. They crouched at the edge, side by side, and looked over.

"That's the house." She pointed to a structure tucked against the hillside to his left. A floodlight had been turned on, illuminating the yard, which was nothing more than the same sandy dirt and scrub brushes.

Except for a truck parked out front. Engine running. Door open so the dome light was on but there was no one inside.

"How many men were there?"

She sucked in a breath. "Two that I saw. But I thought I heard more voices than that." Fear lived in the quaver of her voice.

He'd never known what it felt like to be so scared and hoped for her sake that her son would come out of this unscathed. If Patrick could help him through it— before he left town when they were safe again and he was back in Albuquerque—then he'd do what he could. Maybe it would be enough to keep the kid from having nightmares.

"How many rooms?"

She briefly described the layout, but it sounded like she'd seen only part of the house. "I'm sorry. They shoved us in one room, and then when we left we just found the closest door and ran for it."

"Why did they want you? Did they say—"

The back door swung open.

One man strode out, dragging a smaller person with him. A child.

Her hand grasped his arm. To get his attention or for solidarity? He didn't know. She whispered, "Rick."

The name she used to call him, so long ago. There

wasn't time to absorb the way it reassured him. Warmed him, even.

"We have to get him."

"I will." He watched the man tug the boy along toward the truck. "Stay here." Patrick unclipped Tucker's leash and dropped it to the ground. Then he clicked his tongue again and patted his leg.

Tucker moved with him, keeping beside Patrick's leg in a perfect heel, where he tracked with every footstep Patrick made.

There was no time to call for backup or check if he even had a cell signal right now. If he and Tucker were going to take this guy down and get the boy out of harm's way it would be together. In lockstep.

They were partners. Each watching the other's back.

Patrick kept his head low, weapon drawn, in a jog that ate up the sandy dirt between him and the truck. Jennie's son.

He'd have only a split second to react when the man saw him. Patrick would have to take that second and use it to his advantage. Act before the man could hurt Nate.

The gunman shoved Nate toward the truck.

The boy cried out, a sound that rang across the mountainside as clear as the night sky.

Patrick took two more steps and brought his gun up just as another man emerged from the house.

"Hey!" Jennie screamed down at the house. "Hey, I'm right here! Come and get me!"

Patrick nearly faltered. What was she doing?

"Mom!" The boy screamed for her, the sound so full of fear that it hurt to hear.

A gunshot rang out, whizzing above Patrick's head.

He hit the dirt and Jennie screamed.

THREE

She hit the ground and dirt wafted into her mouth. Jennie spat, getting back up to her knees immediately. "Nate!"

Patrick was already up, staying low as he ran toward her son with the dog close to his side. Headed right for the man with the gun. "State police! Put it down. On the ground. Put the gun down, now!"

She didn't even have a gun and she wanted to obey him. His voice carried that much command.

The gunman with her son froze. Nate cowered by the truck wheel, the engine still running. It hurt to see him so scared, even as her brain reminded her that it was good he'd curled into a smaller target. Patrick might not know who the boy was to him. *Should have told him.* But he would protect Nate.

"I said, put it down!"

She caught movement to her left, out the corner of her eye. Another gunman had emerged from the house. She couldn't make out his features, but the stance wasn't friendly. The second man held a gun in one hand, down by his side. Had Patrick seen…

"Hands on your head!" Busy ensuring their safety

by disarming the first bad guy, Patrick hadn't even acknowledged Nate yet.

The man by the house raised his weapon.

Jennie grasped a palm-size rock and stood, hefting it
as she rose so that the rock sailed across the distance between them and hit the second man square in the chest.
Thank you, softball. The man yelped and staggered back.

His gun went off as he reeled. Patrick fired a round
of his own, causing the man to pitch forward and stumble down the stairs. The gunman toppled to the ground,
where he lay moaning. Patrick glanced from the bad guy
beside him to the one at the house.

But it was too late.

The man by him launched up and into the front seat of
the truck. He hit the gas and the vehicle lurched forward.

Nate dove out of the way, and Jennie had to watch
in horror as the truck raced past. The wheel, so close.
She tore down the mountainside to her son. He hit the
ground, well clear of the truck as it sped closer to the
house.

"Thank You, God. Thank You." She fell to her knees
and gathered up her son in her arms as she watched the
second man, the one Patrick had shot. The last thing she
wanted was for any of them to get a bullet in their back.

Nate was safe—or would be in a second. That was
what counted right now. The rest would come later, when
she figured out why Patrick didn't seem to think Nate
had anything to do with him. She wondered why he
didn't know Nate was clearly his son. He'd known she
was pregnant the night he left town, right?

The truck slowed. Patrick raced toward it, Tucker
running fast beside him. Jennie watched as the second
man, the one she'd hit with the rock, clambered up and

hauled himself over the side of the truck, narrowly landing in the bed.

Patrick yelled after them but didn't shoot.

Jennie almost wanted him to. These men had kidnapped her. They'd terrorized Nate.

She twisted to look down at him, then shuffled the boy in her arms to lay him down. "Patrick!"

He ran over, commanding the dog to "guard" as he dropped to his knees beside her. "What is it?" Patrick grabbed something from his belt. He flipped a switch and the flashlight illuminated. He moved it so the side of the beam lit up her son's face. "He's unconscious?"

Jennie just nodded as tears rolled down her face. "He must have rolled and hit his head on something. I thought he was just getting out of the way of the truck."

He squeezed her shoulder. "I'll call for—I have no signal."

"It's spotty up here." She patted Nate's face. "Baby, wake up. Mama's here." He didn't like her calling him "baby" since he considered himself a big kid these days. A young man, even. He puffed up when the pastor called him that.

"Maybe there's a phone in the house?"

She didn't know if Patrick wanted an answer to his question. She kept patting Nate's cheek, praying at the same time that he'd just passed out for a second. Shock, not a concussion. "Come on, Nate. Wake up."

He moaned and shifted, his eyes fluttering.

"Hey." When she saw his eyes fully open, Jennie couldn't help but smile. "There you are." She touched her forehead to his, then kissed him, being careful to keep it light just in case he'd hit the back of his head. "Hi, baby."

His brows drew together. She saw the objection in

his eyes before he'd even finished the thought and knew then he didn't have a concussion.

"I know. Don't call you 'baby.' Give your mother a break, okay? It's been a long day." She sat back out of sheer relief, toppled over and wound up slumped against Patrick. Snug in his coat. No gunmen in sight. She was almost giddy, even though they were miles from anywhere with no way to get there except their legs.

Thank You, God.

Nate sat up.

Both of them reached for him. Patrick said, "Easy."

Nate stiffened. "Are you…?"

"I'm a cop." Patrick shone the flashlight on the badge clipped to his belt. "And this is Tucker. He's a cop, too. He's the one who found you after your mom—"

"You fell down the mountain!"

"I know." Jennie groaned, and all the fear and grief rushed back. She didn't know what to do with it and more tears rolled down her face. She gathered her son to her in a hug and reveled in the feel of him.

"I thought you…" His voice thickened and he coughed.

"What happened after?" She leaned back to look at him. She had to know. "Did they hurt you?"

"One of them grabbed my arm and dragged me back to the house." Tears trailed down his face, too, and Patrick handed her a pack of tissues from one of the pockets of his cargo pants.

"He said the boss didn't care about you. He wanted to see *me*. Why, Mom? I don't want to see him."

Jennie touched the sides of his face. "No one is going to take you from me. He didn't, right? I was here. So was Patrick, and Tucker."

Nate's gaze flicked to the man beside her and she saw him make the connection. Yep. He'd heard the name Patrick before. That was her smart little boy.

She said, "You're safe now, right?"

He nodded.

"Tell me what happened."

"You saved me. You, and Patrick. And Tucker." Nate motioned to the dog, who lifted his head. Ears pricked.

Patrick said, "That's right."

Nate stared at him.

Tucker inched forward, his belly still on the ground. He sniffed and then licked Nate's arm. Her son jerked and then chuckled. Sounding more like the little boy from a few years ago than the third-grader she had on her hands nowadays.

Patrick said a soft, high-pitched "Yes" directed at Tucker.

The dog lifted to stand, his face level with Nate's. In one long swipe, he licked Nate from his chin to his hairline.

The boy erupted into laughter, winding his arms around the dog's neck. She saw Patrick give Tucker a hand signal and figured with the open palm that he'd asked the dog to stand still for a hug.

Her heart melted.

No matter what they'd been through tonight, she was glad for this moment. God had brought Patrick and his dog here. Something that had made Nate laugh. They offered more comfort than she could provide right now. *Thank You, Lord.* It was an unexpected gift she would be forever grateful for. Regardless of how things might turn out, this meeting had been sweet.

"Patrick…" she began, no clue how she was going to

ask him why he didn't seem to care, or maybe even realize, that Nate was his son. Maybe this wasn't the time
for that conversation anyway.

Before she could continue, he stood. "I'm going to
check the house for a phone. Tucker, guard."

Patrick made a quick search of the house. Thankfully
it was small, barely larger than a cabin. Jennie and Nate
had spent hours here, fearing for their lives, while two
men with guns burned coffee in the kitchen.

He wanted to see me.

The boy's words reverberated in his mind. The gunmen had been waiting for something. Or, more likely,
someone. If they'd had no cell signal, the two men had
likely hung here waiting for their boss or some other
person to arrive. After that, who knew what would have
happened?

He didn't want to know and was glad it hadn't come
to that.

Patrick wrinkled his nose at the coffeepot on the
counter—the source of that smell—and headed back out,
more than ready to personally guard Jennie and her son.

He strode back to them. "No phone inside. We'll have
to walk to my car. I'll drive you two back to town, to
the hospital."

Jennie nodded.

Patrick crouched in front of the boy. "You okay,
buddy?"

The edge of fear was still in Nate's eyes. "Are you
really a cop?"

Patrick could understand Nate's hesitation to go with
him—a stranger with a gun—after being held by two

of them. Yes, he was far different than those men. He had a badge, after all. But fear wasn't normally rational.

He kept his voice soft. "I am a cop. I know you're scared, but Tucker and I are going to make sure you and your mom get to safety. No more bad guys, okay?"

Nate nodded, relief in his eyes. "Okay."

Patrick glanced at Jennie. She looked like she wanted to say something, and he figured he knew what it was. Something that might put the boy's mind at ease.

"You know what?" Patrick asked. "Your mom and I are actually old friends. We knew each other in high school."

"Your name's Patrick?"

Jennie said, "Um…maybe we should…" Could be she was embarrassed because she'd done nothing, said nothing, when her father had run Patrick and his mom out of town.

Patrick glanced at her son. "Yes. I'm Patrick."

The boy stared up at him. "Patrick is my dad's name." He then looked to his mom.

Patrick just stared at the little boy.

He heard Jennie whisper, "Rick."

The name, *her* name for him, sliced like a blade. He sucked in a breath and turned to her. "What…?" He couldn't formulate a question. Didn't even know what to say.

"Patrick…"

He glanced at her. "What…is this?"

"This—" she touched the boy's shoulder while the kid looked up at him with wide eyes "—is your son. Our son. The one my father told you about before you left town."

Patrick stared at Jennie. Her father had told him… what?

Jennie blinked. "Please say something."

He had a son?

Or was he supposed to ask "Why didn't you tell me?" or "Why didn't you try to find me?" Patrick couldn't voice either, and didn't know if he should in front of a son he hadn't even known about.

"He ran me and my mother out of town."

"Which left me alone and pregnant." The hurt on her face was apparent.

When he hadn't even known anything about this?

His brain couldn't catch up to what was happening, let alone have a coherent thought right now.

All this time. I had a son.

Did she think he wouldn't have stuck around? Or asked her to *go with him*? He'd done one of those, suggesting she run with him, but she'd chosen her father out of fear.

And she'd raised her son in the town where that man—her own father—sold drugs.

"I'm guessing your father just *loves* the fact I'm his grandson's dad."

Nate's face dissolved.

Jennie sucked in a breath.

Patrick wanted to call the words back. As if that was even possible. "I'm sorry. I'm sure you all have a wonderful time at family dinners."

Now he was making it worse.

Tucker whined.

Patrick rolled to his heels and stood. "It's best if we head to my car. We can talk on the way, okay?" He held out his hand to Nate. What did he say to a boy he'd just met, who was his son? He was in shock.

Thankfully the boy took his hand and Patrick helped him to his feet. He didn't let go of the kid's hand. Instead, he shook it. As though this were some kind of official meeting, and they weren't standing outside an abandoned house after he'd been kidnapped.

"It's really nice to meet you, Nate." Patrick meant it. Regardless of what Jennie had done, the years she'd denied him the chance to know his own child—and how that made him feel—the boy didn't deserve to be in the middle of that. She'd known she was pregnant and she'd still chosen to stay with her father?

This was unbelievable. He deserved an explanation, but that would have to come later. When they were safe.

Patrick crouched so he was nearly eye level with the boy. "I'm glad you're all right, and that I could be the one to make sure you're safe."

"It's...nice to meet you, too."

Patrick straightened and Nate stared up at him.

"Am I gonna be as tall as you?"

Jennie touched his shoulder. "If you are, you'll eat me out of house and home. I'll be broke." She laughed, but Patrick didn't totally believe she thought this was funny. Still, he knew her attempt at humor worked when Nate relaxed and turned to her.

"I'm having a growth spurt."

"You're *always* having a growth spurt."

Patrick grinned, not really feeling it but needing to do what was best to put Nate at ease right now. When he glanced at Jennie, he saw the same need in her eyes. The times she'd smiled for her son, or reassured him, when circumstances were far from good.

"Are you okay to walk?"

Nate nodded. Jennie said, "I think so." She touched her temple. "My head hurts, but I'd rather get out of here."

Patrick snapped the leash back on Tucker and then led the way, the two of them behind him. Holding hands. Reminding him they had a connection without him. He'd been denied knowing his son, while they'd lived for years sharing that bond of family and unconditional love.

Jennie had lied to him, withholding the fact she was pregnant the last time they'd spoken. Then she hadn't even responded to his letters.

She'd basically told him she'd wanted nothing to do with him. Then he'd made his last-ditch effort to convince her, and she'd had her father try to pay him off while he ran Patrick's mother out of town in a grab for her land.

Now it made sense. Jennie had known she was pregnant. Her father had offered him a payout. Money Patrick hadn't accepted and was certain her father would never have parted with anyway. Because her father had wanted him out of the picture? He'd wanted to… What? Raise the boy himself?

Patrick shuddered. He'd been manipulated.

There was far too much bad blood between him and Jennie to ever salvage anything from their past, despite the fact the attraction remained.

She and Nate could have died tonight. He was tempted to thank God he'd been the one sent here. But he didn't believe anymore.

A loving God would never have allowed Patrick to leave town not knowing Jennie was pregnant with his baby. Her father had wanted Patrick out of her life but had never gone that far before. Patrick now understood why he'd suddenly been willing to part with so much money just to get rid of him. Patrick hadn't accepted the money. Her father had been so eager to see him gone.

Patrick was going to make sure he had the relationship with his son that he'd always wanted with his father. Someone who made him feel safe and loved.

That was what he'd tried to give Jennie, in his own way. How many times had he told her they'd needed to get away from her father?

Now, he didn't want anything to do with her. He would be Nate's father, but Jennie was not going to be part of Patrick's life.

Not after what she'd done, keeping the truth from him.

"Patrick!"

The second she called out, he realized why. A vehicle made its way up the road, headed for the house.

"Come on. Nate, Jennie. We need to run!"

FOUR

He didn't even care. Jennie could think of nothing else. She was right. He'd acted shocked, but that was probably only for Nate's benefit. She kept hold of her son's hand as they hustled to Patrick's car.

Every sound. Every shuffle, or snap. Jennie whirled around, expecting a gunman. Meanwhile, beside her, Nate walked straight. Eyes straight. Body taut.

They'd finally outrun their pursuers.

She squeezed Nate's hand. "Hey. You okay?"

He nodded, and a million questions roiled through her head. Why had they been taken? Who was behind it? What had they been waiting for? Who was the "boss" and what did he want with Nate?

"Hungry?"

No answer.

"Yeah, me neither," Jennie said. "Hot chocolate, though. Now that sounds like a good idea."

He exhaled, and she might've seen a flash of a smile. Her eyes had readjusted to the darkness so she could make out her son's features.

Him. Her. They were the whole world as far as she was concerned. They had Jesus, so what else did they need? Some might think that was a cliché, but for the two of them it was everything.

The man walking with his dog in front of them, leading them away from danger, wasn't part of their lives.

She figured Patrick probably had as many questions in his mind as she did. Yes, they'd sprung the news on him at a bad moment. Not the worst, just bad. Compassion meant she should try to see things from his side, but the truth was that he hadn't wanted to know. Why be so surprised about his son now? It didn't make any sense to her. Obviously a nine-year-old boy was his. What kind of a girl did he think she had been back then?

Her father's daughter.

She hadn't been that girl since her dad had died. Since her brother had joined the army and never written. Never called. Jennie had long since realized she had no one but herself and Nate.

The last time she'd tried to find Patrick, she'd gone so far as to hire a private investigator. Never mind that Patrick hadn't seemed to want to know. It was the right thing to offer him a relationship with his son.

The investigator had happily taken a chunk of her inheritance money. A few weeks later he emailed to say he hadn't been able to find Patrick Moreno.

Officer Sanders.

No wonder, considering he'd changed his name. Why had he done that? Though, shouldn't a private investigator worth his salt be able to find someone even after a name change? If he'd been in witness protection, or something, Patrick would never have come back. But he had. So how hard could it have been to find him?

Apparently, she'd just needed to be kidnapped.

"Mom."

She glanced down, realizing she was squeezing her son's hand too hard. "Sorry, bud."

Patrick clicked the locks on his small SUV. He loaded Tucker in the back, and then held the door while Nate and Jennie both climbed into the back seat.

When he got in, he turned and asked, "Are you cold, Nate?"

"A little."

Patrick stared at him for another second, as though absorbing the sight of a boy he now knew was his son.

I'm sorry. The words stuck in her throat.

No matter what justification she felt for the fact he hadn't known about Nate, she did feel guilty he didn't seem to have known. He'd been genuinely surprised, flipping upside down everything she thought she understood about what had happened the night he'd left.

What her father had told her.

He really hadn't known she was pregnant?

Patrick started his vehicle and set the heater to full blast.

Jennie wound up taking off Patrick's jacket before they got to the hospital, where he turned to her. "You guys go in. I need to call the sheriff."

Jennie shoved the door open. As Nate climbed out, the dog whined, his nose against the wire that divided the seats from the trunk area.

Nate said, "Bye, Tucker."

Patrick glanced over. She knew that look on his face. The first expression that even resembled the boy he'd been. Sure, his features were the same. But he'd grown up so much. Nine, nearly ten, years and he was…a man. A handsome man.

Nate and Jennie walked into the hospital and got

checked in. When she mentioned they'd been kid-napped, the woman at the desk blinked then snapped up the phone. "I should call Sheriff Johns."

"He's already been called," Jennie said. "There's a cop outside. I think he'll be in shortly." She realized that she didn't know if Patrick was planning on coming in. He hadn't said that, specifically.

"He's my dad." Nate's chin lifted. "He's a *cop*, and he has a *police dog*."

The double doors whooshed open. Jennie turned and watched as Patrick strode in. Nate tugged at her hand. She let go, and he moved to his dad.

Jennie winced. But it was too late.

Nate slammed into Patrick, arms wrapping around his middle. Patrick lifted the boy up. Nate immediately tucked his head into his father's neck, one hand grasp-ing Patrick's shirt.

"Ma'am."

Jennie spun around and saw the nurse.

"If you'll come this way."

She wasn't going anywhere without Nate. Jennie held out her hand…but Patrick would have to put him down. She dropped her hand to her side. Wow. She might actu-ally be jealous. No, she was just exhausted. They'd been through a horrifying day.

"Let's get you seen to." The woman led her to a bed, surrounded by a curtain. "I'm sure your husband will take good care of your son."

Still, as the woman ushered her in, Jennie turned to Patrick and mouthed, *Be nice.*

He frowned and carried their son to the next bay. Jen-nie tugged on the curtain so she could see. Patrick laid

Nate on the bed. He grasped for his father's hand and scooted over so Patrick could sit beside him on the bed.

It was the trauma. That was why he was latching on to Patrick—who hadn't even looked at her. She'd told her son plenty of stories about his dad. After all, what child wouldn't be curious about an absent parent? He'd seen pictures of his father. Heard all the stories about Patrick's football team wins. Now Nate never missed a home game.

His father was here. Everything he'd ever wanted. And on a night like tonight? She didn't blame him for holding on tight. This man had rescued him.

So why did Jennie feel like she was going to be sick?

The doctor pulled back the curtain. "Nathan Patrick Wilson?"

Patrick stiffened, hearing his own name as his son's middle name. Nate stiffened as well, which he figured was for a whole different reason. Patrick shifted on the bed to face him. "Hey. The doctor just needs to make sure you're all right. Okay?"

Nate looked at him. "Mom's the one who's bleeding."

Maybe it was fear, or maybe he was the kind of male who needed the woman he cared about to be seen to first. Either way, the outcome was the same.

The doctor glanced at Jennie in the next bed over. Then he looked back at Nate. "That your mom, Nathan?"

The boy nodded.

"I'm going to have a nurse take a look at you while I look at your mom's leg. Is that good with you?"

"Yes."

Patrick figured the doctor had read Nate's wariness. That was a good quality in someone who needed to treat injuries and illnesses but also had to have a care for the emotions and mental state of his patient.

The nurse checked out Nate, who had a few scrapes and bruises along with a sprained wrist. It was the bump on the side of his head—one that neither Patrick nor Jennie had noticed in the dark—that worried both her and the doctor. Nate was admitted overnight, while Jennie was cleaned up. Her leg was bandaged, but her injured head needed pain pills.

She came over and sat on the end of Nate's bed.

The nurse gave the boy a shot to calm him so he could sleep and, minutes later, his eyes fluttered closed. He fought it. Struggling to stay awake. "Mom."

She leaned over and kissed his cheek. "Good night, buddy."

Patrick knew Nate had been in good hands with his mom. And yet she'd denied him the chance to know his son. "You should have told me."

"I thought you knew." She gritted her teeth, whispering back, "And I *still* tried to find you anyway. Now, right when we're kidnapped, here you are. Waltzing in with your *dog* to save the day. Well you can go back the way you came. We didn't need you before, and we don't need you now."

He laughed, but there was no humor in it. "Not happening."

She really thought he would leave when he'd just met Nate? No way. Seriously. *No. Way.* Not in a million years.

"So tell me why you were kidnapped, and maybe I can figure out exactly how much danger you put *my* son in."

She shook her head and got up. The second she put weight on her leg, she winced.

"Sit back down."

"Don't tell me what to do." She glared at him. "You chose to leave. I did the best I could, alone and pregnant, with no one but my *father* to ask for help." She kept her voice low, so she didn't wake Nate, but her tone dripped with angry sarcasm. "You can probably imagine how that went. But you don't know. Because you weren't there."

"Is he why you were kidnapped? Some kind of turf war?"

Her father was a drug dealer the sheriff hadn't managed to put in prison while Patrick was in high school. If things were the same, Jennie was probably still caught in the middle all the time. And Nate? Patrick didn't even want to imagine what back-and-forth the boy had been subjected to.

"That would be difficult. Since my father died when Nate was two. He doesn't even remember his grandfather, so I'd appreciate it if you quit bringing him up."

Her dad was dead?

"And you still didn't find me."

"That would be difficult, *Officer Sanders*. Considering I didn't even know your name. Why did you change it?"

Patrick said, "That's why I wrote you all those letters. So you'd know how to find me. In case you changed your mind, which is what I was hoping. But I never heard back from you."

"Maybe that's because I didn't get any letters."

He was about to reply in kind, his tone now hard as hers and just as sardonic. But Nate rolled over in his sleep and tucked himself against Patrick's side, his hand on Patrick's arm.

He stared down at those small fingers. Tiny nails, smaller than he'd ever seen. A scar on the knuckle, long since healed. Evidence that he'd lived a life.

One Patrick had missed.

Jennie said, "I tried to find you." After a pause, she added, "You knew where I was."

He'd also known who she'd lived with—a father who had no moral compass and an even lesser desire to do anything but make money by any means necessary.

He lifted his gaze to hers and saw tears in her eyes. "I didn't know I had a son."

Pain flashed in her eyes. He realized the implication of his words. He'd have come back for Nate, but not for her. The truth was, that had proved correct. He'd stayed away. Because of her father.

His mom had taken him to Albuquerque to stay with his aunt. Changed their names to his mom's maiden name, Sanders. She'd gotten a job as a waitress and he'd worked while going to school. Twice as hard as everyone else. Twice as determined to become a cop and put men like Jennie's father away.

"Now I do. Your secret is out, and I know about Nate."

Patrick had to let go of the pain. Get along with her, enough that Nate could have some semblance of a peaceful life as he was shuffled between his parents.

The curtain fluttered and a nurse appeared. She stepped aside to admit the sheriff.

Bitterness left a sour taste in Patrick's mouth, but he swallowed against it. "Sheriff Johns."

The old man nodded. "Officer Sanders. You found them. Good job." He glanced at Jennie.

She tried to smile.

Johns looked back at Patrick. "Everything okay?" He frowned. "Is Nathan okay?"

You mean, Nathan Patrick Wilson? He wondered if the old man knew he was Nate's father. Could be he'd planned this. Brought Patrick here, so he could meet them. Probably not. Maybe the reason was far more sinister.

Patrick turned to Jennie. "Tell me who those men that kidnapped you were."

Her mouth dropped open and she paled. "You think they'll come back?"

"Now, Officer—"

Patrick interjected, "I'm taking a witness statement, if you don't mind."

"I do mind." Johns rocked to the balls of his feet and then back. "You were brought here for one search and rescue job. You found them, and now they're good. You can go, Officer Sanders. Before I call your lieutenant in Albuquerque and tell him you overstayed your welcome in my town."

Patrick just stared at him.

What was going on?

FIVE

I didn't know I had a son.

Jennie wanted to collapse into the nearest chair and just cry. At least now he knew her father was gone.

She looked at her son, holding his hand while the sheriff and Officer Sanders—it was much better to think of him like that—duked it out over who was going to talk to her.

"Go ahead and call my lieutenant, Sheriff. I'll wait."

Jennie heard Patrick shift and glanced over to see he'd folded his arms. Determined. Refusing to back down. Exactly the kind of man Nate needed in his life. Someone who could teach him to be a good man. Patrick hadn't been there for her when she could have used that kind of man in her life. None of the other men around her had been anywhere near good. Not her dad. Not her brother.

Patrick had been the breath of fresh air she thought she'd needed back then, even if it hadn't lasted. In comparison, her brother, the train wreck, had disappeared just after he'd graduated high school—right before her junior year—and joined the army. She'd only seen Martin once since, but on several occasions he'd called, asking for money. One time he'd been in a jail cell in Georgia, needing to be bailed out. But all that was years ago. Until last summer, when the army called her a few times.

She hadn't called them back.

Martin hadn't been a part of her life for years, and she had no intention of inviting him in again now.

The sheriff's words cut through her thoughts. "—do you hope to achieve here? You've done your job."

"So you insist on pointing out."

Was he going to tell the sheriff that Nate was his son? Jennie didn't think that was any of the old man's business. Especially considering the way he'd tiptoed around the problems she'd been having out on her property.

Jennie twisted to face the sheriff. "I've asked Officer Sanders to help me and Nate." Yes, it would be because Nate was his son. And no, she hadn't specifically asked him. But Patrick was on board, even if he intended to blame her through the whole thing.

She continued. "The same men who've been trespassing on my land took me and my son from our house. They kept us overnight, trying to scare us. They chased us. They shot at us. And I think they were going to take us to meet someone." She folded her arms, trying not to talk so loudly she woke Nate. "I don't want them coming back, or trying again. I want Nate to be safe."

"It's over now," Johns said. "There's no reason to believe you're still in danger."

"And when they drive onto my back forty again, causing trouble, making noise and a mess? What then?" She didn't go there much. But that didn't mean she wanted bad guys on her land, or anywhere near her son. "I'm supposed to just let them do whatever they want?"

"They're still out there?" The sheriff glanced between her and Patrick.

"They ran off."

The sheriff huffed. As though Patrick should have saved the two of them *and* arrested those guys, as well. In the middle of a gunfight. "I thought you had a K-9 with you."

Patrick's lips pressed into a thin line.

Jennie wasn't interested in a battle between the local sheriff and Patrick, who represented the New Mexico State Police. What she wanted to know was why the sheriff had been blowing off her concerns for weeks now.

"Have you received any calls from the DEA?" Jennie asked. "I left all the information when I called them, but they never called me back."

The sheriff blinked. "You called the Drug Enforcement Agency?"

"Sheriff—"

Whatever Patrick had been about to say, the sheriff cut him off. "It's trespassers. That's a local problem, and it's going to have a local solution." He shook his head, looking exasperated. "Everyone knows those boys have dirty federal agents on their payroll. You probably tipped off these guys, and that's why they kidnapped you."

"I thought it was trespassers." Jennie tried to look innocent, with a side of oblivious. She wasn't sure it worked. "You're saying they could be drug runners? I know my father used to transport narcotics through town using back roads and people's land. I thought you shut all that down."

Also, since her father had died, a lot of his associates had scattered, leaving a void in town. The rest of what had happened to the drug trade locally...she had no idea. She'd been a busy twenty-year-old single mom trying to figure out how to make enough money to support herself and her son.

Sheriff Johns shrugged. "Who knows what kind of men they were? Could just have been a couple of bikers, or transients. People looking for passage through the back country."

"We know what kind of men they were." Patrick stared down the sheriff. "Both Jennie and I saw their faces. So we'll need you to supply us with your collection of mug shots, and we're happy to ID them."

Jennie nodded. "Yes, we're happy to tell you who it was. Then you can bring them in."

"Good." The sheriff didn't look like he thought that would be a problem, but he also didn't seem happy, either.

She wasn't sure if he was on the up-and-up or not. She'd always thought he was a good guy, or at least tried to be. "Then there will be two fewer dangerous men out there."

Johns nodded. "We try. Right, Officer Sanders? Every day, chipping away at the bad element. The job is never done but we do what we can to stem the tide. Especially in a place like this, where good people live."

Maybe Johns thought *she* had something to do with it. Like this was a turf war and she was some kind of drug queen. Jennie would have been scared if that idea hadn't made her want to laugh out loud.

"And," Patrick said, "we'll know who their associates are as soon as we know their names. Which gives me a shot to identify this boss they were going to take Jennie and Nate to see."

Neither of them mentioned Nate being taken alone. That would come, and she got the feeling Patrick was as reticent to overshare with the sheriff as she was.

Sheriff Johns hadn't protected her. He'd only brushed her off, insisting things weren't that bad. *Just a few high school kids, Jennie. I'm sure of it.* Then they'd come to her house at night.

She noticed Patrick's gaze on her. A slight frown shifted his brows, but she knew if she leaned into his concern, that would just give her permission to fall apart. And that was the last thing she needed to do right now... when she should be strong for Nate.

For Nate.

Patrick would make sure his son was safe, and that was all that mattered.

She was scared. Really scared. Patrick could see the fear on her face, and it made him want to protect her.

He pulled out his phone and typed a quick email to his partner, copying in their lieutenant. He needed Eric here to help him figure this out and he wanted the lieutenant to sign off on it. But he included the personal revelation. No point hiding the fact when he'd later ask for a vacation so he could get to know his son. He had enough accrued days that he would be able to take a couple of weeks off at least.

Judging by the look on Jennie's face, she wasn't going to say no to him hanging around. And if that meant he had his gun on his hip and his dog by his side, she'd probably feel a little better still.

He turned to the sheriff. "So you'll get me those mug shots?"

"Why wouldn't I?"

Patrick clenched his jaw. No point arguing with the man, even if he insisted on making everything a battle of wills. Was he just an old sheriff, set in his ways, or was there a reason Johns wanted to take care of this himself? Sounded like there wasn't. Or, if there was, the man was inordinately slow at getting results.

What was up with that?

Patrick needed more information if he was going to figure out why those men had taken her and Nate, who their boss was and what it had to do with trespassers. But he would find out. Otherwise he'd have to go back to his office, and his home, knowing there was still danger on Jennie's land. Right at his son's doorstep.

"Great. I appreciate the aid," Patrick said. "I'll be sticking around to make sure both Nate and Jennie remain safe until the men that took them are behind bars. Along with everyone they work with."

No, he wasn't a one-man army. Still, he had every reason to see it through. Jennie wasn't married. She was doing this alone when she could have the bonus of someone else there to share the load. As it had been with his mom—also a single mom after his father had died—she very much *could* do it all by herself.

But that didn't mean she *had* to.

The sheriff repeated, "Great." Though from the look on his face things were far from great. "I'm glad for the assist."

If the sheriff of his hometown had *anything* to do with what had happened to Nate and Jennie, Patrick was going to figure it out.

Out the corner of his eye, he saw her take a half step back and glance over. Reacting to his words?

Of course, he was sticking around.

Her eyes were wide with surprise. But why? Obviously he cared about both of them. Nate, more so. There was no sting of betrayal when he looked at the boy. But he didn't want anything happening to either one. Nate needed protection, and he needed his mother with him.

Patrick had no intention of coming between them. Even if he and Jennie had to have a hard conversation about how this could've happened, it wouldn't change what he'd missed out on with Nate. Talking through it would help them get past it. But it wasn't going to get back time.

What was done was done. Now it was all about getting to know Nate and being a good father.

She had to know that.

Patrick said to the sheriff, "I'll send you the location of the house where they were held…"

Johns was already nodding before he even finished. "I'll go there personally and see if I can find anything that will tell us who these guys are."

"I already walked through it once, but I was moving quickly so I might've missed something. Or they could have come back after." His phone buzzed and he looked at the screen. Eric was on his way.

The men could be at the house now. Or they could have cleaned up what was left.

The sheriff might find nothing at all.

Patrick was tempted to thank God that he'd found Jennie, and then her son. That Tucker had caught the scent and Nate was safe in the hospital. But he'd left faith behind as well when he'd left town.

Despite the blessing of now having so much in his life, and it coming so unexpectedly, he couldn't thank God. Not when He was a God that Jennie believed in.

She was the one who'd kept the truth from him. Did God really want that from His people?

The sheriff said, "Both of you, come by my office. I'll get you on the computer so you can look at mug shots. All that stuff is digital now."

"I'm not leaving Nate." Jennie took hold of the boy's hand, as though she was about to be dragged from his bedside. Separated from him against her will.

Did she think he hated her that much?

"I can do it," Patrick told her. "But Nate will be here at least until tomorrow, right? If we make sure he's safe— maybe one of your friends can sit with him—you'll be a help to me. You spent longer with those men."

She got that look in her eyes. The one a witness got before they announced they were refusing to testify and wanted nothing at all to do with the case. Because fear had gotten the best of them.

Patrick said, "My partner will be here tonight. If Nate has a familiar face with him, and there's an officer I trust on the door, could you go with me?"

It was plain in her frown that she didn't like it. "I… Yes. I could do that."

He figured that meant it was possible, though she clearly didn't want to. He couldn't blame her. Patrick hardly wanted to leave Nate's side now that he knew the boy was his son.

He studied the sleeping child, seeing the line of his nose and the set of his eyes. It made him want to cling hard to him and never let go. But what kind of life would that be for either of them?

Patrick stood. "I'm going to walk the sheriff out."

Jennie nodded.

Patrick didn't go far. Just enough that she wouldn't be

able to hear the conversation, but he could still see the curtained-off area where she sat with Nate. She probably needed some time alone to be with him. They'd been through an ordeal, and there was a chance it wasn't over yet.

Sheriff Johns squared up on him, chin raised. "Something you need?"

"Any idea who might be behind all this?"

"Trespassers? No. But now a kidnapping?" Johns shrugged. "I guess you'd better ID them."

"And you're fine with state police working a case in your town?" He'd met more than a few small-town sheriffs. They all had their own way of doing things. And differing opinions on the assistance they'd like from state police.

Except this wasn't assistance. It was Patrick's case now.

"If it keeps them safe, of course." A flash lit the sheriff's eyes. "And you can tell me if she has anything to do with this."

"Excuse me?"

"The daughter of a man who ran the drug trade in this town for *years*." He huffed. "She's either involved, or she knows who is. That's why I called you. So you can use your resources to investigate Jennie's involvement in all this."

SIX

The curtain pulled back. She'd been expecting Patrick again, but it was Beth. Jennie jumped up from the chair as soon as her best friend entered. Relief nearly sent her to her knees. At just a familiar face? Yes, considering this familiar face was the least dramatic person Jennie had ever met.

"Rough night?" Beth probably meant it as a joke, but it didn't sound like she thought it was funny. "I couldn't believe it when I saw the state of your house. I called the sheriff right away." Beth pulled back, her attention on Nate now. "How is he?"

"They gave him something to knock him out. He was pretty stressed. Thanks for coming. He'll need a friend here if he wakes up and I'm not back yet."

"Was that really…him?" Beth wandered over to the bedside.

Jennie nodded. Her friend knew all about Patrick.

"Talk about *whoa.*"

"Yep."

Beth had been new in town when they'd met at the library. Jennie had been there with Nate, around four at the time. They'd instantly clicked. Bonus: Beth hadn't known anything about Jennie's father and his criminal activity. Though she'd told her friend *everything*, which was how she knew about Patrick. Double bonus: Beth had reintroduced her to Jesus Christ and told her how He had saved her.

Jennie had gone to church every Sunday since. Faith was everything to her, and God had showed up time and time again over the years.

Beth frowned. "What is it?"

"I just…" Jennie gathered her thoughts. "I've seen God do so much. Why would I question whether or not He's going to show up, even in this?"

Her friend smiled. "I'm so good at giving counsel, I don't even have to say anything."

Jennie burst out laughing then clapped a hand over her mouth. Her friend gave her another quick squeeze. "Thanks." Jennie blew out a breath. "I needed that."

"After being kidnapped?" Beth shook her head. "I can't believe that happened to you guys. I thought this was supposed to be a safe little town. First, they're trespassing, and then they escalate to kidnapping. I can hardly believe it."

"I'm just glad the sheriff actually called the state police for help."

"And they sent—" Beth glanced at the curtain, then whispered "—Nate's father."

"He knows. Nate was actually the one who said something."

Beth frowned. "Patrick didn't know?"

"He had no idea." Jennie sighed. "Patrick grew up here. It makes sense that the state police sent him."

"And it turns out Nate's dad's a cop. A *handsome* cop."

"Those things will make him a good father?"

Beth said, "You know what I mean."

Yeah, she did. Jennie had to admit the man he'd grown into wasn't just cute. He was pretty much breathtaking. She had to quit thinking about him. She didn't need the distraction. Not when gunmen had held them—terrorized them—for hours.

Mom!

She could still hear him cry out for her when she'd fallen down that mountainside. Tears filled her eyes.

Beth's warm hand touched hers. "You're both safe now."

Jennie thought about Patrick and the fact that he was there. "No, we're not."

Their lives were in danger. Their hearts were in danger.

Though she had no intention of being vulnerable with Patrick, he still represented a threat.

Jennie squeezed her eyes shut. She heard Beth whispering prayers, covering them both with God's love and protection. That strange dichotomy between what they possessed, by virtue of being God's children, and yet being able to ask for those things in even greater measure—and so much more.

Thank You.

Patrick cleared his throat.

Jennie said, "One second." She kissed her son goodbye and exchanged another hug with her friend.

"Beth's already met my partner." Patrick motioned to the man beside him.

Her friend blushed, but there was no time to decipher that as Patrick continued his introduction.

"This is Officer Eric Fields."

Eric wasn't as tall as Patrick, his features darker. He grinned and stuck out his hand. "You're Jennie."

His whole demeanor caused her guard to slip a little. "I'm afraid so."

He chuckled and they shook hands, though his gaze drifted to the still-open curtain and the spot where Beth sat beside Nate. "I'll watch out for Nate. And your friend in there."

Patrick said, "Eric is going to stand guard until we get back."

Considering the badge and the gun, and the fact the guy put her at ease the way a friend should, she nodded. "Okay." She turned to Patrick. "We won't be gone that long, though. Right?"

"Just long enough to get you and Nate fresh clothes and then swing by the sheriff's office to ID the men who held you."

She figured the quicker they went, the quicker they would get back. Hopefully before Nate even woke up. She was exhausted, but still the reserves to get things done for her son's sake kept her going. Soon enough she would crash, and probably sleep for a couple of days.

Would Patrick stay with Nate while she did that?

Eric said, "Nice to meet you."

"You, too."

Patrick led her away. "Let's go. The quicker we get this done, the quicker we can get back here."

She glanced at him.

"What?"

"Nothing. I agree with you, that's all. I actually thought the same thing a second ago."

"Great minds think alike?"

Did he remember? Years ago, they'd constantly had

similar ideas. It had been a pillar of their relationship, that connection. Now, she wasn't so sure. Maybe there was a piece of it still there, but life had taken them in completely different directions. Even if she wanted to salvage something, she wasn't sure there was anything there to work from.

They fell into silence as they made their way outside. Patrick scanned the parking lot, one hand on his gun. Making sure Jennie was safe.

As they approached his SUV, Tucker barked.

"I should take him over to that grass. He's been cooped up for a bit."

She nodded and leaned against the car, watching Patrick walk his dog.

Fatigue weighed on her. Jennie had to fight it off, stomping her feet to keep awake. As a bonus, the movements kept her warm, since she'd given Patrick his jacket back.

Across the lot, a car sat with its engine running. Jennie frowned. The man inside, was he watching her?

"What is it?" Patrick glanced in the direction she was looking while Tucker walked close enough to brush against her leg.

She leaned down to pet the dog's head. "Probably just me being paranoid."

"Maybe."

The car set off and the driver pulled out of the lot.

"Like I said—" Jennie reached for the door handle "—it's probably nothing."

But she wasn't so sure.

When he asked Jennie for directions to her house so he could forgo GPS on his phone, and she gave Patrick the street where she'd lived in high school, all thoughts of that other car disappeared.

His foot let off the gas and he turned to her.

"Yes." The tight tone of her voice matched her body language. "I live in my father's house."

"I'm not passing judgment."

She huffed.

"It's not like you still live with *him*. Right?"

Patrick winced and headed for her place. Probably not the best thing he could have said. Maybe she'd grieved for her father. A lot of people whose parents weren't nice to them, or even good people, still grieved the loss. A bad parent was still a parent. Sometimes they were all a person had.

The house was dark when he pulled onto the lane. Set back from the street, the single-level ranch house had a stucco exterior and red-clay roof tiles.

He parked and glanced over at Jennie. Her eyes were shut, her breathing shallow and steady. He didn't want to wake her but there wasn't much choice. "Hey." He gently shook her shoulder while Tucker sniffed at the open window behind him.

Jennie came awake fast.

"It's okay. It's me."

"Rick?" She glanced around. "Oh. We're here. That felt like five seconds of sleep."

"Sorry. Do you want to take a nap while we're here? Tucker and I can stand guard if you want to rest."

"I don't even want to take the time out to shower." She wrinkled her nose. "But I probably should."

Patrick grabbed his door handle. He didn't need to be distracted by thoughts of how cute she was. The teen girl he'd been so enamored with had grown into a beautiful woman. Too bad he'd abandoned the idea of a relationship. Why be vulnerable again when what they'd had already destroyed him?

"Let me check out the house first. I'd like you to wait by the front door."

"Oh. Okay."

She might not agree, but she did as he'd asked while Patrick gave Tucker the command to roust anyone who might be hiding in the home.

It was a task they'd done a hundred times.

When Tucker returned to him, tail wagging in expectation of his reward, Patrick gave him a rubdown. "Good boy. Yes, you are a good boy."

The dog sat.

Then Tucker raised up to almost shoulder height and snagged the treat from Patrick's fingers. The dog lowered back to stand on all four paws, clearly pleased with himself that he'd earned this unique reward.

Patrick patted his head. "Go play."

"What does that mean?"

He turned to Jennie, who'd shut the front door behind her. "It means we're done with work, and he can just…be a dog." The animal sniffed around, then trotted down the hall. "He's probably looking for Nate, since he knows his scent now."

Jennie trailed down the hall.

Patrick had never been in the house before. The decorations were Southwestern, with lots of color and Mexican tile on the floor. Jennie clearly liked cacti and succulents. Pots of all sizes decorated nearly every surface, even the round dining table.

He found her in the main bedroom, gathering items from her drawers, which she set in a big canvas tote bag. The logo on the side was from Grand Canyon National Park. Patrick found Tucker in Nate's room, sniffing under the bed.

"What did you find, buddy?" He crouched and found a single battered tennis shoe along with two toy dinosaurs. On the wall were posters of zoo animals but the bedspread seemed to be dedicated to his favorite video game.

"I've been looking everywhere for that." Jennie took the shoe from him. "Thanks."

"Tucker is the one who found it."

She rummaged in the closet and came up with a matching shoe. Then she pulled pajamas and clean clothes from the dresser. "I'm surprised Nate can find anything in here."

Patrick grinned. "I'm pretty sure my bedroom looked exactly like this when I was a kid."

He'd been into sports, too, but nature was a passion of his. Animals. Being outside was his preference, and he did it as much as he could—which was fine with Tucker.

Patrick couldn't put into words how it felt to know Nate shared his interests. He knew what they were going to talk about. And what kind of shows they would watch together the first weekend they spent with each other.

The bittersweet pang in his chest shouldn't have been a surprise.

He walked through the rest of the house, despite Tucker's assessment that it was safe and he could relax.

Tucker followed, and Patrick let him out the patio door so he could sniff around there, as well.

Even when he and Jennie had been dating, she'd always come to his house. Mostly when his mom was working—which explained a lot of the trouble they'd gotten into. Being alone with the girl he'd thought he loved had been a heady experience he'd been too immature to realize was risky.

But the result?

He couldn't deny the fact that, without those mistakes, Jennie wouldn't have had Nate. He wouldn't have a son who had suddenly become his whole world. And how was that even possible? He'd gone from not knowing his boy and feeling like he was so alone in the world to having a family. All in one night. Jennie was the girl who had gotten away. Now she would be a part of his life forever, in one way or another.

And Nate would always be his son.

Patrick heard the shower come on. He didn't blame Jennie for wanting to clean up. She'd been kidnapped and injured. She probably wanted to wash off the stress along with the grime of the past day. And it would help to wake her up.

He didn't begrudge her wanting to get back to Nate as quickly as possible, either. Patrick felt the same way.

Ten minutes later she emerged in fresh clothes, her wet hair hanging loose over her shoulders. Patrick slid the patio door open. "Tucker, come!"

He heard the animal's tags jingle before he saw him.

In the distance, multiple sets of headlights flashed across the expanse of land he knew was behind her house.

Patrick stepped outside. He heard Jennie come out after him. She gasped.

"It's them. The trespassers." Fear threaded through her tone. "They're here again."

SEVEN

Jennie needed to get back to her son, not dragged into another kidnapping. The men who'd taken her and Nate had warned her off a few times from "meddling" in what they were up to on her land.

"I'm calling the DEA again." She stepped back inside. "And this time, someone had better call me back."

She was sick of being blown off. Having her instincts questioned, like Johns telling her it was nothing but high school kids. No way. She knew what danger smelled like.

That might sound crazy to some, but she'd been raised in a home with a drug dealer. Her brother hadn't cared one bit. Jennie, on the other hand, had developed an instinct for danger. Grown men in multiple trucks thought they could do whatever they wanted to on her land.

Well, she wasn't going to just stand around and allow her son to be placed in danger. Not again. Where was her phone? She didn't know where she'd put it the last time she—

"Jennie." Patrick snagged her arm and tugged her around until she faced him, shaking her head.

Her breath hitched and only a sob came out. Patrick's expression softened and he pulled her in for a hug. Jennie backed up, shaking her head. "No. Don't." She'd fall apart if he hugged her.

"I'm fine." She wound her arms around her waist.

"You don't have to be."

"It doesn't matter. Nate is the only thing that matters and we need to get back to him." She wiped tears from her face. "After I call the cops."

"Jennie, I am the cops." He pulled out his phone and tapped the screen. "I reported the activity to my lieutenant."

That was it? All her problems solved with a simple message?

Jennie wandered to the hall and grabbed the duffel she'd packed. Her and Nate. Just the two of them. Patrick didn't even care enough to mention the fact she'd made a nice home for her son. He knew the kind of father she'd grown up with. After he'd died, she'd put her heart and soul into this house, redecorating what she had money to do bit by bit. Coloring her walls with leftover paint that the hardware-store owner passed on to her. Yard sales and secondhand-store furniture.

She'd finished it with pillow covers she'd sewn herself. The plants were all in pots she'd made. Experiments and castoffs she couldn't sell. Nate said those were his favorites.

Jennie glanced around the living and dining room. Patrick stood in the center, staring at her. After the shower, she'd put on her favorite shirt, and he hadn't even reacted. He'd loved her when she'd been young and beautiful. Now she was just Nate's mother. A woman he used to know.

"I hated this house when I was growing up."

"I know." Why was he looking at her like that?

She couldn't decipher his expression and there was no point trying. This man was a stranger. "I changed every single thing about it. Even knocked down the wall that used to divide the living room and kitchen, making it open plan."

"You want to talk about renovation right now?"

"No. I want you to know that I made something I'm proud of. A life for our son that has nothing to do with anything associated with my father. Not since he died."

"Okay."

"My brother might've thought what Dad did was cool, but I did *not*. And I don't want it *anywhere near* Nate."

Patrick nodded. "I know you wouldn't put him in danger."

But she had. "I thought I was doing the right thing, calling the sheriff. When he did nothing, it was logical to go up the chain. Call the Feds."

Patrick nodded again. It was like he had no opinion at all. Was this what he did with criminals? Maybe he thought she was lying and this was an interrogation. *Please, Lord.* She didn't want him trying to throw her in jail. Or worse, taking Nate from her.

Dread settled over her. Was that why he was still here?

Patrick glanced at the framed picture over the living room mantel. "Do you have a camera?"

"Yes." She'd taken that picture. Finally, something about her and her life here that he might actually appreciate.

"Get it. We can take pictures of those trucks on your land, get evidence of who they are and show it to the sheriff."

"Are you serious?"

"Quickly, please. We need to catch them in the act." He was looking at her with a soft expression she didn't understand. "You're beyond exhausted, and I'd like to get you back to Nate before I also run out of steam. Otherwise we'll both need sleep right when Nate needs to see one of our faces."

She wanted to make a quip about a son and that special bond they had with their mother. But even "beyond exhausted," she knew that wouldn't be fair to Patrick.

Jennie got her camera. And because she needed help where she would actually get something in return, she also grabbed her Bible. That was the place she should be looking for reassurance and answers. For peace and hope for the future.

Not in Patrick, who'd left once. He'd proved she couldn't trust him. *God, he can't let Nate down. I couldn't bear to watch Nate go through that.* It was the last thing her son needed.

Jennie could withstand a whole lot of hurt. But she knew what it felt like to lose a beloved parent.

It was why she'd done everything she could to make this house a home her mother have loved. All through the process, she'd told Nate stories of his grandmother, who'd passed away when Jennie was in middle school. Then he'd asked about his father. Why hold back from him? She'd had good memories. Now Nate could make good ones of his own.

She just had to keep herself from getting hurt in the process. As much as she could, at least. That meant holding back any feelings she might have for Patrick. Refusing to give in, even the slightest, to anything that had the potential to grow into what it had once been.

Love she'd never forgotten.

That she could never allow to be again.

Patrick needed to get out of this house. Bright colors, small touches that brought the whole place to life. Including the photo over the mantel, his favorite view in all of New Mexico. The mountains surrounding their town, where they'd hiked together so many times.

Compared to his apartment in Albuquerque, this house was a home. Somewhere he'd actually want to return to at the end of the day. Instead of the barren rooms where he "lived" that were nothing more than a place to leave his stuff.

Something snagged his attention on a pot on the floor in the corner. He picked it up and rotated it in his hands. The clay was misshapen, but sturdy. It had been painted royal blue with a dusting of yellow over the top half.

"Nate made me keep that one."

"You made it?"

She nodded, her eyes puffy and her face still damp from her tears. He had to look at the pot again, because she was so beautiful it actually hurt to look at her. "It's beautiful."

"I don't know about that. But he wouldn't let me start over. He insisted we fire it, and he painted it himself. Gave it to me for Mother's Day." She sniffed. "He said he learned at church that God takes broken things and makes them beautiful."

Tears blurred Patrick's vision. His mom had said something similar to him once. She still believed it, but he'd never been able to grasp that truth for himself. Life always held him back from believing.

"We should go." He set the pot down and cleared his throat. "Tuck."

The dog trotted in from the kitchen.

"I'm ready." Jennie waved the camera at him.

"We won't interfere. I don't need you in danger, so you won't be anywhere near the line of fire, but I can't leave without taking a look to see if your instincts were right. Then we'll get over to the sheriff's office."

She nodded. "I trust you."

The words settled like lead might in his stomach. He rubbed his abdomen as they stepped out front and she locked the door. "This is a spare key. I have no idea where my purse or my phone are. And my wallet is in my purse, as well."

"You think they were stolen the night you were taken?" He pulled out his phone. "I can have Eric come and change the locks."

A shiver rolled through her. "Why take my purse and phone? Do you think they're going to, like…steal my identity?" Fear was stark on her face.

"We'll find out." He wasn't supposed to make any assurances to the victim. Not when it was a promise he might not be able to keep. But her saying, straight-out, that she trusted him? Patrick wanted to promise a whole lot.

He loaded up Tucker and then sat in the driver's seat with the engine running while he studied the map on his phone.

In the span of a few hours, everything had changed. He wanted to tell her he'd be there for her. Whatever she or Nate needed. Like requesting a transfer and getting a position in this more northern part of New Mexico. A place he'd promised himself he'd never come back to.

And now he wanted to live here, as close as possible to Nate. Permanently.

As close as Jennie would let him be.

Patrick cracked the rear windows so Tucker could smell the breeze while he drove. He headed for the main road and then took a dirt track that cut across her land and threaded toward the back of her sixty-some acres. "Anything out here I should be wary of?"

She fiddled with the strap on the camera case in her lap. "Just a dozen or so cows. Nate doesn't really enjoy the part where they're taken away. I haven't explained to him about hamburger yet. He likes to name them, especially the babies." She said, "I thought about sheep, but this is the *way* wrong climate for them. Doesn't your cousin live in Scotland?"

Patrick nodded. "Yeah. Neil isn't a sheep farmer, though. He's a cop like me, and a K-9 handler with the Edinburgh police. They use Airedales, as well, which is why I got the idea for Tucker. No one believed me that training a terrier would be worth the work it was going to take, but he's more than proved himself over the past six years."

And not just because he had gotten Nate back, to Jennie and him.

"You never left your home. You just made it your own." He didn't know why he'd said that, but it was out now. There was no taking the words back.

"I love my home. And that's not even about it becoming mine at a time when I had nothing. I couldn't afford to move. Not on what I was making back then, going to art school. Trying to raise Nate." She fell quiet for a second. "Still, I'll always think of my mother more than my father when I walk out here. The house is mine and Nate's now. It doesn't remind me of him at all."

The dirt road disappeared beneath the headlights.

Jennie put her hand on his arm. "Slow down a little."

He eased off the gas. "What is it?"

"A wash."

The SUV dipped down and they traversed what he realized would be a river—if it actually rained here. There was no snow, so no runoff. On rare occasions when the weather was wet, this would be a running stream. Right now it was only a dip in the road.

He hit the gas and they climbed up on the far side, bumping over a couple of ruts. If he hit one too fast, it could bend or crack the axle. Should that happen, they would be in serious trouble.

"I'm not sure how close we'll get," he told her. "I'd rather go in with the lights off, but we might run into a hazard and either get stuck or flip over. And if we leave the headlights on, they'll see us."

He slowed to a stop and studied the terrain. The headlights on the far edge of her land were still a ways off.

"This dirt track goes all the way back there, where they are." Her voice trembled. "But I don't think I want to meet them."

"That's probably a wise choice."

He eased the SUV to a stop and then put it in Reverse. Back to the wash, where they went down onto the dry riverbed and up the far side.

As they crested the incline on the other side, he saw lights to his left. "Someone else is out here."

The lights shifted and one pair split off into two pairs. Four beams. But not spaced the way headlights were.

Those were dirt bikes.

He heard the roar of engines cut over the sound of his own and the noise brought with it a tremor of foreboding. "We need to get out of here."

He'd barely finished speaking when automatic gunfire echoed across the night sky, a rapid *crack, crack* of bullets headed right for them.

A stream of shots slammed into the back quarter panel. Patrick gripped the steering wheel and slammed on the gas.

EIGHT

Jennie twisted in her chair to see where the bullet cracked the window. "Tucker!"

"He okay?" Patrick's voice was strained. "Tucker?"

The dog whined, turning around in the back. Nervous. He barked at the roar of engines.

"It's okay, buddy." Jennie hadn't been around dogs all that much. Tucker put his nose to the wire separating the rear of the vehicle from the back seat. Too far for her to reach. "It's okay." She didn't know what else to say.

"How many are there?"

Jennie surveyed the scene behind them. "Four, maybe. I can't see that well." It was pitch-black. The headlights on the dirt bikes dipped and moved so fast she could barely keep track of them. It reminded her of strobe lighting.

She turned back to Patrick, his gaze pinned on his side mirror. He seemed to be waiting for—

Patrick jerked the wheel to the left. The back corner of the SUV clipped one of the bikes. Blasts of gunshots erupted and the headlight flashed as the bike flipped over.

"You got him."

"I know." Patrick had two hands on the wheel. He seemed to know what he was doing. The confident, capable police officer. But that didn't remove the danger.

There were three more. "I can't believe they're running around like this on my land."

The bikes kept chase.

Patrick said nothing, driving steady. Checking his mirrors every few seconds. "Herding us."

"Off *my* land." Hot anger boiled in her stomach. How many times had she called Sheriff Johns and he'd said it was nothing but teenagers?

That wasn't what this was.

These were adults who thought they could do whatever they wanted on *her* land.

"I'm not leaving. They're the ones who don't belong here." Three bikes pursued them. "They're not trying to kidnap me again. They're up to something here, right? They don't want me to see what it is." She folded her arms and huffed out a breath. "I'm not just going to be some helpless victim."

Not only had she not been raised that way, Jennie wasn't raising Nate that way. Her son needed to know how to be both strong *and* kind. It was rare to find someone who possessed both qualities.

"I know." Patrick's tone was a cross between someone trying to placate a crazy person and someone resigned to a situation they couldn't control. "But that doesn't mean this is the time to fight back."

Excuse me? "You want me to just sit here?"

"Honestly? Yes." He sighed. "I don't want any of us getting hurt by these guys. Right now, they're leaving us alone. If we can get out of here without any more gunshots aimed at us, that's the best scenario. They're letting us leave. See?"

Jennie studied the dirt biker out the left back window. The one on her side had a huge semiautomatic gun strapped across his back.

Stalemate? Was that what this was? She wanted these men—and the ones who had kidnapped her—to pay for the fear now running through her veins. She was flushed, sweating and freezing at the same time. Like her body didn't know what to do.

She never wanted Nate to experience this. Not before, when they'd been in that house, and not ever again.

A whimper left her throat. Patrick reached over and took her hand. He squeezed it, then held it, resting on her knee. "It's going to be okay. They're leaving us alone, and we're almost at the road."

True to his word, they bumped up onto the blacktop. Patrick turned toward the center of town.

"Now we go see the sheriff."

Jennie checked behind them. As they drove away, the three bikers sat at the end of the dirt track—no, there were only two now. Had one gone back, concerned for their friend? They were bad guys. They probably cared about nothing. Except money and the power they wielded over people they considered to be weaker.

"What do they want with *my* land? There's nothing special about it, except that it's just land."

Patrick was quiet long enough she wondered if he would say anything. The second he did, she knew she'd rather he hadn't. "Didn't you say your father had used the back forty to transport drugs across the state?"

"And what would that have to do with me now? It's been years." She was glad he'd let go of her hand for the bump onto the blacktop. She didn't want to hold it ever again. Not if he thought for one second that she would bring drugs into her son's life.

It was because she'd been determined to keep those things far from Nate that they'd ended up in this situation in the first place. Trying to do the right thing. That's what had led to the kidnapping.

She kind of wished she'd been there long enough to meet the boss, as she dearly wanted the chance to spit in his face.

Patrick thinks I'm involved.

He knew how she'd felt about drugs. Selling them, trafficking them. It didn't matter where someone was in the chain, it was *wrong*. The people who supplied that stuff preyed on the vulnerable. She didn't want to be around any of that, and there was no way she'd let it near Nate.

He should know she would never do that. Right? But the truth was, they didn't know each other.

Not anymore.

Patrick mulled over everything on the way to the sheriff's office while Jennie's ire bled away next to him. He knew she was scared. He hadn't expected the anger. She was a force to be reckoned with. A strong woman passionate about keeping her son safe—and she was willing to put her life on the line to do it.

No matter how far they moved on from the past, Patrick would always be aware of what he'd lost.

Could he forgive her?

That would be contingent on her allowing him all the way into their family. He didn't want to muddy things.

Once he'd ensured they were safe, he wanted time to get to know his son.

Right now what he needed was information. That was why he didn't delay ushering her inside the sheriff's office. They could have talked in his vehicle, but why be alone and chance getting sucked further into thinking about her?

He should be doing his job.

"Sheriff." Patrick got his attention and explained what had happened at her house.

Johns lumbered to a side office and leaned in. "Melanie, be a doll and send Ted over to Ms. Wilson's ranch. Tell him to be careful."

"Copy that, Sheriff."

Then he crossed over to a desk and waved them over. "Let's get you all set up here." He jiggled the mouse on an ancient-looking computer and then pecked with two fingers to bring up the database.

"You sit. I need to talk to the sheriff," Patrick said.

Jennie glanced at him but didn't argue.

As she looked through the mug shots in the county database, Patrick motioned for Johns to join him out of her earshot.

"What is it, son?"

I'm not your son. Patrick didn't remind him that it was "Officer Sanders" even though he wanted to. "This seems to be personal to Ms. Wilson. Do you have any idea why that might be?"

This sheriff had been in the job for nearly twenty years now, according to the news article framed on the wall. He had to have known Jennie's father. After all, he'd insinuated she might be involved in all this.

What Johns didn't seem to know was Patrick's personal connection to Nate—and it was none of the man's business. Patrick had no intention of giving the sheriff ammunition to have him pushed aside on this case.

He was all in, until Nate and Jennie were safe.

The sheriff glanced from Jennie back to Patrick. "Have you asked her that?"

"I wanted your take first. As the law in this town, you must have an idea who's behind the trespassing. And I know you don't believe it's just kids."

"We'll see what's what when my deputy reports in."

"A bit risky, don't you think, sending someone out there alone? This Ted person, whoever he is, sticking his neck out. You need to send more men before something bad happens."

"It's as risky as taking a civilian into an unknown situation."

Patrick knew then he wouldn't get far calling this man out. He might be a decent sheriff, but he was also stubborn and prideful.

"What information I choose to disseminate to those private citizens in my care is up to me," Johns said. "And scaring a young single mom isn't how I operate."

"You don't think she should exercise caution? You blew her off and she called the DEA."

"Which put her in more danger." The sheriff huffed. "I told her to be careful, and that didn't mean calling in a bunch of cowboy Feds. We both know how quick they are to shoot first, with no intention of asking any questions later."

Patrick shrugged. "What's done is done. The issue here is what will happen going forward. I've got my partner in the mix, but he's watching out for Nate—which is what I intend to do as soon as Jennie has identified those men. What I'd like to know is what you plan to do."

If something needed doing that wasn't being done, Patrick would move in regardless of the sheriff's wants.

The men who'd taken Jennie and Nate and held them at gunpoint, scared for their lives, would be locked in a jail cell as soon as Patrick located them.

"Put a name to the faces, and I'll go round them up."

Patrick pressed his lips together. There wasn't much point belaboring anything with a sheriff who wanted to do things single-handedly.

Could there really be a drug operation in town, akin to what Jennie's father had accomplished? If there was, Sheriff Johns probably wasn't as in the dark as he pretended. Just to save face? Patrick wasn't sure about that. He was probably used to politicking. Holding things close to his vest and then disseminating information in a way that kept his position and respect in town. If it seemed like he was having trouble maintaining order, it probably wouldn't play well for the next election.

Was he planning on running again soon? That would explain him downplaying drug-trafficking across land belonging to a private citizen.

"Hey."

Patrick pulled a chair up to the desk where Jennie sat. "Hey. You okay?"

"I haven't found anything, if that's what you mean."

"Partly. But I also want to know if you're hanging in there."

Jennie blew out a breath and refocused on the monitor. "I'll be better when I'm back with Nate."

"Me, too."

They shared a smile. Patrick wondered if it would

be the first of many, or if things between them would always be tense.

Jennie gasped. "That's one. I found one."

Patrick yelled, "Sheriff!"

She jumped.

"Sorry." Patrick looked at the picture. A man he hadn't had a clear view of in the dark. "Click that."

Jennie tapped the mouse button.

He raised his eyebrows at the name Carl Andrews. "Wasn't he friends with your brother?"

NINE

"My brother?" Jennie turned, aware of the frown on her face. Given the last day or so, she figured she looked like a recently showered person…who had been through the ringer. Scared for her life. Running across a mountain. Falling down said mountain.

Not exactly date-night ready. But then, she hadn't done that in so long she probably had no hope.

Maybe in another ten years, when Nate was out of the house, she would find a nice man. Settle down. Though, when she pictured that dream, it was Patrick standing on her doorstep with flowers, ready to take her out.

Cue another frown.

"Ms. Wilson."

She blinked and glanced at the sheriff. "I'm sorry… what was that?"

"I asked when the last time you saw your brother was."

How did she even begin to count that? Years. More than a decade. "Longer than the last time I saw Patrick." She saw him wince but kept her attention on the sheriff. "Martin left for the army right out of high school, and he's three years older than me. So it's been a long time."

"He never came back to visit?"

"I called him when my father died," she said. "He never even came back for the funeral."

"Wow." Patrick shook his head. "I remember him being a piece of work, but that takes the cake. The army surprises me, though. He got in so much trouble in high school I'm surprised he managed to have a career in the military."

"I always figured he either straightened up his life and just didn't want anything to do with home or family. Or he dropped out of the army, maybe even ended up in jail again, and still didn't want anything to do with home or family."

Either outcome, same thing. It meant she had no brother in her life. And considering how Martin had treated her—and the things she was pretty sure he'd done for their father back then—she figured that was no loss. Nate didn't need an uncle like that in his life.

"This isn't anything to do with my brother. He hasn't come back to town, right? Or he'd have probably come asking for money." She didn't know how much more plainly to say it. "Carl Andrews and whoever his associate is work for someone. But it has nothing to do with Martin. I can assure you of that."

"Okay." Patrick nodded. "Sheriff, do you know this Carl Andrews? If we have an idea who his associates are, or where we might find him, we'll be closer to bringing him in."

While they talked, Jennie scrolled through the mug shots to try to find the second man. There might be a way for her to look at Andrews's known associates in the police database, if the sheriff had them connected in this system.

She didn't know if that function was even part of this computer program, but it was possible. She'd put together her own database of customers she sold to directly through her website, as well as stores she sold to on consignment. So how hard could it be to find a box to click in this program?

Her thoughts drifted back to her brother. Why? She'd meant what she'd said about this having nothing to do with him. Was that because she didn't want to believe Martin would do something like that to her? Maybe he was angry that she'd inherited everything.

But it wasn't like that was her fault. When the will had been read, she'd found out that the house and all the property, which had been in her mother's name, had been left to her. She hadn't believed it, either. All their father's death had done was pass ownership of everything officially to Jennie. She hadn't even known that her father had withheld that information from her. The land had belonged to her grandfather—her mom's dad. Her father hadn't owned any of it.

Because he hadn't wanted the authorities to be able to seize anything?

Jennie had made it her own. Her father was deceased. There was no point in being angry with him for keeping her home for himself. If he hadn't died from that heart attack, would she ever have discovered the truth?

Jennie studied the photo on the screen. *Not him.* She clicked to the next one and shook off the thoughts that had crowded in her mind.

"Rick." She realized what she'd said and turned. "Patrick." Of course, that was what she'd meant.

He broke off his conversation with the sheriff about BOLOs, whatever those were. "Yes?"

"I found the second man." She got up just for the sake of moving, paced a few steps and turned.

Patrick and the sheriff both stared at the screen. Patrick said, "Michael Danes." He clicked the mouse. "He and Andrews have priors for assault and illegal weapons possession."

Jennie was ready to be done with this whole ordeal. Sheriff Johns and Patrick were both cops. They could take care of Carl Andrews and Michael Danes while she went back to her son and her work. Life would return to normal, but now her son had a father in his life and Jennie had gained the added peace of mind of a cop hanging around the house.

And given what had happened during the past twenty-four hours, he could stay for as long as he wanted. She was ready to feel safe again.

So long as her heart stayed safe, also.

Johns turned to her. "Do you remember either of these guys?"

"Of course. They were the ones who held us in that house." She swung an arm in Patrick's direction. "And they shot at all of us."

"That's not what I mean," Johns said. "Did they work for your father?"

She blinked. Not the question she thought he would have asked her. "How would I know that? It isn't like I was part of his business."

"Maybe you could think back. I know he's been dead a while, but these men might be his associates."

"What would it matter if they were? Like you said, he's been dead a while. Which means that has nothing to do with this—" she pointed at the floor "—what's happening right now, that's putting my son in danger. And you need to do something about it."

"If you were worried about putting your son in danger, then perhaps you shouldn't have gotten involved in the first place," the sheriff shot back.

Patrick started to butt in.

Jennie didn't let him. "I didn't invite them over for dinner. These men dragged me from my house. It's your job to arrest them."

"I'm just glad your actions didn't get your boy killed." Johns shook his head and huffed. "Calling in the DEA. I don't know what you hoped to achieve with that."

Patrick turned to the sheriff. The move put him shoulder to shoulder with Jennie. It occurred to him that it was the two of them now facing off against the sheriff. Not two cops and a civilian. Just Patrick and Jennie, together, as though the rest of the world was on the opposite side.

He had no time to think about how often they'd done that before. Mostly against her father, or teachers who came down on her for being a criminal's daughter, as though her parentage was her fault.

Patrick said, "Now that we've identified the two men, it's time for us to go back to the hospital. I need to check in with my partner, and Jennie wants to see her son."

He left out the part about Nate also being his son. It was still none of the sheriff's business.

Johns held up his hands. "I still need statements from both of you, full written accounts of what happened out there tonight. At the house where you were held, and at your house, Ms. Wilson. So why don't you both take seats and I'll get you some coffee while you write it all down."

Patrick glanced at Tucker, lying in the corner with his chin on his paws. Eyes open, trained on him. He looked about as ready to get out of there as Patrick was.

He checked his phone. "I suppose we can get the paperwork done real quick before we go." When Jennie turned to him, he said, "I'm sure Nate won't wake up until early morning. Isn't that what the doctor said?"

She pressed her lips together and nodded. About as happy to be there as the dog.

"But we won't be having any more cracks about the Feds, okay?" He stared down the sheriff. "What's done was done, and Ms. Wilson did what she thought was best after the *sheriff's department* failed to aid her. Everyone has the right to feel safe in their own home."

"I've been out on her land," Johns said. "All I saw was tire tracks."

"Yes. Because there were vehicles on my land." She lifted her chin. "Ones that didn't belong to me and did not have my permission to be there. Whether you found anything or not, that doesn't mean there wasn't anyone out there."

"I never said you were making it up."

"No, but it seems to me you were supposed to take care of it. You didn't, and my son had a *gun* waved at him. Because he was *kidnapped*."

She strode to the water cooler and stood staring at the wall for a minute, breathing hard.

"This may need to be a federal case." Patrick folded his arms. "Or, at the least, that it's now an investigation that will be undertaken by the state police."

The sheriff started to object. Probably more bluster. Patrick said, "After all, you have a huge county to patrol and I'd guess not nearly the staff to keep everyone who lives in it safe at all times."

"You try doing my job."

To his credit, the sheriff did have the decency to look guilty that Jennie and Nate had been hurt. Still, as far as Patrick was concerned, if he was going to continue doing things "his way," he'd have to accept the fact that Patrick would find it suspicious they hadn't been able to leave yet. And that Jennie had essentially been blown off.

Whether that was because the sheriff hadn't had time to look more deeply into her concerns—and hadn't known they would escalate to kidnapping—or for nefarious reasons, Patrick didn't know.

He needed to make the guy think everything was fine. Patrick grinned. "I don't know if I'd like it. Would I be able to bring Tucker?" He waved at the dog, who lifted his head after hearing his name.

The sheriff glanced at him, then back at Patrick. "Depends. Can he flush out those guys?"

"Yes. If you know where they're holed up."

Johns's eyes widened.

"It's part of his training."

"I thought he just found missing people, like he did with Nate."

Patrick shrugged. "He's had a lot of different training. You'd be surprised what he can do." He was intensely proud of his dog and the fact that Tucker had proved himself over and over again. Yes, that was mostly because he'd been forced to do so. Not many had believed an Airedale could do this job, despite the fact other police departments used them and had since World War I.

Some people didn't like change.

Patrick studied the sheriff as he situated Jennie with a piece of paper and a pen to write out her statement.

Patrick probably would've said he himself was one of those people set in their ways. At least until his entire life had been upended. He would say the sheriff was likely one of those people, too. There were a lot of cops who'd been doing the job for years and did that job even better with twenty or thirty years under their belt. Then there were the ones who'd be doing the department a favor if they put in for retirement.

He knew which one he'd prefer the sheriff here was. Especially considering how he'd likely get in the way as they worked to locate the two men Jennie had identified. The sheriff could cause them a whole host of problems.

Perhaps the man would be content to stick in his office and not mind that it was Patrick and his partner who found Carl Andrews and Michael Danes. Perhaps not.

Patrick's phone rang and he pulled it from his pocket. The screen showed his partner's last name: Fields. He swiped and put the phone to his ear. "Sanders."

Jennie looked over. He mouthed *partner* and she went back to writing. Fast. Maybe as fast as she could so they could get out of there.

"You there, bro?" Eric asked.

Patrick turned away from her. "Yeah, I'm here. Everything good?"

"This middle-of-nowhere desert is really where you grew up? I mean, there are some seriously beautiful ladies out here." He cleared his throat.

"That's Jennie's friend."

"Yeah, her, too," Eric said. "Can't believe you grew up here."

"Keep your focus, okay? This isn't something I need you distracted on."

"Hundred percent, bro. I'm paying attention to the kid. You know, the one with your nose, who I still cannot believe is your son. She really kept it from you? She seemed so nice, and you tell me she's this…what? A bold-faced liar?"

Patrick moved out of earshot, but where he could still see Jennie. "She's not a liar. And yes, I told you he's my son."

"Does Tucker like him?"

Patrick thought back to the dog's reaction to his son. "Yes."

"Good enough for me. He's a way better judge of character than you."

Patrick frowned. "Will you focus?"

"Bro—"

"Pay attention. They were kidnapped yesterday, so you need to be vigilant. Whoever wanted to talk to Nate might come back and try to get to him again."

"I know that. I also…"

"Eric. What is it?"

"Yeah, Mom. I know that." Eric paused. "I am taking all my vitamins, Mom. I promise."

"Is someone there?" Not just a person his partner didn't want overhearing his side of a police conversation. Someone else. Someone who would present a threat to Nate.

A bad guy.

Eric said, "Yes. You are always right." The tone was the same, but his meaning was clear.

"Are they on approach to Nate's bed?"

"Yes, Mom. It's true." He chuckled. Not good, since the laugh sounded completely fake.

Someone was trying to reach his son's bed. "I'll be there in five minutes. Don't let *anything* happen to Nate."

TEN

Jennie flung the door open before he'd even shoved the SUV into Park. Tucker barked at her as she jumped out, but she wasn't going to stop for anything.

Someone had approached her son's bay in the hospital.

That cop—Eric. The one Patrick introduced as his partner. He'd been on the phone with Patrick when he'd led him to believe someone was approaching.

That was all she knew.

The whole drive over—which felt like an hour but was closer to a few minutes—she'd asked and asked what was happening with Nate. Never mind that he didn't know more than what he'd already told her. Wasn't withholding anything. Patrick had no intention of keeping her in the dark about what was happening to their son. He just hadn't had more information to give her.

"Jennie!"

She heard him race after her, along with the jingle of Tucker's tags, but just kept going. All the way to the alarmed Emergency room doors. How had someone gotten past them anyway?

Patrick touched the small of her back. She didn't look

at him. Not when he did that, and not a second later when the doors slid open. Released by the staff member behind the desk.

Jennie darted between the doors, but Patrick caught her elbow.

Jennie said, "No."

He tugged her around to him, his other hand holding the leash with Tucker close to his side. The dog looked ready to work. "Jennie."

"Nate—"

He cut her off. "You stay behind me." She heard the snick as he drew his weapon. "We don't know who is there. So we're going to let Tucker go first."

She was right behind him, though. No way would she allow anyone to get to Nate if she could help it. But he was correct that he should be the person in front. He had a gun, after all. And that badge on his belt. Tucker sniffed at the floor tiles as they raced down the hall to the bay where he'd been admitted overnight.

She looked around Patrick, but the man she'd met wasn't there. Patrick's partner had worn similar clothes, but now he was gone. A white paper cup lay on the floor, tipped over, its contents spilled in front of the curtain.

Patrick swiped back the curtain, gun raised. Tucker sniffed.

Beth sucked in a breath and blinked away a sleepy glaze in her eyes. Nate lay in the bed, still asleep. Jennie rushed around Patrick and went to her friend, so she didn't disturb her son from his rest.

Beth yawned. "What's going on? I heard someone yell, didn't I?" She looked around Jennie and Patrick. "Where's the other cop?"

"I'm going to find out," Patrick said.

Jennie glanced at him and nodded. Beyond him, a security guard moved into the hall.

"Stay here, watch them and *don't move*," Patrick ordered.

The man seemed a little perturbed but nodded. She didn't know how much help he would be. He had a badge, but only a stun gun on his belt.

Patrick left the man watching over them while he disappeared with Tucker to search for the threat.

"What's going on?"

Jennie looked at Beth. "Patrick was on the phone with his partner, who thought that someone was making an approach."

At least, that was how he'd worded it. But he hadn't known. And where was Eric, anyway? Had he run off after someone? That meant the person hadn't gotten near this hospital bed. Right?

"He needs to find Eric and figure out what happened." Jennie checked on Nate, smoothing down covers that didn't need to be adjusted and laying a soft kiss on his forehead. One he would have groaned about if he'd been awake.

"Oh." Beth rubbed at her eyes.

Jennie glanced at the security guard, who watched them in a kind of detached way while he chatted to the nurse. Of course, he was just a security guard, but she figured Patrick wouldn't have liked it. Still, this man wasn't doing anything she should worry about.

She was just on edge, being paranoid and seeing danger where there was none. Because Patrick was facing down the danger.

And that meant *he* was the one at risk right now.

Something that might be okay with him. But that

didn't sit right with her. No matter that he was a cop, she didn't love the idea that he was in the line of fire. For her, or for anyone else. Maybe that was irrational. Or silly. Either way, it was how she felt.

The security guard glanced down the hall where Patrick had gone. Jennie peeked around the curtain.

She immediately saw the tension between Patrick and his partner. Even Tucker seemed to be on edge. Or just hyperalert.

Jennie raced over. "What happened?"

Eric ended their stare-down and looked at her. "I saw a guy. He clocked me and broke off his approach, so I followed."

"And lost him." Patrick lifted his chin.

"Back off. *Partner.*"

Patrick blew out a breath that sounded like it might've been a huff of laughter but didn't say anything. Jennie wanted to squeeze his arm—something—but given his body language figured he didn't want to be touched right now.

"You saw someone?"

Eric nodded.

She turned to Patrick. "Maybe it was one of those guys I picked out."

"If we look at the surveillance, you can see for yourself. I'm sure he's on the footage." Eric pointed high on the wall to a surveillance camera.

Jennie looked up. On the bottom of the round lens, a red light flashed. Did that mean it was recording?

She glanced at the security guard, who was still watching her son, then turned back.

Patrick hadn't taken his attention from his partner. "You didn't catch him."

"Hard to do that when he clocked the shield from twenty feet away." Eric motioned to the badge on his belt. "He was two floors down the stairwell by the time I got through the door. No point chasing him when that left the kid exposed."

A muscle in Patrick's jaw flexed.

"Nate is still sleeping," Jennie assured him. "He didn't even wake up." She moved to Tucker and petted him. Maybe if he relaxed, Patrick would, as well.

He turned to her.

"Everything is fine."

"Nate is being targeted," Patrick said. "He's in danger here, the same as he was at your house. We need a safe place to take him."

She nodded. "Okay. Wherever we need to go, we'll go. As long as you and Tucker are with us."

Jennie saw Eric's glance between them. She wanted his friend to think she was a good woman for Patrick's son to have in his life. That she could stand strong and not fall apart at the slightest thing. He didn't need to be saddled with all the work unraveling what was happening and keeping them safe while they did nothing to aid that.

She wasn't going to be deadweight. Some helpless female who couldn't do anything to combat what life threw at her. Together, they would protect Nate.

Patrick turned to her. "I will keep you both safe."

"I know." Her words softened his gaze. He appreciated her faith in him. "You won't let anything happen to Nate."

"To either of you."

She nodded. "Okay."

* * *

Okay. So much faith in him. Too bad he didn't have faith in himself.

"She's quite a woman."

Patrick turned back to his partner. "You and I are going to have serious problems if anything like that happens again."

"You think I should have been in two places at once, protecting the kid—who is fine, by the way—and catching the guy who tried to approach?"

Patrick clenched his teeth. He didn't have a better idea for what Eric should have done. In fact, Patrick would likely have done exactly the same thing for the chance to catch whomever it was that had tried to get to Nate.

"I get this is personal," Eric said. "You've never indicated you'd have compromised judgment when it's personal, and I doubt you will. But I'm here to be a sounding board, okay? If you need impartial judgment."

"What I need is a safe place to take Jennie and Nate when they release him. Somewhere they can lay low and actually rest, and I can know they're safe while we find these guys and figure out who's behind this."

"Now you want my help again?"

Patrick nodded. "I need it."

They were partners. Eric was right. This was personal—in a way that was unprecedented. And like every other difference between them, they would work their way past it. At the core, they were two cops. Despite personal differences, they'd been trained the same way and had the same goals.

"Okay, then," Eric said. For them, it was basically an apology. Things were good now and they would move on. "I'll get you a copy of the surveillance footage. See if there's a good angle on this guy's face."

Patrick held his hand out. "I appreciate it."

Eric shook with him, then went to the elevator while Patrick returned to Jennie and Nate. They were like a tether. He didn't want to be too far from either of them. Not for long, at least. Just enough time to figure out what was going on.

Beth stood. "I'm going to go get some coffee. Do either of you need anything?"

Patrick shook his head.

"No, but thanks." Jennie gave her friend a smile.

He took the empty chair and Jennie leaned one hip on the bed in front of him, angled toward Nate. He gave Tucker a command to lie down beside his chair.

Tucker leaned his chin on the bed and Patrick heard him sniffing. Only after he'd done that did Tucker lay down.

Jennie smiled at him. Patrick was tired enough to want to stare at her and not care that she'd see him do it.

He tipped his head to the side. "How are you doing?"

"I feel about as tired as you look."

He felt his lips twitch. "So pretty good, then?"

She smiled back. "I'm not fielding that one. Hit me with another."

"I told Eric we need a safe place to say when Nate is released."

"I don't want to stay here long, but I know he needs medical attention. If the doctor thinks he should be in the hospital then I won't argue." She traced her thumb on the back of Nate's hand. "Even though I have to admit, all this makes me want to gather him up, run away and hide."

"That's understandable," he said. "You want to keep him safe."

Didn't all parents want to safeguard their children? But it was impossible to protect them from everyone and everything that might harm them.

Jennie said, "That's not the best for him, though. He can't live life tucked away from the world. He'll never learn to be strong that way."

"It's still okay to want to protect him. You should want that." He was finding he wanted it, also. Not just because Nate was vulnerable and in danger. Eric was right about this becoming personal. Patrick could do his job perfectly fine even when the victim was someone he cared deeply about. He'd be inclined to pray just to cover his bases, but that didn't really mean he had faith.

"Jennie?"

"Yes?"

"Will you pray, please? I'd like to know we're covered, but I don't want to be a hypocrite." He needed to admit where he stood with that. "I haven't gone to church in years."

"Because of me?"

"I didn't leave because of you. It was your father who forced my mother and me from our home, and when I went to talk to him…to confront him…a couple of his guys laid into me. They tossed me on the street."

She gasped.

"It was a long time ago. He's not here anymore, which means he can't answer for what he did." Patrick wasn't going to tell her that being kicked so hard two of his ribs had broken wasn't a big deal, because it was. But not as bad as her father trying to toss money at him to induce him to leave Jennie—and town. When he hadn't taken it, they'd attacked him. "Soon as I got home, my mom drove us out of town. I wrote to you in the car."

A tear rolled down her cheek and she wiped it away. She was quiet for a while then said, "He told me he talked to you. That he told you about the baby, and you didn't want to know. That you asked him for money. Then you were just gone." She sniffed. "I went to your house, but you'd already cleared out and left."

Patrick tugged her up and wrapped his arms around her. Jennie melted against him, her arms sliding around his middle as they held each other. He exhaled a long breath, his cheek against her hair.

Patrick studied Nate as he slept. Eyelashes fanned on his cheeks, his chest slowly rising and falling. Together, they'd made him. Though not under the best of circumstances—understatement—it could not be denied that Nate was astounding. Patrick couldn't wait to get to know his son better.

"Oh. Sorry."

Jennie backed away. "It's okay, Beth."

Patrick turned, cold from the loss of her embrace. And from a simple hug? It made no sense, except that it had been a long time and what they'd had was one of those once-in-a-lifetime things.

Eric stood behind Beth.

"What is it?" Patrick lifted his chin.

His partner crowded in, weaving around Beth as they both said, "Sorry. Excuse me." There was hardly enough space for the four of them and the dog, plus the hospital bed where his son lay.

Eric's countenance didn't allow for argument. Especially when he held out his phone. "The security guard sent the email to you, as well."

Patrick looked at Eric's phone screen. The photo was a grainy shot of the hallway. "Can we get an ID from it, see if it's either Carl Andrews or Michael Danes?"

It might also be the boss, who'd wanted to talk to Nate and hadn't cared about Jennie. Who did that? What more value could a child be than his mother? It didn't make sense that they would want him and not her. Patrick needed to figure out this mess.

Before it got worse.

When he looked up, Eric's attention was on Jennie. Why was he…?

Patrick caught the expression on her face.

"Jennie, do you know who that is?"

ELEVEN

Jennie strode between Beth and Eric, out to the hallway, though it wasn't any less crowded than it had been in Nate's bay. She could hardly believe he was still sleeping. But that was due to whatever the doctor had given him.

"Jennie."

She lifted her arms as though they could hide her face from the world and paced away from where Patrick stood. More attempts at avoidance? *No.* Jennie was going to face her problems head-on. She'd survived so much in the last day and a half. She wasn't giving up now.

She took a couple of deep breaths and then lowered her arms.

"You know who it is." Not a question.

"My brother."

She sank into a chair and covered her face again. Patrick tugged her hands down and she saw him crouched in front of her. Tucker got up and sniffed at his face. Patrick nudged him away and said, "The man on the surveillance video, the one who approached Nate's room, was your brother?"

She nodded.

"How can you know that? It's been years since you've seen Martin."

So she was either lying or she was guessing? Jennie didn't know which was worse. "It's him. I know it is."

"The image is grainy." He glanced at the photo on the phone. "I guess it might resemble him."

She sat back in the chair and tugged her hands from his. It didn't matter that Patrick didn't believe her. The picture was of her brother. And now that she thought about it, the whole thing made sense. Not hurting them. Wanting to see Nate.

But Martin was in the army. This had been going on for weeks. Longer than any leave he'd have, right? She hadn't seen her brother since he'd left and didn't know much about army life. But she figured he couldn't just leave his job—or posting—or whatever, and come home for weeks at a time.

"Maybe he's done with the army."

"But he hasn't tried to contact you."

She shook her head. "I have no idea why. If he has, I didn't know it was him."

"What is it about that picture that makes you think it's Martin?"

"The fact I know my brother?"

"Is that a question?" When she didn't answer him, Patrick said, "I knew your brother in high school. He was three years older, but I remember what he looked like then. But this guy?" He shook his head. "I can't say for sure."

"My dad had pictures of him in uniform. I think Martin sent them to him. I have them in a drawer somewhere, so I could show Nate. But I never have."

"And you think that man is Martin?"

"Yes, I do."

He didn't believe her, though, did he? And that hurt a lot. Jennie had been getting used to having Patrick here, supporting her. Helping. It had been a matter of hours, but that was evidently enough time to become dependent on another person. Not just because they'd been in danger, but because she hadn't been alone as a parent anymore.

Now Martin was back?

Instead of coming to the house and ringing the doorbell like anyone else, Martin was involved in something that included trespassing on her land. Then he'd had them kidnapped, and now he was threatening Nate's life?

"I don't want him coming anywhere near me." She stood, lifting her chin as Patrick stood, as well.

Beth had gone back to Nate's bedside, something Jennie would be forever grateful for. Eric stayed at the curtain, another man determined to protect them. But there was nothing in her appreciation for him that even came close to how she felt about Patrick.

That just meant this man in front of her, Jennie's son's father, had the ultimate power over her. Him doubting her identification of that man showed he had the ability to hurt her.

It had crushed her the day she had realized he'd completely cleared out and left her alone—and pregnant—still living in her father's house. Even now, he had the ability to destroy her.

And if she continued to let him into her life, and her heart, that would only get worse.

Until the day he wrecked her all over again. When he inevitably fought her for custody of Nate. He was a cop, while her family was nothing but criminals. There was no way she would win.

Patrick frowned. He looked about to say something when Eric broke in. "It's Martin Wilson?"

Patrick turned to his partner. Jennie exhaled, glad to be relieved from his scrutiny.

"That's what we believe."

Now he believed her? Jennie chose to just be grateful he no longer had that knowing stare aimed at her. The one she figured could see past what she was saying to her deeper feelings. Desperation. Fear.

Both *totally* attractive things. Not.

She wasn't interested in attraction. She didn't need any of that—especially not from a man who had hurt her so deeply in the past. Sure, he would no doubt be a good father to Nate. But that didn't mean he would stick around for Jennie. Literally or figuratively.

There was just too much pain in their history. Miscommunication or not, it would always be between them.

"Let's find out what we can from the army."

Eric nodded.

"Once we have that, we'll be a step closer to figuring out what's going on here."

"Ms. Wilson?"

She turned to find the doctor standing there. "When is Nate able to be released?"

Ready to get back to her normal life, she wanted to take him somewhere they could both rest.

"We'll have to see how he's doing when he wakes up, but it's possible he can go home later today."

Jennie crossed her arms in front of her, trying not to be cynical about doctors or hospitals. She needed to let him do his job. Her fingers grazed across the bandage on her elbow and she winced. "Thank you, Doctor."

Patrick stepped around her and questioned the doctor about things to watch out for with Nate and when he might need to be brought back in.

She turned away, trying to tamp down the frustration. *He's being a good dad, remember?* Plus he was new at this, and cops tended to take charge of situations. She had to repeat the question in her mind four times.

Jennie strode past Nate, glancing over to make sure he was all right. Still sleeping. Beth had her gaze on the other police officer—the one down the hallway. Eric paced, the phone clutched to his ear. She assumed he was asking the army about her brother or talking to his boss.

"Hey." Patrick touched her shoulder. "It's good news that Nate might be released. Right? Are you okay?"

Jennie didn't have the mental energy for a deep conversation. "I'm going to stay by Nate. Please let me know when we're leaving." She went to sit with her son.

She'd done everything she could to have a different life than the one she'd had growing up. Her father had never included her in his "business," but she'd seen enough. That kind of stain spread, and she'd felt its cloying stickiness on her too many times.

That life wasn't something she wanted anywhere near Nate. Not when he'd been born, not now and not ever.

No matter what her brother tried to do.

Fear for his son clouded out everything. Patrick knew exactly how Jennie had felt when she walked out of the bay where Nate slept. That need for space, emotional and physical. A much-needed second in the middle of all that was going on to just take a moment and process.

He had a son.

That son was in danger.

Tucker whined, leaning his body against the side of Patrick's leg. He reached down and patted the dog's head.

Now they knew it was Martin Wilson. But did they? Sure, Jennie's brother might be the man who had come onto this hospital floor to see his nephew. A child he'd never met.

That didn't mean he was the person behind their kidnapping, or whatever was going on with the trespassers on her land.

Patrick didn't think it was a coincidence. The son of a man who'd been the local drug dealer—kingpin, maybe—for years, strong-arming locals out of their money.

Preying on people. Ruining more lives than just Jennie's and Patrick's. Martin had learned how to be a man from his father. He'd run off to the army, but even that kind of structure didn't change who a person was at their core.

Was Martin his father's son, or had he done what most people struggled to do and broken the cycle of how he'd been raised?

Eric wandered over. Patrick met him halfway with Tucker so Jennie didn't have to listen to whatever was said. He'd figure out how to tell her later. Though, from the look on her face, he imagined she knew a lot of it.

"I spoke with an MP at the base where Martin Wilson is *supposed* to be."

Patrick stilled. "What?"

"Fourteen months ago, he went AWOL. Came back from a deployment, went on leave. At the end of the two weeks, he never reported in. He'd left his phone—everything—behind on base, only had one bag of clothes. They haven't been able to find him since."

"He's here."

Eric grinned. "It was very satisfying to inform them of that fact. Even though it's not like we were looking for the guy." He folded his arms. "They're sending over a couple of MPs. Boots on the ground."

"Assistance?"

"They're interested in Martin Wilson being put in cuffs. Evidently he needs to answer some questions about an incident that happened in Afghanistan."

But they weren't going to help with whatever Martin had been up to for the fourteen months since anyone had last seen him.

Eric nodded at the expression on Patrick's face. "Yeah. Pretty much."

He shook his head.

"Don't need their help anyway, right?" Eric said. "Only there's really no way to actually say that without sounding whiny and then making people wonder if you think maybe you *could* use their help."

"We don't need it."

Eric nodded. "Exactly."

"Did you figure out accommodations?"

"You really should check your email. I got you a local short-term rental I booked under an alias I used for the last undercover job."

That had been over toward Arizona, and everyone involved was in jail now. There wouldn't be any blowback or a risk of anyone showing up for revenge.

Patrick let out a huge exhale. "Thanks."

"All the information is in your in-box. Address, door code. Everything."

"And you?"

"I've been thinking about that." Eric scratched at his chin. "If her brother was here, and he's trying to make contact with Nate for whatever reason…" Before Patrick could argue with him, Eric continued, "Means he could be watching."

"Waiting for us to leave, so he can make an approach," Patrick said. "What are you thinking?"

"It involves you giving me your car keys."

"You think pretending to be me will fly?" Patrick grinned.

At least Eric hadn't offered to take Tucker, to complete the ruse. Eric and Tucker had a somewhat antagonistic relationship. They were like two kids, or siblings, each one intent on annoying the other until one or the other had the upper hand.

Patrick said, "You want to pretend to be me, and draw him out. It'll only work if there's someone on the other end to catch him."

"Or it'll be enough to draw him away, give you guys time to get to the house."

"A distraction."

Eric shrugged one shoulder.

His partner was willing to put himself in harm's way so Patrick could get Jennie and Nate to a safe place?

"I looked into the father."

Patrick said, "Yeah?"

Eric nodded. "He used the land, and neighboring lands he…acquired, to transport drugs."

"Including the land he got from my mother."

"Never legally. It's not like Jennie inherited everything he had and is now some kind of land mogul. She doesn't own your old house. She got the house she grew up in and the land around it. That's all in her name now, because it was left to her by her mother."

"So her father strong-armed the town into getting what he wanted, but never on paper. You think the sheriff was in his pocket?"

"If he was," Eric said, "Martin could be up to the same thing. Took over Dad's business after he died. Kept it running through a middle man. When things got heated in the army, he split and came home to run it in person."

"Sounds like some mob boss still giving orders from prison."

"Only he was in the military."

"It's a pretty good cover," Patrick said. "No one would think he was behind it, given he's either across the country or deployed."

Even Jennie hadn't given her brother a second thought. Until he was brought up.

"The MP I spoke to told me they tried to contact Jennie to find out if she'd seen him, but she totally ghosted them," Eric said. "Never returned any calls. He said they spoke with the sheriff, who told them to leave her alone. That she was done with her family."

Patrick felt his eyebrows rise for about the hundredth time. Yet more surprises. "Maybe I was wrong to doubt him."

"Are you going to trust him with this now?"

Patrick shook his head. "No way."

"Okay, good. I was worried for a second."

"If I thought we needed a task force, I'd make a call. But Jennie was right to contact the DEA. They'll want the case if a Wilson is operating in this county again, transporting drugs."

Eric nodded. "We keep her and Nate safe. The army picks up Martin, and the DEA can mop up the rest of them. The sheriff will probably take credit for the whole thing, when we all know who the real hero is." He tried to pet Tucker, but the dog only sniffed at his hand.

"As long as Jennie and Nate are safe."

Eric glanced in their direction. "Mmm. I can see why you might feel that way."

Patrick nudged his partner's shoulder. "Focus. You already let Martin get away once."

"But they are safe. Right?"

Patrick nodded. "Yeah."

Eric pretended he didn't care about the slight. "Let's figure out how we're going to keep them that way."

Patrick grabbed his phone. "Let me call Johns first. See if he has anything from the house and make sure it's been secured."

He figured the men on dirt bikes had cleared out, but he called anyway. There was no answer. Patrick couldn't go check on what was happening. He and Tucker needed to stay with Jennie and Nate.

"Give me your keys." Eric motioned with his fingers. "I'll do double duty, lead Martin away and check on the sheriff."

Patrick dug his keys out. "Please be careful."

"You just don't want to do the paperwork if something happens to me."

"I'm more worried about Tucker. You give him more treats than I do."

Eric laughed as he walked away. But Patrick couldn't join in. Not when instinct told him even one second of a slipup might end in the worst way.

Right now, distraction could cost someone their life.

TWELVE

Patrick shoved the curtain aside and stepped in. Tucker padded to Nate's side and set his chin on the bed.

"Look who it is." The words died on her lips as she realized Patrick was wearing Eric's jacket, holding a ball cap with the word Police across the front.

All his attention was on Nate.

Jennie said, "He woke up a couple of minutes ago. He's still pretty groggy."

Patrick approached the bed. "Hey, buddy."

"Hi." Nate moved his hand and stroked Tucker's head.

She figured her son didn't know what to call him. Patrick or *Dad*. She squeezed Nate's arm, wanting to tell him that they were all new at this. Still figuring it out. This was going to be a whole lot of trial and error.

She said, "The doctor signed off. They're releasing Nate as soon as the nurse comes back with the paperwork and they get a wheelchair up here."

"I can walk."

"You don't think it might be cool to ride in one?" she asked him. "Because that's the only way you're getting out of here."

Nate made a face, his lips mushed together.

"Yeah, yeah." Jennie grinned. If he was giving her that expression, then he felt pretty good. The lasting effects of being kidnapped would show themselves, and likely wouldn't be physical. But that was a worry for tomorrow. Right now she was concerned about where they would go.

Before she could ask, Patrick eased down onto the side of the bed. "How are you feeling, Nate?"

"Pretty good." His little boy face crinkled into upset.

"What?" Patrick leaned forward. "Tell me what, buddy."

"I—" He glanced at her. Why the guilty look on his face?

"Whatever it is, it's okay," Jennie said.

"I don't wanna go home." He sounded like the little boy he had been, using phrasing he'd grown out of lately.

Jennie pushed away the rush of…grief. And the sheen of tears. He'd lost the feeling of comfort and safety in his own home. That was definitely a reason to grieve.

Patrick answered before she could reply. "My partner found us a place to go. A short-term rental, where we'll be safe."

"Is Tucker going to be there?"

Hearing his voice, the dog jumped up to set both front paws on the side of the bed. Nate laughed.

Patrick said, "Tucker. Off."

The dog hopped down just as the nurse and an orderly came in. The nurse handed Jennie the discharge papers and the orderly helped Nate into the wheelchair. Her son seemed more tired than anything else. Jennie's injuries stung, but she didn't care about that when Nate had a bigger knot on the back of his head than she did. *No concussion.* She had to remember that.

Thank You, God. Keep us safe. Please.

Jennie accepted the paperwork, stuffing the pages in her purse without even reading them. Patrick took the bag she'd packed for herself and Nate and slung it over his shoulder even though he had Tucker's leash, as well.

She walked by Nate's shoulder as they made their way out. "Are you going to tell me what the plan is?"

Patrick glanced over. She wondered if he was even going to answer her whispered question.

"Or why you're wearing Eric's jacket."

"I drew the line at swapping pants," he said. "Especially since he's four inches shorter than me."

She grinned. "And that?" She motioned to the ball cap.

"Oh." He looked down at the hat in his hand. "I almost forgot." He shifted the duffel on his shoulder, and they were off again. The hospital orderly wheeled them in the direction of the elevator.

"Nate."

Her son turned, the hope in his eyes almost too much for her to handle. At just his father's mention of his name.

"Do you wanna wear this?" Patrick asked.

She didn't know if he was aware he'd used the same words as Nate. Stress, fear and anxiety changed how a person spoke and behaved. She wanted her son to meet his father under normal, calm and carefree circumstances. But this was what God had given them.

"It's for me?"

"Yeah, buddy." He settled the ball cap on Nate's head.

"Cool!"

Jennie chuckled then covered her mouth with her hand. It was probably a disguise. A way to claim his son and keep Nate's identity under wraps as they left the hospital and headed for what amounted to a safe house.

"Mom! Look at it!"

"It's very cool."

Patrick glanced at her, an expression on his face she hadn't seen in a long time. Behind Nate and the orderly, she reached over and took his free hand. She gave it a squeeze, then loosened her grip. Patrick didn't.

He kept hold of her hand all the way to the elevator, and only let go to push the button so they could go down.

"So you and Eric traded jackets?"

"And he took my car."

She knew there was more he wasn't saying. Patrick wanted to keep them protected, so he was having his partner drive his car. If someone wanted to get to them, they would follow "Patrick."

Or the person might stick around, thinking he'd gone. They would look for Jennie and Nate, who were the real targets.

There was a lot about police work she would never understand. But Patrick had managed to find her and Nate on the worst night of their lives. Now Nate looked at him like his father could do anything. Certain that Patrick could make a plan to keep them safe. The expression looked a whole lot like hero worship.

Jennie would know, because she felt the same way. She always had. And it was clear now that maybe she always would.

That was the deep-down truth. But the wall between that and what she allowed herself to feel was the pain she'd endured for years, thinking he'd abandoned her.

Despite the fact it had been her father's doing, she just couldn't get past the pain. The loneliness she had suffered, raising her son by herself.

Right now was about him getting to know Nate—alongside protecting him. He loved Nate and would be part of his life—and hers because of it. But he'd moved on with his life. Jennie didn't know if she would ever be able to move on with hers.

Not with the hurt so fresh.

Patrick wasn't here for her, and he wasn't sticking around to get into a relationship. When she fell in love again, it would be with someone for whom she would be the priority. The one that someone was wholly devoted to and would never leave.

As much as she might want things to be otherwise, she had to face facts.

That someone wasn't Patrick. It never had been.

The elevator doors slid open and the orderly wheeled Nate inside. Patrick moved alongside the man in his scrubs. They both shifted at the same time, blocking the doorway so she had to wait to enter. Finally it cleared, and Jennie shifted to follow.

Someone grabbed the back of her jacket, tugging her away from the elevator doors. "What—"

Whoever it was shoved her before she could turn, and she stumbled. Nearly fell.

"Jennie!" Patrick's voice rang out. Tucker barked.

She looked back to see Tucker race out between the doors before they slid shut. Gone. She glanced at the man standing behind her.

One of their kidnappers!

Tucker growled.

The orderly blocked his way to the closed doors. Patrick resisted the urge to shove the man aside.

"Mom!"

Patrick turned to Nate, still seeing in his mind the second she'd been dragged back. Pulled away from the elevator.

"What happened? Where is she?"

"I don't know." Patrick wanted answers to those same questions. He moved to the panel of buttons. Emergency stop? Or should they just try to go back up? "We need to—"

The orderly cut him off. "Don't press any of the buttons."

Patrick turned to him, wondering why the man's tone sounded so threatening. "Why wouldn't I—" He knew the answer to his question and didn't need to finish saying it.

Behind Nate's back, the orderly had a gun pointed at him and his son. Not one of them in particular. But the fact he could shoot either—probably faster than it would take Patrick to pull his gun—wasn't good at all.

He didn't know what to say except, "Don't."

Cold rage settled over him, along with a healthy dose of fear. If something happened to Nate, while he stood there…forced to watch.

His son of only hours—all Patrick had ever had with him—would be dead. Because he'd failed. If Jennie was somewhere, safe and alive, Patrick would have to tell her.

She would never forgive him. Not when he'd promised to take care of them both.

His fingers drifted to his own weapon. But what could he do? Start a war that would result in far too many innocent casualties.

The gunman saw it. "Put that on the floor. Slowly. Then kick it toward me."

Patrick shook his head as he studied the man's face. Not one of the kidnappers Jennie had identified. This man wasn't Martin Wilson, Nate's uncle, either. So who was he? Another man on Martin's payroll. Living on the proceeds of those ill-gotten gains, thinking he could do whatever he wanted with no repercussions from the law.

"You think I'm going to disarm myself?"

No cop worth anything would do that, no matter what was at stake. It was the same as the government's principal not to negotiate with terrorists. Patrick was never going to give all the power to a bad guy with a gun.

Not. Gonna. Happen.

The cop he was, and the father, would never do that. Not when possession of his own weapon meant protecting the innocent here—his son.

"Don't think you've got much play here." The gunman smirked. "So unless you want cop brains all over the elevator, you'll do what I say."

He wasn't going to kill Nate. Whether by principal, which meant he had at least some convictions even if it wasn't much, or because he'd been ordered not to kill the boy... Did the why even matter?

Patrick had that one thing working in his favor. And he was going to use that to get Nate to safety, put this man in cuffs and find Jennie. That was the only acceptable outcome here. Even when all hope was lost, there was always a way to find a victory. His cop mentor had taught him that.

They saw ugly every day. It was easy to forget that there was still good in the world. Right now Patrick needed hope *and* a second chance.

Was this guy one of the dirt bikers, here to get revenge for his maimed friend?

He hadn't counted on them when he'd made his plan, determined to get Nate and Jennie safe from whatever her brother had planned.

Now he realized exactly how thoroughly he'd miscalculated, even with Sheriff Johns providing a female deputy to go with Eric and act as Jennie's double.

Now his K-9 partner was with Jennie instead of here to help him search for her.

First he had to disarm this guy and get Nate to safety. Then Patrick was going to rescue her. Tucker just had to protect her until he got there.

Nate shifted, still sitting in the wheelchair. *"Dad."*

Before the gunman could react, Patrick said, "I'll get you back to him soon, buddy." He had to play this like the kid was just his charge. Not that he was Nate's father—a man with everything to lose if this went wrong.

Or if the gunman recognized precisely how much leverage he had.

Nate sniffed. Patrick wouldn't blame him if he gave away too much. That wouldn't be fair. He was a smart kid, but even a rookie cop could unintentionally divulge information in a high-stress situation.

"I'm not going to let you take the boy." Patrick motioned at Nate with a flick of his fingers. "You think I won't get fired if I let something happen to him?"

The gunman's lips puffed out, his expression belligerent. "You think I care?"

"I'll be better off dead with benefits for my family than alive and disgraced, with nothing. So go ahead." Patrick patted his shirt—underneath which was a vest.

Any second now, the elevator doors would open. He needed a distraction. Anything. Something. The upper hand, even for a split second, to get the jump on this guy.

The gunman studied him, probably trying to figure out if Patrick was just reckless or if he was actually serious.

Anything to buy him a few extra seconds.

"What's the plan, huh? Take him to your boss. For what?"

"What do you care?" the gunman asked. "You'll be dead."

"Answering a question with another question. Typical." Patrick rolled his eyes. It probably didn't look right. He wasn't sure if he'd actually ever rolled his eyes before in his life. "But I don't think you'll get far. This is a hospital. Cops. Security. They're all here, protecting the woman and her son. You know, considering they were kidnapped and all."

The gunman's lips twitched. "Heard about that. Shame I wasn't in on it."

Patrick didn't like the look in his eyes at all. The only source of comfort was the fact that Tucker was likely protecting Jennie right now. No way would anyone be able to take her again, not with his dog there.

Nate twisted in his chair to look at the man. He reached down for the wheels and turned them opposite directions, rotating the wheelchair toward the gunman.

What was he…?

"You're going to die. The kid and me are leaving."

Patrick pressed his lips together. *At least say it right.* "That's not going to happen."

"Then you'll be dead before the doors open."

He wasn't sure that was true. Patrick wondered if he'd ever killed anyone before, and if he had the stomach to do it now. Still, regardless of the perceived threat level he had to get this situation resolved.

The only thing Patrick could think to do was pray. *I asked Jennie to pray. You were supposed to be protecting them.*

He wasn't sure how he'd feel about a God who didn't come through for His own children.

"You're dead, and the kid comes with me. If I don't call to say I have him, they kill the mom."

The bottom dropped out of Patrick's stomach.

Jennie.

THIRTEEN

Jennie felt the poke of the gun in her side. She gritted her teeth and tried to think past the barking. "Tucker."

"You tell that dog to shut up." His punishing grip squeezed her arm as he dragged her down the hall. The gun barrel glanced off her ribs.

She sucked in a breath through her nose. "Tucker, be quiet."

The dog leaned forward, ears lifted. Teeth bared as he barked again at the man holding her.

A nurse exited a room in front of her. "What is going on out…"

The gunman's breath hissed in Jennie's ear. "Act natural."

A sob worked its way up her throat. She coughed it back down. Jennie covered the action with her hand and waved the woman off.

Nothing to see here. Just a police dog obviously agitated.

"Tucker." She didn't know what to say to him. Would he even listen to her?

"You shut him up, or I will." He yanked on her arm, squeezing the bandage over her elbow. Jennie cried out.

"Hey!" the nurse yelled.

Three steps from the stairwell—not the spot Jennie wanted him to take her to—the nurse yelled, "Where you guys going?"

The gunman, a man who'd kidnapped her and didn't care one whit if she lived or died, swung around. Cameron? Carl? She didn't remember his name from the police database. All she cared was that his move put Tucker behind him.

The nurse's gaze darted between Jennie and the man who held her in a tight grip. She had a cell phone in her hand. Had she called security?

The nurse put her hand on her hip. "You're just gonna leave without giving me a hug?"

As though behind them both, Tucker wasn't growling to indicate a serious threat.

The nurse was stalling. Jennie said the first thing that came to mind. "You know I'd never do that to you, girl." As though this woman was a longtime girlfriend. Someone she cared about the way she cared about Beth. This nurse was going up against an armed man. She'd read the situation and she was putting her life on the line to intervene.

"We should find that handsome officer so he can come get his dog," the nurse said.

Yes, we should.

"You gonna let her go so she can say bye to me, and I can call that cop?"

Wow, Jennie thought, this woman might be the bravest person she'd ever met. She could've broken down and cried right then and there.

"No." The gunman tugged her backward, to the door for the stairs.

Tucker barked.

"You back off, dog."

No, don't do that, Tucker. But how did she get him to intervene in a way that didn't lead to this horrible man trying to hurt him?

"I'm not going with you." She whispered the words, her gaze wholly on the woman. Pleading with her, and letting the gunman know she wouldn't cooperate.

Praying with all her might that the nurse would understand what was going on.

That she had, in fact, already called security and was just delaying this man. Waiting for them to show up.

Jennie lifted her chin. "Tucker won't let that happen."

"So I fire this gun. Kill you. What happens to your boy then?"

"I'm not letting Martin have him." With her eyes she pleaded with Tucker to…what? He flashed those intense dog teeth and growled.

The man chuckled. His only response to her comment regarding her brother, or his opinion of the animal. It seemed like there was something he knew—or thought he did—that she didn't know yet. Or he was determined to be smug.

Either way, she had to get out of this. Fast. Preferably with no one being hurt in the process.

"On second thought," Jennie said, "take me to my brother. I want to see him."

"Good choice."

She'd find a way to break free of his hold and grab Tucker's leash instead, or this guy would haul her all the way to wherever Martin was hiding. After she spit in her brother's face for what he'd done to her family, she would figure out how to get away.

Everything she'd learned years ago in that very basic self-defense class escaped her now. She could remember a stretch or two—that she couldn't do—from the six months Nate had decided he wanted to be a ninja and she'd taken him to martial arts classes at the local gym.

Then he'd decided he loved animals more and wanted to be a vet.

She was a million percent sure right now that he was going to decide unequivocally that he wanted to be a cop. Probably a K-9 handler. She wouldn't blame him at all. If she was honest with herself, Patrick made her want to be one, too. He and Tucker were both heroes.

"Sir." The nurse looked stern now. "You need to let this woman go."

They were almost at the door. Tucker barked again, his back to the door. Determined not to let them get through. *Good dog.*

Jennie wanted to shake her head, vehemently, at the nurse but she didn't want Tucker to get hurt. Then Jennie would likely be pushed down a flight of stairs. Just because he wasn't there to kill her, didn't mean he needed her hale and hearty when she got wherever they were going.

Behind the nurse, a security guard armed with a stun gun stepped into the hall.

Her heart sank.

Jennie lifted her hands. *Do it. For Nate.* "Everyone just calm down."

"That's right." The gunman dragged her back another step. "Move, dog. We're leaving. Anyone who stops us is going to die!"

"You don't have to do that. Let's just go." She didn't want this to cost anyone their life.

Unless that was what he wanted? Maybe this scene had been inevitable. He hadn't had any plans to go downstairs and this was all just to cause a distraction.

So that someone else could take Nate.

But her son was with Patrick. Nothing would happen to him, not with a cop in the elevator. She wanted to squeeze her eyes shut, take a second and pray, but there was no time. "Please." She could only muster that one word.

And then he tugged her back again. Tucker barked.

The man lifted the gun, so it was pointed past her. At the nurse.

Self-defense. Jennie bent her knees a fraction. In one move, she grabbed his wrist, twisted her hips and swung his whole body around. He basically fell over her. But he was so heavy, she collapsed to her knees and he rolled, arm around her now.

His arm tightened so she couldn't inhale.

Jennie tried to get away from him. The gun went off and someone cried out.

"No!" Jennie had no idea what had even happened.

The gunman waved his weapon around. Tucker closed in, barking loudly enough to make her wince.

"Shoot him!" That sounded like the nurse.

A man said, "I'll hit her!"

Jennie tried to scramble to her feet and get out of the line of fire. She couldn't think. The gun slammed into her temple and her vision sparked with stars.

She wasn't going with this man. She was going to fight the way Tucker was, for her life and for the life of her son. His father. Her family.

Jennie jabbed back with her elbow and hit something

solid. The gunman grunted. A heavy weight slammed into her. Maybe the gunman, too. Warm fur. *Tucker.*

Jennie hit the floor and everything went black.

Patrick was so focused on protecting his son from the man with the gun, he didn't see how it began. He heard a grunt and before he realized what Nate was up to, his son had moved.

Nate gripped the wheel bars, turned the chair with a twist and flung out one leg. The gunman groaned and fell back against the wall, but he didn't go down. Nate didn't have enough momentum or strength to do any damage. But it was sufficient to distract their assailant.

Behind the gunman, the elevator doors slid open. Patrick dived. He slammed into him and took the guy to the ground.

They hit the floor in a tumble. The man grunted again. Patrick grabbed his wrist and wrestled for control of the gun. He didn't exactly play fair, elbowing the man in the stomach so he struggled for a breath, but the life of his son was at stake.

The gunman roared.

Tucker barked.

"Tucker!" That was Nate.

Patrick slammed the gunman's wrist on the floor and the weapon skittered away. He lifted up and off the guy, then turned him onto his front and secured him with cuffs. He then patted him down; no phone, no wallet. Not even a gum wrapper.

"Nate?" He glanced back and saw the empty wheelchair. Where was…? Nate peered around the corner, still in the elevator but out of the way of flying bullets. "You okay?"

The boy stepped out, looking nervous.

"He's cuffed. He won't hurt you."

"I heard Tucker."

A second later, Patrick's dog rounded the corner, his leash dragging along the floor behind him, and raced over. Patrick retrieved the discarded gun and tucked it in the back of his waistband. Then he motioned for Nate to come to him. Tucker got there first, skidding on the tiled floor when his paws lost traction and slamming into Patrick's leg. "Hey, Tuck. Did you do a good job?"

Nate giggled. Patrick figured he was less likely to go into shock if he kept moving. Processing. When a person froze up, problems occurred. So he picked up the leash and said, "Let's walk."

Nate eyed the man lying prone on the floor.

A security guard approached. "State police?"

Patrick nodded. "Officer Sanders."

"We've got another one of these guys upstairs. Secured him and called in the sheriff. He's sending someone over to pick him up."

He wanted to ask about Jennie. "They should take this guy, as well."

"This your case?"

"Johns needs to question them, since they're locals and so were the victims. I'm going to stick around and work protection."

"Mom!"

Patrick turned and saw her approaching across the lobby, walking with a nurse.

Nate collided with her halfway, wrapped his arms around her middle, and they hugged. Tucker strained at the leash to go, too. Patrick had to make sure the gunman wasn't going to try anything. But before he turned back to the security guard, and the job he was there to do, he met Jennie's gaze. He mouthed, *You okay?*

She nodded, relief clear on her face, and called back, "Tucker saved me."

"Can you take charge of this guy?" He motioned from the security guard to the cuffed man. When the guard nodded, Patrick pulled the gunman to his feet and rounded on him. "Who sent you here?"

The man stared ahead, saying nothing.

Tucker growled.

"Does the name Martin Wilson mean anything to you?"

A flicker in the skin around his eyes indicated... something. But he still said nothing.

"What does he want with his sister and nephew?"

Patrick didn't much care about motive, but if Martin had something planned then Patrick needed to know what that was. Knowledge being power, it also meant it'd be easier to take care of Jennie and Nate. To keep them safe for good.

Clearly, there was something Martin wanted but didn't yet have. And it seemed that he was still trying to get it.

"Fine." Patrick took a step back. "I guess you can tell the sheriff instead."

"Sure," the guy finally said. "After he calls my lawyer."

A sheriff's deputy strode in, and Patrick explained everything. After the deputy had the security guard—whom he apparently knew—confirm it all, he took the gunman and the weapon.

Patrick turned to where Jennie now sat, Nate close to her side. Both sipped from paper cups, and a doctor was crouched in front of Jennie. She shook her head then caught Patrick's stare.

He took two steps toward them and his phone rang. It was Eric. He answered, lifting one finger for her to hang on while Tucker kept going. She gave him a short nod.

"Sanders." He clicked his tongue for his dog to wait.

"No one followed us. We drove around town a few times, I dropped off the deputy and she followed while I circled again," Eric said. "You guys good?"

"It was probably quiet for you because all the focus was on the hospital."

"I'd like to know how it didn't work. I make a pretty convincing Patrick Sanders, thank you very much."

"Sure you do." He smiled to himself. "I don't want to contemplate it, but I think the uncle wants Nate." Even as Patrick spoke the words, the knowledge settled in his stomach like old fried rice. His son was the target.

"You and that dog of yours get them to the house."

"While you work with the sheriff on interrogating the two men he now has in custody."

"Sounds good."

Effectively they'd given each other orders, but it was how their partnership worked. Mutual cooperation and mutual respect. They were equals. Except for Tucker, who had one master and did not think his relationship with Eric required cooperation.

Another smile.

It occurred to Patrick then that he was happy here. Something he'd never have believed would happen in his hometown. Had someone told him that a visit home would involve danger, so many feelings he'd never anticipated and more joy than he'd thought possible, he'd have thought they were crazy.

And yet, this was exactly where life had brought him.

That made him wonder if Jennie might be right to believe in God.

Had He given Patrick all this, when he'd never even asked for anything?

"Later." Eric hung up.

Patrick stowed his phone, ready to get Jennie and Nate to safety. Unless she needed to be admitted to the hospital, he could do that as soon as possible. She tossed the cup in the trash, took Nate's hand and they met him halfway.

Patrick bent his knees to meet his son's gaze. "You okay?"

"Uh-huh." Despite his words, Nate moved closer to Jennie's side. Tucker shifted in as well and sniffed the boy's face until he giggled.

"Worried about all this?"

The boy worked his mouth. Almost like he was chewing on what to answer. He shrugged one shoulder.

"How about you keep me safe, like with that wheelchair move in the elevator, and I'll keep you safe?"

"What wheelchair—" Jennie started to ask.

Nate cut her off, standing a little taller. "Okay."

Patrick nodded. "Okay."

He needed to get the kid a police badge of his own, so he could feel official. Then he'd have the conversation with him about being brave versus being smart.

He glanced from Nate to Jennie. "Ready to go?"

Jennie nodded. "I'm good."

Nate wound one arm around Patrick's waist. That he was still holding on to his mom while he hugged Patrick meant she was tugged up against him.

Patrick wrapped his arms around them both.

FOURTEEN

Jennie gasped awake. Panic clouded her vision. She breathed hard, glanced around and then remembered where she was. Safe.

She heard the jingle of tags and sat up in the bed. Nate lay beside her on the comforter, under a thin blanket instead of as she was—under multiple heavy covers to keep warm. Tucker lay in the hall, just outside the open bedroom door, scratching at the side of his head with his back foot.

Everything was fine. *You're a good dog.* The nurse had told her how Tucker had jumped on the gunman's back, sent both Jennie and her assailant crashing to the floor and enabled the security guard to take down the kidnapper.

My hero.

Jennie lay back and breathed. A moment of calm in the midst of this storm. They were in a safe place. Nate was good. Everything was good.

She repeated the words in her mind.

Everything is good. She mouthed the words then whispered them to the quiet room before she pushed the covers aside and got up.

Not exactly ready to face the world, but hiding never solved anything. Burying her head in the sand wasn't going to make her brother go away.

Tucker passed her on the way to the door. She reached down and ran her hand along the dog's back as he moved toward the bed, then turned to watch him hop up on the bed and lie down beside her son.

Jennie opened her mouth. Only the thought of Nate waking alone, as panicked as she had, stopped her from calling the dog off the furniture.

Instead, she left them sleeping together and located the hall bathroom. All the while, she tried to figure out what on earth her brother even wanted from her.

Why come after her son? Why take them both, not harming them apart from terrorizing them, and then try again in the hospital? There had to be a reason, but she couldn't see what it was.

Jennie didn't have money. All she had was her mother's land that had been left to her. If they were trespassing, maybe that was what they wanted? Easy access to her back forty. Maybe Martin wanted the house. She had no idea.

It wasn't like she'd been left a fortune—just a paid-for house. Definitely an asset. Especially considering she'd been a young single mom trying to get an online business going that paid utilities and left something over for food and a tiny fun-money budget. Was that what Martin was after?

Jennie wandered through the house, looking around but mostly trying to find Patrick. Surely he hadn't gone far if he intended to protect them.

She found him in the kitchen, stirring something in a big fry pan on the stove, his back to her. Taller. He'd filled out in the last ten years. In a way that she wasn't ashamed to admit—at least to herself—made her mouth water.

Yeah, she was still very attracted to him.

And why not? The boy she'd loved was now a good man. A cop. On the right side of the law, unlike every other man who'd been in her life. He was like a breath of cool desert air. Light in an otherwise dark life.

Since she was admitting things to herself, Jennie decided to quit being in denial. She did want him back in her life. There was a lot of pain associated with his having left her alone and pregnant. Especially since it was the result of a lie. They'd have to work through all that. But she was willing.

Patrick was the perfect missing piece to their family puzzle. Not just the right piece, but the *best* piece. Considering how long they'd lived without him, there was really no time to lose.

Patrick should know how she still felt about him being a part of their family…for good. For real. Forever.

But then, maybe he didn't feel the same way.

She had to fight those age-old inadequacies. They reared their heads whenever there was a risk to be taken, a chance that could turn out wonderfully if she actually measured up. If Jennie threw caution to the wind and went for it. Things that were scary were usually the ones that were worth doing—like raising her son by herself.

But could she take the risk when Nate's heart was on the line here, too? If she and Patrick had only brokenness between them, her son would be able to tell.

Maybe it was better not to say anything at all.

Jennie sucked in a breath, a sniffle. She wasn't crying but Patrick heard it and turned.

His curious expression softened. "Hey. You okay?"

She didn't even know where to start answering that. There was only one thing to say at a time like this. "Is there coffee?"

"Half a pot."

She hunted for a mug in the cupboards. "I'll probably be awake all night, anyway, considering how late I slept. I doubt caffeine will make much difference now."

"Maybe we could…watch a movie later? Just because we're hunkered down waiting for the sheriff to find your brother doesn't mean we can't distract ourselves. And Nate."

She glugged milk into her mug and then sipped. As she drank those few mouthfuls, she used her free hand to put the milk back in the fridge.

When she turned back and lowered the mug, Patrick had a wide smile on his face. "What?"

He shook his head, grinning. "Nothing."

"Hey, coffee is the nectar of life for moms. Probably cops, too, right?"

"That is true. But I can't say I've ever enjoyed it that much." He motioned to her mug with a tip of his spatula.

She eyed the pan. "Is that breakfast or lunch?"

"Well, it's after two. But I'm still planning to call it brunch."

"Sounds good to me. Brunch is yummy."

"I'll endeavor to not disappoint you."

I don't think that's even possible.

"What?"

She blinked. "What?"

He turned back to his pan.

What just happened? She was willing to let him proceed with his tactic of letting it go. There was so much to talk about. Still, this probably wasn't the time for heavy conversation. Maybe she should just keep things light. And let him do the same.

She leaned against the counter. "So, you cook?"

He glanced over his shoulder. "It was that or eat take-out forever. So I had my mom teach me the basics."

Jennie had loved Patrick's mom. She had been warm and loving to Jennie, though never would have replaced Jennie's memories of her own mother. His mom had been accepting, no matter that her father was a criminal no one could bring charges against.

Hopefully that wouldn't hold true with her brother, as well.

What would Patrick's mom think of her now? She didn't want to be all needy about it, but right before they'd left town, things had been…frosty. Now that Jennie knew her father was the one behind their breakup, she understood. Patrick's mom had allowed her opinion of Jennie to be clouded by how she felt about her father.

"What is it?"

Jennie shook her head.

Patrick turned off the stove and closed the distance between them. If he was any nearer, they would be touching. "Tell me what."

"Nothing." She wasn't going to brush him off, though. "Everything."

"I know what you mean." He squeezed her elbows for a second, then dropped his hands, determined not to push anything. If she wanted him closer, she would let him know. "It's been a wild couple of days, where you've had barely any time to think. Let alone work through what has been happening."

Jennie shrugged. "That is true. You're probably used to it."

"Because I'm a cop?" When she nodded, he said, "Most police work isn't nearly as exciting as what you've been through. I've had more than a few tough shifts over the years, so I'm kind of used to it. In a way, at least. Not your normal couple of days, though."

"No. It hasn't been. Our lives are quiet." Tears gathered in her eyes. "This wasn't supposed to happen. I mean… Martin? Really? I've had nothing to do with him since he left, and I like it that way. Why would he come back now? It doesn't make sense that suddenly he shows up, and now he wants to meet Nate?"

He led her to a chair at the table and dished out some of the food he'd made. Just a simple egg scramble. No bacon—which was why Tucker was currently content protecting Nate and not waking the boy up to get in here and locate some smells. And a sample.

Whatever drew the animal to his son, Patrick didn't blame him. He was grateful Tucker had bonded with the boy and was determined to protect him.

One less thing for Patrick to worry about. There were plenty of other things, but with that one, he had yet another reason why maybe he should thank God.

"You're safe." He touched her hand between bites then said, "You're here, and your brother doesn't know where you are."

She nodded.

He decided to just ask her what was occupying his thoughts. "Do you think God protected you?"

"Of course."

"But it's not like everything was fine. I mean, it wasn't exactly terrible, either…" He wasn't sure what he was trying to say. Just that while things hadn't been all right, they also could have been a whole lot worse. Maybe he just wanted her opinion.

She took a sip of her coffee. "I think… I mean I fell down the side of a mountain. I have a couple of scratches and nothing worse. Nate was in the company of serious gunmen. Anything could have happened, especially if we hadn't gotten back to him in time. All he has is a bump on the head. If that wasn't God's work, looking out for us, then I don't know what is."

"I wanted to pray. When you were pulled away, and the elevator doors shut. Maybe God helped Nate swing his chair at the gunman and distract him."

"He and I will be having a talk about that. It was dangerous. He should never have put himself in jeopardy like that."

"I know. I even agree with you. He's a child and it was my job to protect him."

She shook her head. "That's not what I'm talking about."

It wasn't? Patrick figured he should have taken care of the gunman himself. And he had, but not without Nate's assistance. His son was as good as a deputy, or an honorary partner, at this point. He was full of gratitude that the boy had the fortitude to take action like that.

But he should never have been put in the position where he'd needed to do it.

Jennie sighed. "Never mind. It's over, right? You said we're safe here."

Patrick figured they probably needed God's help with that, as well. "You are."

He didn't want her to worry. Plenty of things could potentially go wrong. Part of that involved the answers from Eric, about his interviews with the gunmen they'd arrested, and from the sheriff, due to call back as soon as he and his deputy were done looking around Jennie's land.

She pushed a chunk of potato around her plate, quiet for a moment before she said, "I tried to find you."

Patrick turned to face her. "But we changed our names."

They'd done it so her father wouldn't be able to threaten them anymore. He'd gotten their land, so he probably would have left them alone anyway. But his mom hadn't wanted to take any chances.

Jennie and Patrick had talked this through already, but at a time when their emotions had been fresh. Now seemed more like the time to give each other the gift of understanding. To give each other grace. The first step toward building something good out of everything that had happened.

"After my father died, I hired that private investigator. I always wondered if he didn't try all that hard. Or if you'd hidden really well." She shrugged one shoulder. "Maybe he took my money and never searched for you at all. Just sent me that canned email about how there was no trace."

They were both at fault. "I'm sorry you were alone. Sorry about what I missed, but also that I didn't get to be here and help you."

"I'm sorry, too."

He squeezed her hand. When he moved to tug his away, she held on tight.

"I was about to go to your house and tell you that I was pregnant, but my father told me you came over already. That you'd been and gone, and I'd missed you."

He nodded. The afternoon they'd beaten the snot out of him because he'd refused a payout her dad would never have given him anyway, and dumped him in the street like trash, he'd limped home to find his mom had already packed the car.

"He said he told you about the baby, and you didn't care." A tear slipped from the corner of her eye. "He even said you asked for money to leave me alone."

"And you really believed him?" The question slipped out before he could decide if it was a bad idea to say it aloud. She had hired that private investigator. Maybe, deep down, she'd known something wasn't right.

"No. Of course not." More tears slipped free. "I went to your house, but you were already gone."

"I sent you letters."

It was her turn to nod. He figured because he'd told her about the letters earlier. Then she said, "I never got them."

"And I never knew you were pregnant." Yes, he was restating what they knew, but it brought with it so much sadness. He just had to get it out. A thought occurred to him. "I wonder if my mom did."

"I think she hated me in the end. Or blamed me for what my father did to the two of you."

"You think if she did know, she'd have purposely not told me?" Patrick wasn't sure. But he did know people in pain did strange and stubborn things sometimes, thinking it was the right choice. "I guess maybe she might've not wanted us to be tied to your family forever. Never able to separate our lives again."

She looked away.

"What's done is done, Jen." But he needed to talk with his mother. "We *are* tied together, and it's a good thing. Nate is amazing. There are a lot of things about what happened that I would want to change, but he isn't one of them. I should have been here. You shouldn't have had to do this alone."

Jennie let go of his hand to wipe her tears away. "Thank you."

"You raised Nate all this time." He leaned close to her and touched her cheeks. "Thank *you*."

Tucker barked. Patrick was out of his chair before it even registered what that particular sound meant. Followed by a series of barks, it usually indicated danger. Tucker needed to alert him to something.

He reached the door to Nate's room and saw the boy, sitting up in bed.

"What is it?" Tucker was at the window to the backyard.

Still barking.

"You're awake." Jennie moved around him and crossed to the bed. "You were probably dreaming."

Nate turned a pale face and shocked expression to Patrick and shook his head. "It wasn't a dream. Someone was out there."

FIFTEEN

Jennie sat beside her son. His face was pale, his chest rising and falling rapidly. Patrick came over, as well. They'd been close just a second ago, and it had been sweet. Now she wanted to glare at him for putting their son in danger. To remind him that he'd promised they would be safe.

But it wasn't Patrick's fault. No, this was down to her brother, which meant it was more Jennie's fault than his. Neither option was all that rational of a conclusion considering her brother was an adult she hadn't seen in years. Martin made his own choices. He was the only one to blame for this.

Patrick stood over the bed. "What did you see, Nate?"

The boy looked up at him. Scared. Did Patrick not know how imposing his tall figure was, standing over the bed like that?

Jennie twisted to face Nate. "Tell us. Okay?" She kept her voice soft and touched his shoulder.

"It wasn't a dream, Mom."

"I know you think—"

"I *know* it wasn't."

Jennie pressed her lips together. Patrick touched her shoulder. He said, "Please tell me what you saw, Nate."

"A man." Nate swallowed. "In a blue jacket."

"Hair color?"

"Brown."

Jennie bit her tongue and kept quiet while Patrick basically interrogated Nate. Was it a dream, or had it actually been real?

"Outside the door," Nate said.

She looked over at the French doors that led out to the backyard. Tucker stood, his focus on the door, his body straight and tight. As though the second Patrick opened it, he would bolt.

"I'm going to take Tucker and look around outside, okay?"

The dog understood enough of what he heard that he bounded over, tail wagging. Animated now, excited to get to work. Patrick got a leash, hooked it on Tucker's collar and led him outside with a command to "Look."

Was there really someone out there? Jennie knew what her son believed, but she didn't want to agree even though there was a high chance he'd actually seen someone. There was no way her brother had found them this quickly, right?

She looked at her son, who stared at the door where his father had gone. She forced her face into a wry expression. "Did you really tackle an armed man in an elevator with a wheelchair?"

Patrick had mentioned a wheelchair move, but she'd had to put the pieces together herself. She didn't know whether to be proud of the man she was raising or horrified.

He blinked. Distraction accomplished. "Saul taught me how to do it."

"Ah." Nate's school friend had a condition that left him wheelchair-bound. He also played in a kids' wheelchair basketball league. "He taught you how to face down gunmen?"

"There was only one. Dad needed my help."

She wanted to groan but forced it back. "That was very brave." And foolish. And he should never have done it. But she knew now that Patrick blamed himself.

"I couldn't hurt him. But I turned like Saul does and kicked him." He frowned. "It didn't really work."

She found the wherewithal to smile. "I'm sure your dad appreciated your help."

He gave a small shrug with one shoulder. "I think he was mad."

"Sometimes adults look and sound like they're mad, but they're actually scared. It can be confusing. You know what I could use?"

He eyed her. "What?"

"Hot chocolate for breakfast."

He grinned, all trace of that earlier fear gone now. "Do you think we have marshmallows?"

"We can certainly look." She figured he needed to use the bathroom, so she said, "Meet me in the kitchen?"

They went their separate ways, but her mother's senses tracked his movements. Like when he locked the bathroom door. When the toilet flushed. She watched out the window, but couldn't see Patrick or Tucker.

Jennie didn't want to be too far from her son, so she met him in the hall and they moved together to the kitchen. She'd have liked to hold his hand, but he hadn't appreciated her doing that for a few years now.

She set the kettle going, and found enough of what she needed to make this work before Patrick came back in.

There was someone out here.

Tucker strained on the leash, his nose scenting the air as they jogged across the yard. At the far end was a path and a tiny gate they could both hurdle if they had to. But Tucker didn't go near it.

He only moved through the yard, looking for a scent. Over the berm that had been covered with decorative boulders, shrubs and desert bushes.

"Tuck."

The dog halted and Patrick crouched by what had snagged his attention on the ground. A footprint. Just one thick-treaded print, by itself, angled toward the side of the house.

They walked that direction, all the way around to the front door.

Nothing.

When it was clear he wasn't going to find the intruder, Patrick commanded Tucker to heel and they went back to sniff at the gate. Just in case. But there was nothing out there to track.

He'd seen a figure on the far side of the berm when he first stepped out, but there was no one around now. And if Tucker couldn't find a scent, then Patrick would only be walking around and looking randomly. Taking him farther and farther from the house where Jennie and Nate now had no protection.

Once inside, he took Tucker's leash off and fired off a quick text to his mom before he found them in the kitchen. Before Nate turned around, Patrick gave Jennie a small shake of his head.

Still, simply because he hadn't found anyone didn't mean there was no danger.

Tucker moved to Nate, who leaned against the counter by the silverware drawer. The dog turned and sat with his back to the boy, resting against his leg the way Nate rested against the counter.

Patrick said, "That means he trusts you."

Nate petted the dog's head, a frown on his face.

"He's turned so you're behind him. It means he trusts you won't try to hurt him while his back is to you. Like watching his back. The way he's watching your back."

"Did you find the man?" Nate asked.

"No, buddy. I didn't." Patrick quickly added, "But that doesn't mean it was a dream. Just that whoever was there ran off before we could catch him."

Nate was silent.

"You okay?"

Nate shrugged.

"Do you…want a hug?" Patrick shrugged as well, wondering why he felt so nervous.

Across the kitchen, Jennie poured hot water into three mugs, but he knew she was listening. Patrick hugged his son. Their son. She glanced over and shared a smile with him. They'd covered a lot of ground—especially with their earlier conversation. Things were in no way settled, but it definitely felt like they were getting somewhere. He'd thanked her for raising their son. Of all people, Patrick knew what it was like to be raised by a single mother. That also meant he understood how hard it would have been for her over the years.

"Hot chocolate?" She turned, holding the three mugs.

Nate slid onto a stool. "Mom makes the *best* hot chocolate."

Jennie smiled as she slid his mug over then pushed one toward Patrick. His fingers glided over hers. Warmth. Those tingles he remembered from high school.

They might be adults now, but the rush of attraction was still there.

"Are you going to drink yours, Mom?"

Jennie jerked out of her musings, her cheeks flamed. Before anyone could comment, Patrick's phone rang. When he pulled it out, he saw it was his mom, replying to his text with a call. "Hey, Mom."

Across the breakfast bar, Jennie stiffened.

"Patrick. I thought you were out of town, working."

"I am. I just had a question, though." Was there even an easy way to ask this? He should probably just rip off the bandage. "I'm in Erwin."

She was slow to respond. "What…would you be doing there?"

"There was a missing boy and his mother." Patrick reached over and rubbed Nate's back, between his shoulder blades. "It was Jennie."

"Jennie." His mom breathed her name. Patrick wasn't sure what to make of it.

Jennie took her mug to the sink, where she stared out the window.

Given Nate might have seen someone outside who could still be there despite Tucker's search, Patrick got up and moved to her. He motioned for her to come away from the window. She sniffed and wiped her cheeks before sitting beside Nate.

Patrick took up her spot. "Jennie has a son." Before his mother could ask, he said, "I have a son. His name is Nate."

Jennie reached out and took Nate's hand in hers.

"And he's missing?"

"No, Tucker found him." Patrick and his son shared a smile. "He's safe, and so is Jennie." *Maybe.* His brain insisted on reminding him their safety was currently tenuous at best. He needed Eric to call back, or the sheriff. In the meantime, he was on point protecting them. And while there was definitely nowhere he'd rather be, it would also help if he could investigate this and find her brother.

Talk to the two they had in custody from the hospital. Look for the other man who had taken them.

"Just…wow." His mom exhaled, the rush of breath audible against the phone's microphone.

"I know. It's a lot to take in. I'm having trouble believing it myself, even though he's sitting right in front of me."

"He's there?"

"He looks like me."

Nate's eyes filled with a kind of wonder Patrick didn't even know how to feel. But he was getting there. And it was probably written all over his own face, as well.

"Let me show you. Turn on your video chat." Patrick tapped the screen to change their phone call to a video call. Then she'd be able to see her grandson. He moved around the breakfast bar and pointed the camera at the two of them while he stood behind Nate, his arm over Nate's shoulder.

"I can hold it." Nate took the phone.

The camera image loaded and his mom's face came into view. "Patrick?"

"We can hear you."

Nate smiled wide. "Hi."

His mom gasped. "Hello."

"I'm Nate."

"Hi, Nate," she said. "I guess… I'm your grandma."

Nate chuckled. Patrick hugged his waist. His son said, "Hi, Grandma." It was tentative, but the most beautiful thing he'd ever heard in his life. Except for Jennie, years ago, telling him that she loved him. Two wondrous things he'd been given.

It felt like his heart was going to burst.

His mom started to cry. "Grandma." She smiled wide and dabbed at her face. Just like Jennie had done.

He glanced at Jennie, but she didn't look at him. Two women he respected. Loved, even. In a way, he always would love Jennie. That was something he'd known since they'd driven out of town. She had been everything he'd needed and wanted in high school.

It astounded him that he now had a second chance. It made him want to believe there really was a God, and He had actually blessed Patrick with everything he needed to fill all those empty, lonely places inside.

"How can this be?"

Patrick moved to the side so he could ask her a question where it was a bit more private. "When we left Erwin, did you know that Jennie was pregnant?"

His mom blustered. "Of course not. Her father nearly killed you. And now you have a son? Just another way to bring you around to her way of thinking."

Jennie let out a whimpering sound. She raced from the stool, down the hall to the bedroom. A second later, the door slammed.

"That was mean." Nate hopped off the stool and stood.

"She didn't mean it," Patrick said. "She doesn't know what's been happening here." And as soon as he could explain it all to his mother, along with what had happened for Jennie since she'd learned she was pregnant, surely his mother would soften toward her.

His mom said, "How could you not have known, Patrick? How could she not have told you?"

He and Nate stared at each other. Torn between their mothers. He was tempted to pray that split wouldn't result in tearing them apart. "I'm going in the other room. Will you get Tucker's toy?"

Nate nodded.

His mom, thankfully, remained silent. Patrick needed to wade carefully through this.

Nothing was going to shake what they were building.

In the bonus room the owners had fixed up like a rec room, Patrick turned the video call back to a regular phone call and put the cell to his ear. "You need to listen to me, Mom."

Nate came in with Tucker's tug toy, and the two started to play. Thankfully out of earshot. Patrick said, "You have to understand that Jennie thought I knew she was pregnant. Her dad told her I asked for money to go away."

She gasped. "You would never have accepted that money, and he would never have given it to you."

"I know that. She faltered in her belief in me and I have to figure out how to forgive her for it. We were gone, and she never got my letters."

His mom fell silent.

"I have a son, Mom."

Nate glanced over from nudging balls across the pool table while Tucker sniffed the carpet underneath. His son and the dog who'd adopted him. There was no going back now.

"I can't believe this." The anger had dissipated. She sounded sad now.

"You need to see Nate in person. Then you'll realize what a great job Jennie did. He's amazing."

The boy blushed, his attention elsewhere, but clearly listening to every word of the conversation. Maybe Patrick didn't have as much work to do as he'd thought. His mom did, though. Nate wasn't the kind of kid who would accept a grandma at odds with the mother he adored, the one who had saved his life.

A scream rang out from the kitchen.

"Mom!"

Patrick hung up and raced after his son. He'd thought she was in the bedroom.

"Tuck!" The dog responded by getting in front of Nate in a protective stance. Patrick ushered both of them into the hall bathroom. "Stay here."

"But—"

Patrick cut him off. "I love you. Please, stay here with Tucker." To the dog he said, "Guard."

No one would get through that door.

Patrick raced down the hall. "Jennie!"

SIXTEEN

She heard him call her name. *Rick*. Jennie turned from the sink.

He raced into the kitchen and practically skidded to a halt.

"Nate." It wasn't a question and yet it was. Where is he? How is he?

"Stop!"

She paused, her foot raised to step toward him. Jennie looked down. Right. She'd dropped a glass in the middle of her freak-out and now there were shattered pieces all over the floor. But was that the point? "Where's Nate?"

He moved to her. "In the bathroom with Tucker. He's safe, and Tucker is guarding him." He stopped and surveyed the room as though attempting to figure out a problem. "What happened?"

"I saw my brother. Outside the window. There were two of them."

She wanted to ask if he was sure Nate was okay, but would that even be helpful? Not likely. Jennie needed to get around the glass and get to him so she could make sure. Not that she doubted Patrick. Of course not. After the last couple days, and what she'd just seen, she needed to reassure herself.

Jennie braced her weight and hopped up to sit on the kitchen counter. She scooted to the end and jumped down. Not the most hygienic of moves, but she didn't want to step on broken glass.

Patrick met her. When she landed, he swept her into his arms.

And didn't let go.

She lifted her chin. "Rick…"

"He's here."

She nodded. That should be the focus right now. The fact her brother was here, along with another man. That meant Patrick was outnumbered. "We should make sure Nate is safe."

"You think Tucker will allow anything to happen to him? At least not without a whole lot of barking to alert me that something is up?"

Jennie relaxed a little, which only served to bring her into closer contact, still tucked against him. Safe in his arms.

He slid his arms from around her and stepped away. A second later, he touched the side of her head and kissed her forehead. "I should call this in. Get backup here."

Jennie flushed. In the heat of the moment she could hardly remember the reasons why falling for him all over again was a bad idea.

Patrick pulled out his phone. She walked to the hall. "Nate? You okay?"

"Yeah, Mom!" His voice sounded shaky, but he was all right. "What's happening?"

"I just dropped a cup, okay?" She didn't want him to worry that his uncle and one of the kidnappers were outside. He would only freak out even more now than he had before. Like she was right now.

"Stay there for another minute. There's broken glass out here and I don't want Tucker to get a cut."

"Okay!"

Giving him a job, and something to focus on—an animal to take care of—would keep him occupied while Patrick figured out what they were going to do.

Jennie got a broom and dustpan from the utility closet to sweep up the glass. She'd been so shocked at seeing her brother trying to hide out of sight. But she'd seen both him and his friend. They were getting ready for something. Preparing to come in, and take Nate from her? She would use this broom, and not for sweeping the floor.

If Martin thought he was going to kidnap her son, he would regret facing her.

The bravado bled away pretty quickly, though. Replaced by the jitters and the shakes. She glanced over at Patrick, jabbing buttons on his phone and muttering to himself.

"What is it?"

"Eric didn't answer." He lifted the phone to his ear. "I'm calling Sheriff Johns."

She'd figured his partner and the sheriff were busy interrogating the men that had been captured at the hospital. But she had also thought that the sheriff was going to her house to check things out. She wasn't a cop, so she'd have no idea what the situation was until Patrick got off the phone and she could ask him.

The same way she planned to ask what the deal was with his mother.

Jennie kept sweeping as she blinked away tears. Hearing his mother's voice over that call had hit her harder than she'd anticipated. She'd been swept up in the tide of it. The love she'd had for his mom, a woman who had meant so much to her back in high school. Jennie had lost her mother at a young age, so she barely remembered her.

Patrick's mom had filled a void, providing support. A sounding board. Maybe she'd told her too much, and his mother had put two and two together when the intimidation started to heat up. She'd figured out it was all Jennie's dad. Then she'd taken her anger and frustration out on Jennie, seeing her as part of the problem instead of what she'd wanted to be.

Part of their family.

Tucker let out a sharp bark.

"No! Tucker!" Her son's cry followed.

Jennie dropped the broom and ran to the hall. The back door, at the end of the hall, was wide open. She raced to it. Before she could run out, Patrick tugged her away. "Stay here."

Because that worked so well?

She followed him outside, but stood on the top concrete step and tried to find…

"Nate!"

Where was he?

Tucker barked again as he faced off with her brother's friend—the second one of her kidnappers. The man kicked out at the dog. Tucker latched on to the kidnapper's pant leg.

Patrick planted his feet wide. "Police! Let me see your hands!"

Jennie searched the whole area for a sign of Nate. Where was he? Still in the house or out here? Maybe he was still in the bathroom.

But when she checked, she didn't see him.

Back at the door, she looked outside again. Nothing. "Nate! Where are you?"

No reply.

"On your knees! Hands behind your head!"

The kidnapper knelt.

She ran over. "Where is my son?!" Her foot caught on a rut in the dirt and she sprawled over.

"Jennie!"

She looked up. "I'm—"

The kidnapper tackled Patrick from behind. A single shove, and Patrick stumbled. Tucker barked and the man raced into the trees.

Instead of following him, Patrick sprinted toward her. She thought he was going to help her to her feet, but he ran inside.

Jennie followed him, but Tucker beat her inside.

When Patrick reappeared, holding a shirt belonging to Nate, she shook her head. Her brother was still out there, and Patrick was messing with a shirt? "You should have gone after that guy. You could have interrogated him until he told you where Nate is and what's going on."

Patrick closed the gap between them and touched his lips hers. "Get your shoes."

What was…?

He held the shirt in front of Tucker's nose. "Scent." The dog stuck his snout in the shirt, nostrils moving. Jennie could hear him taking in air.

She realized what they were doing and ran for some shoes.

The second Tucker moved back from the shirt, Patrick said, "Find."

* * *

The familiar pull of Tucker on the end of the leash settled his stomach, at least some. Up ahead was another neighborhood. Streets. People who could be witnesses. This was work. This, they could do. The worry of a parent was unfamiliar, and Patrick didn't know how to begin to control it.

Last time Nate had been missing, Patrick had been a cop and Nate the victim. Now Patrick was both cop and parent, with the victim being his son.

If Eric was there, he'd be taking lead.

If he'd answer his phone.

Patrick gritted his teeth. He glanced back to make sure Jennie was right behind him. She was flushed, probably more with worry than exertion. She wasn't unfit. But she had hit her head recently, and been knocked out. He'd have to make sure she remained all right. Otherwise she would become a liability that would delay him finding Nate.

Then again, Patrick had zero intention of letting her out of his sight.

Okay, God. If You really are there, then I need Your help. Keep us safe. Together. Help us find Nate.

He wondered then what "together" meant. Here with each other…or more than that.

Tucker took a left turn. Patrick should load the GPS on his phone and figure out where they might be headed. He unlocked the device and handed it to Jennie.

"Find a map. Figure out where we might be going, yeah? But be careful. You don't want to trip and twist your ankle."

She nodded.

He faced forward again, trying not to think about that

kiss. Heat of the moment. He knew she'd been scared. How else was he going to reassure her? Maybe it was selfish, and it was actually him who'd needed reassuring.

Would he have to apologize later?

"We're almost to the edge of town. After that we're in the middle of nowhere," Jennie said. "But there's a road up ahead."

So Martin could have taken their son along this route to get him to that road, where presumably he'd had a car waiting. Or he was being shuffled into another house.

Patrick picked up his pace. "Are you good?"

"Yes." That breathy voice had returned. "Let's just get him back."

Nate was the priority. Over everything, including their safety and their emotions. He knew if the rescue wound up costing him a future relationship with Jennie in some way, it didn't matter. As long as they got Nate back.

He wasn't prepared to give up anyone's life except his own. Though he knew what Tucker was prepared to do to protect the ones he cared about. The dog was relentless, and Patrick knew he wouldn't care if he had to give his life for any of them.

Jennie could stay back. Patrick and his K-9 were going to get their boy. There was no other result that was even remotely acceptable.

"How did it even happen?"

He didn't look at her, just kept going. Right to Nate. "I don't know."

Except that he'd been distracted. She'd seen her brother out front, along with a friend of his. Had that been the distraction? Get Patrick away from Nate, leaving the boy exposed. But Nate had been in the bathroom.

Which meant either Martin or his friend had to have opened the unlocked back door. Perhaps Nate heard the sound and thought the coast was clear enough to come out. Or at least enough to take the dog out the back.

"We'll find him, right?"

"Yes." He realized how short the word had sounded. But he couldn't explain because his phone rang. She handed it to him. "Sanders."

"Hey." It was Eric.

"Where have you been? Martin came to the house. Somehow he found out where we were and he took Nate. We're in pursuit." It physically hurt to say the words.

"I'm on my way. I'll do that 'find your phone' thing and track your location."

"Okay." He managed to navigate through to the settings to enable that feature without slowing down too much.

"Backup would be good." So long as Eric could get here in time. There was a serious chance this whole thing would be over before he showed up. "What about the sheriff?"

"He found nothing at Jennie's house. No one on the land, no one in the house. Just a bunch of tire tracks. Someone was there, but they're gone now."

Patrick frowned. "And the guys from the hospital?"

"I just came out of interrogating the second one. That's why I didn't answer. Because I was getting answers."

Patrick heard a tone there, at the end. "But?"

"Yeah." Eric sighed. "Word is, he's more ruthless than the father—who had a serious reputation himself. And the brother is worse."

"I know." Patrick had lived it. Being beaten and then run out of town.

"You said he has Nate?"

"Yep."

"I'll be there, fast as I can."

"Thanks." Patrick ended the call and handed the phone to Jennie, so she could look at the map again.

Out in front of him, Tucker pulled on the leash, still chasing the scent trail Nate had left behind. One that apparently wound through this end of town. And not in circles. They were heading somewhere specific. If they went too far, or if there was an interruption in the scent, they would lose precious seconds finding it again.

God, help us.

Patrick was desperate enough to call on God when he wasn't sure he believed in Him. It might not be faith, but it was a start at least.

"What did he say?"

Patrick scanned the area around them. Tucker took another turn. He told Jennie what Eric had said about her brother.

She said nothing until, "This, up ahead, it's the end of…" Jennie's voice trailed off.

"I see that."

Town just…ended.

The last street, last house. Then nothing but dirt and shrubs. Like the landscape he'd found her in last night, which felt like weeks ago but had only been a day.

Tucker barked.

Across the street, a paneled van had been parked on the dirt shoulder at the side of the road, the door on the side still open. He couldn't make out what was inside. Patrick unclipped Tucker's leash and commanded, "Find!"

Tucker darted across the street toward the van and hopped in.

Jennie made to rush after him, but Patrick slid an arm around her waist. "Wait." He pulled his gun as men emerged from every hiding spot. Behind parked cars. A waist-high brick wall to their right. Someone in the van yelped. Tucker barked and growled.

Patrick spun around. There were at least eight men surrounding them, all armed. He shoved Jennie behind him, but they were everywhere. Martin's hired help? They looked like thugs. Street dealers. Men who'd do anything for the right price.

"Nate!" Jennie's cry rang out.

Patrick looked over at the van and saw a gunman drag Nate out onto the street. The boy stumbled but didn't go down. Tucker hopped out, barked once and sat beside the boy. Patrick gave him a hand signal that meant "Stay."

Patrick glanced around at the men gathered. "Let him go."

"No," a man's voice called out.

Jennie gasped as Martin Wilson came into view.

Her brother lifted his chin. "You'll be putting your gun down now." He grinned without humor. "You're surrounded."

SEVENTEEN

Jennie tore her eyes away from her son and stared down her brother. "Why are you doing this?"

Tears rolled down her face. Intellectually she'd known her brother was behind this, a "head" knowledge she had understood. Now her heart knew. The realization brought with it the deep sting of betrayal. Her brother was the one who had repeatedly put her and her son's lives in danger.

Now there were guns pointed at them. Nate was scared. So much so that she could hardly meet his gaze. What was she supposed to do? The mom bloggers never covered how to emerge unscathed from a crowd of angry armed men.

They were shady looking, with scruffy hair and dark circles under their eyes. Baggy clothes with stains. The kind of people she didn't want to stereotype, but if she was walking through town with Nate she would have crossed to the opposite side to steer clear of them. Along with saying a prayer that they would find help, if that was what they were looking for.

Then she looked at her brother. Exactly the same kind of man. What had happened to him? The army? His time since then? Maybe she was staring now at the person he had been all along.

Her son moaned. The dog shifted, moving closer to Nate so he could lean on the boy's leg.

Jennie wanted to drop to the ground and start bawling. Though it would likely look and sound more like scared whining.

As her brother stalked toward her, Jennie realized she had no idea what they were supposed to do.

Patrick still had his weapon out.

Martin's gaze was on him as he lifted his gun. And pointed it at *her*. "You're gonna put that down now."

A muscle flexed in Patrick's jaw.

She tried to speak, but nothing emerged except a moan.

Patrick shifted his grip. The gun slipped around in his hand, rotating until he held the butt of it. One of Martin's men snatched it from his hand. The man kicked his foot into the back of Patrick's knee. He fell, hissing in pain, but making no other sound.

Jennie moved to put her hand on his back. As he stood, she held his arm. "Why are you doing this?" she asked her brother again.

Martin only sneered.

"What do you want?" She shook her head, struggling to believe him capable of involving family in his business affairs. He had to know how she would feel about him kidnapping them. Seriously. How could he not know?

He didn't answer her.

She said, "Why don't you just leave us alone?"

"No can do, little sis."

"You and I are *not* family. This isn't what family

does. And the second you thought I wanted you—" she waved her arm, encompassing all of the men around her real family "—and *this*, you gave up the little piece of me that I *might* have considered giving you." She shook her head, vehement now. Shocked to her core that this was happening to her. After all she'd struggled through. The way they'd grown up. The life she'd had with just her and Nate.

Her brother had walked out of her life a long time ago.

"I have to say, I missed the way you get mad at every single thing I do." Martin tipped his head to the side then zeroed in on her with a hard stare. "No, wait. I don't miss that."

"You have to know the army is looking for you. This is only drawing attention to yourself." She wanted to wave Nate over. To have him run to her so she could hold him. But what if he got shot? She didn't want to do anything that would induce these men to hurt her son. Or to hurt Patrick…again.

"I know how to run my business."

"Using *my* land?"

"That land belongs to both of us," he said. "I have as much right to it as you do."

"That's not true. You are no part of this family. Something that was entirely your choice, which you never even bothered to tell me about. You just left. So even if it wasn't completely legally mine, you'd have no part in the ranch. Because you gave it all up."

"Jennie." Patrick's soft voice penetrated, but only a little.

She shifted to square up against her brother again, but Patrick tugged on her elbow. He pulled her close to his side and said, "What do you want, Martin?"

Her brother chuckled. "I guess you have more you owe me than I thought. Including your thanks. Cause you know what? You're welcome." He clapped his hands together, making her jump. "Back together again, right?"

"That has nothing to do with you."

"No?" He grinned.

Why he disagreed, she had no idea. And didn't want to stand around waiting for him to deign to reveal it to them.

"Just tell us what you want." She lifted her chin.

Martin stared at her. "I'll admit, you were a nuisance. Sticking your nose in. Now things are so much worse. Or better." He eyed Patrick. "Depends on how you think about it."

She took a half step back and Patrick put his arm around her waist. She looked at Nate, so sorry that he couldn't be part of the embrace. Tears rolled down his cheeks, causing a new crop to spring free of her eyes and trail down her cheeks. She wanted to mouth *I'm sorry.* As though she'd had any control over this.

God, help us. We need You so badly right now.

She'd forgotten the very thing she had learned all along, raising Nate. Just the two of them. When they had nothing else, they still had everything they needed to get through.

Because they had their Heavenly Father.

I'm sorry, Lord. I should have remembered that You have us in Your hands.

Peace filled her. The kind she'd never felt before.

Patrick lifted both hands. "What do you want?"

"Let's take a ride." Her brother stepped back. "I'll explain when we get there."

"Let Jennie and Nate go with Tucker. Take me."

She wanted to argue that they shouldn't be separated. But maybe he was right. Patrick was a cop. But she and Nate had been together alone for years, and now they had Patrick back she didn't want to lose him all over again.

Martin shook his head. "They come, too."

"Why?" Patrick's tone was hard.

Was he stalling to wait for his partner? Two men against eight was better than one, but it didn't scream "winning team."

Martin waved his gun around. Jennie and Patrick both flinched as her brother yelled, "Get in the van! Now!"

Patrick jolted forward. "Easy."

They walked toward the paneled van. Jennie stuck out her hand. The second she was close enough, Nate grabbed it.

"Tucker, heel."

The dog moved to Patrick's side and walked with him, step for step. Body tight. Eyes alert. He knew something was wrong. And he'd found Nate.

They climbed in and sat in the back of the van.

Nate huddled against her side. Patrick's arms around both of them. Tucker lay down beside his leg. Head up. Eyes still alert.

She reached over and petted his head. "You're a good dog. Yes, you are."

Patrick looked up and quickly realized where they were heading. A fact that was confirmed when they pulled onto the drive in front of the house.

His house.

Beside him, Jennie gasped, her gaze out the window. "That's your house."

"Not for a long time," he said.

Not since her father had forced them from the ranch and from town, as well. At twelve acres, it wasn't as big as her land. But it had been home, and he'd loved living there with his mom after his dad had left. Long enough ago, he didn't even remember the man. Something Nate would never be able to say about him.

Patrick made sure the two in the front—the driver and front passenger—weren't paying attention as he slid his phone from his pant pocket. Tucker shifted. Jennie had praised him, making Patrick practically melt. It was exactly what they'd all needed at that moment. They were all scared, not just Nate. The break in tension of her petting Tucker had made Nate almost giggle.

He thumbed through to his texts, making sure he made no sound, and sent a message to Eric.

The blow came from out of nowhere.

Jennie gasped.

Pain rolled through his head, sparking in his vision and raising bile into his throat. He didn't even feel it when the phone was snatched out of his hand. But he heard Nate cry.

Patrick hissed out a breath and tried to control his reaction to the pain while Tucker barked. He moved his hand blindly and found the dog's flank. "Quiet."

The bark, way too loud, made the pain in his head worse.

When he managed to lift his head, he saw the front-seat passenger had his phone in hand. "Looks like our cop here was trying to call for help."

Patrick waited for the man to pull a gun and shoot him right now, in front of his family.

But the shot never came. Instead, the man rolled the window down and threw the phone out.

Patrick shut his eyes for a second. The guy had to have hit him over the head with the butt of his gun. But he hadn't killed him.

That meant he either wasn't allowed to do anything to them that Martin hadn't authorized, or they didn't want Patrick dead.

Maybe it was that they didn't want any of them dead. But that only made his pain-filled brain wonder what they *did* want with him, Tucker, Jennie and Nate.

Their family.

The van jolted to a stop and Patrick gritted his teeth as the door slid open and sunlight spilled in. He loved that blazing New Mexico sun. Always had. Other places had cloud cover almost all the time. Who wanted to live somewhere like that?

Tucker hopped out of the van and did some business. Patrick would have preferred he'd done it on Martin's shoe but, sadly, that wasn't meant to be.

"Tuck."

The dog trotted back over to stand by him as Jennie and Nate climbed out and huddled close.

Martin called out, already walking to Patrick's old front door. "Get them inside."

The house looked so run down. Ten years of weathering and neglect brought with it a pang of sadness. It was never like this before. His mom might have supported them both single-handedly, but she'd always planted shrubs and made sure the lattice fence and garden rocks were freshly painted. Even if that paint was a castoff from a friend of a friend who worked construction.

Patrick had Jennie and Nate go ahead of him so he could watch their backs. The second they reached the front steps, Martin motioned to Patrick. "Not you. You stay out here."

Good. Patrick wanted to talk to him. He'd rather have done it when his head wasn't pounding and he didn't feel that warm, wet trickle running down the side of his face that he was pretty sure was blood. But he'd take what he could get.

God, help me be strong.

He wanted to rely on God. Patrick had nothing else, not even his own strength, to lean on.

"Dad."

"I know, buddy." He moved to give Nate a hug, but Martin shoved him back.

"Both of you get in the house. Now."

Jennie winced.

Patrick wanted to give her another kiss. Anything but think about the one he'd given her earlier. He didn't need to be distracted right now.

"Can Tucker stay with me?" Nate sounded braver than Patrick felt right now. Perhaps he was gaining strength with everything that had happened.

He'd turned to Martin, who said, "No. Now obey your elders and *get*." He waved at the door.

Jennie ushered him toward it. "Come on, Nate."

Tucker whined, his weight steady against Patrick's leg as Patrick said, "Just tell me what you want." The quicker this was over, the quicker he could get Jennie and Nate out of here. To somewhere safe they could recuperate.

He was thinking Maui.

When Martin didn't answer, Patrick said, "You don't care about anything but yourself, do you? You're trau-matizing both of them." All of them. "And it doesn't bother you one bit."

"Wrong." Martin sneered. "I care about money."

Patrick pressed his lips together, trying not to let disdain for Martin's choices show on his face.

"I care about interruptions in my business. That's where you come in. Since you were good enough to respond to the sheriff's summons, now you'll help me with my problem."

"You coerced him into bringing me here?"

"Not one bit. I hadn't even thought about using a search and rescue dog when I took Jennie and Nate from their house. That was just to scare her so she'd quit calling the cops and the Feds, and then sign her land over to me. Lo and behold, you show up."

Martin lifted his hands and continued, "Lightbulb." He folded his arms across his chest. "You can find my missing truck. She quits calling the law, gives me her land and leaves town. Everyone goes home happy."

"You want me to find a truck?"

This was the first he was hearing about a missing vehicle. They'd played into Martin's hands. Unknowingly, but it was still the truth. Patrick's presence here had made things so much worse for Jennie and Nate. He hadn't wanted his arrival to have done that, even with all they'd gained from him being there.

The truth was out. They would be a family now.

He could explore what was obviously still between him and Jennie—the deep feelings he'd always had for her. They'd never gone away.

Martin shrugged. "I'm an entrepreneur. We have to think on our feet. Two problems, turns out there's one solution."

"You need me."

"Correct."

Patrick's heart sank. "One single hair on either of their heads is touched, and you get *nothing* from me."

Martin laughed. "That's the spirit. There's nothing like a good bargain."

This man was exactly the same as he'd been in high school, but with added experience—which honestly made Patrick more worried right now. Ruthless. Spiteful. He would absolutely hurt them if he thought it would motivate Patrick to do what he wanted.

"I'm supposed to find a truck?"

Martin nodded.

"A truck with drugs in it."

Another nod.

He was tempted to just string Martin along. Instead, he said, "Tucker can't find a truck. And he's not trained to sniff drugs." Since they also didn't have a scent trail, it wasn't as if there'd be anything for the dog to follow. "What do you expect me to do?"

"I expect you to problem solve." Martin waved to one of his guys. "Get me the thing." The man brought him a bundle of material in a grocery bag. Martin held it out. "Here's his sweater. Find this man, I get my truck and the drugs back."

Patrick said nothing.

"If you don't find my drugs, you're all dead." He leaned forward. "All. Four. Of. You."

EIGHTEEN

The hallway closed in around her. Nate huddled close to her side. Gunmen all around. It was dark in here, the walls bare. The floor nothing but broken floorboards and bits of trash.

"It smells in here, Mom."

"I know." She squeezed his shoulder.

Grief rolled through her for what had become of Patrick's house. His mom had taken such good care of it, making sure it was a pleasant place for him to live. A sanctuary from everything that happened outside.

Jennie had modeled her own home for her son on the same principle. A place Nate could rest. Somewhere he *wanted* to come home to at the end of the day, where the atmosphere was one of peace and rest.

Instead, her father had forced Patrick and his mom from their home. Had her brother been using this house since going AWOL from the army?

The man ahead of them shifted. He shoved a door open. "Get in here, kid."

When Nate didn't move from her side, the man reached for him. Both of them stepped back. She stumbled a little but kept them from falling down. She didn't want to know what nasty thing they would land on.

"Let's go, Nate." She tugged him forward so they could enter the room. Safety. Space. Somewhere they could wait together and not be bothered.

"No," the gunman said. "He goes. You're in there." He pointed at a room across the hall.

"We're staying together."

"Those aren't my orders."

"And you do everything my brother tells you?"

"Pays the bills." The man shot her a toothy grin, his stubbled face displaying his amusement. He enjoyed this. She might even be inclined to believe he particularly enjoyed their fear. What horrible things had he done in his life?

Maybe she didn't want to know.

He waved his gun between them and the room. "Now, he goes in there. Got it?"

"No." Anger surged in her. She wanted to stomp her foot. Put her hands on her hips. It worked with a room full of boys at a sleepover. These were just overgrown boys, right? She planned to treat them as such because she was just fed up. "No. We aren't getting separated. My son will stay with me."

The door behind her was shoved open so hard it bounced off the wall. Martin stormed in. "What's going on?"

"You're not separating us."

Beyond him she could see Patrick, standing outside with Tucker. The look of helplessness and fear on his face was surely a match to what was on hers. Neither of them could get their family out of this alone. He'd tried, and they'd slammed his head.

Now there was blood running down the side of his face.

"You'll do as you're told."

Jennie faced down her brother. "Nate is nine years old. He was already kidnapped and terrorized. You're *not* separating us."

She prayed things weren't going to get worse. That her actions now wouldn't cause additional problems for any of them. But this was nonnegotiable. She held Nate to her side.

Martin huffed out a breath. "This is all your fault. I should separate you, considering all the problems you've caused me."

"Because I wouldn't allow you to trespass on *my* land."

He really thought this was her fault? All she'd done was call the authorities. Had she known at the outset that it was her brother, she would probably do the exact same thing as she had before. After all, a criminal didn't get special treatment just because they were family. Especially not when Martin had been absent from her life longer than Nate had been with her.

Seeing him now did nothing more than break her already shattered heart.

The man he could have been was evident when she put him side by side with Patrick. Goodness and evil. There wasn't a greater contrast in life, was there? The ultimate opposites, they would be forever at odds.

She was sad for who he was now—who he thought he should be. The man her father had made him into. She'd had Patrick, and it just hadn't been the same between her and her father. But he'd groomed Martin to follow in his footsteps. To do exactly this.

Still, the life he lived now... On the run, full of not

much besides illegal activity to fill his time. He would have to always look over his shoulder. It was all down to his own choices.

The decisions he'd made.

As much as she wanted to be immune to him, a tear rolled down her face anyway.

Martin ignored it. "I'd have been free to do what I wanted if you'd just *left things alone*. Instead you've caused me so many headaches I have a migraine because of you."

She should have called the army back a year ago. They'd have swooped in and taken him into custody, right? Problem solved.

Martin snickered. "I can see you planning something. Well, you know what? It won't work. So don't waste your energy. Keep your son quiet. Patrick does his job, and you get to go free."

"But you'll continue like nothing is wrong?"

"No. I'll be long gone. One last severance payment for everyone I employ and I go live my life. You'll never see me again."

That was enough to make her smile. He would be gone? "Fine." She had every intention of calling the army and telling them everything as soon as she got to a phone. "Nate and I stay together."

"Get in there."

She looked at Patrick. He gave her a short nod, everything he wanted to say plain on his face. She wanted to mouth the words *I love you*, though she wasn't all the way there. Yet. Those feelings were fast coming back.

Jennie had loved him once. Had that ever really gone away? Giving those words to him now would mean everything to her. Yes, there were qualifiers. She was falling for him again. But complicating it with specifics didn't mean much. In a situation like this, she needed to either go for it or not. Their lives were on the line.

Why not her heart, as well?

He lifted his chin. "It'll be okay."

She nodded back. "Okay."

A pact. They were together. Even if they got separated, they'd stick with each other through this. Come out of it a family. Where it wouldn't be too soon or too complicated. She'd be able to tell him the simple truth of how she felt.

Martin strode outside. His man shoved them into the empty room and slammed the door.

Nate walked around the empty space for a second. He settled against the wall and slid down, knees to his chin. Jennie sat beside him.

"I wish Tucker was in here."

She gathered him to her, holding him in her arms. "Sorry, buddy. I guess he needs to work."

Nate made a *pfft* sound through his lips but said nothing.

"We should pray." She didn't wait for him to agree or disagree. It shouldn't matter whether she "felt like it" or not. The situation was out of control and they needed to hand it over to the One who was in control of everything.

Jennie prayed over them, and over Patrick's work with Tucker, asking God to help them get out of this alive.

Nate said, "Amen."

Jennie shuddered. A vibration of fear she could no longer contain.

Help my son to live.

A gun jabbed into his back. Patrick stumbled away from the house. "Okay. Ease up." He turned to them, hands raised. "You got what you wanted, so just lay off, okay?"

Yeah, he was repeating himself. But it seemed like these guys needed an extra hand understanding. He was supposed to find a truck? Martin knew that didn't have a scent. And a man, from his sweater? Sure, if they could find a place where he'd actually been. If they had no idea where he was, how was Patrick supposed to have Tucker find the scent? It would be like finding a needle in a haystack that could be thirty miles away, for all they knew. And drugs? Tucker hadn't been trained as a drug detection dog, so that wasn't a possibility.

Patrick scrubbed both hands down his face. When he looked, Tucker was leaning forward. Body straight, muscles tense. The hair on the back of his neck stood on end. Any second now he would flash his teeth and growl.

He wanted to let the situation escalate in a way Martin would regret, but that would result in Tucker being hurt. Patrick pulled the long leash from the pocket of his cargo pants and snapped it on. "Heel."

Tucker shifted to his side, but didn't back down. Much.

Martin eyed the dog, then said, "We got a problem?"

"What do you think?"

"I think you're going to find my truck."

Patrick didn't even know where to start with that. "He can't find a vehicle. Or a man who's been in a vehicle. If the windows were rolled up, there's no scent. And he's not trained to find drugs."

"He's a search and rescue dog, right? So search for my truck and rescue my drugs."

Patrick blew out a breath. What did this guy expect him to do? It literally wasn't possible. "Do you have an idea of the location where he is, or somewhere he was, like, when you last saw your friend?"

There were a million other questions rolling around in his head, but that was a pretty good start.

"I'll give you what I have."

That sounded more like a threat than an intention to share information. This man was a dangerous loose cannon. After all, he'd lived under the radar for the better part of a year since he'd walked away from the army and disappeared into civilian life—the criminal underworld.

"And I'll have to figure out how to do the impossible, I guess."

Martin shrugged. "The alternative is I kill you and Jennie, take Nate and raise him as my son."

Patrick surged forward. Tucker did the same, barking at Martin.

Jennie's brother lifted his gun and pointed it at Patrick's face.

That was the only thing that stopped him from tackling the guy. Take his son, when he'd just met the boy? Destroy his life, and Jennie's, and all that could be?

"No." He practically stared down the barrel of the gun. Never a good spot to be in. Even with a K-9 partner by his side, Patrick was in serious danger.

"Mmm. I agree."

So this was about control, then. "Just give me what you have and let me do my job. Then, you *will* let us go. Unless you want the army crawling all over this place and breathing down your neck until they finally catch up with you."

"As if they will. I've gotten away with it so far."

"They know you're here." Patrick shrugged one shoulder. "The call's already been made. Wheels are in motion. In fact, it's probably only a matter of hours before they descend on this place en masse."

Boy did it ever feel good to say that to this guy's smug face.

Until Martin slammed the gun down, aiming for the same spot where he'd already been hit. Patrick turned away from him in time. The butt of the gun slammed into his shoulder instead. He grunted at the impact as pain reverberated through his torso.

He straightened. "Everything you have?"

"Good choice." Martin waved to one of his buddies.

The gunman spread a map of the local area on the hood of the van that had brought them here. The kind of map you'd buy at a grocery store. Only this one had penciled lines. Notations. Asterisks. There was a clearly indicated route that cut through the foothills from what had been Patrick's home, across the desert, through Jennie's land, to the highway east of town.

"This is where he was last seen." Martin pressed a dirt-smeared finger north of Jennie's land.

"That's why you were trespassing?" Or, at least, why there'd been an uptick in activity on her land recently.

"He went missing five days ago."

"And you want your drugs?"

"We all have our retirement plans."

Patrick had a lot to do *before* retirement—like get his family back. All of it. The way it should be. But he got what Martin meant. "What's in that truck is your nest egg? How do you know the driver didn't take off with the drugs and he's in Mexico by now?"

Martin pulled out a phone. "GPS. The tracker in the truck went offline. That's how we lost him. Then he never checked in when he should have. But he couldn't have disabled the tracker himself. He didn't even know about it. Besides, he's dumb as a box of rocks. Actually, that's an insult to rocks."

Patrick faced off with Jennie's brother. "Great. Let's go out there and I'll get Tucker to search for a scent. Assuming that item of clothing you've got is even something he can get a scent from."

He was waiting for a hitch in this plan that would mean Martin had no use for them.

So long as his not needing them anymore didn't mean he would execute them all and leave them out here. Or stage some kind of elaborate murder-suicide scene to throw off the sheriff.

"Is the sheriff in your pocket?"

Martin shrugged. "I might do that. If he actually cared enough to try to get rid of me, I'd probably offer to pay him money."

That didn't answer Patrick's question. Not really. "So he just leaves you alone?"

Martin said, "I don't care about him. Find my truck."

"Give me that sweater so I can use it for a scent." That was better than trying to get a straight answer out of Jennie's brother.

Martin looked about ready to slam him with the gun again, but Patrick didn't care. What more could Martin do, or threaten to do, that hadn't already been done to him by the men in Jennie's family? Then there was the damage they'd done to Jennie. To Nate. They'd been through enough—too much, in fact.

One of the men retrieved the grocery bag holding the sweater.

"Ready to go, Tucker?" He needed to get the dog excited about work. Focused on Patrick, and not the fact he wanted to be in the house with Nate.

I know how you feel.

Martin's phone buzzed. He pulled it from his pocket and muttered under his breath. "The sheriff is headed here. Everyone load up. Now!"

"What about Jennie and Nate?" He wasn't going to give them back to the sheriff, was he? That would mean he'd lost all his leverage.

"They come, too." He turned to his gunman friend. "Get them. Two minutes. Let's move!"

Patrick was shoved toward a car as Jennie and Nate came out.

"What's happening?"

He got close enough to grasp her hand. "The sheriff is coming."

But the happiness on her face was short lived.

One of the gunmen grabbed Nate around the waist and hauled him away from them.

"Mom!"

NINETEEN

"Nate!"

She'd been shoved into that room. Then, only minutes later, she'd been dragged back out. Now Jennie didn't even know what was happening.

The sheriff is coming.

Patrick moved with her. But Martin stepped in front of them, blocking the path to their son. Who had been ripped from her arms.

"Move!" She screamed in her brother's face, tears streaming down her cheeks once again. Maybe they hadn't ever stopped. "You can't keep me from my son."

"Get in the van." Martin looked deadly serious, like he was inclined to shoot whenever he decided to.

She halted, though everything inside her wanted to shove him out of the way—gun or no—and race for Nate.

Her son was currently being dragged away. He kicked and screamed against his captor, struggling to break free of the man's grip. A man who looked like he'd go up against a biker without breaking a sweat. Ruthless. Evil, maybe.

Did she believe in her heart that Martin would actually kill her if she ran for Nate? Maybe not. But he would shoot to maim her.

"Let's go. In the van. *Now.*"

Jennie's body jerked with the force of his order. A sob worked its way up her throat, but she didn't let it out. Crying wouldn't help.

Tucker barked. Jennie sniffled and Patrick tugged her toward the van. Didn't he want to go after Nate? Instead, he was hauling her toward the van. Doing what her brother ordered them to do. Why? Johns was on his way, so that meant they should delay as much as possible to ensure they were still there when he showed up.

The sheriff wasn't in on it. She'd wondered before, but if Martin was purposely avoiding him then the man was a threat to Martin's plans. He wasn't in Martin's pocket. If he was, then it wouldn't make sense for them to run.

She turned to glare at Patrick. *Nate.*

"I know." It was like he knew what she was thinking. Probably it was written on her face. *Good.* He said, "Come on."

He wanted to help Martin by cooperating?

Patrick tugged her on, the muscle in his jaw flexing. Tucker hadn't moved when they had, causing them to bump up against him. The dog barked at the man currently holding Nate where Jennie couldn't reach him.

"Tuck. Heel."

Her brother motioned with the gun. "You keep that dog in line. And no commands to bite anyone."

"He isn't a protection dog. He finds people."

"Good." Her brother nudged the gun into *her* back. "Now get moving." Then he told the man holding Nate, "Take a walk."

The man nodded. He already knew what that meant?

Jennie watched, her eyes stinging they were so wide, as Nate was taken from her between the house and the dilapidated old garage Patrick's mom had used for storage.

Martin shoved them to the van. "Get in."

She spun around instead. "Don't let that man hurt him. And don't you let him even *touch* my son. That is your nephew. If you have any good inside you at all, you won't leave him in the hands of someone who could hurt him." Or worse. Some wounds healed. Others were never visible to anyone else, and yet the bearer carried the pain for years.

God, please. Not my son.

Martin shoved her back again. The gun glanced off her collarbone and his other hand slammed into her, toppling her over into the van. Backward, so she fell awkwardly.

Patrick sucked in a breath, sounding like he was in pain. Tucker's tags jingled. Jennie pushed off the floor of the van and winced at the ache where she'd landed.

"Let's go!" Her brother's voice rang out.

Patrick climbed in the van, and she heard Tucker move around her. Jennie curled up. After a second, she realized she was crying.

"Okay." Patrick gathered her into his arms. "Come here, Jen."

She sucked in a choppy breath and let the tears flow.

He pulled her close and held her in the strength of his arms, one hand rubbing up and down her back as the van rumbled along.

"Nate." Her voice was barely a whisper, more like a moan. She squeezed her eyes shut and prayed he would be safe. Unharmed. She could no longer pray he wouldn't be traumatized by this. That was a fact they would all now have to live with. It was real, and it was going to be part of Jennie's future as a mom.

Because they *were* going to get past this. She would get Nate back and they'd move on. With Patrick in their lives.

No matter what, she was going to have God to thank for everything if they were all alive. Life went on.

Jennie lifted her forehead from Patrick's neck and pushed off his shoulders as she sat. She wasn't going to fall apart anymore. Not when God would always be there for her.

"Hey." He touched her cheeks, wiping away tears.

Jennie didn't have any words. She touched her forehead to his and shut her eyes.

"It's gonna be okay. I'll find his guy, and his drugs, and all this will be over."

He wanted her to believe that? Maybe she did and maybe she didn't. But she could agree on faith that the assurance would come later. Despite the circumstances. Despite the prognosis.

That was what faith was.

"The sheriff will show up at my house. Eric, too. They'll realize what's happening and track us all down. This many people together won't go unnoticed for long."

She nodded and lifted her head, opening her eyes. "Thank you for being here."

He'd been called to this job because of his position. Not because of her—at least, not that she could surmise. All she wanted to think about was Nate. But Patrick had come. He was the only man she'd ever loved. Her son's father.

She touched his cheeks then pressed her lips to his. "Thank you."

"There's nowhere else I'd rather be."

God, keep our son safe. It was like a mantra, rolling through her head over and over again.

Patrick held her gaze with his. Soft. Determined. "I'm not leaving. No matter what. I'm going to do this for your brother, and we'll get Nate back. That's nonnegotiable. Okay?"

Like him, she could hardly contemplate losing her son.

"I'm not leaving."

She lifted her gaze. Why repeat that? Unless he was coming to care for her, as she was for him. Probably she was way past that right now. Falling for him, when she'd been in love with him for more than ten years?

Jennie was going to trust him. "Good."

The van bounced over a rut in the dirt road and her mouth bounced against his. Her cheek slammed into his jaw. He gritted his teeth. "Sorry."

Jennie squeezed her eyes shut. "Let's just pray for Nate."

"Okay." His arms tightened for a second, imbuing her with another dose of comfort as she spoke her prayer aloud until the van pulled to a stop.

Patrick kissed her forehead and she opened her eyes, shifting so the gunmen and her brother didn't see how close they'd gotten. She felt better, but that didn't even touch the fear she held for Nate. Nothing would cure that. Not until her son was back in her arms.

Safe.

She pulled away, but Patrick still felt her weight against him. Shared warmth. The echo of the feelings roiling inside him. Nate, alone with a dangerous gunman. Held captive until Patrick found this truck, its driver and the drugs inside.

The van door slid open. She scooted away from him, but he touched her arm. "Let me get out first."

He wanted to protect her. It was an imperative now. There was nothing else he could do but keep her as safe as possible. *God, help me keep them both safe.* It was coming more naturally now to lift up a prayer. Something to be thankful for, even in the middle of everything that was happening. Faith grew in him, incrementally with each new occurrence.

Except it seemed like things were only getting worse, not better.

Tucker hopped down.

"Heel." Patrick shortened the distance between them and kept the tension on the leash. Now, more than ever, Tucker needed to know that Patrick was the one in charge.

With his free hand, he kept Jennie behind him, hopefully out of the line of fire. She closed in, one hand on his left hip as she peered around his right shoulder. Close enough she could touch her cheek to his arm.

Martin came over.

"This is where the truck was last seen?" Patrick asked.

They weren't too far from the back portion of Jennie's land. Maybe five miles. They were parked in a dirt lot of an abandoned bar, shut down long enough ago that the windows were boarded up and what remained had been smashed by rocks—probably thrown by local kids messing around.

This place? Jennie's father had reigned as king here. Not surprising Martin had gravitated toward it. Seemed like he'd been trying to take over his father's empire. Resurrect the old days. Because he wanted to be as lucrative as his dad or because he simply missed the old man? This might even have been the place Martin had been living in since he'd walked away from the army. Squatting in an abandoned building was no kind of life, no matter how much cash he had from illegal operations. It wasn't like he was putting it in a savings account for wherever he moved next.

Patrick didn't want Martin trying any of his father's methods for keeping people in line on him, Tucker or Jennie. Or Nate.

God, help us.

Martin studied him. "So eager to get started?"

"Let's just do this. The quicker I find your stash, the quicker we're all done with this," Patrick said. "You know the cops are on your heels. It's only a matter of time before the sheriff's department—and the army—is breathing down the back of your neck."

Martin grinned. He pulled out his phone and made a call. When the recipient answered, the only thing he said was "Do it." Then he hung up and looked at the scenery to the west.

An explosive blast shuddered the sky. The fireball rolled up into the air from a structure over there, and wind blew at them in a single gust.

Jennie huddled closer to Patrick's back. "Was that the garage?"

Nate. His son hadn't been inside. But that didn't mean Martin lacked the means to make good on his threats.

"Don't worry about the sheriff, or anyone else finding us," Martin said. "I'm not."

Well, he was. Patrick was also worried about Eric.

His partner was smart, but that didn't mean he couldn't ever be caught unawares.

"Give me the bag. Tucker can get started."

If there was even a scent to find and the truck driver had been traveling with the windows down to leave a trail, and recently enough that the scent would still linger. And yet, given everything Jennie had told him had been going on, it must have been long enough at least one weather front had rolled across this desert.

There was probably nothing left to find.

He still figured the most likely thing that had happened was that the man had taken the drugs and made a run for it. He was likely hiding in Mexico, or somewhere he could stay under the radar, and off-loading the merchandise to someone who would pay cash and ask no questions.

Patrick just had to string Martin along long enough for Eric to catch up with them. Or the sheriff, the DEA or the army. Patrick was feeling pretty equal-opportunity about their rescue.

But help would come.

I believe, Lord. Help me do this.

Martin's guy gave him the grocery bag containing the sweater. Patrick bemoaned the fact he'd never trained Tucker to fake finding a scent. Maybe they should try that. Though, it would be seriously difficult to get a scent dog to do the work under a separate set of commands when there was nothing and he had no idea where to go because he wasn't following anything. Go in circles? Go for a run?

That was a problem for another time.

"Scent." He held out the bag.

When Tucker had sniffed the contents enough, Patrick handed back the bag and they set off.

Tucker headed for the building. He circled around, sniffing the wall in a couple of places.

"He isn't in there."

Patrick didn't look back at Martin. "Doesn't matter. This could take a while. That's why I wanted to get started. If your man is miles from here, we could be doing this all day."

"Okay." The tone was like he'd said "So?"

Patrick tried not to glare at the sarcasm. "I just want to know Nate is all right."

He followed Tucker away from the highway and into the desert. There wasn't a road out here. Had the man he was looking for walked out into the middle of nowhere?

He didn't like the scenarios going through his head.

"Me, too," Jennie said. "I want to know Nate is okay."

One glance at Martin, walking behind them, told Patrick the man didn't much care what Jennie or Patrick intended to do. Patrick said, "You need me. And Tucker. One command and he lays down."

"One command and your son starts bleeding."

Patrick pressed his lips together. "Just let me know he's all right."

It took Martin a minute to make the call. When it was answered he said, "Yeah. Put the kid on."

Patrick glanced back.

Jennie held the phone, now on the line with their son.

"Hi." Relief washed over her face. "You okay?" She listened, her lips pressed into a thin line.

After a minute, Martin snatched the phone back and hung up. "Now you know."

Patrick set off in a slow jog. Tucker had something.

He picked up his pace for another twenty minutes, until they were almost two miles from the building by his guess. That was when Tucker found the man.

Patrick saw him first. Before anyone else could catch up and see, he tugged on the leash. "Heel." When Tucker came to him, Patrick said, "Good boy," and petted his head.

Tucker was confused. He hadn't sat to let his master know he'd completed the task.

Patrick praised Tucker as if he had, while he tried to figure out what to do.

The truck was nowhere in sight.

"What is it?" Martin picked up his pace and approached.

Jennie didn't look like she was doing very well. Her face had flushed, and she was breathing hard. He figured she needed to sit, with Nate on her lap.

"Well?" Martin waved at the desert in front of him.

"He's right there." Patrick indicated the area where Tucker had stopped. A man lay on the ground, facedown. "Is that your guy?"

He knew the answer to that, even before Martin rolled him over. And then kicked the dead man in the leg while he yelled out his frustration. "Where are my drugs?"

TWENTY

Jennie turned away from the dead man. Bile rose, anyway, and she had to pace a few steps farther to an out-of-the-way spot where she could spit. There was nothing in her stomach to deposit on this middle-of-nowhere land, no matter if she wanted to throw up or not.

He was dead. Really dead. Not that there was a midpoint where someone was partially dead. Especially when they'd very obviously been out here a while given the flies.

"You okay?"

She turned to Patrick. His expression was one of sympathy. He didn't think less of her for reacting like this to a dead guy?

Jennie managed to nod. "I'm good." As soon as she could swallow, she would be even better.

There was so much going on, though, the state of her stomach didn't really rate. A dead guy? That was a little higher on the scale. She wandered to Patrick and leaned down to pet Tucker. "Is he really dead?"

He nodded. "Sorry. It looks like he hit his head, or maybe was struck."

"So he might have been murdered? Like someone killed him and stole the truck?"

Martin let go of the dead man, done searching the guy's pockets. And his shoes, for some reason, that were now discarded on the dirt. He strode to her. "This was betrayal, not murder. This man worked for me, and I take his death seriously."

"Great." It came out before she could call it back, sarcasm threading through her tone. She couldn't believe anything about her brother now. Who he was. How he was. All of it churned her insides even more than that dead guy.

She folded her arms over her stomach. "You care about your people's lives, but not the lives of your own family? Isn't that just great."

"Don't comment on things you know nothing about."

She shrugged. "People do it all the time online." Why did he care what she said now? He barely thought about her.

Martin shook his head. "If I don't get my money, who do you think is going to die?" He slapped his chest. "This part of your precious *family*."

"You don't care about my life, so why should I care about yours?"

She shouldn't but did. And when did care have anything to do with a person's worth? That wasn't how feelings worked.

"Why will you die if you don't find it?" She was careful to keep her tone even. He was like a bomb about to explode at any moment if she did or said the wrong thing. "Tell me."

"The men who gave me those drugs expect payment.

If I can't get it from sales, it comes out of the collateral. My life."

That sounded like a horrible business model. She wished she'd never asked. Jennie could have lived her whole life never knowing that was how the drug business worked. Then again, given her family history, she probably should have put that together. If she'd spent any time at all actually thinking on it—which she hadn't.

"You were nothing but a memory." She faced him down. "Now you're a nightmare come to life."

She'd tried to get him to realize he was hurting his family. Martin didn't care about their lives, even just the tiniest bit. He was oblivious to what he was doing to the people he should always care about, no matter what. Martin cared about nothing but himself. And money. He had no conscience, not anymore.

The only person who had always cared about Jennie, no matter what? Patrick. He and Nate were the only people she could say the same about for herself. Unconditional love. That was what they'd given each other.

Jennie paced away from her brother. Patrick held out his arm, so she walked into his embrace, eyes shut tight to try to block everything out and just focus. Pray. Believe in faith for her son.

But she could get no clarity.

Jennie gave him a squeeze and pulled away. She walked farther. Away from the dead man and her evil brother. She kicked at the ground and tried to wrestle through what she wanted to say to God. She was at the point it was tempting to start making demands, but it didn't work like that. Her Father in Heaven wasn't going to acquiesce just because she tried to force Him to.

Please.

It was all she could manage.

A spot on the ground caught her attention. Dark colored. Not something she usually saw out in her desert. She didn't have the time or the heart to care, whatever it was. Jennie kept going and stomped on it because that was how much she shouldn't care. Not at all. Until she saw another spot.

This whole thing had ruined her ever wanting to hike, camp or try practically any other outdoor activity again. Though, when she got Nate back—not *if*—she'd be happy to do anything he wanted. It didn't matter how she felt. As long as Patrick came, too, she would be safe.

She glanced back at Patrick, but he was in a hushed conversation with Martin. Strong. He'd been disarmed, but that hadn't taken much away from his presence.

Neither man looked happy, both faced off with the other, but she didn't like the tension in Patrick at all. She wanted him to be relaxed. The man she loved should be safe and secure, no worries. Wasn't that the goal in life? Of course not, because bad things happened anyway.

She blew out a breath, wanting to kick at the ground again. "I want my son back!" She wasn't ashamed to yell the words to whomever was listening. Her brother. All of them. Who cared about Martin and his stupid drugs? "I want my son back *now*!"

One of the nearby gunmen snickered.

Great. He thought she was an emotional woman throwing a tantrum. She was, but it was justified.

Jennie stomped toward him. He backed up two paces. "Whoa. Calm down."

"Jennie!" Her brother snapped the word at her.

She swung around to him and yelled like she would have done when they were kids. "What?"

"We're closer than we've been in weeks. Calm down."
He scrubbed at his head.

Jennie moved to him. There was another spot on the
ground, between her and the…deceased man. He'd been
out here awhile and she—

Don't think about that.

She stared at the ground. "What is *that*?"

Patrick moved closer. "Looks like blood droplets.
Probably from the dead guy." He looked at Martin. "If
we follow them, there might be a trail. Maybe he crashed
the truck and tried to walk for help. Could be it was an
accident."

Martin studied the ground.

Jennie walked back to where she'd been. "There are
more over here. They go this—"

A shot blasted. She froze, too late to avoid it. Dirt
had already kicked up from Martin's shot at the ground
faster than she ever could have moved.

"Easy!" Patrick said.

Martin waved the gun. "Jennie, get back here. You
wander off too far, you're as dead as that guy. I'll leave
you out here for the birds."

He saw her shiver. Patrick wanted to do the same,
but held himself steady as they followed the blood trail.
Would it lead to the source?

He wanted this done. No more gunmen pointing
weapons at him, or Jennie. Not even to shoot the ground
by her feet and scare her. Patrick wanted Nate back in
his arms. All this over with already. *Please, Lord.* He'd
been stubborn for so long, it felt freeing to not have to
rely on himself for this.

He could simply trust.

Martin studied the ground, content to let his men watch his back. But how long would that last? He was motivated to get his drugs. To save his life. Patrick had thought—from what he'd said—that this was about a nest egg. In a way, it was. But only in the sense that it would keep him alive when the men who'd supplied him with the drugs demanded payment.

"It doesn't have to be like this, you know."

Martin eyed the ground as they walked. Tucker thought they were out for a stroll. He'd never been interested in blood before and didn't seem to be now. He kept turning his head to look back. Making sure Jennie was okay?

Martin said, "This the part where you offer me witness protection?"

"You think you've got enough on these guys to warrant that?" Patrick wasn't afraid of him. Not when God was in control. And no matter what happened, God would still be in control. "Because we can protect you."

Martin scoffed.

"It doesn't have to be like this," he repeated. "The police can search for this truck much more effectively, especially if it's out here in the middle of nowhere. We don't have to walk miles and miles."

It was cold, and the January wind whipped at his face. Soon enough they'd all have red cheeks and chapped lips. Not devastating, but so unnecessary.

Most of this could have been avoided. Patrick tried not to get angry, but it was there.

"These people don't have to threaten your life. We can get the drugs off the streets. We'll protect you, and maybe even try to talk the army into not putting you in prison for deserting your obligation and disappearing.

If you testify against whomever you got the drugs from, we can make sure they stop. Cut off the drug trade and get more of those substances off the streets."

It was poison, and it killed every day while it sucked in yet more people to the tangled web of addiction. No one wanted that. But Martin, following in his father's footsteps, could be a whole other story. Maybe he didn't care. He was just out to make money.

"That's how you think you'll talk me down?" Martin asked. "Offer me a minimum wage life under a new name, some nobody in some nowhere town? Stop me from hurting any more people." Those last few words were said in a high, whiny voice.

Patrick bit down on his molars. "It's the right thing. After what you've done? I doubt you'll be free even a year before you die. And here you are, racking up even more charges. Digging your hole deeper." Anger got the better of him. "I hope you fall in it."

This guy was going straight to military prison when the army caught up and he finally had to explain what those incidents in Afghanistan were about. Patrick figured they had charges in the works and Martin had essentially slipped bail.

Then there were the civilian charges. He could've disappeared. Instead, he'd resurrected a legacy of crime and death just to make a buck.

Guys like him were the kind of people Tucker flushed out every day. People with no regard for others, only themselves.

Patrick leaned down and petted his dog's flank.

Tucker barked.

Patrick looked at him, then at the expanse of land in front of them. "What is it, buddy?"

He thought he saw something up ahead. Probably just a critter Tucker smelled, but he walked faster. Shrub brushes collected together, as though congregation was more important than height. A bundle of sand shinnery oak stood together. The dirt behind looked like it might be a path, or some kind of fire road.

Old. Abandoned.

"The truck!" Jennie moved to his left, staying out of Martin's arm reach. He didn't blame her for that.

They all circled the bushes and saw the truck, on its side. Patrick looked in the front windshield and said, "There's blood on the window."

The open door at the top was the passenger side. Was that how the dead man had climbed out? The driver's door was smashed against the dirt.

"I think he hit a rut and flipped over. Hit his head." And still managed to climb out and walk or crawl to where he now lay? That was some determination. Patrick almost admired the man.

"Check inside." Martin waved his gun from pointing to Patrick's torso to the truck.

"Secret compartment, like the old bootleg days?"

"Get in there."

Patrick walked to Jennie instead, leading Tucker. "Can you please hold the leash?"

The frown on her face indicated she was about as excited about this as he was. Patrick handed over the leash, then leaned down and quickly touched his lips to hers. He whispered, "It'll be okay."

She shot him a wry look, but it was soft.

Patrick went back to Martin. Before he climbed to the open door and got in, he wanted all the information. "Any guesses on where this stash is hidden?"

Martin clearly didn't want to answer but he said, "Under the floorboard behind the front seat."

Patrick looked at the sky and sighed. When he retrieved the drugs, would Martin simply shoot them and walk off with his stash? Patrick didn't like the idea that they would be left for dead out here. *I'll raise your son as my own.* The thought of that made him want to throw up as Jennie had done when confronted with the dead body.

"Let's go, cop."

Patrick pressed his lips in a thin line. "You don't have to try bargaining with these guys. It can end differently... with you doing the right thing."

No more loss of life. No more threat.

"Your nephew doesn't need to be an orphan."

He heard Jennie's soft gasp but couldn't comfort her right now. Patrick needed to eliminate the threat here first. Otherwise it was all over.

Martin said, "As long as I'm alive, what do I care?"

"If that guy is hurting him—"

"Get in the truck and get my drugs." Martin pointed the gun at Patrick's face. He realized then that it was his gun.

"He's right," Jennie called out. "You don't have to do this." *To Nate.* She didn't say it, but he heard the words anyway. They made his chest hurt in a way it never had before. "It's not right. You're only causing more pain. Don't do this."

One final plea for her brother to do the right thing. But it fell on deaf ears. Or stubborn ones.

Martin shifted the gun from Patrick to her. His own sister.

Patrick realized what was about to happen. He moved,

instinct firing his muscles. He ran for Jennie and Tucker, determined to protect them.

The gunshot cracked like a firework. Without thinking, Patrick tackled Jennie.

Pain shot through his shoulder as he fell toward her. Tucker yelped at them. Jennie screamed as the two of them hit the ground together.

TWENTY-ONE

It took Jennie a second to realize she was screaming. She sucked in a breath—which caused the noise to cease for a second—and blew it out the way she had when she'd birthed Nate. Everything that had just happened rushed back in one go.

Martin. Tucker. Patrick.

Focus.

"Patrick." She touched his shoulder with one hand, pushing at his weight, and pressed two fingers to his neck with the other. The man she loved. The one who had saved her life. "Rick…" Calling him that was so natural now, even if it was little more than a breathy moan. "Rick."

His weight was heavy on her, and she felt a steady pulse. Tucker barked. The wet feel of… *Don't think about that.* A buzzing noise interrupted her thoughts. Patrick still hadn't moved or even moaned. She turned his face to her and patted his cheek. "Wake up. Please wake up."

"Cops!" One of the gunmen beat feet away from them. Scurrying off to try to escape what was inevitable.

"No, they're army!" someone else shouted.

Whoever it was, Jenny didn't much care. Either way, they were the good guys and she wanted these bad guys to leave. Or at least not try to hurt any of them again.

Tucker barked. He sounded agitated, and she realized she was learning his temperaments. Jennie looked at her brother, who had tried to kill her. Gun pointed, trigger pulled, actually *fired a shot* in her direction. She couldn't believe it. So much so that it wasn't just Patrick's weight causing her to be breathless.

Martin stared up at the sky, his jaw hard. His reckoning was coming. But not before he told them where Nate was. Still at Patrick's house, or somewhere else?

Jennie would get her son back. She would. *God, keep my son safe until I get there.*

Patrick groaned. Jennie rolled him off her, onto the ground beside her. Tucker leaned forward on his four paws. After a second of tension, he barked twice. The action caused his front paws to lift off the ground as he announced his displeasure at Martin.

"Tucker!"

She didn't want her brother to hurt him. What if Tucker got injured and Patrick wasn't conscious enough to intervene?

Patrick groaned again and she heard him suck in a long breath. The next sound from him was a moan.

Jennie didn't know if it would work, but she said, "Tucker, come!" using a loud, commanding voice like Patrick did.

The dog glanced at her.

"Come."

He started toward her.

Jennie peeled off her sweater. When she turned back to Patrick, she tried not to react. Tried. A whimper escaped her lips. She balled up the fabric and pressed it hard against his shoulder, leaning on him with as much weight as she could.

He moaned again, his eyes focused on her.

"You were shot. Don't move." Jennie looked at the sky. A helicopter? Whether it was the army or the state police, she didn't care. "Help is on the way. Just hang tight, okay?"

Most of the gunmen had fled.

She looked around for her brother and saw him climb the side of the truck. Patrick had done it much more easily. It took Martin a couple of attempts before he managed to haul himself to the open door so he could drop inside.

Those moments Patrick had been beside the truck and she'd been by her brother and the other gunmen, even holding on to Tucker's leash, had been some of the scariest of her life. Now her brother was behind the windshield. Trying to get the drugs? She glanced at the helicopter. The authorities were closing in.

Soon there would be nowhere to go.

She turned back to Patrick. "Are you okay?"

He nodded. Jennie wasn't sure she believed him.

"You need to be okay." She held the sweater tight. Patrick lifted a hand and placed it over hers. She said, "You have to be here when I get Nate back."

"I…" He gasped a breath but didn't finish, pain washing over his face.

Her heart soared just at the idea that he still cared about her. There was no time for that to sink in, though. Not the full extent of what it would mean for them. For their son, and the future.

She leaned down and touched her lips to his in a fast kiss. "We'll talk later. When things are safe."

Her brother rooted around in the cab of the truck.

His men had disappeared. In the distance three big Humvee-looking vehicles kicked up dust as they approached in formation. The helicopter was closer now, circling around them.

Those men would swarm over this whole area. Martin would be locked down.

She couldn't let him be taken by the authorities without telling her where that man had taken Nate.

She looked at Tucker. "Stay." Then she clambered to her feet. She stumbled but managed to stay standing. What should she do? Martin had dropped the gun before he climbed into the truck. She swiped the weapon from the ground and realized it was Patrick's. Jennie moved around to the windshield and planted her feet.

She raised the weapon and pointed it at the glass. "Martin!"

He looked up. A split second of fear crossed his face, and then he turned back to his search.

"Tell me where Nate is!"

He didn't respond. She said it a couple more times, but got no response.

Jennie redirected her aim to the bottom corner of the windshield, in front of the steering wheel. She squeezed the trigger and fired a shot.

Jerk. Exhale. She fixed her stance and readied to fire again. She took a long breath and let it out slowly. Calm. That was what Nate needed right now.

"Tell me!"

Her brother shifted. From behind the windshield

she'd just shattered, he turned to face her. His first shot slammed a baseball-size hole through the windshield.

She yelped and jumped out of the way. He still had his gun.

The second shot was closer. Jennie dove for the ground. She saw him climb out the door, and she lifted her arm. Empty hand. Jennie looked around for the weapon.

As soon as she had it in her grasp and lifted it, he'd disappeared out of view. She ran to the truck and saw him beyond it, sprinting away at full speed, hauling a duffel bag over his shoulder.

Tucker's dog tags jingled.

He passed her, racing after her brother.

"Tucker!" Martin would surely shoot him. Right?

The helicopter circled in front of her brother. She heard a yell, but didn't know where it came from. As Jennie watched, the dog launched himself at her brother and took him to the ground.

A gunshot rang out.

"Tucker!"

Patrick gritted his teeth and rolled. He managed to get up and stumble toward Jennie as white spots floated across his vision. His teeth ached, he was clenching so hard.

He nearly went down but snatched the gun from her. She gasped.

Patrick moved to Martin and Tucker, giving his dog a quick pet.

Martin groaned. His legs shifted, but he couldn't get up with the weight of Tucker on his back. Patrick noticed a knot forming on Martin's forehead.

Patrick held out his hand to the dog. He had nothing

to give Tucker, so he rubbed the sides of his face and put his own close. "Good boy."

His equilibrium shifted and Patrick nearly fell forward. Nausea rolled in his stomach and he had to admit his shoulder screamed fire right now. He pushed out a breath between his teeth and planted a knee.

He waved a hand for Tucker to back up. "Down."

The dog moved off Martin. Patrick stuck a knee in Jennie's brother's back.

A uniformed man approached. "Hands up!"

Patrick lifted one hand. "New Mexico State Police."

"You're Officer Sanders?"

He nodded. "She's with me."

Jennie flushed with relief. Even dirty and bedraggled, her expression full of fear and adrenaline, he thought she'd never looked more beautiful.

Standing around them was a crowd of uniformed state police, interspersed with a lot of camo-dressed army guys. Some had MP bands on their arms. All had high-powered rifles.

"We'll take that guy off your hands." The soldier held a hand out, and Patrick clasped his forearm. The guy practically hauled him off his feet—a sergeant. Ready to take Martin into custody. Finally. Well, Patrick was the one who had found him.

They weren't going to take Martin away until he told them where Nate was.

When he turned to see them cuff Martin and lift him up—a whole lot less gently—Patrick said, "Where is Nate?"

The army guys glanced at him. Patrick kept his focus on the man who would've been his brother-in-law. He even might still be now, after Patrick and Jennie figured everything out. And got their son back.

Patrick took a step. The movement sent pain through his torso. He was assuming there was no serious damage. He'd been shot in the shoulder and was pretty sure the bullet had gone all the way through—out the back. The best scenario. It wasn't naïve to think like that—it was hope.

He grunted. "Will that guy kill him?" Patrick needed to know.

Jennie sniffed back tears.

"He's your nephew, Martin. You turned him over to that guy? You want me to bring you up on more kidnapping and accessory charges on top of all the trouble you're already in?" He was personally involved in this case. Patrick wasn't going to be the one to pursue this, given the army was involved, but he would make sure the full force of the law came down on Martin Wilson's head.

"I want a deal. Then I'll tell you where he is."

Patrick got in his face. "No deal. You shot me, and you had your guy kidnap my son. Twice. Where is he?"

He wasn't going to threaten the man in front of this many people. That wouldn't go down well. Patrick would find it hard to support his family if he were fired—or thrown in jail himself.

But Martin knew what he implied.

"Where is he?"

Given the gunshot wound, Patrick couldn't fight him. Martin was cuffed anyway.

Maybe a few days ago he'd have wanted revenge. Before Patrick learned that trust in God was his best weapon.

Make him tell me.

It was an honest prayer, but maybe not theologically correct. Patrick needed all the help he could get right now.

"Sanders!"

He turned again and saw Eric running toward him. Behind Eric, Sheriff Johns walked a cuffed gunman toward their huddle. The sheriff had a wound on the side of his face, as though the guy had fought being cuffed and Johns had taken the man down. Eric had a smudge of dirt on the front of his shirt.

Patrick swayed, light-headed all of a sudden. Jennie lifted his arm on his good side and stood under it, holding him up.

Eric stopped in front of them.

"We need to find Nate."

Patrick was glad she'd said it. He wasn't sure he could put the words together right now.

"Your man needs a hospital." The army sergeant passed Martin off to one of his men and came over to Eric. He motioned to indicate Patrick and said, "You should take him in. We've got this covered, and the sheriff can round up Wilson's men."

"We need to find my son." Patrick forced the words out through gritted teeth. "Martin knows where he is."

"Martin says differently," the sergeant said. "Told me he doesn't know where his man took your boy."

"*His* nephew." Tucker leaned against his leg, but Patrick would probably pass out if he touched his dog's fur right now. That was the side where he'd been shot in his shoulder.

The sergeant nodded. "I'll keep working, but if he asks for a lawyer, there's nothing I can do. He won't get a deal. I'm sorry." He looked apologetic, even as he shrugged it off. "He's coming with me."

Eric waved a cell phone. "We found this on one of the gunmen. We can track every cell it communicated with in the last three days. Get all their GPS locations and figure out who isn't here. Maybe we can find Nate that way."

"That will take too long."

"We have all these guys—" Johns shifted the man he held "—so maybe one of them will talk."

The cuffed gunman laughed. "What's it worth? Cause I want a deal, too."

Patrick wanted to punch him. Not constructive, but it was how he felt.

Jennie straightened her shoulders. "Tell us where he is." She should have sounded distraught. Instead, she sounded strong...and full of grief. "Don't you have people you care about?" she asked the gunman. "How would you feel if one of them was in danger?"

The gunman's lips quirked, and he huffed.

"Can Tucker find him?"

Patrick squeezed his eyes shut as he thought it over through all the pain in his shoulder. "We need something to get a scent from, and we can start from the last place he was seen."

Eric pulled out his keys. "I'll drive."

Patrick opened his eyes and met his partner's gaze.

Eric said, "We'll find him."

He nodded. Patrick had no intention of stopping until he found Nate. He would probably keel over on the way, but he wouldn't back down.

They started for the car. Eric ran ahead and drove over the desert they'd walked, back to pick them up.

They had no idea where Nate was. None of the gunmen had talked, and Martin either didn't know or refused to say. *I don't care.* It wouldn't stop them from finding him.

Eric drove to the rental house and went inside with Jennie to get a shirt, or something Tucker could pick up a scent from. Patrick shifted in his seat to face Tucker, in the back of Eric's SUV. "Hey, buddy."

Tucker sniffed Patrick's face, then licked his cheek. Normally that wasn't okay—because it was gross—but Patrick realized a tear had rolled down. Better that it was gone when Jennie came back.

"You wanna find Nate?"

The dog whined. Probably just a reaction to the tone of Patrick's voice—a brokenness and fear he'd never heard from his handler before.

Jennie brought a shirt back, and Eric drove them to Patrick's old house. He couldn't think about the past. This was about Nate, not his own feelings.

Eric pulled up behind the house.

Patrick had Tucker scent the shirt. "Is that Nate?" The dog took a big sniff, reacting in a way he never had before. Tucker knew who wasn't there. "Are you ready, Tuck? Wanna go? Ready? Let's go!" The dog bounced up and down, tugging on the leash. "Tucker, find!"

The dog raced ahead of him. Patrick fought the pain and led the way, leading Jennie back to their son.

On the most important search of all their lives.

We're coming, Nate.

TWENTY-TWO

Jennie was exhausted. Tucker was the only one who didn't seem to be. The dog had energy for days. Patrick and his K-9 partner raced ahead. Eric came second, with Jennie behind him. She didn't even know how Patrick was still functioning.

He'd been shot. Her life with him had flashed before her eyes as she'd pressed her sweater into his wound.

Now he was walking around?

"You love him, don't you?"

She glanced over to find Eric watching her as they both trotted along, trying to keep up with Patrick. "Um… what?"

Her brain wasn't exactly firing on all cylinders right now. She watched Patrick ahead of them. Love him?

"I always have. Not much changed, even after he left town. As much as I wanted to hate him for leaving me alone, I never really did. And now I know what happened, and why, there's no animosity there at all."

This was good. They were racing across the desert behind Patrick's old house—actually heading in the direction of her house. The distraction of conversation helped her not think about how much her legs ached. She would collapse eventually. Hopefully not before they found Nate, because that would only slow down the search.

Eric eyed her. "He's a good man."

"I know that." She huffed out the words, breathy now that they'd been running for nearly fifteen minutes. "Probably the best man I know."

Patrick was better than anyone and everyone she'd ever met—except Nate. Father and son were tied on that scale.

God, help us find Nate.

"Because he's your son's father?"

She shot Eric a look. That's what Patrick's partner thought of her? Jennie only appreciated Patrick because of his biological connection to their son? If it was true, it was also completely shallow. She could separate the two.

If she only acknowledged him because of the fact he'd fathered Nate, that meant she saw no additional value in him.

Jennie would never shortchange Patrick like that. He had so much honor and worth. His mom had raised a good man, regardless of how she'd felt about Jennie. They could get to a place where Nate would have his grandmother in his life, and two parents that respected each other and loved him.

Underneath it all, Jennie would still feel that same pain she'd always carried. Knowing what she'd lost, because of her father. What she could never have back.

There was simply too much hurt between them. Her family had tried, at every opportunity, to destroy Patrick. Her love wasn't stronger than the pain he'd endured—or the grief over all he'd lost.

He would never forgive her.

She picked up speed, ready to get to her son. She'd

seen Tucker search a couple of times now. Given how he was acting, he clearly had something. *Nate.*

Despite how sweet Patrick had been, this was about him and Nate. About bringing a grandmother into her son's life. And having the chance for him to get to know his father. They'd slipped back into old habits on a few occasions, with those wonderful hugs. The times he'd kissed her forehead.

But this wasn't about a relationship between them. And it never would be when she couldn't believe his feelings were real. Not just because she wanted Nate to have a true family. She'd never trust his affection had no strings.

"Is Patrick going to be okay?" Jennie asked.

"If he isn't, we're here for him anyway. Right?"

Jennie nodded.

She figured by now that Patrick couldn't hear their conversation. He'd have reacted—hopefully well—to something she had said. Or he was just focused. Concentrating, as she was, on praying for Nate with every step, despite being drawn into a conversation with his partner. That was probably Eric's attempt to distract *her.*

"Thank you." She glanced at him again. "For being here." She motioned in front of her, toward Patrick. "For both of us, and Nate."

If something happened to Patrick, Eric could continue. Jennie wouldn't know the first thing about going up against a dangerous gunman. Though, she had to admit she'd done pretty well when faced with her brother. But that was different.

She'd have said he couldn't possibly try to hurt her, but he had.

Jennie fought a sigh. Later, she would cry over the lack of love between her and the only sibling she had.

She recognized where they were headed. "That's my house." Nate's house. "Do you think that's where they went?"

"We'll find out. And if he's not there," Eric said, "we'll move on and find him."

Jennie swiped at the tears on her cheeks and nodded.

Patrick turned. "We need to search the house." His face was pale. As she watched, he started to keel over.

Jennie ran to him and ducked under his good shoulder, as she had before. "I've got you."

"We need to get in there."

Eric said, "I'll go."

"Tucker can clear the house and find Nate."

"If the door was open." Eric shot him a knowing look. "I'll go inside and leave the door ajar. Once I'm out of sight, tell Tucker to come in. At least he'll be a distraction to the man holding Nate. At best, I can take the guy down and he can find Nate."

"You take the man." Patrick nodded. "Tucker will find Nate."

Relief rolled through her. The wash of it was like sunshine on a cold day. Sudden warmth and happiness. *Nate.* They were so close.

Was he really inside?

She couldn't even contemplate the worst that could have already happened. That didn't bear thinking about. Not when God had brought them this far.

You did, didn't You? Thank You.

There was one final hurdle, but she was grateful anyway.

"Copy that." Eric didn't waste any time. He raced over

to the house, head low and gun drawn. Should they have called for backup? Maybe there was no time. Also, she didn't want the man holding Nate to freak out at multiple approaching cops and wind up hurting Nate in a way that none of them could recover from.

She shivered just thinking about it.

Eric kicked in the back door and moved inside. Patrick showed Tucker the shirt again, so he could get Nate's scent. "Tucker, find!"

She held her breath as the dog darted across the yard. "It'll be okay."

She nodded. "I know." More just to say the words aloud than because she believed them. "It has to be. I can't lose him the way I lost you."

His arm squeezed her. She reached up and took hold of his hand. Patrick turned his face so his mouth was against her cheek. "You didn't lose me."

Inside the house, a gunshot rang out.

Then another answering shot.

Jennie sucked in a breath. "Nate."

"Hold on."

Jennie's whole body shuddered. Patrick held her tight in his one good arm. "Just hold on."

He wanted to go inside the house and help Eric.

Right now he would be a liability, and Jennie had no way to defend herself. Tucker was in there, and Eric.

"Hold on." He said the words a third time, repeating the mantra as much to her as to himself as seconds ticked by like minutes and it felt like an hour before Tucker let out one short, sharp bark.

Where was Eric? Who had been shot? Patrick had

more questions, but standing took a lot of brain power. It *hurt*.

They made their way to the house. He had to grit his teeth with each step, and he knew the dental bill alone after all this would be killer.

But if they got Nate back, it would also be worth it.

Eric appeared in the doorway, clutching his arm. "The gunman is dead."

"You got hit?"

"Just a scratch. Unlike you."

Patrick wasn't going to banter right now. "Tucker found Nate?"

Eric nodded and moved aside. Jennie let go of Patrick and he swayed. His partner led him to the hall and he collapsed against the wall. Probably bleeding on the drywall paint. Leaving a smudge. He tried to turn to see where Jennie had gone, but pain tore through him and he hissed out a breath.

Where was Tucker?

And where was Nate? It had been hours. He wanted his son back.

"I'll step out and call this in," Eric said. When Patrick glanced over, he added, "Dead guy is in the dining room."

"Copy—" Bile rose and he couldn't get any more words out.

"You need an ambulance."

He needed his son.

"Nate!" Jennie called out to the boy. It sounded like she was running through the house. Frantic. Searching. Was he hiding? Had that man told him to duck inside some closet and stay there?

Patrick turned the other direction and saw Tucker sitting by the kitchen at a door. Waiting for him? No. He'd found Nate, right? "Tuck."

The dog barked. His body moved the way it did when his tail wagged. But he stayed in that "Sit" and he didn't break it.

Nate was there.

Patrick tried to push off the wall, but he couldn't control his weight and started to keel over. He slammed into the other wall and cried out, "Jennie, he's in here!"

He heard her coming. Down the hall. The patter of her feet closing in. "Tucker." He breathed out his dog's name.

Patrick couldn't move. Pain sparked tears in his eyes. He needed to get to his son. Given all the blood, he was going to scare the boy witless the second Nate saw him. He frowned, gasped a breath and tried not to lose it as Jennie raced past him.

"Laundry room."

She didn't even pause, just sprinted to the door and petted Tucker. Then told him to get out of the way.

Patrick heard the shuffle, pushed along the wall and looked around the corner.

He managed a couple of steps. His dog sniffed his hand, but Patrick didn't have the strength to even pat his head.

He made it to the table, braced his weight and kept going to the kitchen counter. He grabbed the dish towel hanging on the oven and pressed the towel against his wound. The pain made him want to throw up, fall down or pass out. Perhaps all three. He settled for sliding down the wall.

Jennie opened the door. Nate was huddled in the corner where Patrick could see he had no visible injuries but looked seriously pale. She crouched. "Hey." Nate's gaze shifted from her to Patrick. Jennie touched Nate's shoulder. "You okay?"

Nate said nothing. His cheeks were red over the pale color. Patrick couldn't tell if they were flushed from fear and crying or if he'd been slapped around. Told to stay where he was. Scared enough he couldn't move now.

Patrick swallowed down nausea the pain was causing. "Hey, buddy."

Nate's gaze shifted to him again.

"I hurt my arm." There was a whole room between them, but he kept his voice low. "Will you go see the doctor with me?"

Nate looked at his mom, then back at Patrick. He chewed his lip. "He told me not to move."

"He's gone now." Jennie touched Nate's cheeks. "That man is not going to hurt you anymore."

Tucker wandered in and stopped by Patrick's boot. He motioned with a flick of his fingers. "Go."

The dog trotted to Nate and licked the boy in the face. Nate squealed and giggled. It was subdued, but it was there. "Hi, Tucker."

The dog sniffed his son's neck and then lay down by his side. He put his paw on Nate's lap. Not something Patrick normally allowed, asking for affection like that. But this time he let it go. Clearly the two of them had something special, and right now it seemed like it was more important for Nate to feel safe than anything else Patrick might have to correct in the ornery Airedale's training later.

Eric came in. "Ambulance will be here in five."

Patrick tried to nod. His consciousness faded toward black, but he fought it for every inch of hold it wanted to take. "Thanks."

Jennie shifted. He heard her pet his dog, his good boy and the best dog ever. *Yes, you are.* Then Patrick felt warm fingers touch his cheeks. "Hey there. Hang on, okay?"

He tried to focus on her face. Couldn't make his eyes do what they were supposed to. "Love you." He needed her to know. No matter what, he'd always loved her.

And he always would.

"Is Dad okay?"

Jennie held steady to Nate's hand, clutched in hers. "The doctors just need to make sure. But they said he's awake, right? So that's good."

He'd told her he loved her.

Jennie wanted to curl up and cry. It just hurt more, knowing neither of their feelings had ever changed. But that still didn't mean he forgave her for what her family had done to him.

Or for putting their son in danger.

Jennie led Nate down the hall to Patrick's hospital room. At the door she said, "Do you want me to go first?"

If Patrick was bandaged and hooked to machines, it could be scary.

Nate shook his head and didn't let go of her hand. He'd stuck with her as much as possible in the last day or so since they'd found him at home. She didn't blame him. Jennie wasn't feeling much like being separated from her son right now. Later they would need to work through those feelings. Right now they were just enjoying the closeness of having each other back.

Jennie held the door open.

"Hey, guys." Eric pushed off the wall, an easy smile

on his face. "Good timing. I should be going." He ruffled Nate's hair and hurried out.

"What was that about?"

Patrick grinned. It was strained, but there. "He has a date with your friend Beth."

Jennie turned to the door then back. Patrick laughed, and Nate leaned against her hip while his father groaned. "Ouch. That does not feel good." He smiled down at their son. "Hey, buddy. Have you been taking care of Tucker?"

Nate nodded.

Jennie moved forward with him, close enough Patrick could hold out his hand and Nate could lean in for a gentle hug.

"I'm okay."

"Me, too," Nate said. "We stayed at the rental house last night. They have DVDs."

"Anything good?"

Nate shrugged. "Will you be out soon?"

Jennie nearly smiled. It sounded like Patrick was in jail, not in the hospital. Patrick returned her smile. "I hope so." His brow furrowed. "Do you think maybe… when I am, you might want to come home with me and see my house?"

Jennie's stomach hardened. She opened her mouth to say something, but no words came out. What was she supposed to say?

"You and your mom could stay in my guest room, and you could see where Tucker lives."

That sounded nice but didn't exactly answer the questions rolling through her mind.

Patrick glanced at her, some of those questions on his face. She still wasn't sure what she should say.

Nate answered for her. "That could be good." He looked at her.

She nodded. "I like it." For her son, she could do anything.

Nate smiled. The first time since being kidnapped. He wandered to the chair and plopped onto the seat, slouching down.

She was about to pass him his backpack, so he had something to do, when she felt Patrick's warm fingers touch hers.

She let her gaze slide to him.

"Yeah?"

Jennie nodded. He tugged her closer. Enough she got the message and leaned in.

"Ella tried to kiss me at recess," Nate said. "I didn't let her because it's gross."

Patrick's eyes flashed with a smile. Jennie tried to smile back, but it wavered. Patrick whispered, "You know how I feel. How I've always felt."

She shook her head. "After everything my family has done to you?"

He studied her face. "I'm thinking since your father and brother haven't been in your life for a long time, maybe ever, that makes me and Nate your real family."

He really thought that? Tears filled her eyes. "I got you shot."

"Jennie, you didn't hurt me. I'm guessing this—" he wiped the tears from her cheeks "—is because you actually love me."

"I never stopped." She grasped his wrists, determined to hold on tight and never let go. "I've always loved you, and I always will."

"Good." Patrick tugged her to him and kissed her.

"You're the one for me. I knew it in high school, but I know it even more now. I want us to be together. For real."

Jennie nodded. "Me, too."

"Marriage, Jennie. We need to give Nate a real family." Patrick kissed her again. "The family neither of us had."

"Do you really think we can do this?"

"Yes." He sounded so sure. "If we do it together."

Jennie's heart soared. She had everything she'd ever longed for, right here.

EPILOGUE

One Year Later

"Go, Nate!" Jennie jumped up and down, but it was short lived given how exhausted she felt. She watched her son from the sidelines as he ran with the ball, avoiding all the other kids on the opposing team trying to snatch his flag.

"Run! Run!" Beside Jennie, Patrick's mother cheered, also. Then she turned to Jennie and they shared a smile.

It had taken some time, but the two of them had rebuilt trust, and now Nate's grandma was a huge part of his life. Mostly trying to balance being the "fun" grandma to make up for everything she'd missed and not letting things get out of control. Too many snacks wasn't good for anyone. But Jennie was enjoying watching them figure it out as they got to know each other.

As for the letters Patrick had written, Jennie figured her father had thrown them away. However, there was no way to ever know. So she'd let that go. Along with the rest of the hurt.

She sat on the blanket, letting out a satisfied sigh.

The ring set fit snug on her left hand. Patrick had slid it there nearly two months ago now. Longer than either of them had wanted to wait, but it was for the best and gave them all time to adjust. They were different people now than they had been, building a relationship with God and with each other.

They were a family for real, both Jennie and Nate having the last name Sanders. Nothing of who she had been was a part of their lives now. How could it be, when that life had been loneliness and dishonesty and this one was filled with life and blessing?

Jennie lay back on the blanket and closed her eyes, overwhelmed to the point of exhaustion. Well, that wasn't the only reason.

Thank You, Lord.

So many blessings.

She woke to a strange sensation. As soon as she opened her eyes, she realized what it was. "Tucker. I told you how I feel about you licking my face." She shoved the dog away playfully and sat up.

Patrick crouched by her, dressed in his state police uniform. "I brought sandwiches."

She was about to thank him when pandemonium erupted on the flag football field. Barely seconds later Tucker had stolen some kid's flag and made a run for it while all the players and the coaches chased him. Nate fell on the ground, laughing.

Patrick sat by her, tugging her to his side. "You were asleep when I got here. Tired?"

She didn't like the worry on his face. "Yes, but it's not bad."

"What…?" He didn't finish.

Jennie leaned in, touched both his cheeks and spoke close. "I'm pregnant."

Cheers and congratulations erupted along with laughter on the blanket. And not just from his mother.

* * * * *

Carol J. Post writes fun and fast-paced inspirational romantic suspense stories and lives in sunshiny central Florida. She sings and plays the piano for her church and also enjoys sailing, hiking and camping—almost anything outdoors. Her daughters and grandkids live too far away for her liking, so she now pours all that nurturing into taking care of two fat and sassy cats and one highly spoiled dachshund.

Books by Carol J. Post

Love Inspired Suspense

Visit the Author Profile page at LoveInspired.com for more titles.

TRAILING A KILLER

Carol J. Post

My grace is sufficient for thee:
for my strength is made perfect in weakness.
—*2 Corinthians* 12:9

Acknowledgments

Thank you to my uncle Danny Post, who showed us around Matlacha and Pine Island and gave us the inside knowledge that only a "local" can have.

Thanks to my sister, Kimberly Wolff, who not only helped me plot this book but also let me drag her around South Florida for research. You're the best sis ever!

Thank you to my editor, Dina Davis, and my critique partners, Karen Fleming and Sabrina Jarema, for making my stories the best they can be.

And thank you to my husband, Chris, for keeping romance in my life for the past forty years.

ONE

Erin Jeffries moved down the two-lane road that spanned the eighteen-mile length of Pine Island. Sheets of rain slapped across the windshield, the final fury of a storm that had pounded the area for most of the night.

Ahead of her, a metal post stood at the edge of the sidewalk, devoid of whatever sign it had held yesterday, and stubborn fronds clung to battered palm trees. A hodgepodge of limbs, metal, wood and plastic littered the roadside.

Florida had seen worse. This one was only a category three, but it still packed enough punch to be dangerous. If the report she'd gotten was accurate, someone was trapped in the rubble of a building that had collapsed. He would probably come out of the experience with a new respect for Mother Nature. If he came out of it at all.

At the northernmost tip of the island, Erin navigated a gentle left turn. Charlotte Harbor lay to the right, invisible behind the rivers that flowed down her windows. She glanced in her rearview mirror. The top of a crate peeked over the back seat of her RAV4. Her white German shepherd was inside.

"Almost there, Alcee."

Maybe the current band of rain would move past them by the time they had to exit the vehicle. If not, she and Alcee would still do what they needed to. Emergency personnel ventured out as soon as conditions were safe, not necessarily comfortable.

Erin lifted her foot from the accelerator. Capt'n Con's Fish House lay to the left, and the grassy area beyond offered boat trailer parking. Main Street continued farther, but public access ended there. A sheriff's vehicle sat off the roadway, ensuring no one ventured past the no-trespassing sign. Erin could get through with her badge identifying her as a detective with the Lee County Sheriff's Office. But today she was acting in a different capacity.

As she drew to a stop, the deputy exited the vehicle, head tilted downward beneath the hood of his rain slicker. Erin cracked her window enough for conversation. The deputy had just started to give her a curt nod when a smile spread across his face.

She and Joe had started with Lee County a year ago, both in patrol. Nine months later she'd made detective, at least in part due to the glowing recommendation the department in Sunnyvale, California, had given her. Though their paths didn't cross that often, they'd stayed on friendly terms, friendly enough for Joe to keep trying to match her up with his former neighbor.

Joe glanced at the dog in the back. "I take it you're not on duty."

"Not with Lee County. Alcee and I are volunteers with Peace River K-9 Search and Rescue. We're looking for hurricane victims." One, anyway. She'd gotten the call right after daybreak and had been ready to respond within ten minutes.

"Every mandatory evacuation, there are always people who think the *mandatory* part of that phrase doesn't apply to them." He shook his head and, after wishing her success, waved her through.

Erin raised the window and crept past him. Her destination was on the last small street branching off Main, a large older home that had been converted to apartments.

She made a left onto Boca Vista and drove past the first residence. When she stopped behind the sheriff's vehicle sitting in the next drive, she released a low whistle. The building in front of her seemed to have tipped forward, the two upper stories falling onto the first. Rafters, joists and studs jutted outward from the jumble like broken bones.

Her hope that the rain would slack off by the time she arrived hadn't materialized. She reached for the slicker in the seat beside her. Alcee's search-and-rescue vest wouldn't do anything to keep her dry, but at least the big, fat drops weren't cold. Florida rain in August was just wet.

Erin shrugged into her raincoat. As she stepped from her car, a deputy rounded the corner of the house and called a greeting. She'd met him when she started with the department, but hadn't seen him since. They worked different shifts in different parts of the county. She struggled to pull up a name. Hidden beneath the rain slicker, his nameplate was no help.

"Erin, right?"

"You have a good memory." She gave him a sheepish smile. "Better than mine."

"I had just one name to learn. You had a whole department." He extended a hand. "Alan Drummond."

She accepted the handshake. "So what do we have?"

"I've only been here about fifteen minutes. We got

the call from one of the residents in town who didn't evacuate. He got out at the crack of dawn, during one of the lulls." Drummond nodded toward a white Dodge Ram sitting next to the cruiser. "With the truck parked here, he's afraid someone might have been inside when this came down."

"Have you heard or seen anything?"

"Not a thing. I've circled the building, calling out, but haven't gotten a response."

"If anyone's there, Alcee will find them." She opened the back door of her SUV and unfastened the latch on the crate. "Come."

Alcee jumped out, undeterred by the pouring rain. Beneath the vest, eagerness rippled through her sleek body as if she sensed the importance of what she was about to do. Erin bent to scratch her neck and cheeks. "You're a good girl."

As Erin moved toward the wreckage, Alcee pranced next to her. The dog would do her work off leash.

Deputy Drummond followed. "We've been in touch with the owner of the building and are working on contacting his tenants. I ran the tag on the Ram, and it came back registered to someone in Cape Coral. I don't know why it's parked here, unless he moved and didn't update his address."

Erin pointed at the pile of rubble. "Seek."

The dog didn't hesitate. As she gingerly made her way upward, boards shifted under her, but she maintained her footing.

Erin's heart pounded. *God, please help her.* Working around collapsed buildings was dangerous, and dogs had been hurt. But it was more than that. She really wanted

Alcee to succeed. Whoever might be trapped in that building *needed* Alcee to succeed.

The two of them had finished their search-and-rescue training a year and a half earlier, and although they'd participated in several searches for lost children and elderly people with dementia, the missing person had always been found in one of the other teams' grids. This time she and Alcee were alone. But the dog was ready. She'd practiced this scenario dozens of times, with a trainer hiding in rubble. She'd passed every test and graduated from the program.

Except this wasn't a simulation. It was the real thing, with a real life at stake.

Drummond watched the dog for several minutes, then returned to his vehicle. Erin stayed rooted to the spot, pleas for help circling through her mind. Her primary prayer was that there weren't any victims. Her follow-up was that if there were, help would reach them in time.

As she waited, the rain abated, then stopped altogether. Steel-gray clouds blanketed the sky, a small patch of brightness barely visible at the eastern edge. She slipped out of her rain jacket and laid it over the hood of her vehicle to dry. Maybe that last band was the end of it.

A rumble broke the silence, the distant sound of helicopter rotors beating the air. The volume and pitch increased as it grew closer. It was likely one of the local news stations.

She joined Drummond at his vehicle. "Anything new?"

"So far all the tenants are accounted for except a single, older gentleman. The calls go straight to voice mail. The Ram belongs to his grandson."

Erin nodded. "Maybe the grandson came to pick him up and they left in the grandfather's vehicle."

She returned her attention to her dog. Alcee's movements had grown more animated. She was sniffing with new vigor, head down, nose tracing a jagged path. She'd locked on to a scent.

Erin's pulse picked up speed, and her heart beat in her throat. Alcee's first find. At least, her first find that involved a real injured person, not a trainer pretending to be trapped.

The dog pawed at a board, released three barks and sat. That was her indication—bark and sit.

Erin turned to Drummond, unable to keep the tremor from her voice. "Alcee's found a survivor. We need debris-removal people."

"Already done. A construction company's on the way with a crane."

As if in response, the deep roar of an engine drifted to them. A half minute later a truck turned the corner, a crane mounted in its bed. Turner-Peterson Contractors, according to the sign on the door. She met the driver at the road.

"Someone's trapped, right up there."

She pointed to Alcee sitting atop the debris like a furry sentinel. She'd stay until Erin released her.

A pickup truck bearing the same signage as the first arrived. It remained parked at the road while the other driver maneuvered the crane truck into position.

Erin retrieved a rope toy from her vehicle and held it up. "Alcee, come."

The dog made her way down as carefully as she'd ascended. Erin couldn't tone down her smile. Warmth swelled inside her—love for her dog and pride in what she'd accomplished.

Less than three years ago Alcee was training to be a companion dog for the blind but wasn't getting it. They'd tried training her for narcotics detection, and that hadn't gone much better. Fortunately, her trainers had recognized that, with her curiosity, endless energy and toy drive, she was better suited to a search-and-rescue career.

Erin dropped to her knees and wrapped her arms around the dog. "Good girl." She held out the twisted rope with the ball affixed to the end and let Alcee play a game of tug-of-war. Then she relinquished the toy and put the dog in a down-stay. They'd both remain out of the way of those working to free whoever was trapped.

The helicopter Erin had heard earlier passed overhead. She'd been right. Bold letters on the belly proclaimed it belonged to one of the local stations. It turned and made several slow passes. If they were looking for a story, they'd found one.

For the next half hour the workers used the crane to remove rafters, beams and joists from the pile, careful not to disturb the stability and cause further collapse. It was like a giant game of Pick-Up Sticks. Erin fought the urge to chew her nails, a habit she'd broken years ago but was tempted to start back up.

The simulations she and Alcee had done at the training facility near LA didn't include removal. Watching the men's painstaking work, praying they didn't disturb a board that would cause the pile to come crashing down, was nerve-racking.

A news van turned onto Boca Vista and drew to a stop. Two people hopped out, a man with a video cam-

era and a woman with a microphone. Erin stepped into
the shade of a mango tree and pressed her back against
its trunk. If she took off Alcee's vest, maybe they'd assume she was a curious neighbor and leave her alone.

The reporters gave them a cursory glance, then approached Drummond. Whatever the deputy told them
was lost under the noise of the crane truck. When they
moved toward her, she turned away and held up a hand.
"No camera." The last thing she wanted was to have her
face plastered on national TV, for reasons that had nothing to do with shyness.

The woman extended her arm toward her associate,
palm down, and he lowered the camera. She offered
Erin a warm smile. "What a beautiful dog. I hear she's
the one who discovered the victims."

Erin responded in the affirmative, then fielded several
questions about search and rescue in general and Alcee
in particular. Which was okay. She could talk about her
dog forever, as long as there were no cameras. While she
conversed with the reporters, Deputy Drummond sum-
moned an ambulance and the men continued to work.
Suddenly, one of them bent over and shouted something
into the debris. Erin couldn't make out the words over
the sound of the equipment.

The rescuer straightened, hands cupped around his
mouth. "I can't see anything yet, but we've got someone. He's alive and conscious."

Erin released a breath she hadn't realized she'd been
holding. *Thank You, Lord.*

The reporters moved in that direction and the camera clicked back on. Deputy Drummond approached the
collapsed building. "Ask if he's alone."

The worker crouched to engage in a brief conversation and then rose. "His grandfather is with him, five or six feet away. He's frantic about the old man. Says he stopped talking to him a few hours ago."

Erin frowned. Two victims, one seriously hurt, maybe even dead.

The EMT who'd driven the ambulance joined the conversation. "Ask him if he's injured."

Several seconds passed with just the rumble of the truck's engine and the whir of the crane before the man straightened again.

"He says he's fine, just get his grandpa out. But it sounds like he's having trouble breathing."

The EMT radioed for an additional team, and the men continued their tedious work, opening a larger path to the victims. The second ambulance arrived, and paramedics readied two stretchers.

Finally, the first of the victims was free. He struggled into an upright position, and the paramedics rushed to assist. When they reached the victim, he waved them away. Erin could guess where the conversation was going. The guy was worried about his grandfather and wanted all the attention focused on him.

Some words passed between him and the paramedics. Whatever they said must have penetrated the guy's panic, because he finally allowed them to help him down.

Once on level ground, he looked up. His gaze locked with hers. Suddenly, the ground wasn't level anymore. Her whole world tilted. His apparently did, too, because he froze midstride. His eyes widened and several emotions skittered across his face.

She took several stumbling steps toward him. Cody Elbourne hadn't been her first love, but he'd been her deepest. Then she'd ended it. With that free spirit she'd inherited from her hippie grandparents and four years of college to look forward to, she'd wanted to keep her options wide-open. So after one magical summer, she'd severed contact, a decision she'd questioned more than once over the past twelve years.

Just before she reached him, she jerked to a stop. Now wasn't the time for a reunion. The man had just been pulled from a collapsed structure, and she had no idea what injuries he had.

He lifted a hand toward her, wincing with the motion. "Erin."

Although he allowed the paramedics to ease him onto the stretcher, he remained in a seated position. His T-shirt was plastered to his skin, muscles outlined beneath as he gripped the edge of the gurney. The light brown hair she remembered as being soft and full of body hung in limp, wet strands. He'd likely had a miserable night, lying trapped while pounding rain seeped in through the debris.

A soft whine drew her attention downward. Alcee looked up at her with a question in her dark eyes. Her dog was used to providing emotional support—easing loneliness, calming fears, even settling Erin down after one of her frequent nightmares. But this was different. Alcee likely sensed something was off but didn't understand what.

Erin placed a reassuring hand on the dog's head, offering a smile to back it up. She was all right. At least, she would be, once she recovered. The problem was, the moment Cody's eyes met hers, her universe had shifted, and it still hadn't realigned. It probably wouldn't for some time.

When she straightened, Cody was watching her. "What are you doing here?"

"Searching for survivors." Of course, he already knew that. "I left California a year ago, settled in Fort Myers."

"Oh."

Just *oh*?

Questions tumbled through her mind. What was he doing here? Had he come back permanently, like she had, or was he just visiting? And why Southwest Florida, where they'd both vacationed and fallen in love so many years ago?

Before she could voice any of those thoughts, one of the paramedics slipped a blood pressure cuff over Cody's arm. Erin moved to the end of the stretcher, well out of their way as they did their assessments. The reporters observed from a distance. They'd probably stay until they got a complete story, which wouldn't be until Cody's pops was free.

She hoped it would be soon. Although Cody cooperated with the paramedics, worry lined his face, and his gaze kept shifting to the crane and the men working on the wreckage.

She lightly touched the back of his hand. "They'll get him out. They're good at what they do."

He gave her a weak smile. "I'm just worried about him. He hasn't said anything for several hours. I'm hoping he's unconscious and not…" His eyes dipped to his lap and his fists clenched. "I won't let these guys take me until I know Pops is all right."

"Your grandfather, is this the one I knew?" If she could keep him talking, it might help him keep his sanity while he waited.

"Yeah."

Of course it would be. All he had was his maternal grandparents. His dad's parents had been as absent in his life as his dad had been. His mom ran a close third.

He tilted his head toward Alcee. "I take it the dog is yours."

"She is." The sides of Erin's mouth lifted. It was an involuntary reaction every time she thought of her sweet German shepherd. "Cody, meet Alcee."

He grinned down at the dog. "I'm pleased to meet you, Alcee, especially since you saved my life." Cody's focus bounced back up to Erin, and his smile faded. "I'd fallen asleep, or maybe passed out, then heard a dog barking somewhere above me."

"That was Alcee." Erin patted the dog's back, then pressed the furry body against her leg in a one-armed hug. Almost an hour had passed, but the love and pride she'd felt when Alcee alerted hadn't lessened one iota. "The authorities called us out to see if anyone was trapped."

She resisted the temptation to add *even though everyone was supposed to evacuate*. The best thing Cody could have done for his grandfather was gotten him to safety. If anything happened to the older man because of Cody's carelessness, he'd carry that burden the rest of his life. She wouldn't wish that on anybody. She knew about regrets.

Cody shook his head. "For a while, I didn't think either of us was going to make it. With those gas tanks blowing, I was afraid the whole place was going to catch fire."

"Gas tanks?" Deputy Drummond stepped closer,

brow creased. "There aren't any gas tanks. The heating and appliances are electric."

Cody's face mirrored Drummond's look of confusion. "But there were explosions, about five or six of them close together. Then groans and creaks and finally the pop of splitting wood. The floor tilted, and bits of plaster rained down. Next, the building collapsed."

The deputy's lips pressed together in a frown. He unclipped his radio from his shirt and called Dispatch. "We need an investigator from the Bureau of Fire, Arson and Explosives. One of the victims reported hearing explosions just before the house came down."

Erin shifted her gaze to the home next door. A couple of shutters were gone and a piece of fascia was dangling from the front porch. The roof had taken a hit, too, with patches a shade or two darker where shingles were missing. The home on the other side was in the same condition.

The contrast between those houses and the one where she was standing was startling. Until a few minutes ago, it hadn't made sense.

But maybe there was a reason only one home out of hundreds had been destroyed. Maybe Mother Nature wasn't to blame. Or maybe she'd had some help.

But why? Had someone set out to simply demolish the house?

Or had they been after the people inside?

Cody drifted on the edge of consciousness. Something nagged at him, but trying to analyze what it was required too much effort. Where was he? He wasn't at home. The sounds and scents around him were foreign. But he didn't have the will to decipher those, either.

Awareness advanced, and with it, pain. Everything hurt. The worst of it was confined to his torso. And his head. Yeah, definitely his head.

His chest, too. No, his heart, as if someone had squeezed, shredded, then stomped on it. Pops was gone. It couldn't be true. But the grief pressing down on him said it was. Cody opened his eyes with a groan.

A nurse stood with his back to him, facing the rolling bedside table. He spun and met Cody's gaze for the briefest moment before stepping toward the back wall.

The man had brought lunch. A plate sat in the middle of a tray, a plastic cover hiding whatever was beneath. A packet holding a napkin and silverware lay to the side, along with a beverage. The lights were off, the natural light struggling in through the narrow window offering the only illumination in the room. On such a gray, dreary day, even that was minimal. But the shadows were fitting. Anything else would seem out of place, disrespectful to the memory of the man who had raised him.

Sometime this evening, Erin would return. She'd promised to check on him when she finished her day. At the thought, his spirits lifted just a little. She was the only person in the entire state who understood what Pops had meant to him.

Cody craned his neck backward to check out his visitor. Latex gloves covered his hands, but he wasn't wearing a nurse's uniform. With pants in a nondescript blue-gray color and a button-up shirt in a tiny plaid pattern, he was probably maintenance. His beard was neatly trimmed, and wavy blond hair flowed from beneath a baseball cap, almost touching his shoulders. Was a ball cap approved hospital working attire? More likely in maintenance than nursing.

The man fiddled with something on the wall, then hurried away, hitting the switch on his way out. The room brightened. Maybe someone had reported a problem with the lighting. The guy they'd sent wasn't very personable. But Cody wasn't in a talkative mood.

Pops had made it as far as the operating room, then died in surgery. Ruptured spleen. He'd spent four years in a Vietnamese POW camp, followed by dangerous military missions in places he couldn't even talk about because the US was supposedly never there. And a hurricane took him out.

Footsteps sounded in the hallway, growing closer. Between the solid, rhythmic footfalls was another sound he tried to place, the more rapid click of something against the vinyl tile.

Erin stepped into the room holding a leash. Alcee walked next to her, toenails making little scrapes against the floor. Cody's heart rolled over and his chest clenched. He really needed a hug. He squelched the irrational thought as quickly as it had come.

Erin cast a glance toward the doorway. "Who just left your room?"

"Hospital maintenance. I guess I had some lighting issues. Why?"

"Alcee growled when he passed."

"Maybe he reminds her of someone she doesn't like."

"Maybe."

She stopped next to his bed, and the dog burrowed her nose under his hand. He obviously wasn't on the people-she-didn't-like list.

He scratched her head and neck. She still wore her vest, its block lettering clearly labeling her a service dog. "So the Dynamic Duo is finished with all its rescue missions?"

"Yeah. We did a couple of searches farther north, where the storm made landfall, but both buildings were empty. We just came from there."

She looked the same as she had that morning—khaki pants and the blue Peace River K-9 Search and Rescue T-shirt, her hair woven into a thick braid that went two-thirds of the way down her back. It had been long when he'd known her before, too. Now it was several shades darker than her natural medium shade of brown, and she'd added a deep auburn-colored tint. It looked good on her. Actually, everything about her looked good.

She pulled up a chair and commanded Alcee to lie down. The dog complied immediately. After her performance this morning, he didn't expect any different.

Erin gave him a tentative smile. "How are you doing?"

He pressed the button to raise the back of his bed. The pain through his torso stole his breath. Though he tried not to show it, her wince said she noticed.

"I'm okay, all things considered." He released the button and drew in a shallow breath. "Three broken ribs, several bruised ones and a doozy of a headache."

"You have a concussion?"

"Probably. They did a brain scan."

"Find anything?"

He grinned. "I do have one."

She returned his smile. "A healthy one?"

"There's a little swelling. I got knocked half-silly with a joist from the second floor, then hit my head on the coffee table on the way down."

She winced. "Ow. Double whammy."

"I'm pretty sure the broken ribs are from that same joist. After clunking me in the head, it landed on my side and kept me pinned until you guys arrived."

"What are they doing about the head injury?"

"Keeping an eye on me. At this point they don't think I'll need surgery."

"Good. And your grandfather?"

Her presence had chased away some of his grief. Now it pounced on him with a fresh vengeance. "He didn't make it. Ruptured spleen."

She cupped her hand over his and squeezed. "I'm sorry." The sadness in her eyes underscored the heaviness in her tone.

The teenage Erin had been all about fun and didn't have a serious bone in her body. At the time, she'd been just what he'd needed. With a dad who'd deserted him before he started kindergarten and a mom whose popping in and out of his life had done more harm than good, that carefree abandon had drawn him to her like metal shavings to a magnet. Of course, that same carefree abandon was the trait that had kept her from continuing their relationship beyond that one blissful summer.

But the way she was looking at him, her hand warm over his, the intervening years must have changed her. She'd matured. There was a seriousness that seemed to now be an intrinsic part of her personality, as if she'd learned the hard way that life wasn't all fun and games.

"It's my fault he's gone." He swallowed hard under the pressure of the guilt bearing down on him.

She squeezed his hand. "Hindsight's always twenty-twenty. Don't beat yourself up. People who haven't been through a hurricane don't realize how deadly they can be."

"I knew. I've lived here in Cape Coral for the past

eight years." He'd gotten sick of the Chicago cold and left Gram and Pops for the warmer climate.

He'd had a reason for choosing the Charlotte Harbor area. He'd met Erin in nearby Punta Gorda after his high school graduation when their grandparents stayed in the same RV park. Upon arriving eight years ago, he'd searched for her on social media and even checked parks in the area to see if her grandparents had come back. They hadn't. So he'd closed the door on that season of his life.

Erin had said if it was meant to be, their paths would cross again. They had now, and he was still reeling. He'd thought of little else since the moment he'd looked up and seen her standing there with her dog. At one time it would have been a dream come true, but eight years and one ex-wife later, those doors had closed. Erin wasn't the only one whose life experiences had changed her.

He reined in his thoughts. "What I didn't count on was Pops's stubbornness. He was supposed to be waiting out the storm at a friend's house thirty miles inland. I didn't find out he'd decided to stay in his apartment until we were already catching the outer bands. I went there, planning to bring him home with me."

"I take it that didn't work."

"Not at all. The more I prodded him, the more he dug in his heels. You might remember Pops had a stubborn streak the size of the Mississippi River."

She gave him a sympathetic smile. "I do. But I also remember how much he loved you and your grandmother."

"He did." Cody hadn't always known it growing up. Pops had been stern and gruff through those years, a strong disciplinarian. Whether that sternness was innate or due to his experiences in the military, Cody wasn't sure. But with his own anger and rebelliousness, he'd needed a lot of tough love, and Pops had provided it, something Cody hadn't appreciated until he was almost grown.

He shook his head. "I wasn't about to leave him alone. So I stayed." He heaved a sigh, inducing a wince. "I'm the reason Pops was here. When Gram died last year, he took it hard. I couldn't stand the thought of him up there by himself. He finally gave in and moved two months ago. If I'd left him in Chicago, he'd still be alive."

Before Erin had a chance to respond, a sheriff's detective walked into the room. Alcee rose, tail wagging, and Erin greeted him by name.

He returned the greeting. "So this is your dog. I heard you two were on site first thing this morning. Good work. But it looks like someone other than Mother Nature might have been involved. We've already started an investigation. You'll be working it, too."

Cody looked from the detective to Erin. What would search and rescue have to do with investigating the explosions he'd heard?

The detective nodded in his direction. "I'm Detective Manuel Gonzales. I see you've already met Detective Jeffries."

"Detective?" Granted, he'd just suffered a head injury, but things weren't adding up. "I thought you worked for Peace River something-or-other, with dogs."

She smiled. "I do. One dog, anyway. But that's on a volunteer basis. My work with Lee County Sheriff's Department is what pays the bills."

Detective Gonzales circled around to the other side of the bed. "Do you feel up to answering a few questions?"

"Sure." He'd had better days, but nothing was keeping him from talking. Other than the pain that stabbed through his side with every breath.

The detective pulled up a chair and removed a small, spiral-bound notepad from his pocket. "The Bureau of Fire, Arson and Explosives is still early in its investigation, but there's evidence of charges being set."

"Charges?"

"Explosives. C-4, dynamite."

Yeah, he knew what the man meant. He was just having a hard time accepting that what killed his grandfather might have been intentional.

Erin was apparently having the same problem. "Why would someone bring down the building, especially with people inside?"

Cody's mind spun. "Maybe there wasn't supposed to be anyone there. Pops's car was in the shop, having some mechanical work done. His friend's daughter was supposed to pick him up, and they were going to head to her dad's house. Then I found out Pops had changed his mind, and I went right over to get him. When I pulled up, the last resident was leaving. The place looked abandoned."

The detective frowned. "You saw someone leaving the building?"

"I even talked to him. He asked if I was staying, and I told him I was there to pick up my grandfather. The guy wasn't from around here. He had a heavy Northeast accent, like New York or Boston."

"Can you describe him?"

"Stocky build. About two inches shorter than I am."

"And you are?"

"Six foot even."

He paused to jot down the information. "What else?"

"He was wearing a yellow rain slicker. Sunglasses, too, which was odd. We were getting hit by one of the outer bands, so it was raining pretty hard. The slicker's hood was pulled up, leaving the guy's features in shadow, but I could see he had some facial hair. Whether a full beard or a goatee, I couldn't tell."

"Color?"

"Light brown, dark blond."

"What kind of vehicle?"

"None. He left on foot, headed toward Main."

"If you saw him again, do you think you could identify him?"

"It's doubtful."

After a couple more questions Cody couldn't answer, the detective stood with instructions to call if he remembered anything else. He'd almost reached the door when Cody stopped him.

"Wait. There were sandbags."

The detective turned. "Pardon me?"

"When I got to my grandfather's place, I noticed sandbags. But they didn't seem to serve any purpose, just one or two resting against the pilings underneath the house, instead of stacked to form a barrier." The structure had been constructed like a lot of them close to the water, built to accommodate a storm surge without flooding, as long as the surge wasn't too bad. The arrangement of the sandbags had looked odd at the time. Now it seemed sinister.

The detective made some more notes. "Maybe they weren't there to protect the house. Maybe they were hiding what would destroy it."

After Gonzales left, Erin eyed the tray on the table next to her. "Have you eaten?"

"No. They brought it while I was asleep, and you got here right after I woke up."

"Don't let me keep you from your lunch."

"I'm not hungry."

"You need to eat." She smiled. "Even though it's hospital food."

He wrinkled his nose. "Cold hospital food."

"The covers help keep the food warm. This one's on crooked, though. Did you already check it out?"

"I haven't touched it."

But maybe he'd take a few bites, just to make her happy. He removed the cover and looked at the grilled cheese sandwich. It was cut in half on a diagonal, the pieces angled with a disposable bowl in the space, likely holding soup.

He took a bite of the sandwich. Whatever warmth it had held when it was delivered was long gone. At least it was something that didn't taste bad cold. He finished one of the triangular-shaped halves.

Maybe the soup had held its heat better. He peeled off the plastic lid and tore open the silverware packet. Alcee rose, sniffing the air. When he put the spoon into the soup, she released a sharp bark.

Erin ran a hand down the dog's back. "What's wrong, girl?"

"Maybe she's hungry." He moved the chunks around with his spoon. "Looks like vegetable beef. I'll give her some of the meat if it's okay with you."

Erin frowned. "She's not hungry. I fed her right before coming up here." Her eyebrows were drawn together, and her face registered equal parts confusion and concern.

"Hey, I don't mind. If not for her, I'd probably still be

buried in rubble, soaking wet and half-starved. Instead, I'm lying here in a nice dry hospital gown, enjoying a cold cheese sandwich and a lukewarm bowl of soup."

He scooped up a spoonful and brought it toward his mouth. Alcee erupted in a frenzy of barking.

"Wait." Erin's hand shot out and gripped his arm.

"What?"

"Don't eat that." Her eyes were wide with panic. "Something's wrong with it."

He lowered the spoon. "Are you telling me your dog sniffs out trapped people *and* tainted food?"

"It's possible. She started training as a guide dog, then was changed to detection. She was too energetic for both of those careers and finally landed with search and rescue. Whatever she alerts to, I trust her one hundred percent."

"Do you really think somebody poisoned my food?" No offense to her dog, but the idea was too far-fetched to take seriously.

"I don't know. But Alcee thinks something's wrong, and she doesn't act like this without good reason."

He put the spoon back into the bowl and lowered his hand to his lap. A sense of uneasiness settled in his stomach, that hollow-gut feeling that came when something bad was lurking right around the corner. "But I don't have any enemies."

"Someone just brought down a building with you inside."

"That wasn't aimed at me."

"Look, Alcee is smart. Shortly after I got her, she alerted me to a gas leak. She feels something is wrong with your soup, so we're taking it seriously."

She pressed the call button for the nurse and snagged

a pair of latex gloves from a box on the wall. After putting them on, she snapped the plastic lid back onto the soup container.

A nurse entered the room and approached the bed. "Can I get you something?"

"Yes." It was Erin who answered. "We need two sterile, sealable plastic bags."

The young woman raised her eyebrows but didn't question the unusual request. Erin's commanding tone discouraged any argument. After a moment's hesitation, she nodded and left the room.

Erin scanned their surroundings.

"What are you looking for?"

"Anything that might reveal your identity."

Cody did his own search. A dry-erase board hung on the opposite wall, his doctors' and nurses' names written on it. But as far as he could tell, his patient chart wasn't in the room. That information probably came in and out on the tablets carried by the medical personnel.

Erin eased back into her chair. "What about your wallet and phone?"

"Everything's in a plastic bag in that bottom drawer, along with the clothes I was wearing when they brought me in."

Erin pulled her phone from her purse. "We're getting Detective Gonzales back out since I'm not on tonight." She tilted her head toward the soup. "This is going in for prints and the soup for a toxicology workup. And you're having around-the-clock police protection until you get out of here."

He lifted his brows. For someone who'd waltzed back into his life just that day, she was being awfully bossy. But he didn't have the gumption to argue. The events of the past twenty-four hours had him pretty shaken up. "And if the report comes back clean?"

"Then we were extra cautious for nothing. I'll choose safe over sorry any day."

She placed the call, then put her phone away. "I don't know what's going on, who set those charges or why."

Her gaze locked on his with an intensity that wouldn't let him look away. "But I do know this. If that soup is found to be tainted in any way, for you, this threat just got personal."

TWO

Erin pushed a wheelchair toward one of the elevators in Cape Coral Hospital, the rubber soles of her boots making muffled taps against the vinyl tile. She'd gotten permission to pick Cody up from the hospital, take him to retrieve his truck, then escort him home. It was her responsibility to make sure he wasn't followed.

"I'm glad to be getting out of here." He shifted in the chair. "Another day and I'd have been climbing the walls."

He'd been scheduled to be released yesterday, but the doctor had held him one more day, wanting to make sure there weren't any complications. Two and a half days in the hospital had stretched his patience. He obviously didn't do well with confinement.

"So where is Alcee?" Cody angled a glance over one shoulder, but couldn't twist enough to make eye contact. He winced, then released a pent-up breath, gaze straight ahead again.

He'd be sore for a while. Besides the cracked ribs, nasty bruises marked both arms. With the bedsheets pulled up past his waist and the hospital gown above that, those were the only ones she'd been able to see, but she was sure there were others. Considering what he'd been through, he was blessed to have fared as well as he had.

"Alcee's with my neighbor. She keeps her while I'm working."

"You're on duty now?"

"Yep. My job is to make sure you get home safely." A marked unit would respond to secure the area, then follow them to Cody's.

The crime scene techs hadn't lifted any viable prints from the soup container, which didn't come as a surprise since the guy had worn latex gloves. The food service people likely had, too. And the toxicology report wouldn't be back for several weeks.

Hospital surveillance tapes weren't any help, either. The cameras had captured the supposed maintenance person, but he'd managed to keep his head down in all the footage. Though his face wasn't identifiable, hospital personnel were able to verify he wasn't one of their employees, which made his presence suspicious.

She stopped in front of the bank of elevators and pressed the down button. If it was up to her, Cody wouldn't even go home. "What if he knows where you live?"

"Then he'd have waited to attack me when I'm there alone rather than in a hospital ward with people all around. He doesn't know who I am or where I live."

"Unless he looked at your wallet."

"He didn't get that far. He was still standing at my food tray when I woke up. I think I startled him, and that's why he didn't get the cover back over my food properly." He attempted another backward glance.

"That's assuming he tried to poison me. I'm still not convinced."

The elevator dinged, and she shook her head. He was either way too trusting or liked to live in denial. Or maybe it was just plain stubbornness. He'd accused his grandfather of having a healthy dose of the trait, but he'd inherited some of it himself.

The elevator doors opened. An elderly couple and a woman with a teenager stood inside. They stepped to the edge to make room for the wheelchair, and Erin rolled it forward.

A short time later she wheeled him through the automatic glass entry doors. A midafternoon thunderstorm had passed through earlier, and walking out of the air-conditioned comfort of the hospital was like stepping into a sauna. Florida wouldn't offer any relief from the heat and humidity for at least another month or two.

She turned to follow the wide walkway to her right. The main entrance was tucked into the V where two wings joined, a large circular drive in front. Inside the circle several palms rose above a floor of neatly trimmed shrubs. Her county-assigned Ford Explorer waited up ahead. She'd pulled it through a short time earlier and parked at the curb.

After Cody was situated in the vehicle, she returned the wheelchair. He turned to her as soon as she slid into the driver's seat.

"When we get to Pops's place, I need a few minutes. I want to retrieve some of his things. I also need to stop at the bank on the way home. I finished a remodel job the day before the storm, and the customer made his last payment in cash. I have an envelope with almost two thousand dollars locked in my glove box."

She frowned at him. "I don't know about the bank, but hanging out at your grandfather's place is out of the question."

The Bureau had finished collecting its evidence yesterday. The construction workers had even made a somewhat clear path to what had been Cody's grandfather's apartment. It had been the only way to get them both safely out. But the fact remained that there was a killer out there somewhere. And whether Cody was willing to admit it or not, he was a target.

"You said they're clearing the area before we arrive, making sure no one's waiting for me."

"That's beside the point. We're not going to let you dally there."

"All I need is ten minutes. There are keepsakes I don't want to lose, memorabilia from Pops's years in the military, letters, photos."

She cranked the car, then wound her way past the series of medical buildings and doctors' offices to come out on Thirteenth Court. "Whatever is there, it's not worth your life." She sighed. Judging from the stubbornness on his face, she was wasting her breath. But she continued anyway. "Somebody brought a building down with you inside."

"And no one believes that was aimed at me."

"Someone just tried to poison you."

"We don't know that. Not until the toxicology report comes back. You trust your dog one hundred percent. I'm more of a show-me kind of guy."

She shook her head as she eased to a stop at a traffic light. Soon they'd be headed toward Pine Island, where his grandfather had lost his life and where Cody could well have joined him. And Cody was going to remain in denial until he had irrefutable proof.

"What about the man in your room? Law enforcement thinks you're in danger, or they wouldn't have posted a Cape Coral police officer in the hall." She heaved a sigh. He was a lot more exasperating than he'd been when she'd known him earlier. "If the man didn't intend you any harm, what was he doing there?"

Some of the stubbornness fled his features. She didn't give him a chance to regroup.

"We've made contact with the apartment owner and two of the tenants. The others haven't returned yet. But based on preliminary interviews, out of the six apartments, your grandfather lived in one, and one was vacant. The other four were occupied by a single mom with two kids, two middle-aged sisters, a retired couple and two guys. The man you saw isn't a resident there."

"What about the two guys?"

"Tall and lanky, not the build of the guy you saw leaving."

The light changed, and she stepped on the gas. When she glanced over at Cody, a muscle worked in the side of his jaw as if he was clenching and unclenching his teeth.

Finally, he shook his head. "How did he find me? Let's assume the guy I saw leaving set the charges. He wouldn't have known Pops and I were inside when the building collapsed. I told him we were both leaving."

"The story hit the news. Your names were withheld, pending notification of your grandfather's next of kin, but everyone in Lee County knows there was one rescue and one fatality."

She made a left onto Pine Island Road. "Or maybe he came back to survey his work and witnessed the rescue."

It was possible, especially if he'd used binoculars and stayed hidden by foliage. She hadn't been looking for suspicious observers, because there'd been no reason to assume anything sinister. Her focus had been on her dog, then on the men working to free victims. After that, Cody had occupied every thought. He was still unwittingly injecting himself into far too many of them.

"He'd assume you'd be taken to Cape Coral since it's the closest hospital. Dressed in his fake maintenance uniform, he was able to move about freely. The hospital isn't filled to capacity right now, either." Not like during the December to April snowbird season, when Florida's elderly population grew exponentially.

She sighed. The conversation had gotten sidetracked, and he hadn't agreed to get in his truck and go straight home. Now she had less than thirty minutes to tunnel her way through his stubbornness.

"Why don't you specify what you're looking for, and we'll get whoever's in charge of cleanup to keep an eye out for it."

He shook his head, jaw set and eyes hard. "If I don't get the stuff today, it'll be gone. I'm not taking that chance."

"You're putting yourself in unnecessary danger." She clenched the wheel and reined in her emotions. She usually prided herself on keeping her cool. But this wasn't a random witness she was dealing with. It was Cody. And she still cared for him. Always would.

He was silent for several moments. Maybe her arguments were getting through to him. When he finally spoke, his tone was low.

"How are *your* grandparents?" He looked at her hard, gaze boring into her.

"They've settled here in Florida. Mimi had a stroke, but she's doing well, finishing her rehab."

In fact, they were the reason she was in Florida. After almost three decades of traveling, they'd bought a place in a senior mobile home park and put down roots. Two months later her grandfather had had a heart attack. Rather than her parents bringing them back to California, Erin had left her position as a K-9 officer with Sunnyvale Police, paid the penalty to terminate her apartment lease and took off, pulling a small U-Haul trailer behind her RAV4.

The move wasn't quite the sacrifice it appeared to be. She'd wanted to put some distance between herself and her past mistakes and at the same time escape the fallout from her latest relationship fiasco. The fresh start had accomplished the latter. Unfortunately, the nightmares had made the cross-country move with her.

Cody nodded. "I'm glad you still have your grandparents."

His words were sincere, but she could read the meaning behind them. She didn't have just her grandparents. She had her parents, too—loving, supportive ones. Based on what Cody had told her, he'd never had a father, and his mother had abandoned him more times than he could count. Now that his gram and pops were gone, whatever he pulled from that wreckage might be all he had left of his family.

He'd lost enough. She wouldn't make him give that up, too.

She heaved a sigh. "Ten minutes. And I'll be timing you."

"Not a problem. I'm in no shape to be doing anything too major. I know where the boxes are, because I helped him move. With all the clearing those guys did getting to Pops, it won't take me long to find what I'm looking for."

The other unit would wait, and although her supervisor wouldn't be any happier with the situation than she was, he'd expect her to do exactly what she was doing. If she forced Cody to go right home, she wouldn't put it past him to head back over as soon as she left.

When she reached Pine Island, there wasn't much more activity than there'd been two days ago. Her electricity in Fort Myers had come back on that morning, but power hadn't been restored here yet. Some of the residents were likely staying away rather than enduring the heat and humidity without air-conditioning. She couldn't blame them. Last night had been pretty miserable.

Eventually, the road curved. To her right, three boats bobbed in a light chop, their occupants fishing. Docks extended out over the water, signs on their ends declaring them private. To her left, a vehicle sat in one driveway, but the other homes were still abandoned. A marked unit waited at the edge of Main, the same place Joe had occupied when she'd spoken to him Sunday. Another one sat in front of the demolished apartment building. No one had followed them. Erin had been checking her mirrors from the time they left the hospital.

After stopping next to the white Ram, she stepped from the vehicle, eyeing the caution tape cordoning off what remained of the structure. It was there for safety's sake, with the newly added no-trespassing signs to discourage snooping and reduce liability. Two uniformed deputies approached from the properties on either side.

"All clear. We're just going to look at his truck since it sat here unattended for some time."

Erin nodded toward Cody. "He's going to grab a couple of things while you do that."

Cody ducked beneath the tape, then maneuvered his way across the pile of debris. For the next several minutes she shifted her gaze between him and the deputies at his truck. While Cody searched, one man worked on hands and knees, looking behind each wheel, and the other checked beneath the hood.

Finally, Cody straightened, brows drawn together and lips pressed tight. Sweat beaded on his face, likely from pain as much as the Florida heat. The handle of a metal box was clutched in one hand. "This has Pops's keepsakes from his Air Force days." He set it aside and returned to his search.

A couple of minutes later he made his way down with what looked like an armload of photo albums and placed them on the hood of her Explorer. "There are a few of us in the top one."

"Really?" Her heart fluttered. He'd held on to them all these years. At least, his grandparents had.

"I didn't know Pops had them until I was helping him move. We were taking a break, and I flipped through them." He gave her a half smile. "We have Gram to thank. She was the historian of the family."

He stepped toward the destroyed building. "I want to get their letters. Then I'll be ready to go."

She glanced at the cops checking his truck and then down at the albums. "Do you mind if I look?"

"Help yourself."

She picked up the album he'd indicated and turned back the cover. This one was devoted to Cody. The first page held a school picture, "first grade" in neat script below. Others followed, showing his progression in age.

Baby pictures were absent. Those were the years before he came to live with his grandparents. His mother was obviously a poor picture taker. Based on what Cody had told her years ago, she'd been a sorry mother, too.

After several photos of teenage Cody enjoying various activities, she turned the page to find her own face staring back at her. Cody was behind her, bent so his chin rested on her shoulder. He held her in a tight embrace, arms wrapped around her waist. The love in his eyes was obvious, even in a twelve-year-old picture.

She'd been in love, too. She just hadn't been ready to make it exclusive. Too many years of watching her mother give up who she was to accommodate a rigid, demanding man had made her gun-shy.

Erin had thought she could put what she had with Cody on hold and have the option of returning to it at a later date, both of them unchanged. As if love was something that could be stored on a shelf, then taken down sometime in the future, dusted off and revived. Life didn't work that way. Over the past twelve years a lot of water had gone under the bridge, and it only flowed in one direction—forward. Never back.

She turned the page. In the next photo she and Cody were huddled together on a porch-type swing, her head tilted toward him, one leg extended. Everything about her, from her pose to her facial expression, shouted *carefree*.

Carefree had been an illusion. In her determination to avoid the constraints that marked her mother's life, she'd picked users and losers. One bad choice had almost gotten her killed. But sometimes it was the unseen wounds that bled the worst.

Erin glanced up as a red Toyota Tacoma turned onto

Boca Vista. She stiffened in alert readiness. But the driver didn't show any interest in what they were doing beyond a brief glance in their direction.

The tension fled her body. The man looked nothing like the guy at the hospital. He was clean-shaven, and his hair was dark and close cut. Probably a neighbor. Someone who belonged here.

Cody made his way toward her with the box he'd retrieved earlier, along with a second one. After placing them on the ground in front of her, he straightened, lips pursed and eyebrows drawn together. "I just thought of something Pops said the night of the storm. A couple of days earlier the owner of the building told him he wanted everyone gone. No one was to wait out the storm in their apartment." He frowned. "Maybe it doesn't mean anything. Maybe he didn't want the liability if something happened."

Erin finished the thought for him. "Or maybe he planned to have the place destroyed to collect the insurance money and didn't want to hurt anyone."

It was possible, even probable. They'd know more after checking out the guy's financial situation. The detectives were already on it. That was always the most logical place to start in situations like this.

She glanced at the deputies who were now squatted at the two open doors of the Ram, apparently looking under the dash. "Did you not lock your truck?"

"No. I was getting Pops and leaving right away. After my half-hour fight with him, I forgot about it."

She nodded, thankful the deputies were being so thorough. "Have you thought about funeral arrangements yet?"

"I have an appointment with the funeral home tomorrow. Pops belonged to a church here, so I'll get in touch with his pastor. When everything's over, we'll have his body shipped back to Illinois to be buried with Gram." Sadness filled his eyes. "I'm going to miss him. I can't tell you how often something crosses my mind and I think about telling him. It still doesn't seem real."

Erin's heart twisted. At one time she'd have drawn him into a comforting hug. Instead, she put a hand on his shoulder and gave it a squeeze.

She remembered Cody's grandparents well. She'd even heard several of his grandfather's stories. He'd been tough and crusty, what she'd always imagined an old military vet would be. But when it had come to Cody's grandmother, the man had had a soft spot that Erin had found cute. He'd directed quite a bit of that softness Erin's way, too.

"Let me know when the funeral is. I'd like to come." She wouldn't miss this opportunity to pay her final respects to the man she'd liked and admired as a teenager.

She'd be there for Cody, too, not because she'd broken his heart twelve years earlier, but because he looked grieved. Maybe even a little lost. And it struck a chord in her.

One of the deputies approached wearing a frown. Erin's stomach tightened. "Did you find something?"

"Possibly. It looks like the dash might have been tampered with." He tilted his head toward Cody. "Take a look at this."

They followed the deputy to the truck, and Cody slid into the driver's seat. "You're right. It's like it's not quite tight. It's hardly even noticeable, but I know my truck."

Erin pursed her lips. "There'd be exterior damage if

it was storm related. It sounds like someone might have removed it and didn't get it reinstalled properly."

Cody frowned. "I have a tool kit in the back. If you have some latex gloves, I can open it up and let you guys have a look inside."

His eyebrows drew together and creases of worry formed between. He reached across the truck to check the glove box. After finding it locked, he opened it with the key. An envelope lay inside, along with the owner's manual and some loose sheets of paper beneath.

Tension fled his features. That envelope likely held the two grand he'd mentioned.

After donning the gloves, he went to work on the dash, grimacing with the awkward movements. Soon he had the upper and lower portions removed. "I'm no wiring expert, but I'd say this isn't factory installed."

Erin watched him loop one gloved finger around a small bundle of wires wrapped in black electrical tape. It had been tucked into the left-hand side of the dash, next to the door. Each end disappeared into a connector, attaching it to other wires.

Cody backed away, and one of the deputies stepped forward. "I'm pretty sure I know what we have going on here." He leaned down to look into the long, flat space directly beneath the top of the dash, then pried loose a thin rectangular box. He held it in one gloved hand for everyone to see. "This is a tracking device."

Erin grasped Cody's wrist, an icy wave of dread washing over her. "Someone went to a lot of trouble to be able to find you at any given time. Is your personal information on anything in your truck?"

"Just my registration and insurance information. And it was locked in my glove box."

She released a pent-up breath. At least Cody hadn't made it easy for the creep. But the danger was far from over. In fact, it was just beginning.

"Now do you believe me when I tell you you're in danger, that I'm not just blowing smoke?" He couldn't deny it anymore. He'd have to face the truth and take her warnings seriously. She almost felt vindicated.

But when she looked at his fear-filled eyes and drawn features, whatever satisfaction she might have felt fled. Cody had finally accepted the danger he was in. And it had clearly shaken his foundation.

Cody walked toward his truck, clipboard clutched to his chest. Yesterday Erin had escorted him home, along with two deputies. They'd made sure he wasn't trailed and kept watch while he fed a wad of fifties and twenties into his bank's ATM.

No one had attempted to follow him. Of course, whoever was after him was probably counting on the tracking device to do the job. By now the killer probably knew the device led nowhere except the sheriff's department.

Erin had advised him to lie low. Law enforcement would be driving by his house regularly, looking for suspicious activity, but they couldn't provide him a full-time bodyguard. To be totally safe, that was what he'd need.

Remaining locked away inside his house wasn't an option. While he'd been in the hospital, requests for hurricane damage estimates had poured in. Today he was taking care of the first half dozen. The meetings, note-taking and measuring were tasks he could handle. By the time he had to do any physical work, he hoped to be fully healed.

The house behind him was one he knew well. Six

months ago he'd completed a master bath addition. Saturday's storm had sent an oak tree crashing through the middle of it. His customer's brother owned a tree trimming and removal business, so the oak was already gone. And Cody had made arrangements from his hospital bed to have his own guys temporarily secure the opening to prevent further damage.

He climbed into his truck and tore off the top two sheets from the legal pad attached to the clipboard. They held measurements, notes and rough sketches that wouldn't make sense to anyone except him. After sliding them into the folder on the passenger seat, he put another address into the GPS.

The folder beside him was titled *Hurricane Estimates*, but only two of the sheets inside were the completed pink copies of his forms. The rest were pages similar to the ones he'd just added—jobs that were too extensive for spur-of-the-moment pricing.

So far it had been a productive day. Although the Gordons were longtime customers, the other people he'd visited were new. Hurricanes weren't fun, but they were great business boosters for the construction industry.

He wove through North Fort Myers, making his way toward Edison Bridge, which would take him south into Fort Myers. He'd started his day meeting a homeowner on Pine Island. Erin wouldn't have been happy. But he'd stayed well away from Bokeelia, where his grandfather had lived.

The island itself held four unincorporated towns, with Bokeelia at the far northern tip, Pineland below it, Pine Island Center below that and St. James City at the southernmost tip. If anyone had been watching for him to return to his grandfather's apartment building, they'd have been disappointed since he hadn't gone anywhere near there.

Unless they were keeping an eye on the only bridge on and off the island. But that wasn't the case, either. At least, not that he could see while driving. He'd looked. He had no intention of being reckless.

Now that he was off Pine Island, spotting him wasn't going to be so easy. In a large metropolitan area consisting of three good-size cities, it would be like looking for the proverbial needle in the haystack.

He eased to a stop at a traffic light. Three more estimates in Fort Myers and it would be time to get ready to meet Erin for dinner. He'd lined it up yesterday, after she'd followed him home. All that remained was choosing a restaurant. He was leaning toward his and Pops's favorite place, which also happened to be dog-friendly.

He wasn't sure what an appropriate thank-you for saving his life was, but she'd have turned down anything too extravagant. Of course, she'd turned down dinner at first, too. She was clearly not in the market for a relationship. At least, not with him. Maybe she already had a significant other.

That was fine by him. It had taken a few times of getting the foundation kicked out from under him, but he'd eventually gotten it—a quiet, stable life alone beat the emotional roller coaster he'd found himself on too many times. His mom, then Erin, then his ex-wife. For some reason the women in his life tended to not stick around.

Cody clicked on his right signal and turned onto North Tamiami Trail. Getting Erin to finally agree to dinner had required his assurances it wasn't a date and his insistence that Alcee accompany them. Erin hadn't had a preference. Once she finished her shift, they'd meet at the pet-friendly Blue Dog Grill and enjoy a late dinner on the patio overlooking the canal.

Soon, the wide expanse of the Caloosahatchee River lay ahead, sun sparkling off its surface. The road split into two separate bridges, northbound and southbound, a dual concrete-colored ribbon slicing through the view. He began his ascent in the farthest lane to the left. Past the lunchtime busyness and too early for the evening rush hour, traffic was moderate.

The slope leveled out, and high-rises stabbed the sky in the distance. An abundance of palm trees covered the landscape, creating a floor of green, fronds standing out against the pale facades of the buildings. Fort Myers wasn't called the City of Palms for nothing.

When a vehicle roared up beside him, Cody slanted a glance in that direction. A gold-colored older Camry fell back to match his speed. He looked again, and the driver peered at him through amber-tinted sunglasses, blond hair brushing his shoulders.

Cody's heart leaped into his throat, and he jammed down hard on the brakes. At the same moment the Camry swerved into him.

The crash of metal striking metal reverberated around him, and he fought to maintain control. The space between his truck and the concrete guardrail shrank. His front bumper's left corner impacted with a bone-jarring crash that sent the rear end of the Ram around in an arc.

He clutched the wheel in a steel grip, hoping all four tires stayed on the road. The world spun past him—water and sky, asphalt and oncoming vehicles, more water and sky, then roadway again, taillights in the distance.

When he came out of the spin, the concrete guardrail loomed in front of him. A fraction of a second later the truck jerked to a halt, its hood crushed, steam escaping from beneath. Most of his side window was gone, dime-size pieces of it lying in his lap. An intricate road map of cracks spiderwebbed across the height and width of the windshield.

Cody peeled his shaking hands from the steering wheel one finger at a time. Someone had just tried to kill him. Had the other driver hoped to run him through the guardrail into the Caloosahatchee River some fifty-five feet below? If the barrier had been metal instead of concrete, he'd have succeeded.

Cody hadn't seen the man's eyes, but he'd recognized the hair. The glasses, too. Dark plastic frames with yellow-tinted lenses. They'd looked out of place in the driving prestorm rain. But they hadn't been there to block out the sun's glare. Their purpose had been to impede identification.

Even so, the guy wasn't leaving anything to chance. He was determined to eliminate his only possible witness.

A figure stepped into Cody's peripheral vision, and he turned toward the broken passenger window with a start. The guy was big, close to Cody's age but with an additional thirty pounds of muscle. In the rearview mirror, two vehicles were stopped behind him and another man approached, a phone pressed to his ear.

The large guy held up a hand. "Sorry to scare you. Are you okay?"

"I think so." He wasn't sure. He hadn't had a chance yet to take inventory. His side hurt, but it had been hurting before, along with several other protesting parts of his body.

The other man joined them. He was older, maybe

midfifties, and not nearly as large. "I've got 911 on the phone. Do you need an ambulance?"

"No, just police. Tell them to look for an older gold Camry with the driver's side smashed in. Did either of you get a tag number?"

The larger man shook his head. "All I can say is it looked like a temporary tag. I wasn't close enough to read it."

"Me neither. But the police could still put out a BOLO for the car."

The man finished the call and pocketed the phone. Cody released his seat belt. Maybe he should have stood and made sure he could walk before he turned down that ambulance. He pulled the handle and pressed on the door with his shoulder. It didn't budge.

The first guy gave it three hard yanks from outside and finally had it open enough for Cody to squeeze through. After walking back and forth in the emergency lane a few times, he was satisfied. Nothing seemed to hurt any worse than it had before.

He pulled out his phone. Both of the men had agreed to hang around and talk to the police as witnesses. But Cody had another call to make, one he dreaded. Erin would chew him out big-time. But he had to call her. He was supposed to meet her and Alcee for dinner and had no idea how long he'd be tied up.

Before she'd left his place yesterday, they'd each pro-grammed the other's number into their phones. She had his so she could keep tabs on him, and he had hers so he could call at the first sign of trouble. He hadn't planned for trouble to find him this quickly.

Thirty minutes later the familiar blue Explorer made its way onto the bridge. By then the police had taken statements from the two witnesses and they'd left to go about their day. The wrecker was sitting behind his truck, lights flashing, while the driver worked with the cables.

Erin stopped some distance back, well out of the way of the tow truck and police officer, who was just now leaving. She jumped from the car and walked toward him, gait fast and stiff. Was it concern he saw? Anger?

"Are you all right?"

Now that she was close, he could see it—worry. Her gaze flicked down the length of him and bounced back up to his face. Warmth filled his chest, and he scolded himself. That concern would be there even without their history.

"I'm fine. Someone came into my lane."

Okay, that was sugarcoating it.

"On purpose?"

He sighed. No sense denying it. "I think it was the guy from the hospital."

She frowned. "You shouldn't be out running around. It's not safe."

"I've been doing estimates for hurricane damage."

"Where?"

"North Fort Myers, heading down to Fort Myers."

"Where else?"

He winced. "I started on Pine Island."

She clenched her fists. "What were you thinking?"

"I wasn't joyriding." His volume matched hers. "I've got a business. It's not going to run by itself."

"And who's going to run it if you're dead?"

His shoulders sagged. She was right. But what choice did he have? "Do you know what happens to the construction industry in the wake of a hurricane? There's more work than any of us can handle. We're swamped for months afterward."

"Then lie low for a few weeks. The work will still be there."

"The first step is doing the estimates for the insurance companies. If I don't do the estimates, I won't be the one doing the work. I could lose hundreds of thousands of dollars. I can't recover from that." Two years ago, maybe. But not now. His ex-wife had seen to that.

Frustration burned a path through his chest. "Why is this guy after me, anyway?"

"Because you saw him leaving the day of the storm."

"But I wouldn't be able to identify him. Not with the rain slicker hiding his head and part of his face. Add the sunglasses and, as far as I'm concerned, he could be anybody."

"He doesn't know that, and he's probably not taking any chances."

The wrecker driver approached, a clipboard in one hand. "Do you have a body shop you prefer?"

"No." He'd never had to use one. Other than a minor fender bender the year he turned nineteen, he had a perfect driving record. He hoped this one wouldn't go against him. "I live in Cape Coral."

"Then we'll take it to West Coast Collision on Country Club Boulevard."

"I know where it is." He signed the paperwork and watched the man walk back to his truck.

Erin tilted her head toward the unmarked Lee County vehicle. "Come on and I'll take you home. But I'm still insisting you need to find some other living arrangements, preferably somewhere away from Lee County."

"I'll think about it." Not that it would change anything. He couldn't walk away from his business, regardless of whatever danger he found himself in.

He walked with her toward her SUV. "Do you mind taking me by Enterprise? I need to rent a car. I still have a couple of appointments in Fort Myers. I'll just be late."

"I don't know." Though her gaze held sternness, there was humor behind it. "If you don't have wheels, you'll have to stay home." As she walked toward the vehicle, her smile faded and she grew serious. "We're trying to solve this thing. The arson investigators are handling the explosives end of things, but Lee County is working on your grandfather's homicide."

Cody's step faltered. *Homicide*. The word sounded so cold and unemotional. It was used to describe people on TV—characters on crime shows, strangers in the news.

It didn't belong paired with the most important man in Cody's life.

THREE

Erin's sneakered feet pounded the pavement, and her braid bounced against her back. Friend and neighbor Courtney Blake jogged next to her, and Alcee was on-leash about six feet in front of them. To their right, the sun hadn't yet climbed above the treetops. But the early hour didn't deter the dog. She loved her runs, whatever time Erin could work them in.

Almost a week had passed since Cody's accident, and there hadn't been any more threats. It helped that he was staying well clear of his grandfather's old place. He also wasn't going out alone. Until this was over, one of his guys would accompany him on all of his appointments. The fact he was driving around in a rented car didn't hurt, either. Once he got the Ram back, they'd have more cause for concern. *If* he got the Ram back. According to Cody, the adjusters hadn't determined yet whether it would be repaired or totaled.

Without slowing, Alcee made a sharp right onto the sidewalk that bordered Linhart Avenue. Across the street two blocks ahead, a paved drive led through the sports fields that lay tucked behind Fort Myers High School. The area provided a great place to run, and even though school had started the prior week, they wouldn't have to share the space with any students this early.

Alcee wasn't the only one enjoying herself. Running had been one of Erin's passions for almost a decade. During that time, she'd completed several half marathons and numerous charity races in LA. Now she needed to find some in Florida.

When they reached the back road onto the school grounds, Alcee slowed, waiting for the command to cross Linhart. At this early hour traffic was nonexistent.

"Go."

The dog trotted across the street. As they jogged past the baseball field with its green block wall and Fort Myers logo, Erin turned to her friend. "You doing okay?"

"Fine." She was winded, but she was keeping up.

It hadn't taken Erin long to find a jogging partner. Shortly after she'd moved into her home four months ago, she'd run past Courtney's house several doors down and found her working in her yard. They'd struck up a conversation and instantly hit it off. In the weeks that followed, Erin introduced Courtney to running, and Courtney introduced Erin to Jesus. Erin got the better end of the deal. By far.

Without slowing, Courtney took a swig from the water bottle she kept clipped to her waist. "I saw you guys on the news the other day."

"Yeah." This morning was the first time their schedules had coincided since the storm. Between Cody's grandfather's death and the rest of her caseload, she'd been slammed. "Remember me telling you about my brief romance here the summer after high school?"

"Cody something-or-other." When Erin nodded,

Courtney's eyes widened. "He was the guy who was rescued? I thought he lived up North."

"He moved here eight years ago."

"Wow. You both end up in South Florida, he gets trapped, and you and your dog rescue him. What are the odds?" Courtney shook her head, but a smile curved her lips. "Looks like God might be giving you a second chance."

Erin threw her a doubt-infused glance. "I'm not looking for a second chance, and I doubt Cody is, either."

"Why not?"

"I don't know his reasons. I can just tell he's not."

"And what about yours?"

"You know mine."

"Those reasons don't apply to Cody."

Erin looked at her askance. "How do you know?"

"Everything you've said about him. He sounds like a really nice guy."

"They're all really nice guys at first." Unfortunately for Erin, she'd never grasped how to tell when that niceness was a facade. She was a good cop and liked to think she had a decent business head. Sadly, that wisdom and good judgment didn't always carry over into her personal life.

So she was determined to keep her focus on her job, church, Alcee and running. And try to stick mostly with female friends. Life was a lot safer that way, both physically and emotionally.

Courtney frowned at her pessimism. Relationship woes were one of the things they had in common. After pizza and a sappy movie one Friday night, Courtney had shared hers, and Erin had relayed her own pathetic history. Not all of it. Some things she hadn't told anyone except her immediate family. And the therapist her parents had insisted she see for a brief time.

In spite of what she'd held back, she'd still given Courtney more of her life history than she'd given anyone else. But there was one big difference between them. Courtney trusted God to bring her Mr. Right. Erin trusted God to help her continue to be happy with her single status and not try to change it.

They followed the road's leftward curve. The Edison Stadium entrance stood before them. At the fence that circled it, they turned around to head back the way they'd come.

When they turned from Linhart onto Holly several minutes later, Erin's house stood in the distance. It wasn't impressive. In fact, just the opposite. She'd gotten a great deal on the place because it had needed so much work, inside and out. It was a small two-bedroom, two-bath, concrete-block exterior. Someday she'd have it stuccoed.

When she reached her driveway, Erin said her farewells to her friend. "I'll be in touch." Rather than set hours, her shift times varied depending on what was happening. "We'll shoot for the day after tomorrow."

As Courtney continued down Holly toward her own home, Erin slowed to a walk and made her way up the drive. Her yard was where she'd focused her attention. The hedge of sea grapes separating her property from the one next door had been there when she arrived. So had the oak in front and several palms. But the house's foundation had been bare, the lawn sparse and weed-ridden.

Over the past four months she'd seeded and fertilized, added some robellinis to the palms already there and created circular beds around each of the trees, filled with crotons, bromeliads and ornamental grasses. Ixora lined the house, each shrub a riot of vibrant red blooms.

She loved her yard. Eventually, she'd love her house, too. She just didn't know how to get there. The idea of letting a strange man inside made her break out in a cold sweat. It had even induced a couple of nightmares. That was something she should have considered before buying a fixer-upper.

After unlocking the front door, she walked into the out-of-date interior to shower and get ready for work. She and the other detectives were making progress on Cody's case, but it was slow. They'd talked to Jacob Whitmer, the owner of the apartment building, twice. He'd inherited the house from his parents years ago, then converted it to generate some income. An insurance claim would have offered an even bigger payout. Whitmer had been their prime suspect. Then they'd executed the search warrant yesterday and found several letters that had changed everything.

Turned out Whitmer's claims that the place held too much sentimental value for him to let it go were true. For the past six months Donovan Development had been trying to buy it. Judging from Donovan's follow-up letters, Whitmer hadn't budged, even when the offer went to double the market value.

With no more motive, Whitmer had fallen off the suspect list and Donovan had landed on it. If the man wanted Whitmer's property badly enough to offer an exorbitant price, maybe he'd decided to remove the obstacle by having the building destroyed. Chances were good he had an acquaintance with shoulder-length blond hair and a neatly trimmed beard.

Today she'd stake out his business, and she was taking their only witness with her. She'd already arranged it. The change in plans meant Cody had to reschedule appointments, but he hadn't objected. He was willing to do anything that might bring him a step closer to getting justice for his pops.

Two hours later she sat in her Explorer at the convenience store kitty-corner from Donovan's business. She'd chosen a parking space at the end, next to the trash container, where she wouldn't tie up any of the store's prime parking spots and where no one on the other side of the street was likely to notice her presence. Cody sat in the passenger seat staring through the front windshield at an angle, watching everyone who came and went.

He lowered the binoculars to his lap. "Right build, longish hair, but the wrong color. And no beard. Of course, he could've shaved his beard and dyed his hair, but I can tell you he's definitely not our guy."

Erin nodded. "The guy pulling up while we're here is pretty much a long shot, but I figured we'd give it a try. And if nobody gets to it before I go in tomorrow, I'm going to show the composite you did yesterday to Jacob Whitmer."

He frowned at her. "Don't get your hopes up."

She'd finally conned him into having the sketch done, even though he'd insisted he didn't have enough details to make it worth their while. His brief glance through the Camry's tinted windows hadn't given him anything more than he'd gotten from the other two encounters. After thirty minutes of sketching, the artist had a guy with wavy, shoulder-length blond hair and a beard, information Cody had already provided verbally.

He watched an SUV pull into the parking lot diagonal from where they sat. "What does this Donovan guy look like?"

Erin took her iPad from where she'd laid it on the dash and turned it on. After touching the screen a few times, the About page of Donovan Development's website displayed there. She handed the tablet to him.

Cody shook his head. "Definitely not the guy from the hospital."

"No." She'd already checked out the company's website and its owner. Middle-aged with balding hair and a roundish face, he looked nothing like their suspect.

Two men exited the SUV. Cody ruled them out with one glance through the binoculars, then grinned at her. "Surveillance isn't very exciting, is it?"

"You have no idea."

"I'd rather be demoing a kitchen."

She smiled. "So would I."

His laughter filled the car. "That makes an interesting picture—you in safety glasses, sledgehammer in hand, swinging for all you're worth, debris flying everywhere."

The picture was more than interesting. It was appealing. More so on some days than others. Although for stress relief, running offered the same benefits.

Five minutes after disappearing inside, the two men who'd arrived in the SUV stepped out the single glass door and headed to their vehicle. As they waited to exit the parking lot, a pickup truck pulled in. When the driver got out, Cody picked up the binoculars, then leaned forward, tension radiating from him.

Erin's pulse kicked into high gear. "Our guy?"

"I think so."

She didn't have the advantage of the binoculars, but viewing him from where she sat, she saw two- or three-inch lengths of wavy blond hair curled from an elastic band at the base of his skull. The man brought a cigarette to his mouth and took a long, deep drag. A cloud of smoke curled around his face and head. She shifted her eyes to Cody, gauging his reaction.

He tightened his grip on the binoculars. "Come on. Turn this way, just a little."

As she looked back at the man, he flicked the butt to the side, then pivoted ninety degrees to grind it into the asphalt with the toe of his boot.

"Beard?" She was a little too far away to tell.

"Yeah. It's him. I'm positive. At least as sure as I can get with what I saw of the man."

Erin picked up her radio. "I'm calling for backup." Cody's ID would be enough to warrant bringing him in for questioning and finding out what kind of alibi he had for the night of the storm and the time stamp on the hospital surveillance footage. If he owned an older Camry with damage on the driver's side, that would clinch it.

Cody dropped the binoculars, concern etched into his features. "What if they don't arrive in time?"

"Then we'll follow, let the uniforms make a traffic stop." She wouldn't approach the guy without backup, especially while responsible for Cody. The man was wanted for murder. He probably wouldn't surrender without a fight.

For the next several minutes she sat with her gaze glued to Donovan's front door. They were so close. Within the hour, it could all be over. Cody could have his life back.

She glanced over at him. Once the danger was over, would he want to keep in contact? Would she?

She knew the answer to the last question without even

thinking about it. Unless he'd changed a lot in the past twelve years, Cody was like her friend Courtney—one of those gems that didn't come across one's path often. She had no doubt they could continue a friendship, as long as Cody could accept her hang-ups and not push for more than she was able to give.

The glass door across the street opened, and a man stepped out. Cody raised the binoculars. "It's Donovan. I recognize him from the website picture."

Donovan held the door open, and the blond guy joined him on the front stoop, his back to the road while they carried on a conversation. A siren sounded in the distance, and Erin cranked the vehicle. By the time the man turned to head to his truck, their backup wasn't more than a block or two away.

She put the vehicle in Drive and eased toward the road, ready to follow if needed.

When Cody looked through the binoculars again, his eyes widened. "Wait. That's not him."

"What?" Her voice sounded shrill in the confines of the SUV. "Are you sure?"

"Call them off. There's a large scorpion tattoo on the left side of the guy's neck."

As Erin radioed a frantic message to Dispatch, two Punta Gorda police cars came into view. The man with the ponytail opened his driver door, casting a glance at them over his shoulder.

The vehicles slowed, and Erin clamped down on her lower lip. If the real villain was anywhere nearby, the presence of the officers would tip him off.

Suddenly, the lights and sirens died and the cruisers sped on past.

Cody released a heavy sigh. "I couldn't see the tattoo until he turned to walk back to his truck. The guy at the hospital didn't have one."

"Maybe he just got it."

Cody shook his head. "It looked old, even a little faded. A tattoo that size, with that much ink, there'd still be some redness and swelling if it was new."

Erin updated Dispatch. As the two cruisers left the parking lot and continued down the street, she returned to the place she and Cody had waited for the past hour.

Cody put his head in his hands. "I messed up big-time. From now on, I'd better stick to construction."

She laid a hand on his shoulder and gave him a playful push. "Hey, trust me, you're not the first person to make a mistake like this. It happens all the time."

His cell phone rang, and he looked at her in silent question.

She smiled. "Go ahead. You're not on the clock."

He took his phone from his pocket and swiped the screen. "Hey, Bobby."

For the next several minutes she listened to the one-sided conversation. Based on what she heard, he was making plans to go out, or changing plans, and this Bobby was going to pick him up. It didn't sound like it was work related, which meant it wasn't essential. When Cody ended the call, she was frowning.

He ignored said frown. "I had lunch with a friend scheduled for tomorrow. It's now changed to Friday."

"You shouldn't do it then, either."

"He's picking me up, and we're staying in Fort Myers. Bobby and I do this once or twice a month." He squeezed her shoulder. "If it's any consolation, he's a cop. The only threat going out with Bobby poses is that for the past year, he's been trying to match me up with one of his fellow patrol officers."

Erin laughed. "Sounds like Joe, one of the guys I know from Lee County. He's been wanting to introduce me to a friend of his ever since I came on board. I figure if I tell him no enough times, he'll get the hint."

"Not if he's like Bobby. Bobby thinks *no* means *ask me later.*"

At least she and Cody were on the same page as far as relationships went. That friendship she'd been thinking about earlier was looking more and more feasible.

Cody returned his attention to the business across the street, and she followed his gaze. Traffic there had been pretty sparse and didn't look like it was picking up. They'd maybe give it another hour, get some lunch, then come back this afternoon.

"When are you going to let me make good on that thank-you dinner I promised you and Alcee?"

She looked over at him. He'd already assured her it wasn't a date. There was nothing wrong with dinner out with a friend. "How about tonight, after I finish my shift?"

"You're on."

"Have you decided on a restaurant?"

"I'm thinking about Blue Dog Grill."

She frowned. "That's too close to Pine Island."

"It's on Matlacha."

"Which the bridge to Pine Island goes through."

Cody twisted to face her. "We need a place that's dog friendly."

"I'm sure there are other dog-friendly restaurants in the Cape Coral area."

"Yeah, but I know Blue Dog Grill. Pops and I ate there

regularly. I can't take you guys somewhere that I haven't checked out first." He gave her a toothy grin.

She wasn't going to let him sway her with his charm and playfulness. "I'm not going to intentionally put you in danger."

"You'll be armed, right?"

"That's beside the point."

"Look, I won't be in danger. The guy who's after me recognizes my truck, which is still in the shop. And it'll be getting dark by the time we get there." The grin was back. "I'm treating you to dinner. Don't look a gift horse in the mouth."

She sighed. He had some good points. Once he got his truck back, it would be different. In the meantime, maybe she could allow him that little bit of freedom.

"All right." She frowned. "But at the first sign of danger, I *will* say 'I told you so.' And you'll be on restriction until this time next year."

If she had her way, she'd keep him locked inside his house until everyone involved in his grandfather's death was behind bars. But that wasn't an option. All she could do was urge him to be careful and not take any unnecessary chances.

She shook her head. Keeping Cody corralled was turning out to be one of her hardest assignments yet.

Cody backed the rental vehicle from his drive, Erin in the seat next to him.

"I figured you'd have gotten a truck."

He shrugged. "It's only a week or two. By that time they'll have mine fixed or, if it's not repairable, give me the funds to replace it. Until then, I don't plan to haul around any lumber."

In the meantime, he was enjoying his new set of wheels. They'd given him an Acura TLX. It was nice and sporty, the kind of ride that would impress the ladies. If he was looking for ladies to impress.

As he made his way along Pine Island Road, a series of canals lay to the right. That was pretty typical of the area. The narrow, man-made waterways created waterfront living for the maximum number of residents and offered easy access by boat to Charlotte Harbor and ultimately the Gulf. If Fort Myers was known as the City of Palms, Cape Coral should be the City of Canals.

Cody had his own boat, sitting on its trailer next to his garage. He'd last had it out two weeks ago, when he and Pops had gone fishing. The Starcraft wasn't likely to see water again anytime soon. He'd promised Erin he wouldn't go anywhere alone. Sitting in a boat out in the open, whether he was with someone or not, didn't seem like a smart thing to do.

He looked in his rearview mirror at the dog stretched across his back seat. Hopefully, the car rental company wouldn't have a problem with the occasional canine passenger. Just to be on the safe side, he'd vacuum up any white fur she deposited on the charcoal-gray leather.

Erin sat in the seat next to him. The final rays of sunlight slanted in through the front windshield, lighting her hair with a goldish-red glow. Instead of having it confined in her typical braid, she was wearing it down, flowing around her shoulders like a river of fire. She was gorgeous. Twelve years, and she still had the power to take his breath away.

He shook off the effect. This wasn't a date, and he wasn't going to treat it like one. He'd moved far past any thoughts of trying to resurrect teenage dreams.

"I hope you both brought your appetites. The Blue Dog is known for its fresh seafood. It was Pops's favorite place to eat."

"I'm starved. I fed Alcee when I got home, but that doesn't matter. If she's offered a second meal, she never turns it down."

When Erin and Alcee had arrived, he'd insisted on driving. It was bad enough she'd had to drive herself to his place. He'd never invited a woman to dinner, then not picked her up, date or not.

The road rose, and he navigated the last stretch of bridge before reaching their destination. Ahead of him, the sun sat perched on the horizon, streaks of orange and lavender staining the sky.

Matlacha hadn't changed in decades. Colorful little shops and restaurants lined both sides of the two-lane road. The community had been founded as a fishing village and had maintained that relaxed ambience. It was something Cody loved, a welcome reprieve from the city.

He turned on his signal and waited for a single car to pass before turning left into the Blue Dog's parking area. August was in the middle of the off-season. A few months from now the area would be bustling with activity as the population swelled with tourists and snowbirds enjoying the mild South Florida winter.

As soon as they opened the Acura's doors, tantalizing aromas filled the car. Erin drew in a deep breath, eyes closed. "If I wasn't hungry before, I am now."

She stepped out and clipped a leash to Alcee's collar. Then the three of them approached the yellow building trimmed in blue and green. Block letters near the door spelled out Blue Dog, a paw print between the two words. The sign hanging from the gable bore the establishment's logo—the dog called Blue inside an oval, the white rubber boots on his front feet a nod to the fishing history of Pine Island and Matlacha.

As they neared the entrance, Cody stopped her. "Wait here with Alcee."

He stepped inside, and the hostess greeted him by name. "I'm so sorry about your grandfather. We were shocked to learn what happened. I hope they catch the guy."

"Me, too." Hers weren't the first condolences he'd received. A few days after the storm the media had released Pops's name, and the news had spread quickly among those who knew him. Given the circumstances, Cody still hadn't been listed by name in any of the reports.

He looked past the hostess into the dining area and the patio beyond. At this late hour several tables were empty. They wouldn't have to wait to be seated.

"I'm with a friend and her dog."

"Bring them around. Teri will meet you on the patio."

Cody walked out the door, then led Erin around the right side of the building, where a sidewalk wove between a metal storage container and the air-conditioning unit. He grinned down at her. "The doggy entrance."

When they stepped onto the patio, their server was already standing at one of the small round tables, two menus in her hand. They both sat. Erin gave Alcee a hand motion, and she positioned herself between their two chairs, head resting on her front paws.

Erin glanced around and nodded her approval. "This is nice."

Cody agreed. Potted plants lined the patio, and triangular pieces of canvas stretched above, strings of white lights accenting the spaces between. Dock line strung from post to post sectioned off the eating area from the canal. Across the water, palm trees rose above the mangroves, their fronds silhouetted against a smoky gray sky. It was a tranquil setting, even romantic, which wasn't necessarily a good thing. The last thing he needed to be thinking about was romance.

After Teri had taken their orders, Erin looked down at the dog lying between them. "This is a treat for Alcee. Though she looks at me with those pleading eyes, I rarely give her table scraps."

Having heard her name, Alcee stood and stared at Erin, head cocked to the side and one ear lifted. Erin leaned over until she was almost nose to nose with her. "Yes, we're talking about you. Cody's determined to spoil you."

Alcee tilted her head in the other direction and released a long *"Arrrrrr."*

"That's right. You're getting dinner number two."

"Arrrrrooo."

Cody grinned. "She's talking to you."

"We have these conversations on a regular basis. I have no idea what she's saying, but she seems to know."

Cody leaned back in his chair. Now that the sun had set, the air had cooled slightly, making the temperature comfortable in spite of the humidity. Two other tables were occupied, the patrons speaking in hushed tones. Other than the occasional words that drifted their way, the night air was silent.

Erin released a long, contented sigh. "This is so peaceful." She rested her chin in her hands. "It's like the crickets are even hesitant to disturb the silence."

"We don't have the crickets like we used to. From

what I've been told, some kind of exotic lizard was introduced that pretty well wiped them out."

Erin frowned. "That's sad."

He thought so, too. The cricket songs formed a backdrop for so many of the memories they'd made. Cuddling together on a bench overlooking the canal at the RV park surrounded by palms and mangroves, watching the sun drop below the horizon. Walking hand in hand on the Harborwalk that wound through Laishley Park or just sitting on the swings while his grandfather did early-evening fishing from the pier.

That was where he'd kissed her for the first time, there at Laishley Park, right in front of the palm tree sculpture honoring those who'd experienced Hurricane Charley. Two palm trees, one standing upright, the other bent at a ninety-degree angle by the wind, metal fronds extending straight in line with the trunk. The sculpture held meaning for Erin. She and her grandparents had been there to experience the devastation.

Erin gripped the top of the straw and slowly stirred her tea, spinning the lemon around in lazy circles. Her gaze was fixed on the glass, but the distant look in her eyes said her thoughts were elsewhere.

She spoke without looking up. "I've thought about you over the years, wondered how you were, what you were doing."

"Same here. I even looked for you on social media."

Her eyes met his. "I'm not there."

"So I discovered. You're one of the few millennials in the US that doesn't have a profile somewhere online."

"Safer that way." Her gaze dropped to her lap.

He paused, sensing a story behind those three words, but she didn't elaborate. She would share when she was ready. Maybe. Whatever experiences she'd had over the past twelve years, they'd changed her. She seemed more reserved, less open, hidden behind protective walls that hadn't been there when he'd known her before.

She gave him a half smile. "Did you ever take out a post office box?"

The seemingly odd question wasn't peculiar at all. When their summer had come to an end, he couldn't stand the thought of never seeing her again. So he'd tried to convince her to set a date for them to meet up again after she finished school, just to see if that spark was still there.

Even that had been too much of a commitment. Instead, she'd come up with a different plan. If somewhere down the road, either of them wanted to connect, they'd rent a post office box, put a letter inside and hide the key in a designated place at Laishley Park.

"Never did. But I'll admit, when I got to Florida eight years ago, I climbed up on the base of that sculpture and put my fingers between every one of those sideways fronds."

Even though he hadn't expected to find a key, he'd been disappointed when it hadn't been there. He couldn't bring himself to write a letter, though. It had seemed pointless. Instead, he'd met someone else, another free spirit like Erin, someone who'd even looked a lot like her.

He should have known better. For the past year his ex-wife had been backpacking across Europe with her boyfriend, and Cody had thrown himself into work like there was no tomorrow. At least they'd never had any kids, so history wasn't repeating itself—there was no little Cody at home wondering why his mommy didn't love him enough to stay.

"I thought you'd be married by now."

Erin's words were jarring in a she-just-read-my-mind kind of way.

"Been there, done that. Didn't work out. What about you?"

"No husband, past or present."

"No significant other?"

The corner of her mouth ticked up. "Been there, done that. Didn't work out."

He wasn't surprised. Regardless of the changes he'd sensed, her aversion to commitment was apparently as strong as ever.

Their server approached and placed their meals in front of each of them. Alcee's, she set to the side. The restaurant folks had already cut the unseasoned chicken breast into half-inch cubes. The dog rose, nose twitching, sniffing the air. Her tail swished back and forth.

Cody shook his head. "How does she know she's getting some?"

"I told you she's smart."

Erin checked the temperature of Alcee's food, then placed the bowl on the concrete. Throughout the meal, they kept the conversation light, an unspoken mutual understanding.

When Teri cleared away their empty dishes and brought the dessert menu, Erin groaned. "I'm stuffed, but this brownie bottom pie looks awfully good. I could do half."

"Then we'll take a brownie bottom pie and two spoons."

Teri returned a few minutes later and placed the plate

between them. Cody hesitated before picking up his utensil. This probably wasn't what Erin had in mind. He should have asked for two plates. There was something intimate about sharing a single dessert.

But that didn't slow Erin down. In a few minutes the plate was empty except for a few smears of vanilla ice cream and chocolate drizzles.

He laid down his spoon with a satisfied sigh. "I hope Alcee enjoyed her thank-you-for-saving-my-life dinner."

Erin smiled. "We both did."

"And when you solve the case, we'll do a thank-you-for-giving-me-my-life-back dinner."

Her smile broadened. "It's a deal."

He paid the bill and led her toward the parking lot, Alcee prancing ahead of them. When he opened the back door, the dog hopped in and stretched out on the seat. Erin settled into the front, and Cody crossed behind the car. He'd just reached the center of the back bumper when an engine revved behind him and squealing tires snapped his attention toward the other end of the lot.

Twin headlights bore down on him, engine at full throttle. He leaped forward and dived between his vehicle and the next, his right elbow striking the pavement. The pain that shot through his arm and ribs momentarily stole his breath.

When he got back to his feet, Erin had exited and stood facing the street, pistol drawn. The car squealed onto Pine Island Road, its rear end fishtailing. Taillights shrank and disappeared as it sped down the road, headed toward the mainland.

She lowered the weapon and ran toward him, panic in every line of her face. "Are you all right?"

"I think so." He flexed and extended his arm. "I'm

sure my elbow's bruised, but it's not broken. And I've got some ribs that are tired of taking a beating. Did you see the car?" As quickly as it had happened, he didn't expect a tag number, but a description might help.

"Older Camry, gold. Since I just saw the passenger's side, I can't vouch for the damage that would have been sustained on the bridge, but I think it's safe to assume it was the same car."

She called the police, and they waited in the Acura for them to arrive. The tasty meal he'd enjoyed sat like lead in his stomach.

"I'm sorry. You were right." He wasn't too proud to admit when he'd messed up. He hadn't just put himself in danger. He'd endangered the lives of both Erin and her dog.

Erin didn't respond. Silence was better than the "I told you so" she'd promised to give him.

He heaved a sigh, frustration coursing through him. "I feel like I'm carrying around a tracking device."

"When he tried to run you off the bridge, he probably followed you from Pine Island."

"But I was watching."

"It's not that easy to spot a tail if traffic is heavy enough and they don't get too close. Maybe he *does* know what kind of vehicle you're driving now. After you wrecked your truck, it was logical you'd show up at one of the car rental businesses. There wouldn't have been that many to check."

"If that's the case, why didn't he just follow me home?"

"You didn't go home. You had appointments. It would've been too obvious if he'd followed you to every stop. He apparently doesn't know where you live, but he's got your connection to Pine Island. There's only one way on and off, and it runs right through Matlacha. With shops lining both sides of the road, do you know how easy it would be to find a spot where he could blend in but still see everyone who came onto the island? That means you need to stay away from here. No argument."

He nodded. It had been more than a decade since anyone had told him where he could and couldn't go.

It didn't matter. From now on, he'd listen to Erin.

FOUR

Erin paced her living room, phone clutched in her hand. Alcee's head moved slowly back and forth, brown eyes tracking Erin as she paced. She'd been trying off and on for the past half hour to call Cody and kept getting his voice mail. Why wasn't he answering his phone?

Last night, hearing the roar of the engine and the squeal of tires had just about put her in cardiac arrest. Cody had barely escaped with his life. He'd dived clear just as the car zoomed past, almost clipping the rear bumper of the Acura.

Whoever was after him wasn't likely to give up until police could apprehend him. Or until Cody was dead.

Now she couldn't get a hold of him and was about three seconds away from making the twenty-minute drive from Fort Myers to Cape Coral to check on him.

She snatched her keys and purse and headed for the door. Before stepping outside, she tried the call one more time. Cody answered on the first ring.

"Where have you been?" She didn't try to soften the accusatory tone. He'd worried her half-sick.

"In the shower. I'm allowed, right?"

"For thirty minutes?"

"Almost. I'm a little sore. Someone keeps trying to kill me."

"Which is why you need to answer your phone."

In the span of silence that followed, a nudge from the rational part of her brain said she was being unreasonable. Unfortunately, her heart wasn't listening.

When Cody spoke again, his tone was teasing. "Do you worry about all your witnesses this much, or am I special?"

"This isn't personal. I'm responsible for your safety. Not officially, but I'd like to keep our only witness alive long enough to catch this guy."

She winced. *Did I just say that?* "I didn't mean that how it sounded."

The truth was, it was very personal. And Cody *was* special. One of a kind. If she could ever let down her guard enough to trust a man, it would be with someone like Cody. But the walls around her heart were too thick, set solidly in place a decade ago and shored up with each year that had passed since.

"It's all right." All teasing was gone. "I'm sorry I scared you. From now on, I'll text you if I'm going to be unreachable."

Why did he have to be so perfect? Her chest clenched, and she was struck with a sudden urge to cry. What was wrong with her?

Nothing was wrong with her. Over the past minute and a half, she'd experienced the full gamut of emotions—from worry to the point of panic, to massive relief. No wonder she was a little off-kilter.

"Thanks." She drew in a stabilizing breath. "How are you feeling?"

"My whole body's sore, but nothing's broken that

wasn't already, so I've got a lot to be thankful for. And by the way, thanks for not saying 'I told you so.'"

She smiled. It had required a lot of effort. She'd had to take several deep breaths and clench her fists to keep from wrapping her hands around his throat. But Cody had looked so shaken. Besides, she'd been as upset at herself as she'd been at him. She should never have let him talk her into going to Matlacha.

"I had a nightmare." His words cut into her thoughts. "Do you ever have those dreams where you're trying to run away and your legs won't move?"

"Yeah, all the time."

"I saw headlights, heard the squeal of tires. Unlike what really happened, the car in my dream was far away. I had plenty of time to escape, but my legs were stiff and my feet seemed glued to the pavement. No matter how I tried, I couldn't move more than an inch at a time. I woke up in a cold sweat just as the car hit me."

"That's rough. I hope you don't have any more."

She'd had her fair share. Was still having them. Sometimes they were just rehashed memories. Other times her mind used past terrors to write new scripts. Regardless of where they came from, she awoke with a scream clawing its way up her throat and a dog pawing her chest. Alcee was always there for her, no matter how often the nightmares came.

"What are your plans for the day?" She hoped they didn't involve leaving his house.

"I'm returning phone calls and working on estimates and paperwork this morning. This afternoon I'm going to a customer's house."

"Not alone."

"No. My electrician's coming over, and we're head-

ing there together. It's the only job I still have in progress from before the storm."

She frowned. "I don't like the idea of you going out,
especially after what happened last night."

"I went near Pine Island last night. I won't today. I'm
not comfortable with the situation, either. But I've got
bills—a mortgage, a truck payment. I've got to eat. I
can't just not work, and I'm not a big outfit like Donovan
Development, with managers and construction super-
intendents and people I can leave in charge while I disappear for a while. I'm pretty much a one-man show."

She heaved a sigh. She didn't like it, but she understood. If she had to walk away from her job, her measly
savings would dwindle to nothing in a hurry.

"Let me know when you're leaving and when you
expect to be back." That way she wouldn't be worrying
about him as many hours.

"Will do. How about you? What are your plans for
the day?"

"Mimi's being released from rehab this morning, so
I'm taking her and Opa home to their place in LaBelle
and getting them settled in. Then I'm going to see Jacob
Whitmer, your grandfather's landlord."

"I hope it's fruitful."

After saying her farewells and leaving Alcee with
her neighbor, she headed toward the Fort Myers Reha-
bilitation and Nursing Center in her RAV4. A half hour
later she walked from the facility, both of her grandparents in tow, then stopped next to their vehicle. Opa
had stayed the past two months with a widowed friend,
so his clothes and personal items were already inside,
packed in anticipation of bringing Mimi home.

While Erin loaded her grandmother's walker and suitcase into the back, her grandfather opened the front passenger door and helped Mimi in. The red Cube wasn't a typical ride for folks nearing eighty, but there was nothing typical about her grandparents. Opa with his long hair, usually pulled back in a ponytail, and Mimi in her long, flowing skirts, they were throwbacks from the hippie era, but without the drugs.

Until settling in LaBelle, they'd spent the past thirty years in an RV, ready to take off whenever the whim struck. It was a mystery how the two of them produced a man like her father—methodical and organized, unwilling to take risks unless he could control the outcome.

After her grandfather slid in behind the wheel, Erin met him at the open driver door. "I'll follow you guys." The first stop would be the grocery store. After two months away they had a lot of restocking to do.

Opa nodded. "Thank you, Pumpkin."

Erin smiled at the nickname. No matter how old she got, she'd never outgrow Mimi and Opa's pet names for her.

Erin's childhood had been nothing like Cody's. Never once had she doubted her parents' love for her. Her father was an engineer who ran a tight ship but worked hard to provide a good home. Her mother was a stay-at-home mom who insisted she didn't mind the fact that every step she took had to be cleared with her husband.

As good as her parents were to her, Erin had known since preadolescence that she'd never be happy following in her mother's footsteps. Mama never complained but always seemed like a bird who'd had its wings clipped. Erin's main role models had been her hip, exciting grandparents who epitomized the concept of freedom.

Instead of turning the key, Opa sat for several moments, lips pressed together.

"Opa?"

The word was German, but neither Erin nor her grandparents had German in their ancestry. When Erin was young, *Opa* had been her version of *Grandpa*. The name had stuck.

Mimi leaned forward to talk around him. "Your grandpa's afraid I'm not ready to be on my own."

Erin had the same concerns, just hadn't voiced them. Mimi had progressed well in rehab, the stroke's only effects a slight limp and some unsteadiness. It was the latter that had Erin worried.

"Would you feel better if you spent a few days with me?" *She* certainly would.

Mimi shook her head. "We don't want to intrude."

"It's no bother. You'll have your own space in the mother-in-law suite, but I'll be there if you need help. Consider it a practice run for being on your own."

When she'd bought the house four months ago, it was the attached mother-in-law suite that had sold her on the place. With her parents wrapped up in their lives in California, she'd planned for the possibility that she'd need to care for Mimi and Opa eventually.

The next several moments passed in tense silence. Finally, Mimi gave a sharp nod. "One week max."

Erin closed Opa's door with a sigh of relief. A weight had been lifted from her shoulders. Her grandparents were two of the most important people in her life.

After getting them settled into the mother-in-law suite, she headed out. Her first task would be showing Cody's composite to Whitmer.

When she arrived at the CPA firm, the receptionist

led her to the office at the end of the hall. Whitmer stood just inside, arms crossed.

The tightness in his jaw matched the stern pose. "What now? I just talked to one of you guys yesterday."

He hadn't appreciated being their primary suspect. Having police search his home and office probably hadn't gone over well, either.

She pulled the composite from the envelope and handed it to him. "We think this is the man who set the charges that brought your apartment building down. Do you have any idea who he might be?"

The annoyance fled his face. He took the sheet from her and studied it, brow creased. Finally, he looked up.

"I'm sorry. I don't. I wish I could help. I want to catch this guy as badly as you do." He handed the sketch back to her.

"If you think of anything that might help us solve this, please let us know."

"Trust me, I will."

She slid the picture back into the envelope. Something niggled at the back of her mind, bothering her on a subconscious level. She turned toward the door, then spun to face him.

Whitmer had said someone from the department had called him. After the search warrant was executed Monday night, Whitmer had been cleared of suspicion. So who had gotten in touch with him yesterday afternoon?

"Do you remember the name of the person who called you yesterday?"

"Detective Roland."

She drew her eyebrows together. "Are you sure?"

"I'm positive. I have a client by that name, so it's easy to remember."

She shook her head. There wasn't any Detective Roland working for Lee County. Maybe it was someone from the Bureau of Fire, Arson and Explosives.

"What did this Detective Roland want?"

"He wanted David Farnsworth's emergency contact information."

David Farnsworth, Cody's grandfather. A block of ice lodged in her heart. "Who was his emergency contact?"

God, please don't let it be Cody. Anybody but Cody.

"His grandson. Cody Elbourne."

Slivers broke loose and moved through her veins. "What kind of information do you have on him?"

"Name, address, phone number."

"Did you give it to the caller?"

"Of course I did. I'm being cooperative, in spite of the earlier harassment."

Without an explanation, she ran from his office, one hand fishing for her phone.

"Ma'am?" The words trailed her down the hall, but she didn't slow down. When she exploded into the lobby, she almost plowed into the receptionist who'd risen from her desk and was crossing the room, maybe headed to the coffee maker.

Phone in hand, Erin mumbled a "sorry" and hit the door at a full run. She needed to let someone at the department know. Cody needed around-the-clock protection. No, the first call had to go to Cody. She needed to warn him. She hoped it wasn't too late.

Because there was no Detective Roland. Not with Lee County or the Bureau of Fire, Arson and Explosives. There was only a killer determined to eliminate his only witness.

Now he had Cody's name and phone number.
And knew where he lived.

Cody's phone buzzed against the desk in his living
room, notifying him of an incoming message. Leroy, his
electrician, was a block away, waiting at a traffic light.
Cody rose, pocketed his phone and picked up his keys.

He'd spent the morning finishing up estimates, responding to emails and returning calls. He hadn't even
stepped outside. Erin would be pleased.

But he couldn't stay cooped up forever. Bill and
Candy Hutchinson were waiting. He'd started their job
several days before the storm, a master suite expansion.
He'd gotten it weathertight before the hurricane brought
everything to a screeching halt. His subcontractors were
as overloaded as he was.

The next phase of the project would be getting it
plumbed in and the electrical run. Leroy had a short
block of time this afternoon to squeeze in the appointment. He could read blueprints, but meeting in person
would give Cody the opportunity to introduce Candy
Hutchinson to one of the men who would be tromping
around her home and ensure there were no misunder-
standings.

Cody rolled up a set of blueprints and walked to the
front door with them tucked under his arm. Leroy would
be pulling in at any moment. Normally, Cody would
meet him at the job site. That was no longer an option.

Leroy had understood. So had Dale, the guy he used
for cleanup and miscellaneous things that required a
second set of hands. Over the past week Dale had ac-
companied him to several appointments. Cody had been
surprised at the concern these two rough construction

workers had shown. They hadn't even ribbed him about needing a babysitter.

Before opening the door, Cody peered through the vertical blind slats and glanced around his front yard. Nothing looked amiss. Of course, nothing had looked amiss the other times he'd been attacked, either. His assailant had come out of nowhere.

When he opened the door, Leroy's white Silverado wasn't visible yet around the neighboring houses, but he had to be close. Cody scanned the area again, searching for threats. Clouds had begun to gather on the horizon, working up to a thundershower that would likely reach them before the afternoon was over.

The surrounding driveways sat empty. The neighborhood was typical middle class, with kids in school and most of the parents working at this time of day. A few yards from where he stood, three queen palms rose from a large oval flower bed, aloe and other succulents at their base. Between the narrow trunks, he had an unobstructed view across the street.

Leroy's truck cleared a house a couple of doors down and moved closer. Cody locked the front door, then fiddled with the fob until his thumb rested on the automatic start. Leroy was driving from Fort Myers to Cape Coral. The least Cody could do was provide transportation from here.

Besides, the Acura was a fun ride with all its bells and whistles—remote start and driver assistance systems such as lane keeping and road departure mitigation. It even had heated seats. Not that he'd use them. South Florida's temperatures rarely fell below fifty degrees in the dead of winter.

Before he could step off the porch, his phone rang.

Erin's name stretched across the screen. He brought it to his ear with a smile and "Hey, beautiful" on the tip of his tongue. He'd had so much fun with her last night. It had almost been like old times. At least, until someone had tried to kill him.

He dropped the "beautiful" and kept the "hey."

Erin's breath escaped in a rush, making a hiss in the phone. "You're all right."

"Of course I am." He looked around again, half expecting someone to start shooting. Did she know something he didn't? "Why wouldn't I be?"

"You need to leave." The urgency in her tone sent dread trickling through him. "No, wait. Lock yourself inside."

He shook his head. "Do you want me to leave or stay? I can't do both."

"Are you home?"

"Yes, but I'm heading out now."

"No!"

Cody flinched at the sharpness of the word. Erin's panic was shaking his own confidence. "What's going on?"

"Stay inside. And don't go near the windows. I'm having Cape Coral Police sent right away."

She still hadn't answered his question. "What's going on?"

"He knows where you live."

"Who?" His mouth formed the word, but his mind was already racing ahead to how he was going to deal with this new information. If he had to stop working and go into hiding, he'd lose everything.

She barked an order and a voice responded. She was apparently on her radio with Dispatch. Leroy reached his property line. In another few seconds he'd be in Cody's drive.

"My electrician's here."

Leroy began the turn into his driveway, and Cody pressed the remote start. The parking lights flashed and the horn sounded its clipped tone.

The next moment something hot and powerful slammed into him, and he was airborne, sailing in an arc toward the shrubbery. He landed with a thud in front of it. Pain exploded through his body. His ears felt as if they were stuffed full of cotton, and a high-pitched ring sounded from somewhere inside his head. What had just happened?

He sat up as another sound joined the ring, not as high pitched. It came from somewhere in the distance. When he looked around, Leroy's Silverado was parked in the road. He'd just watched the man pull into his drive. How did his truck get out there?

The ringing in his ears was fading, but the other sound grew louder. It was sirens. Emergency vehicles were in the area. Were they there for him and whatever had just happened?

The Silverado's driver door swung open. Leroy jumped out and ran toward him. "Are you okay?"

Cody cleared his throat, not sure how to answer the question. "What happened? I was getting ready to step down off the porch and…"

He swiveled his head to look in that direction, and his heart lodged in his throat, choking off whatever he'd planned to say. All that was left of the Acura was a burnt-out, mangled hunk of metal.

The sirens grew closer. Beyond the house next door,

flashing blue and red lights appeared, probably the result of Erin's call.

He squeezed his eyes shut and moved his head from side to side. Although the ringing in his ears was fading, his brain felt as if it had been slammed around and turned to mush. Someone had just blown up the Acura. No wonder Erin had called to warn him.

Erin! He'd been talking to her when it happened.

He pushed himself onto his hands and knees, and Leroy eased him back down. "Take it easy. You could be hurt."

"I need my phone." Erin would be beside herself.

He scanned the area. The blueprints he'd held lay between him and the porch, the roll bent at an odd angle. His phone had landed beneath one of his viburnum bushes, his keys several feet away.

"My phone's there, under the hedge." Cody pointed toward the house. He couldn't have stood if he'd wanted to. His joints had turned to Jell-O. The broken ribs and other bruises weren't feeling so well, either.

Leroy retrieved the phone, and as he approached, high-pitched shouts poured from it, reaching Cody before Leroy even handed it over. A Cape Coral police cruiser spun into his driveway and screeched to a halt. A second one stopped in the road right behind it.

Cody put the phone to his ear. "Erin?"

A river of words blasted through it, several pitches higher than normal. Actually, a geyser. He didn't understand a single one.

"I'm okay." He struggled to calm his racing heart. "Someone blew up the rental car."

She continued to ramble, sprinkling in an intelligible word here and there—*boom, scared, worried, dead.*

Then there was a hitched breath and what sounded like a strangled sob. Was she crying?

Maybe that was what he should be doing. Or praying, thanking God he was still alive. If he did that type of thing. He didn't.

But he should feel something. Scared, relieved, thankful, shaken. Right now he just felt numb.

He tried to gather his scattered thoughts. "The police are here. I need to talk to them."

"I'm headed your way."

"It's okay. I'm not hurt." He didn't want her driving in a panic.

"I'm coming anyway."

That was fine with him. He wanted to see her. In fact, there was no one he wanted more. How much he longed for her should disturb him. Maybe it would. Later. Now the numbness was fading, and horror was setting in.

If that had been his Ram...

He loved his Ram. He'd bought it right after opening his business. It had served him well, but it was a basic model, none of the upgrades the Acura had boasted.

And no remote start.

If he'd had his Ram, he'd have been sitting in the cab when the engine turned over. And he'd be dead right now, pieces of him scattered all over the neighborhood. A shudder pulsed through him. He wished he could just stay numb.

Two police officers approached, and Leroy helped him to his feet.

The younger of the two spoke. "What happened here?"

"Somebody blew up my car."

"I see that." The officer pulled a notepad from the

shirt pocket of his black uniform. He looked to be close to Cody's age, possibly a year or two older. But his demeanor was much more relaxed. Maybe exploding vehicles weren't a big deal to him. To Cody, they were, especially when he was supposed to have been inside.

"How about starting from the beginning?"

"I was heading out the door, clicked the remote start on the fob and *boom!*" He paused. "Well, that's not the beginning."

He filled the officer in on everything, starting with arriving at his grandfather's apartment the day of the storm and ending with the events of a few minutes ago. "There's already an ongoing investigation with Lee County."

After jotting down some more notes, the officer turned to Leroy. "Did you see anything?"

"Just the explosion. I was pulling into the driveway when it happened. I threw the truck in Reverse, backed up and parked there." He pointed to where his truck sat in the road, the right tires barely off the pavement.

"I assume neither of you saw anyone suspicious?"

"No." They answered in unison.

Whoever had planted the bomb had probably come during the night while everyone was fast asleep.

Cody swallowed hard. His heart rate was gradually slowing, but it would be a while before the shakiness left his limbs. "Someone from Lee County is on her way, one of the detectives. The Bureau of Fire, Arson and Explosives is involved, too."

The Bureau was going to have more to investigate than the charges that had brought down the apartment building. Whoever was trying to kill him had a disturbing preoccupation with blowing things up.

FIVE

Erin stared up at the red light in front of her, hands clutching the wheel in a white-knuckled grip. Moisture coated her palms, and her right leg trembled, maintaining its pressure on the brake pedal. "Come on. Turn green."

She drew in a stabilizing breath and loosened her grip. Cody had said he was okay. Maybe he was downplaying his injuries. But he wasn't dead. And he wasn't hurt too badly to communicate.

The light changed, and after a quick glance in both directions to make sure no one was infringing on her green, she jammed the gas and roared through the intersection.

Learning the killer knew Cody's whereabouts had sent her pulse into overdrive. Hearing the explosion over the phone had almost put her into cardiac arrest. As the seconds stretched into a minute, then two, she'd believed the worst. And twenty-five minutes away in Fort Myers, there'd been nothing she could do beyond what she'd already done—asking Dispatch to call for help.

She made a right onto Colonial Boulevard and headed for Midpoint Bridge, straight ahead. As she descended a few minutes later, the Welcome to Cape Coral sign greeted her, the Iwo Jima Memorial replica next to it, a variety of flags waving in the background. She'd crossed the Caloosahatchee River and was beyond the halfway point. Soon she'd see Cody with her own eyes and be assured he was okay.

The emotions colliding inside her during the moments between the explosion and Cody's assurances had shaken her. As a law-enforcement officer, her job was to defend and protect the citizens of Lee County. No matter how long she served, she'd never become desensitized to the pain of others. It was what made her human.

But this was different. She'd been near hysteria, unable to bear the thought of losing Cody.

Losing Cody? He wasn't hers to lose. She'd made her choice. If she had it to do over again, that choice would be no different.

When she'd come to Florida a year ago, she'd remembered the deal they'd made. But she hadn't wanted to connect. She'd been afraid what they'd had that summer would no longer be there. And afraid it would be.

Twelve years had passed, but nothing had changed. In the ways that mattered, she was the same girl she'd been then, but with even less likelihood of a relationship in her future. Now she wasn't only commitment phobic, she was commitment phobic with baggage. Just thinking about anything that hinted of "forever" almost made her hyperventilate.

After almost getting killed by an obsessed boyfriend, it had been a long time before she was willing to date again. Gradually, she'd gotten back out there. No one had ever hurt her after that. Not physically, anyway. After several casual relationships, she'd met someone wonderful and fallen hard. At least, she'd thought he was wonderful…until she'd caught him in bed with her best friend.

Then she'd fallen even harder. Hard enough she'd almost not been able to get back up.

Whatever she felt for Cody, she'd keep it to herself. If she allowed a romantic relationship to develop between them, she'd come to the same conclusion she had before—that no matter how much she loved him, she couldn't do it. Hurting him like that once was enough.

When she turned from Trafalgar onto Twenty-Second Court, she leaned forward. Cody's house stood in the distance. A white Silverado was parked in the street in front, a Cape Coral police cruiser behind it. She roared closer. A second police vehicle sat in the driveway behind the burnt-up rental car. Other than some dents and gouges and charred paint on one of the garage doors, the house looked undamaged.

She screeched to a halt behind the vehicles on the road. Some people had gathered in the front yard, two uniformed police officers and a man dressed in jeans and a polo shirt bearing a logo she couldn't make out. He was probably the electrician Cody had mentioned. Cody stood among them.

As she sprang from the car, the officers turned and moved toward their vehicles, apparently finished with their reports. She swept past them without a second glance. When Cody's eyes met hers, she had to squelch a sudden urge to throw her arms around him and bury her face in his chest.

"Are you the Lee County person Cody said was coming?"

The voice came from behind her. Several seconds

passed before the question registered, along with the fact that it was addressed to her. She swiveled her head toward the officer who'd spoken.

"Yes." The truth of that emphasized how inappropriate her actions would've been had she acted on impulse.

After a brief conversation with them, where they filled her in on the latest developments, she approached Cody and the other man. She could see the logo now. Jacobsen Electric.

She gave him a nod and turned to Cody. "You're not safe here. You have to disappear."

"And how am I supposed to support myself while I'm gone?"

She pursed her lips. She didn't have an answer. She couldn't even promise him it was temporary. Some people went into witness protection and remained there for years.

"Then stay with me." The words were out before she thought them through.

"No way. This guy means business. While he's blowing things up, he's not worrying about innocent bystanders. I won't put you in danger."

Jacobsen held up an index finger. "While you guys discuss this, I'll wait in my truck."

Cody nodded at the man. "Thanks, Leroy. We still have to go by the Hutchinsons'. I'll just be a minute."

Erin crossed her arms. He didn't need to be going anywhere except away from Lee County. "Staying here isn't an option. I wouldn't put it past this guy to burn your house down with you inside."

His jaw tightened, and his eyebrows dipped toward his nose. "Both my house and I would be safer if I was somewhere else."

"What about out-of-state friends?"

"I've got several, but I don't want any of them to support me. I've had my own source of income since I was sixteen."

Yes, he had. When she'd met him, he'd been working for his uncle, a general contractor, on weekends and during summers and school breaks for the prior two years. He'd had a decent car that he'd paid for himself and already had a skill that wasn't related to sports or video games. She'd been impressed.

He wasn't backing down. "I need to be close enough to run my business, meet with customers and assign work to my subcontractors."

"I have an idea." It was feasible. A way to help him and benefit her at the same time. "I bought a fixer-upper four months ago. I'm living with avocado-green countertops and harvest-gold appliances that are older than I am. I'm amazed they still work. I'd planned to have most of the work done by now, but I haven't even started." Now she could get it done without sacrificing her peace of mind.

She held up a hand. "Before you say no, I've got a gun and a dog. And I have a monitored security system. As long as you stay put, no one will know you're there. I'll pick up what you need or have Lowe's or Home Depot deliver it."

There was only one downside—Mimi and Opa. But no one would be looking for Cody in Fort Myers. And with Mimi's independent streak, Erin didn't expect their visit to last much longer than three days.

Cody stood in silence, thoughts churning behind those brown eyes. Finally, he gave a sharp nod. "All right. I'll cut you a deal. I'd do the work for free in exchange for the place to stay if I didn't have to still pay my bills. Hopefully, by the time I finish your job and am ready to start the next, this will all be over."

Erin expelled a relieved sigh. Cody would be safe, and she'd get her renovations completed without anxiety. At least not the kind that came with the thought of trusting a strange man with access to her haven.

Instead, there'd be the stress of guarding her heart, keeping the walls around it intact enough to be impervious to Cody's charm and good looks and the history between them. But she was an adult. She'd deal.

"All right, then. If you still insist on making that stop you mentioned, you ride with Leroy and I'll follow. I want to make sure you're not tailed."

"I have to get some things together, unless you want to share your toothbrush and deodorant. I also need to grab some tools. Unfortunately, the stuff I used for doing estimates and light work was in a toolbox in the trunk of the Acura."

As she followed him toward the house, a quivery weakness lingered in her limbs. Cody wasn't doing much better. His eyes were haunted, and the color still hadn't returned to his face.

She stepped inside and looked around. She'd been here twice but hadn't gone into the house either time. With its stuccoed exterior and gables in varying sizes, she'd guessed at a modern interior with vaulted ceilings. She'd been right.

"This is nice. Did you build it?"

"I did."

It was an open floor plan, with a large combo living/dining area. The dining room led to a kitchen that was separated from the living room by an eight-foot-high wall. The ledge on top held a couple of model boats, painted wooden ducks and a series of collector mugs.

A shirt was draped over the arm of the couch, and crumbs lined the plate he'd left sitting on his desk. The empty glass on the coffee table had a coaster under it to protect the wooden surface. The house looked lived in, not overly neat, but not messy, either.

"I'm getting my stuff together, so make yourself at home."

He disappeared down the hall and returned five minutes later wheeling a large suitcase. In the living room, he put his laptop in its bag, along with the power cord and mouse, then pulled a loose-leaf binder from a bookcase. "A portfolio of some of the work I've done. It might give you some ideas." He handed it to her with a grin. "At least it'll help assure you that I know what I'm doing."

He continued to a door off the side of the dining area. "We'll take everything through the garage, since I've got tools to get. Fortunately, I've got extras of all of the small stuff."

She followed him through the door into a well-stocked workshop, equipped with a table saw, lathe, band saw, radial arm saw and a few other items she couldn't identify. Two long racks held wood, and a variety of smaller tools hung from hooks pressed into pegboards.

"Now I see why you park in the driveway even though you have a two-car garage."

He gave her a sheepish smile. "This was supposed to be a temporary arrangement, but it's turned into more than five years. Eventually, I'll build a workshop in the back. Then I'll actually have a garage."

Cody loaded everything he needed for the foreseeable future into her car. "One more thing. I've got stuff in the fridge that's going to be spoiled before I get back. I'd rather not have a laboratory going on in there. Have you got room for a few things?"

"I'll make room."

He disappeared inside, then came out wheeling a large cooler. After putting it in the back of the Explorer, he climbed into the Silverado. When they arrived at the Hutchinson home on the other side of Cape Coral, a man was circling the yard on a riding mower. Erin parked on the road and picked up Cody's portfolio. As she flipped through the pages, she studied each photo for ideas. She'd made a wise choice having Cody tackle her projects. He did beautiful work.

Fifteen minutes later the front door swung open, and Cody and his electrician stepped out. A woman followed, presumably Mrs. Hutchinson. By that time the mower had moved to the back side of the house. Though Erin couldn't see it anymore, she could still hear the rumble of the engine through her open windows.

After a brief three-way conversation on the porch, Cody and his electrician moved down the drive. Leroy got into the Silverado, and Cody continued to her vehicle. When he opened his door, a gust of wind swept through, heavy with the scent of rain.

Erin watched him slide into the passenger seat with a groan. Poor guy. The abuse to his body seemed to never end. She gave him a sympathetic smile. "Anywhere you need to go before my place?"

"Not today."

"Good." Heavy charcoal-colored clouds were piled on the western horizon, rolling closer. A bolt of lightning zigzagged downward. Maybe they'd make it home before the sky opened up, but it was doubtful.

Cody was watching it, too. "Once we figure out meals, I'd like to get a list together and pick up groceries. When you're working, I'm happy to do meal prep. I'm a decent cook."

She grinned over at him. "A jack-of-all-trades."

"I learned out of necessity. After growing up with Gram's cooking, TV dinners got old in a hurry."

He didn't mention the period of time he was married. Was his wife a good cook, or had he cooked for her? Erin shook off the thought. Why was she thinking about his ex-wife, anyway?

Cody pulled out his phone. "I'm letting my neighbor know what's going on. I'll ask him to watch the place, get the mail and so on. He won't mind. I've done the same for him while he's been on vacation."

As she made her turn onto 41, the first fat raindrops hit the windshield. Cody pocketed his phone. A bright flash lit the sky to the right, and a boom followed a second or two later. By the time she began her climb up the Caloosahatchee Bridge, sheets of rain slashed against the car. The Edison Bridge lay a half mile to their left, visible on a clear day. But the summer thunderstorm had reduced visibility to about twenty feet.

She glanced over at Cody. One week had passed since his car accident. They were now one bridge over. But this one was the same height, and they were crossing it in pouring rain. Cody stared straight ahead, gaze fixed on the taillights in front of them. His white-knuckled grip on the door handle betrayed his uneasiness.

Erin turned on her signal and moved into the left lane. A concrete barrier separated them from oncoming traffic. Maybe it would be easier for Cody if they avoided the lane nearest the edge of the bridge. She understood trauma and how it could mess with the psyche, making simple things terrifying. She hoped his experience wouldn't be the cause of too many nightmares.

She knew about those, too. It didn't matter how much time had passed. Some traumas burrowed so deep into the subconscious, digging them out was almost impossible.

Finally, water gave way to land, and Cody relaxed.

She gave him a sympathetic smile. "Sorry I had to put you through that."

He frowned. "I didn't expect it to bother me. As a kid, I had a fear of bridges, but I got over it. I had to, living here. But once you started driving up the incline, with water all around, all I could see was the world spinning, then the concrete barrier in front of me, and I remembered the helplessness I'd felt, wondering if it was going to hold."

"It gets easier with time." At least that was what everyone said.

A while later she turned into her driveway and killed the engine. Her place didn't hold a candle to Cody's, but it was home, and she loved it. Besides, the yard looked great.

But Cody wasn't looking at the house or the yard. His gaze was fixed on the car sitting next to her.

"Is someone here?"

"That's Mimi and Opa's car."

His eyes narrowed. "Why is it here?"

"They're staying with me for a few days. Opa didn't feel comfortable bringing her back to their home in La-Belle yet."

Cody nailed her with a glare. "And you figured you'd keep this from me until we got here?"

"I wasn't trying to keep anything from you." Well, maybe she was. If she'd mentioned that Mimi and Opa were here, he'd never have agreed to come.

"Take me back home. You talked me into this, against my better judgment, convincing me you can defend yourself. I'm not going to risk bringing this creep down on a couple of old people."

Erin winced, glad Mimi hadn't heard that comment. She'd never considered herself old. Probably never would as long as she was on this side of the grass.

She heaved a sigh. "We'll be in the house, and they'll be in the mother-in-law suite. It's two separate residences." Sort of. There was an adjoining door between, one she intended to leave open, at least unlocked. "Unless you want to go into witness protection or leave the area, this is the only place you'll be safe."

He crossed his arms but didn't argue. Maybe she should have given him a heads-up. She could have mentioned it when they were leaving his customer's house. It wouldn't have made a difference. He wasn't happy. But he was safe. And that was all that mattered.

Cody leaned back in one of Erin's dining room chairs. Alcee had made her rounds, lying next to Erin, then visiting her grandparents and lastly moving to him. They'd been finished with dinner for some time and had spent the past hour catching up.

Erin rose from the table and addressed her grandparents. "You guys take it easy. Cody and I will have this mess cleaned up in no time."

The plates Cody carried to the kitchen were each scraped clean, a testament to how good the food had been. But he hadn't cooked it. At least, not alone. Erin had called in and taken the rest of the day off. While her grandparents had napped, the two of them had whipped up a large dish of lasagna, oven-grilled brussels sprouts and a huge tossed salad. Putting away all the food he'd brought had involved some skilled rearranging, but they'd done it. Now they were all pleasantly full, and the refrigerator was a little less so.

Cody finished clearing the table while Erin filled a sink with soapy water.

"I have a dishwasher, but it doesn't work. Fortunately, my stove and fridge are still limping along. I'm hoping they hang in there till you finish my remodel."

"We'll make the kitchen first on the list."

Cody was anxious to get started. He'd always enjoyed building things. As a kid, it was models—cars, airplanes, boats, spaceships. Then at age sixteen he'd started working part-time with his uncle building houses. Though Gram and Pops had started a college fund for him, after one semester, he'd decided the college track wasn't for him. His passion was working with his hands, his dream to have his own construction company.

Gram and Pops had supported his decision. In fact, they'd always been behind him 100 percent, even when he hadn't been able to see it at the time. The familiar hollow feeling settled in his gut. Spending the past few hours with Erin's grandparents had made him realize how much he missed his own.

He approached the sink to rinse the dishes Erin had washed. As he stood next to her, his chest filled with warmth, a sense of intimacy. It was the same thing he'd felt cooking with her. Years ago he'd been sure they were facing a lifetime of activities, both exciting and mundane, made special simply by the fact they were doing them together.

But feelings changed, and dreams faded. And nothing lasted a lifetime.

He took the towel hanging from the oven handle and dried the dishes he'd rinsed. The large breakfast nook was separated from the kitchen by a bar. On the opposite wall, someone had made several two-foot-long swipes with a roller, each in a different color.

He grinned and nodded in that direction. "Trouble choosing a paint color?"

"Apparently. But that wasn't me. The sellers had started remodeling but didn't get very far. According to the Realtor, they ended up separating right after that. So I got a good deal on the place."

"Tomorrow I'll make some lists and work up prices." Erin had already taken him through the house, portfolio in hand, and given him her vision of what she had in mind for each room. "By the time you get home tomorrow evening, I might have some samples for you to look at." He paused. "Depending on what time I get my truck back."

It was ready. West Coast Collision had called that afternoon to let him know. He'd been surprised to learn a few days ago that the frame wasn't bent, so the truck was repairable. Apparently, the three-sixty he'd done on the bridge had reduced his speed enough that when he'd struck the guardrail, his front bumper had absorbed most of the impact.

But getting the truck wouldn't be that simple. Erin and the others had come up with a plan. Someone in law enforcement would drive it while the others set a trap, keeping watch in unmarked units at various points along the route to see if anyone followed.

She frowned. "Regardless of when you get your truck, you shouldn't go out any more than necessary. Let me bring you what you need and, if you have to do estimates, ride with your guys."

"Fair enough. But Lowe's is a mile away. I've got to pick up things as I need them, or I'll be working on your project till Christmas. Two years from now."

She let the water drain from the sink and put away the dishes he'd dried.

He waited till she'd finished. "Shall we join Opa and Mimi?"

Using Erin's names for her grandparents felt odd. During their whirlwind summer romance, it had been natural. He'd thought they'd eventually be his grandparents, too. When he'd tried *Mrs. Jeffries* this afternoon, Erin's grandmother had objected. They were *Mimi* and *Opa* to Erin, and there was no reason they shouldn't be *Mimi* and *Opa* to him. Apparently, the fact that he and Erin were no longer a couple wasn't a reason.

When he followed Erin into the living room, her grandfather had the TV remote in his hand, scrolling through the options Netflix offered.

He watched them cross the room. "Mimi and I were wondering about watching a movie. What do you think?"

"Sure." Cody and Erin answered in unison.

As the opening credits rolled, Alcee hopped up to crowd into the space between Cody and Erin. Her tail beat against Cody's legs, and her front paws rested in Erin's lap. The tail slowed and stopped, and she eventually laid her head between her paws, eyes closed.

Over the past two months Cody and Pops had watched

countless movies together. At least, they'd started them together. Pops had slept through the end of every one. They'd laughed about how Cody always had to tell Pops the ending the following day.

If only he'd known how little time they had left, he'd have made more trips back to Chicago over the past eight years. Or never left to begin with. And he wouldn't have wasted so much of his childhood being at odds with the old man.

Pops had blamed Cody's mother. Every time things would almost return to normal, she'd pop back into their lives with apologies and promises. Both were meaningless, because nothing ever changed. Eventually, Cody would wake up to find her gone, a note lying on the kitchen table.

In the weeks that followed, he'd be mad at the world, ready to pick a fight with anyone who looked at him the wrong way. Finally, Pops had told his mother that if she pulled one more disappearing act, to not bother coming back. Cody had been thirteen and hadn't seen her since. At the time he'd thought he'd never forgive his grandfather. In hindsight, it had been the best thing the old man could have done for him.

When the movie ended two hours later, Opa rose. "We're heading to bed." He helped Mimi up and led her the few steps to her walker.

Erin pressed the power button on the remote, and the screen went dark. "How about leaving the door cracked? I want to be able to hear you if you need anything during the night."

Cody watched them cross the living room toward the mother-in-law suite. Though Mimi had both hands on her walker, Opa walked next to her, an arm draped across her shoulders.

Cody smiled. His grandparents had had the same kind of relationship. Pops had been as tough as could be, stubborn to a fault. Gram had been the sweetest person Cody had ever known, but one stern look from her, and Pops had always caved. She'd even gotten him into church, over his adamant objections. Surprisingly, it had stuck. One of the first things he'd done on arriving in Florida was find services to attend.

After Gram passed, Cody had hoped Pops would find happiness again. But every time a widowed lady had shown interest in him, his response had always been the same—"She's not Gram." Maybe that kind of love happened only once in someone's lifetime.

Would Cody ever find the same thing? He'd thought he had. Twice. And he'd struck out both times. He didn't know how to choose them like Pops and Opa did.

While Erin set the alarm and turned out the lights, Cody headed down the hall in the opposite direction Mimi and Opa had gone. His room was the first one. The middle bedroom was set up as an office, with a desk, bookcases and a daybed. The master bedroom was at the end.

He'd just closed the door when two soft knocks sounded.

"Do you have everything you need?" Erin's voice came through the door. "Extra pillows? Blankets? I keep the air set pretty low at night."

He glanced at the double bed with its two pillows and what looked like a handmade quilt. "I'll be fine."

He opened the door. "I appreciate everything you're doing for me. You started out the day living alone and ended it with three houseguests. You're good at going with the flow."

"You three are easy guests, not very demanding." The edges of her mouth quirked up in a smile. "Besides, I'm getting a home remodel out of the deal." After a short pause she continued, her tone serious. "You have no idea what that means to me, what a relief it is to have you here."

He lifted a brow. He wasn't the only good contractor in the Fort Myers/Cape Coral area. He was giving her a deal, but something told him there was more behind her relief than getting quality work at a reasonable price. Whatever it was, he'd probably never know. She'd stashed her secrets behind such thick walls it would take a chisel and crowbar to get to them. Or a jackhammer.

Much later Cody lay in bed, still awake. He'd flopped from one side to the other for the past hour and a half, unable to get comfortable. It wasn't the bed's fault. The mattress was the right firmness. The temperature was perfect, too. He just couldn't shut down his thoughts. If he was home, he'd have a bowl of cereal, maybe watch some late-night TV.

If he was home, he wouldn't still be awake.

Here, there were too many things to occupy his mind. Opa and Mimi were totally different from his own grandparents. But they reminded him so much of them, he couldn't talk with them without the void Pops had left almost consuming him.

Knowing their beautiful granddaughter was sleeping at the end of the hall didn't help. Several times over the past few years, he'd have given anything for an opportunity to spend so much time with her. Now it was bittersweet torment as he fought the emotions her near-ness resurrected. Emotions he had no business feeling.

The mental battles kept sleep from coming. He'd gotten close once. His thoughts had grown random, and he'd slid down the slippery slope of unconsciousness. Then the squeal of tires and the image of his truck slamming into the concrete barrier had jarred him awake. The trip back over the bridge this afternoon had shaken him more than he wanted to admit.

He flopped onto his other side and rearranged the sheet. When he grew still again, a soft, high-pitched whine broke the silence. He held his breath and listened. A few seconds later it happened again.

He tensed, every sense on full alert. The doors and windows were locked, the alarm set. But was Alcee trying to alert them to danger?

He threw back the sheet and sprang from the bed. When he opened the door, the dog was whining in earnest. She was in the master bedroom. There were other sounds, too, thrashing, as if someone was struggling.

Then a moan and a whimper sent his heart into his throat. Something was wrong with Erin.

He charged down the hall at a full run. Her door was open. Two night-lights illuminated the room with a soft glow. The same glow came from the bathroom.

He cast frantic glances around. Except for her dog, Erin was alone. Alcee lay on the bed, paws on Erin's chest. The dog's head swiveled toward him, and her dark eyes begged him to do something.

Erin tossed her head side to side, another long moan escaping her mouth. It was only a nightmare.

"Erin." He rushed to her side, grasped her shoulders and shook her. "Erin, wake up. It's just a dream."

A strangled scream escaped, and her fist connected with his jaw. He stumbled away from her until his back met the chest of drawers.

Erin bolted upright. She held the sheet clutched to her chest, which rose and fell with every jagged breath. Her green eyes were wide, her hair a tangled mass around her face and shoulders. She was unguarded, vulnerable. And absolutely beautiful.

He dragged his gaze from her face and fixed it on the nightstand next to her. A lamp sat in the center, next to it a water bottle and a book titled *Jesus Calling*.

"You were having a nightmare. I think Alcee was trying to wake you up."

The dog plopped herself across Erin's lap. Erin wrapped both arms around her and rocked back and forth, holding on as if she were drowning and Alcee was her lifeline. It was like dusk in the room, or the beginning moments of sunrise. Who slept with three night-lights?

Someone who was afraid of the dark.

His heart twisted at the fear lingering in her eyes, and he moved closer. When he reached her bedside, he stood still, arms tense with the effort of keeping them at his sides when he longed to draw her into a protective embrace.

But it wouldn't be welcome. He knew without asking. Her dog was providing the comfort he wanted to give. Her rocking slowed and stopped. How often did Alcee have to chase away the terrors that lurked in her mind?

"What happened? What were you dreaming?"

"I just had a nightmare." Her gaze dipped to her dog, still in her lap. She made a long stroke down Alcee's back, then reversed the motion, burying her fingers in the thick white fur.

"That must have been one doozy of a dream."

She shrugged. "Just an ordinary nightmare. It's not a big deal."

He pressed a hand to the side of his face. "My jaw would beg to differ."

"I'm sorry I hit you. For future reference, never grab someone who's having a nightmare."

Yeah, he knew that about people suffering from PTSD. Like soldiers who'd seen the horrors of battle. Not ordinary people.

But nothing about Erin had ever been ordinary.

She wasn't military. She hadn't seen war. But apparently, sometime during the past twelve years, she'd experienced her own terrors.

SIX

Cody sat at Erin's dining room table, his computer in front of him. A TV played in the background, the sound coming from the slightly open door of the mother-in-law suite. Except for dinnertime, which they all shared together, Mimi and Opa stayed in their quarters. Alcee had the run of the place and hung out with whoever would give her the most attention.

As he'd promised Erin, Cody had spent the day yesterday coming up with kitchen ideas. Last night they'd gone to Lowe's together and picked out appliances and selected several flooring samples. They'd also planned meals for the next week, and since Erin had the day off today, she was at Publix tackling the lengthy grocery list while Cody worked on cabinet design.

He made several clicks with the mouse, typing in intermittent commands, and a drawing took shape on the screen. Erin had chosen a style she liked from the photos in his portfolio, and he'd taken measurements and done rough sketches. But the two- and three-D renderings he was doing in AutoCAD would let her visualize the image he already had in his mind. It would also give his cabinet guy something easier to work with than the scribbles on the legal pad sitting next to his computer.

Once he finished the kitchen remodel, Erin wanted to modernize the bathrooms, then the rest of the house. The mother-in-law suite would be last, long after Mimi and Opa returned to their home in LaBelle.

The way things were going with the investigation, he'd be living at Erin's indefinitely. Everything was at a standstill. Police hadn't found the Camry, and the traps they'd laid yesterday getting his truck to Erin's had come to naught. No one had showed the slightest bit of interest.

Tracing the phone number of the alleged Detective Roland had led nowhere. The call had come from a burner phone. They'd interviewed the developer also, and none of his associates matched the description of the guy in the hospital.

Alcee slipped through the open door, announcing her presence with the tap of her claws against the linoleum floor.

Cody looked away from his work. "Hey, girl. Are you coming for another visit?"

She tilted her head and lifted an ear.

"Mimi and Opa aren't giving you enough love?"

She tipped her head in the other direction, and that ear lifted. Erin had said she was smart. Cody had no idea how much she understood, but she made it look convincing.

He scratched her neck and jaw, and she pressed her head into his hand. When he stopped, instead of lying next to him, she put a paw in his lap.

He checked the time on his computer. Eleven. She wasn't due to eat for another hour.

"What do you want, girl? Do you need to go out?"

She barked once and trotted to the sliding glass door. He rose to let her into the fenced backyard. She would paw at the door when she was ready to come inside again.

After completing his drawing, Cody lifted both arms and arched his back over the chair. He'd slept well last night. After the previous night, he'd been too exhausted to do anything but. Erin had slept well, too. At least, she claimed she had. But even if her nightmare had returned, she wasn't likely to tell him about it. The Erin of old had been an open book, guard down, the world her playground. That Erin no longer existed.

He clicked the mouse and sent what he'd done to the printer in the middle bedroom. With his tools in his truck, his blank invoices and estimate forms in his computer bag, and his laptop connected to Erin's printer, he was ready for business.

His phone rang, interrupting his thoughts. Erin's name displayed on the screen.

"I'm getting ready to check out. Anything else you want me to get while I'm here?"

"I don't think so. That list we made last night was pretty extensive."

"Tell me about it. My cart's heaping. Food preparation for four is a little different from food preparation for one."

A lot more expensive, too. But they'd all agreed to do an even four-way split—half the bill paid by Mimi and Opa and a quarter each by him and Erin.

"Sounds like you'll make it home before I leave." He was meeting Bobby for lunch at Zaxby's, then stopping by Sherwin-Williams for paint chips. "You're welcome to join us." He laughed. "If I bring a woman along, maybe Bobby will stop trying to match me up with his coworker."

Her laughter joined his. "Thanks for the invite. Although I'd love to be able to bail you out, I think I'll just have lunch with Mimi and Opa. Since your friend's a cop, I'd say you're in good hands."

As he disconnected the call, Alcee scratched against the sliding glass door frame. He slid the door back on its track. "Come on, girl."

She bounded in, tail wagging. Lunchtime was close, and she knew it. The dog had a built-in clock. Cody walked into the kitchen and picked up the porcelain bowl. The white dish with a big blue paw print in the bottom was licked clean.

"Are you ready to eat?" Her head tilted again, and her ear lifted when he said *eat*. That was a word she *did* understand, like almost every other pet in America.

He took a can of Purina ONE from the pantry and popped the top. After he'd dumped the contents into the dish, he glanced at the clock hanging on the opposite wall. He was feeding her fifteen minutes early. If it was a problem, he'd stick to a stricter schedule in the future.

A short time later Erin arrived home with the back of her RAV4 filled with groceries. He met her outside and, after looping several bags over each arm, nodded down at what he held. "You can start putting everything away, since you know where it goes. I'll tote the rest in."

When they finished, it was time for him to leave. He picked up his keys and stuffed his phone into his pocket. "I'll see you in a couple of hours."

"If you see anything suspicious, or are even slightly uneasy, call the police. Then get a hold of me."

He grinned. "You *are* the police. So is Bobby."

"Someone on duty whose sirens and lights can get them there in a hurry."

When he arrived at Zaxby's, Bobby was already inside waiting near the door. The larger man clapped Cody on the shoulder in greeting, and he winced. He was still sore, as much from slamming into the concrete barrier as spending the night trapped in the collapsed building. The dive in the parking lot hadn't helped, either. Neither had being blown halfway across his front yard.

But Bobby knew none of that. Cody had gotten a hold of him yesterday to let him know he'd relocated to Fort Myers and wouldn't need the ride from his house. He would fill him in on everything else over lunch. Soon, they were seated at a table, two plates of wings and fries in front of them.

Cody picked up a fry and dipped it in ketchup. "Did you hear about the apartment building collapsing in Bo-keelia, on Pine Island?"

"Not only did I hear about it, I was on duty, keeping people who didn't belong from venturing back there. I didn't see the story air, but I heard the collapse was intentional."

"It was. I was inside when it went down, even spent a little time in the hospital with a concussion and some broken ribs."

"Whoa. I had no idea that was you. What were you doing there?"

"Trying to convince my stubborn grandfather to evacuate."

Bobby shook his head. "You don't look much worse for wear. How about your pops?"

Cody pressed his lips together. "He didn't make it."

"Ah, man, that's rough. Sorry to hear that."

Cody nodded his thanks. "What have you heard about the case?"

"Nothing. Being in patrol, I'm not involved in homicide investigations."

As they ate, Cody filled him in on everything that had happened. Finally, Bobby sat back and shook his head. "You've gotten yourself tangled up in a mess."

"I know." He was still having a hard time wrapping his mind around it. "I'm not used to having people out to get me. I get along with everybody." At least, once he'd gotten through his troubled adolescent and early teen years. "The last time I had an enemy was in ninth grade when someone tripped me in the cafeteria and I spilled Kool-Aid on Jimmy Thompson's new Izod shirt."

Bobby laughed, then grew silent, thinking as he finished off the last of his chicken. "Have you checked with the planning department to see if the developer sought approval for anything there?"

Cody picked up one of his wings and took a bite. His plate was still half-full. He'd been the one doing almost all the talking.

"I don't know if anyone has thought of that. As a contractor, I know the people there pretty well. I'll see what I can find out. If he's already been to the planning people, he's pretty serious about buying." Of course, the offer Erin said the developer had made to Whitmer showed some pretty strong determination.

"So where are you staying? You said somewhere here in Fort Myers."

"Yeah. I'm staying with someone I just reconnected with, who also happens to be one of the detectives working the case."

"That's convenient. He's letting you live there until this gets wrapped up?"

"Not *he*—*she*. And yes, she's letting me stay until this is over. Actually, she's not giving me a choice. Everything that's happened has her pretty worried."

Bobby grinned. "Hmm. Sounds promising."

Cody shook his head. "It's not like that. There's no romance going on. I've got my own room and so do her grandparents."

Bobby had been around for the implosion of Cody's marriage and had been on a mission ever since to secure him a happily-ever-after. Cody had made it clear he wasn't interested, but his friend still hadn't given up. The man wasn't dense, just determined.

Bobby shrugged. "No romance now, and grandparents to chaperone. But you never know where things might lead." He waggled his brows, which looked more silly than anything. Knowing Bobby, the effect was intentional.

Yeah, one never knew where things might lead. But some paths were so unlikely it didn't make sense to even consider them. Neither he nor Erin had any intention of letting down their guard. He didn't know what was behind her resistance, but he understood his own. He'd had enough people he loved walk away that he wasn't interested in going another round. Life alone was pretty good, as long as he stayed busy and never dwelled on what he'd lost.

Bobby crumpled up his napkin and dropped it on the empty plate. "Well, if things don't work out with this lady, I can always introduce you to my cute coworker."

"Sorry, I'm going to pass on both."

Bobby's brow creased. "Actually, if you were conscious when they pulled you out of the rubble, you might have already met her. Cute lady about this tall." He held up a hand. "White German shepherd dog."

"Erin? That's who I'm staying with."

Bobby bellowed with laughter, slapping the table and struggling to catch his breath.

Cody frowned. "You wanna tell me what's so funny so we can both enjoy the joke?"

Bobby gradually got control of himself. "Erin Jeffries is the woman I've been trying to introduce you to."

"You told me she was in patrol with you."

"She was. Then she moved to detective. I guess I didn't tell you that part." He chuckled a couple more times.

"Do you work with somebody named Joe?"

"You got a last name?"

Cody shook his head. "He's been trying to match Erin up with a friend of his. She keeps turning him down, but the guy's persistent."

The laughter bubbled up again.

Cody waited, his frown deepening. "I'm glad you're finding this so entertaining."

"Sorry, I can't help it." He made a valiant attempt at seriousness, but his lips quivered with the effort. "I'm Joe."

"Huh?" He and Bobby had been friends for four years. How would Cody not know that?

"My given name is Joseph Robert Morris Junior. With my dad being Joe, it was too confusing having two of us in the house, so I was Bobby. Everywhere I've worked, though, they've called me Joseph or Joe." A couple more chuckles escaped. "As much as I wanted to introduce you guys and got nowhere, your paths still managed to cross. God does work in mysterious ways."

Cody's frown returned. God probably didn't have anything to do with it. But crediting the coincidences of life with the intervention of God was what he'd expect from Bobby. His friend had invited him to several of his church's activities over the years. Cody had turned down those invitations the same way he'd rejected the match-making attempts—with a good-natured but firm *no*.

He didn't need church. He was doing all right. He had his work, his hobbies, his friends and his home. But he wasn't just wrapped up in his own life. He'd always been generous with his money, making regular dona-tions to several charitable organizations, at least until his ex-wife wiped him out. That generosity had to rack up some brownie points with the man upstairs. If some people needed more to feel fulfilled, he understood. But the whole religion scene wasn't for him.

Cody had almost finished his meal when a buzz no-tified him of an incoming text. He held up an index fin-ger. "I need to take this, in case it's Erin."

At least now Bobby would leave him alone about the pretty fellow law-enforcement officer. Or maybe not. Now that they were living under the same roof, he'd probably be even more relentless.

Cody pulled out his phone. The notification wasn't from Erin. "Finally. I've had protein powder on back order since two days before the storm. It just got deliv-ered an hour ago." He pocketed the phone. "Would you mind running me by there to grab it? Then you can drop me back by here."

Erin wouldn't like it, but he couldn't expect Lee County or Cape Coral PD to act as errand boys.

Bobby's eyebrows dipped toward his nose. "You sure it's not a trap? It's definitely your package?"

"Yeah. The notification came from the company."

Bobby nodded, but deep vertical lines still marked the space between his eyebrows. "I think you should check with Erin."

Cody scowled. He hadn't asked for permission to go somewhere since he was a kid. But Bobby was right. Erin was doing everything in her power to keep him safe. She deserved to know if he was getting ready to do something reckless. Besides, he'd already vowed he'd listen to her from now on.

He pulled his phone back out and dialed Erin. Her "hello" sounded anxious. Of course it would. She'd told him to call her at the first sign of danger.

"Everything's all right. I just wanted to let you know about another stop I need to make."

"O-kay." The anxiousness had turned to hesitation.

"My protein powder finally arrived. I was going to have Bobby run me by to pick it up."

"Are you trying to get yourself killed?"

He ignored the sharpness in her tone. "We'll be in his truck. I'll even stay inside. Bobby can jump out and grab the box." He paused. "No one knows I'm going over there."

"No one except whoever might have seen that package being delivered."

"Do you really think someone's watching my house twenty-four/seven?"

"Can you guarantee someone isn't?"

No, he couldn't guarantee anything, except that less than two weeks had passed since the destruction of his grandfather's apartment building, and he already couldn't wait to get his life back.

"Don't forget, Bobby's a police officer." His arguments were losing their conviction.

"And he's bringing along an explosives detection dog?"

The last of his resistance fled like air escaping from a balloon.

"I didn't think so." She paused, but not for long. "Some guy blew the supports out from under your grandfather's apartment building, then blew up your rental car. You know how easy it would be to cut open your package, put something inside, rig it to explode the moment the box is opened, then seal it back up?"

He nodded, his lower lip pulled between his teeth. Okay, he was properly chastised.

"Go on to my place. I'll call it in and have a dog check it out before anyone touches it. If it's clean, we'll have it delivered here."

Cody agreed and disconnected the call. Two wings still sat on his plate, but he'd lost his appetite. He said his farewells to Bobby, promising to keep him posted, then walked to his truck. As he slid into the seat, a bolt of panic shot through him. His neighbor Jack was keeping an eye on his place. If he noticed the package on his porch, he'd pick it up and take it home for safekeeping.

He brought up Jack's number and pressed the call icon. After Jack's voice-mail message played, Cody left his own message and then sent a text as backup. All he could do was hope Jack saw the text or missed call before noticing the package. Or that the police arrived there first.

Cody stopped at Sherwin-Williams and gathered

paint chips in the color combinations he and Erin had discussed. Then he headed for her house. Three blocks away the light in front of him turned red, and his phone buzzed with an incoming text.

It was from Erin. Just two words. But they sent a waterfall of dread crashing over him.

Dog alerted.

Cody held open the glass door leading into the building department, and Erin walked through with a nod of thanks. It was her investigation, but Cody was a gentleman.

Friday's package situation had turned out all right. The authorities had evacuated the surrounding houses and defused the bomb without incident.

Since then, she'd thanked God several times that Cody had called her instead of heading over there. Cody probably hadn't. She'd invited him to go to church with her and Mimi and Opa, and he'd declined, saying he needed to get some estimates finished. That was all right. Cody was in the same place she'd been four months earlier. Courtney hadn't given up on her, and she wouldn't give up on Cody.

The killer had acted fast. In the less than two-hour time frame between when the package was delivered and the police arrived with the bomb detection dog, he'd sliced the tape on top, inserted the bomb and taped it back up.

If Cody had opened it, he'd have been killed instantly. If he'd waited until he got to her house, he might have taken Mimi and Opa out, too. Or if he'd opened it in Joe's truck, they'd both have been blown to bits.

At the thought of the Lee County officer, a smile threatened. All along, Cody was the friend Joe had hounded her about meeting. What would've happened if she'd given in and agreed to meet him, if they'd both given in? Where would they be today, enjoying a solid friendship, having moved past their history and settled into an easy camaraderie? Or would their relationship have grown into something more serious? The latter seemed like nothing but a fantasy, far out of reach, but a part of her wanted to believe it was possible.

Some relationships made a lasting impact, causing change that endured for a lifetime. She'd experienced the negative side of that. But what about change for the good? Could a man like Cody undo all the damage of the past, or was she beyond that point? Would he even want to try? He'd suffered his own wounds.

She squared her shoulders and shook off the thoughts. Right now they were at the Lee County Building Department, seeking out details on the plans Donovan Development had for the land the apartment building had occupied. As they walked toward the planning department, Cody greeted each of the employees they passed. Then they sat to wait their turn. Erin didn't expect any surprises. Donovan had already given them the abridged version of what he'd hoped to do, plans he'd scrapped when Whitmer hadn't been willing to sell.

A short time later one of the clerks called Cody by name. After the woman made introductions, they both sat.

Cody leaned forward to rest an arm on her desk. "I talked to Sheila yesterday. She was going to pull the preliminary plans for the project Donovan Development had planned on Pine Island."

The woman rose—Tamara, according to Cody's introduction and her nameplate. When she returned, she handed him a roll of blueprint-size pages. He spread them out on the desk and began reviewing them.

Erin turned her attention to Tamara. "How well do you know Donovan?"

"Just on a professional level. He's been in here a few times for different projects and things he's doing."

"What's he like to work with?"

"He's all right. A little pushy sometimes, but he's a powerful man. Probably used to getting his own way."

Cody rolled up a page, and Erin looked at what was beneath. It was an artist's rendering of what appeared to be a resort. A hotel rose from the center, eight or ten stories tall, with a pool, a couple of restaurants, miniature golf and walkways that curved through tropical plants and a water feature.

Erin lifted her brows. "All that on one acre?"

"No." Cody rolled that sheet around the first. "This incorporates the properties on either side, too."

Erin nodded. "Then he'd own everything from Charlotte Harbor on the north end of Boca Vista to Back Bay on the south."

"With nothing across the street except marshland bordering Charlotte Harbor to the west."

Erin leaned back in her chair. "That's if all three property owners agreed to sell." The owners on either side of Whitmer's apartments hadn't mentioned being approached. Of course, no one had asked. Law enforcement's focus had been on what those owners may have seen the day of the storm.

Cody finished reviewing the plans and handed them

back to Tamara. After they thanked her for her time, they made their way back to the front of the building.

Erin stepped into the parking lot and clicked her fob. "Donovan put a lot of time and money into his plan. I agree with your friend in there. Men that powerful are used to getting their own way."

Cody slid into the passenger seat. "If the two owners on the end agreed to sell, Whitmer would have been the only thing holding up a lucrative deal. And if those offers were as good as the one made to Whitmer, they wouldn't have been happy about him throwing a monkey wrench in the thing. Looks like motive to me."

"But would they have the means or incentive to go to this extent?"

"Money is a good motivator, especially if someone is desperate enough."

"True." Erin cranked the car and backed out of the parking space. "How well do you know the neighbors on either side of your grandfather's apartment building?"

"I know the couple on the left pretty well. They're older. Not as old as Pops. Maybe in their sixties. But they befriended him, even had him over for meals several times."

"What about the owners on the other side?"

"According to Pops, the other neighbor's a single guy. I saw him in passing a couple of times. I waved, and he waved back."

"I think I saw him the day you were getting your pops's things. Dark, short-cropped hair, clean-shaven, drives a red Tacoma?"

"Yeah. Looks nothing like our suspect."

But that didn't mean he didn't hire someone to set the charges. She pulled into traffic, then glanced over at Cody. "I'm going to drop you off at home and go talk to them." By the end of the afternoon, she hoped to find out just how desperate those neighbors might be.

A short time later she backed out of her drive, a grilled cheese sandwich and a plastic container with apple slices lying on the seat next to her, a travel mug of tea in the cup holder, all prepared by Cody. By the time she reached Pine Island, both the food and the tea were gone. She made her turn onto Boca Vista Court and drove to the end.

The red Tacoma she'd watched roll past a couple of weeks earlier was sitting in the drive. She rang the bell and the door swung inward.

"Jordan McIntyre?"

"Yes."

She introduced herself to the man she recognized as the Tacoma's driver. "Can I ask you a few questions?"

"Sure." He motioned her inside.

As he led her to the living room, she took in her surroundings. A leather sectional occupied two walls, and heavy oak bookcases framed a large picture window. Interspersed among the books were vases, figurines and other collectibles.

Pictures graced another wall, an eleven-by-fourteen wedding photo in the center. Judging from the hairstyles and the yellow tint, the picture was at least forty years old. Many of the others were studio portraits, their subject a boy, infant to high school age. Nothing about the space said *midthirties single guy*.

He swept his arm toward the sectional. "Have a seat."

She complied, and he sat at the other end.

"How long have you lived here?"

"This time? Four years."

"Before that?"

"Wisconsin. But this is where I grew up."

She nodded. "Your parents transferred the house to you five years ago, right?" She knew the answer. She'd already looked up the information on the property appraiser's website.

"Yeah."

"Is there a mortgage?"

"No. Mom and Dad paid it off before they retired."

"Where are they now?"

"Montana, I think. They bought a motor home and have been traveling the continent for the past four years." He grinned, showing straight white teeth. "Spending my inheritance."

"What do you do for a living?"

"Framing carpentry. I work for Coventry Construction."

Hmm. One of the contractors who did work for Donovan Development. "How long have you worked for them?"

"I just started ten days ago."

Okay, maybe not.

"They offered me two dollars an hour more than I was getting with Gersham Contracting."

"Why aren't you working for them today?"

"I was this morning. Finished a job, and the next one won't be ready to start till tomorrow. There was a glitch on getting materials delivered. The hurricane has everyone backlogged."

"What year is that Tacoma out there?"

"2017." He smiled again, his demeanor personable. "Three more payments and it'll be all mine."

She returned his smile. "That's always a good feeling. Did anyone from Donovan Development ever contact you about buying this place?"

"Yeah, Donovan himself. He offered fifty percent over market value. Even though it's mine, I didn't think I should unload it without talking to Mom and Dad. But they were good with it, so I told Donovan I'd take his offer."

"What happened with the deal?"

"It fell through, or at least got stalled. The people on the other end agreed to sell, too, but the guy in the middle didn't. It was all or nothing, so the sale never happened. Or hasn't yet."

"How did that make you feel?"

"I was okay either way. I like it here. It's comfortable and quiet. My boat is right out there, tied to the dock on Back Bay. And the place is paid for. What more could I ask?"

By the time Erin left, she'd eliminated Jordan McIntyre as someone likely to be behind the setting of the charges. He had a good job, a house free and clear and a decent truck almost paid for. Nothing about the man seemed desperate.

The other stop didn't provide any likely suspects, either. As soon as Dave and Margaret Smith opened the door, Erin recognized them from her church, though she didn't know them well. That in itself didn't kick them off the possible suspect list. After all, serial killer Dennis Rader not only attended church but was also president of his church council.

But the conversation Erin had with them assured her they shouldn't be on her list of suspects. Dave had retired two years ago from his job as an engineer in upper New York State. He and his wife were enjoying their dream of living near the water in a warm climate. When Donovan had added another $50,000 to his already generous offer, they'd agreed to sell, but they'd been relieved when the deal had fallen through.

Erin made her way off Pine Island and headed toward Fort Myers. She wouldn't eliminate either of the neighbors as suspects completely until they'd been thoroughly checked out, but in the meantime, it seemed she'd just hit two more dead ends. Which meant investigators had been working on the case for almost two weeks and had no solid suspect.

A killer was still on the loose, one who had Cody in his sights.

SEVEN

Cody's eyes snapped open. Something had disturbed him. He lay on his left side in the darkened room, the chest of drawers in the corner barely visible. A soft glow came from behind him.

He rolled onto his other side. His phone lay on the nightstand, its screen illuminated. It was probably a text notification that had awoken him. He swiped the screen. Yes, one unread text.

Two taps later, he bolted from the bed, eyes still fixed on the message:

R U back home? Smoke coming from bedroom window.

He keyed in a frantic reply:

No, calling 911. Be there in 20 min.

The return message came back moments later:

Already called. Just get over here.

He flipped the switch, then squinted in the stark white light. He couldn't show up on the other side of the county in his gym shorts and barefoot. The jeans and T-shirt he'd worn yesterday were draped over the back of the upholstered chair. He struggled into them with shaking hands, then put on his tennis shoes.

When he'd finished, his pulse was still racing, his thoughts flying in a thousand different directions. He'd asked Jack to keep an eye on his place, but he hadn't expected the man to send him a middle-of-the-night text like this. His home, his workshop, all his possessions, the things he'd retrieved from Pops's place—would anything even be salvageable?

He snatched his keys and wallet and ran for the front door. Alcee met him there. As he punched in the code to disarm the alarm, she looked up at him and released a whine. He rearmed the system, and the series of beeps that followed ratcheted up his tension. The vise that had clamped down on his chest the moment he read Jack's text refused to release.

When he swung the door inward, Alcee forced her way into the opening and erupted in a frenzy of frantic barking.

"Alcee, hush." She was wasting valuable time.

He took a deep breath and tried to calm himself down. Firefighters were on their way, maybe even already there, sending powerful streams of water shooting into his home, dousing the flames. There was nothing he could do till they finished.

The place was likely crawling with cops. He'd be safe there. Unless…

A block of dread slid down his throat and congealed in his stomach. He closed the door and pulled the phone from his pocket. Had he paid attention to the sender when reading the text? Or had he, fresh out of a sound sleep, just read the message and panicked?

The conversation was displayed on the screen. Jack's name wasn't. The number had Cape Coral's 239 area code but wasn't programmed in his contacts.

Cody sank onto the couch, the phone still clutched in his hand. Alcee approached and rested her head on his leg, as if trying to console him. It didn't help. The killer had his address and phone number and had played him. And Cody had almost fallen for it. Stupid, stupid, stupid.

The living room light came on, and he heaved a sigh. Now he'd have Erin's chastisement to add to his own. He deserved both.

Erin stepped into the room, eyebrows drawn together and hair in disarray above her silk pajamas. "I heard the alarm beeping, like it had been reset, and Alcee barking. Were you trying to leave?"

"I got a text that my house was on fire."

"From who?"

"I thought it was from my neighbor."

"So you were going to leave to check it out all by yourself. I'm really starting to think you have a death wish." Her voice held an uncharacteristic shrillness. She was going to wake up Mimi and Opa if she didn't tone it down.

"Alcee stopped me."

Erin planted her hands on her hips. "At least someone in this house has some sense."

Ouch. That hurt. He brought up the keypad on his phone. "I'm calling 911. There's a good chance the killer's waiting for me. The police might be able to catch him."

He'd just finished explaining everything to the dispatcher when the door leading to the mother-in-law suite creaked open the rest of the way, and Opa stepped into the living room.

"Everything okay?"

Erin's head swiveled in his direction. "Cody got a text that his house is on fire."

Opa's eyes widened. "Oh, no."

"We think it's a setup." Though her grandparents didn't know the details, Erin had told them that Cody had witnessed a crime and had to hide out for a while.

For several moments Opa stood looking at them. Then he nodded and disappeared back into the suite with his wife.

"How did Alcee know I was in danger?"

Erin sank onto the couch next to him and reached over to stroke Alcee's head. "We have no idea the things animals sense. But you were probably putting out some frantic vibes. She'd have known something was wrong, even without being aware of the specific dangers."

Cody nodded, his hand joining Erin's on Alcee's head. Yeah, he'd definitely put out some bad vibes. He'd been so panicked, his brain had disengaged. If the dog hadn't slowed him down enough to stop and think, he'd have charged right into danger. Alcee had just saved his life for the second time.

No, probably the third.

The toxicology report on the soup hadn't come back yet, so he had no proof. But despite what he'd said to Erin about being a show-me kind of guy, he couldn't deny it any longer. The maintenance guy had put something in his soup. Something intended to kill him. It had been the first attempt on his life, and Alcee had saved him.

Tonight the creep had crafted another way to try to get to him. And Alcee had come through again.

Darkness settled over everything, smothering every last sliver of light. Erin's heart beat against her rib cage, and her breaths came in short, shallow gasps.

It was a dream, wasn't it? Yes. *Just a dream.* It was one she'd had so many times she'd trained herself to recognize it.

But did it always feel this real? Maybe this time it wasn't a dream. Maybe it was actually happening.

No. She asked herself that question every time, because it always felt real. Someone said people didn't feel pain when dreaming. They were wrong.

Because she felt everything in agonizing detail. The gag in her mouth. The ropes biting into her ankles and wrists. Even the bruises from where vengeful fists had taken out their anger on almost every square inch of her body.

He was nearby. She could hear his breathing. Clothing rustled. Was he shifting positions or preparing to approach?

She lay as still as if she were dead. Maybe if she didn't move, he'd forget about her. How long had it been? How much longer would it be? Nights slipped into days, which slid into more nights, the blindfold making every hour the same as the one before it. The only difference was the level of pain.

How long would it take for her spirit to slip peacefully out of her body?

The rustle grew louder. Then there were footsteps. Rough hands grabbed her, pulling her to her feet. No, he'd never let her slip peacefully away. When her legs buckled, he dragged her some distance and gave her a hard shove. A couch caught her backward tumble.

She trembled, waiting for the first blow. It came, and a scream clawed its way up her throat. How many fruitless screams had she released into the duct tape binding her mouth?

Another blow, another muffled scream. And tears she couldn't stop.

Then there was a whimper, different from her own. Light pressure against her chest. A wet tongue traced a path up her cheek. Those sensations weren't terrifying. In spite of the darkness, they were soothing.

And a male voice. Not *his*. This one belonged to someone kind and gentle. He was calling her name, assuring her she was safe, telling her to wake up.

She opened her eyes and bolted upright with a gasp. Two paws slid down her abdomen and into her lap. The darkness was gone in an instant. The remnants of the dream would take much longer to dissipate.

Alcee moved closer and pressed the side of her head to Erin's chest. Movement in her peripheral vision drew a gasp.

Cody stood two feet from the side of her bed, one hand raised. "It's all right. I was trying to wake you up. Alcee and I both were." One side of his mouth lifted. "She's the brave one. I kept my distance."

She gave him a shaky half smile. "That's probably smart."

All the times Alcee had brought her out of a nightmare, Erin had never hit her. In her unconscious but frantic state, she'd somehow known her dog posed no threat.

"Sorry I woke you up." She scooted backward to rest against the headboard, pulse still racing. Alcee followed.

Erin wrapped her arms around Alcee's middle and buried her face in the fur at the dog's neck. Erin still needed her, and the dog knew it.

Alcee wasn't an emotional support animal in an official sense. She'd come through the National Training Center in Santa Paula, known for recognizing the potential in shelter dogs and training them in search and rescue. It hadn't taken long to learn that Alcee helped her with her PTSD, waking her from nightmares, then calming her afterward.

When Erin had made her move to Florida, Sunnyvale had allowed her to take Alcee with her and join the volunteer group, Peace River K-9 Search and Rescue. If Erin had been forced to leave her dog, she still would've chosen to be near her grandparents, but the decision would've shredded her heart.

Cody moved closer. "Is it okay if I sit?"

She nodded. It was okay as long as he didn't pry. She hadn't told anyone about those terrifying ten days. Well, she'd told the counselors. But that didn't count.

It also didn't help.

No, that assessment wasn't fair. The counseling had reduced the frequency of the nightmares, just not made them go away. She'd expected the latter.

Cody seated himself near the foot of the bed, facing her. She was probably a mess—eyes wild and hair sticking out at odd angles like a knotted, tangled bird's nest. No fewer than three night-lights illuminated the room and announced her weakness. She was a cop, someone whose job put her in the path of danger, and she was scared of the dark.

She should feel embarrassed. At least awkward. But with her dog lying in her lap, and Cody sitting three feet away staring at her with those warm dark eyes, she just felt…safe.

"By the way, two nightmares in less than a week is not the norm for me."

"One nightmare a month is too many."

She'd be happy with one a month. Twelve per year. She could handle that. "I think my subconscious is latching on to all the stuff that's happening to you. You're the one with someone trying to kill you, and I'm the one having nightmares about it." She laughed, but it didn't sound natural, even to herself.

Two soft raps sounded against the open door, and she started. It was only Opa.

"Everything okay? I thought I heard you scream."

She smiled wryly. She'd insisted they leave their door open so they could call if they needed her. They'd been concerned about disturbing her. It hadn't happened yet. But she'd woken them twice.

"I just had a bad dream."

Her grandparents knew about her nightmares, even the story behind them. Opa nodded, his gaze shifting to Cody, then back to her again. "It looks like you're in good hands, so I'm going back to bed."

When he left, Cody studied her. His eyes bored into her, as if he was looking past her walls to the brokenness she kept hidden. "What happened?"

She tensed. "What do you mean?"

"What did you experience that was so terrifying your mind keeps taking you back to the same dark place?"

His gaze held sympathy, even pleading. It weakened her resolve. But only for a moment. If weeks of counseling couldn't banish the nightmares, neither would talking to Cody. She had her medicine. It was Alcee.

And prayer. It calmed her thoughts and helped her fall asleep. But the nightmares hadn't stopped, and they weren't any less terrifying. She'd asked God more than once to take them away. So far He hadn't. Maybe they were like Paul's thorn in the flesh, something to keep her dependent on Him.

Through it all, she was learning trust, the confidence that God would protect her, not only physically, but mentally and emotionally, too. She still had a long way to go. But she was making baby steps. Maybe someday, the night-lights would go off.

She ran her palm down Alcee's back, and the dog released a contented sigh.

"Erin?"

She lifted her gaze to his.

"When the case is solved and I return home, I'd like for us to stay friends."

She nodded. She didn't want to let him go, either.

"I want to know you." He rested a hand on her lower leg where it lay hidden by the sheet. "You're not the same carefree girl I met twelve years ago. Something changed you. Help me understand."

She closed her eyes. His hand felt warm through the sheet. The heat spread, chasing away some of the chill that still lingered.

But he was asking for something she couldn't give, to lower her walls and let him in. But her walls weren't made of brick and mortar. They were rebar in solid-poured concrete. It really was possible for someone to be too damaged to fix.

"Please, Erin."

When she opened her eyes, she kept her gaze fixed on

her dog. Cody wanted friendship. Friends shared secrets, right? Except she hadn't shared this secret with anyone.

Her ex was ten years into a twenty-five-year sentence. But she'd lived the past ten years in a prison of her own. One of fear and regret over the choices she'd made. Maybe in sharing, thirty-year-old Erin would find healing that twenty-year-old Erin hadn't been mature enough to receive.

She kept her eyes cast downward, her fingers entwined in Alcee's fur. "I've made some poor choices."

The first was walking away from Cody. If she hadn't made that decision, her life might have taken a different path, and the other events wouldn't have happened.

"My wife cleared out our bank accounts and took off with her boyfriend. Last I heard, they're backpacking across Europe. I've had my nose to the grindstone ever since. I'm still trying to recover." He released a dry laugh. "Trust me, you don't have a monopoly on bad choices."

"Ever make a choice that almost got you killed?" Okay, bad question. "Not including anything in the past two weeks?"

He didn't answer, just waited for her to continue.

She lifted her gaze to a painting that hung on the opposite wall. "I'd just finished my second year of college. A guy I'd been dating for two months got really possessive. After talking to some friends, I decided to dump him."

Her tone was flat. If she kept the emotion out of her voice, maybe she could keep it out of her heart. Then she'd have a chance of making it through the whole story.

"We'd already made plans to visit his family in Washington to do some hiking, camping and white-water rafting. We were then going to venture up into British Columbia. I didn't want to ruin everyone's vacation, so I went, figuring I'd break up with him when we got back to California."

As she talked, she kept her eyes fixed on the painting. It had been there when she'd bought the house. It was a seascape, but not a Florida one. Waves crashed against cliffs, surf spraying high in the air, wild and harsh and unpredictable. Like life.

"He'd gotten wind of my plans and wasn't willing to let me go. Instead of taking me to his parents' house, we ended up at a remote cabin in the woods. When we got there, it was like something snapped."

A shudder passed through her. Cody moved to sit next to her, lifting Alcee's back end from the bed onto his lap. When he slid his arm between the headboard and her shoulders, she didn't resist. There was something comforting about sitting next to him, being nestled against his side. His strength flowed into her, giving her what she needed to continue.

"As soon as we got there, he started hitting me, punching me in the face and head. I was still in the car, hadn't even released my seat belt." He'd beat her until she lost consciousness, then dragged her inside.

"I woke up on the floor of the cabin, feet bound, hands tied behind my back, and mouth taped so I couldn't scream. I doubt anyone would've heard me, anyway. On the way in, we drove for miles without seeing another house." Never had she felt so alone. Or so utterly hopeless. "Every time I woke up, he'd hit me some more, until I passed out again. I knew I was going to die. More than once, that's what I prayed for."

Cody's arm tensed, and he pulled her more tightly

against his side. She turned her face toward him, pressing her cheek into his chest. The terrors lessened their grip on her mind.

"He had me blindfolded the entire time, so I never knew if it was day or night. After I was rescued, I learned I'd been held captive for ten days. I'd drifted in and out of consciousness, but I was always in total blackness. I haven't slept in a dark room since." Even when they'd lost power during the hurricane, she'd kept a battery-operated lantern going all night.

"After it was over, I trained in self-defense, changed my major from chemistry to criminal justice and went to the police academy. Then I settled in Sunnyvale, almost seven hours from my hometown of Anaheim. He's incarcerated, but eventually he'll get out. I'm not making it easy for him to find me."

She leaned away from Cody to meet his eyes. "Now you know why I have no social-media presence."

"I'm so sorry you had to go through that." His jaw was tight, but his eyes were filled with sympathy, even pain, as if he was hurting with her.

She didn't deserve it. "It was stupid of me to go with him. I should have seen the signs."

"We're all allowed mistakes. At some point we have to stop beating ourselves up over them."

"It's hard to forgive yourself when the bad things that happen are your own fault."

A good half minute passed before he spoke again. "You believe that God forgives you for your mistakes, right?"

"Of course."

"How do you think He feels about you not forgiving yourself?"

She pursed her lips, eyebrows drawn together. She'd never considered that. Somewhere in the Bible she'd read the command to forgive others as God had forgiven her. Did *others* include herself? She didn't have an answer.

He continued, his voice low. "Holding on to the past allows it to keep us in bondage. Maybe healing begins when we stop beating ourselves up." The contemplation in his tone said he wasn't only thinking about her. Maybe he had some regrets of his own.

He lifted his other hand to cup the side of her head. She relaxed against him, enveloped in safety. His heart beat against her ear, sure and steady.

Was he right? Was berating herself for her bad choices stopping her from healing?

She drew in a deep breath but wasn't ready to pull out of his embrace. "Thank you for listening and not judging. Other than my immediate family and my counselors, you're the only one I've ever told this to."

"I appreciate your sharing. It means a lot."

His voice was deeper than usual, making his chest rumble beneath her face. A light scent wafted to her, barely detectable—evergreen, citrus and a hint of spice. Maybe aftershave or body wash used during his evening shower.

He'd said he wanted to remain friends. She'd agreed. But what if she wanted more? Cody made her feel safe, which was more than she could say about some of the men in her life. He would never lay a hand on her. But could she trust him to protect her emotionally, too? What did emotionally safe even feel like?

She pulled away, and he relaxed his arms. The air that moved between them felt suddenly cold. She dipped her head. "It's only three thirty. You could get a few more hours of sleep."

"What about you?"

"I'll be awake for a while." After one of her nightmares, sleep was a long time coming, partly because she fought it, afraid to relinquish control to her subconscious. When she left her subconscious in charge, it sometimes took her places she didn't want to go.

She shrugged. "I'll read. Eventually, I'll fall asleep."

He rose and pulled a chair up next to her bed. "I'll sit with you until you do."

She started to object. But the words never made it past her lips. Protesting would be pointless. Cody knew she needed him, and nothing would dissuade him from being here for her.

She took her reader from the nightstand, where it lay next to her devotional book, then turned on her side, her back to him. He rested a hand on her shoulder, the light pressure a constant reminder that he was here.

Cody being such an intimate part of her life was temporary, tonight's comfort even more so. But that wouldn't stop her from relishing it while it lasted.

EIGHT

Erin sat at her dining room table nursing a cup of coffee. Two books lay open in front of her, her Bible and her devotional book. Courtney had recommended both, telling her to start with the Book of John, then work her way through the rest of the New Testament and read one of the daily devotionals in *Jesus Calling*. Each of the passages was written as if spoken by Jesus Himself, and over the past three months, she'd been amazed at how often the message had been just what she'd needed.

She closed the book and opened her Bible. The early morning was quiet, the other occupants in the house still asleep. The two-legged ones, anyway. When she'd risen, Alcee had followed her out of the room.

Erin hadn't bothered to set the alarm. Today started the Labor Day weekend. She'd put in for four days' vacation so she could go camping with Courtney. Those plans had changed. She didn't feel comfortable leaving Cody that long, especially since Alcee would be with her. Courtney had understood and agreed to reschedule once the case was wrapped up.

Erin took a sip of coffee and then set the mug on the table, leaving her hands wrapped around it. Even though her alarm hadn't gone off, she'd awoken at sunup anyway, rested and refreshed. It helped that last night's sleep had been blessedly dreamless.

The prior morning the blaring alarm had jarred her out of a sound sleep. Her reader had still been in the bed, but the chair next to her had been empty. After unloading her past to Cody, she'd picked up her tablet to read and within ten minutes could no longer hold her eyes open. She never got to sleep that soon after a nightmare. If she said his presence had had nothing to do with it, she'd be lying.

Alcee lifted her head from her food dish and padded over to the table. Erin held the dog's face between her hands. "You're a good girl." She inhaled, then wrinkled her nose. "But you smell like Purina."

Alcee responded with a drawn-out *"Aarrrr."*

"Yes, you do. You need a doggy breath mint."

When Erin looked up, Cody was standing at the edge of the open doorway, grinning.

She returned his smile. "I didn't know you were up."

"I've only been up a few minutes. I didn't announce myself, because I was enjoying your conversation with your dog."

He walked into the kitchen and poured himself a cup of coffee. "Am I disturbing your reading?"

"It's okay. I'm almost finished." She closed the Bible. She would read the last few verses later. Over the past three months, she'd almost completed the four Gospels. She was taking it slow, something else Courtney had encouraged her to do. If she attempted one of those complete-the-Bible-in-a-year plans, most of what she read would slip right past her.

She smiled at him. "As soon as breakfast is over, you can put me to work."

She didn't have to report in, but that didn't mean she'd be goofing off. Her new kitchen cabinets were arriving tomorrow afternoon. Cody had one of his guys lined up to remove the old ones today. He'd originally planned to schedule two workers, since excessive tugging, pulling and lifting weren't advised until his ribs had healed. But Erin had insisted on being the second demo person. She had no construction experience, but destroying a kitchen wasn't rocket science. Besides, working alongside Cody would be fun.

He put his steaming mug on the table and took the chair next to her. "I'll be glad to put you to work. A few days of this, though, and you'll be ready to get back to detectiving."

She grinned at his use of the made-up word. "Or I might decide I like construction better than detectiving and apply for a job with you." She drained the last of her coffee and put the empty mug on the table. "I'm hoping the others will make some progress on the case during my days off."

The units that had been dispatched to Cody's house in the early-morning hours two days ago had found nothing. Donovan's lead had gone nowhere, too. Detectives had talked with every contractor who ever bid on his jobs and were now working their way through the employees and subcontractors. Not a single one recognized the guy in Cody's composite. If there was a link between Donovan and their investigation, they hadn't found it.

Erin sighed. "Donovan has the most to lose if the project doesn't move forward, but he always has projects in the works. He says if this one doesn't go through, he's got five others waiting in the wings." She frowned. "What he says is true, which kind of weakens the possibility of him being our suspect."

She deposited her coffee mug in the sink, then picked up her Bible and devotional book. Instead of taking them back to her bedroom, she left them on one of the living room end tables. Besides saving herself the trip down the hall, maybe Cody would get curious and check them out.

Cody called to her from the kitchen. "How about if I whip you up some scrambled eggs? I'll make Mimi and Opa's once they get up."

"Sounds good." She walked back into the dining room, where two flat, rectangular boxes stood against the wall. "I'll work on assembling those shelves we bought yesterday."

After she'd gotten home from work, they'd bought two plastic shelving units. She would use them to keep her dishes and food easily accessible while the kitchen was undergoing renovations.

Erin had just sat on the floor next to one of the boxes when Mimi entered the living room, walker in front of her, Opa behind her.

Cody looked in their direction. "Did our talking disturb you?"

"No. It was the smell of coffee that woke us up."

"There are still at least two more cups in the pot. And if scrambled eggs sound good, I'll have them ready in a few minutes."

At Mimi's acquiescence, Cody added four eggs to the bowl. While Erin sliced into the box with a utility knife and began removing components, Mimi sat at the table and Opa prepared their coffee.

When finished, he sat next to his wife. "Mimi and I are ready to head back home."

Erin stopped, one upright post held aloft. "Are you sure?"

"We were talking about it last night, after we went to bed. It's been a week and a half. We're ready."

Erin nodded, a lump forming in her throat. She'd enjoyed having her grandparents with her. Knowing they were just on the other side of the open door had put her mind at ease, and she wasn't ready to send them out on their own. But it wasn't her decision. She had to trust that Mimi and Opa knew what they were doing. And trust God to watch over them. The problem was, when it came to trust, she was a work in progress.

When breakfast was over, Mimi and Opa disappeared into the suite and came out a short time later with Opa wheeling their suitcases.

Erin looked at them long and hard. "Are you sure about this?"

They both nodded, and Opa grinned. "You guys live with a little too much excitement." He was probably only half joking.

Erin and Cody each took a bag from her grandfather and followed them to the front door. She hugged one, then the other. "Be careful driving."

Her grandfather shook his head. "Pumpkin, I've been driving back and forth to the hospital, then the rehab place, for more than two months."

But this was all the way to LaBelle. Of course, it was only forty-five minutes, a straight shot down Florida 80. And traffic was lighter.

"You'll have to get groceries. Except for condiments, I pretty well wiped out your refrigerator."

Cody put his hands on her shoulders. "You go with them."

"But—" She'd already done the math. She'd be hard-pressed to make the drive to LaBelle and still get home in time to unload the cabinets before Cody's guy got here at one o'clock.

Cody waved away her concerns as if he'd read her mind. "Go on. I'll unload the cabinets, and they'll be ready to remove by the time you get back."

She hesitated for another beat, then nodded. "Arm the security system."

"I will."

"And you'll feed Alcee her lunch if I'm not back in time?"

He smiled. "I always do."

Erin mouthed a silent *thank you*, hoping that he understood how much she appreciated him. Why had she ever given up a guy like Cody? What good had her freedom done her?

It had given her the ability to choose her own path. But what if the best life was the one she'd walked away from?

She stepped from the house with a sigh, then pulled out behind her grandparents. When they walked out of Winn-Dixie an hour and a half later, they had a full shopping cart with several bags lining the shelf beneath. Erin and Opa loaded them into the back of the Cube and drove the remaining seven miles to their park.

When Opa helped Mimi from the vehicle, she looked around, her face lit with joy. There really was no place like home. And Moss Landing was a beautiful park, right on the Caloosahatchee River, with street names like Shark, Porpoise, Dolphin and Bass Drives, and all the amenities one could want.

Instead of making her way up the ramp into the double-wide mobile home, Mimi met Opa and Erin at their vehicle's open back door.

Erin frowned at her. "What are you doing, Mimi?"

"Getting groceries. I'm fully capable." She grabbed a bag of produce and hung it over one of the walker arms, then added one to the other side. When she moved away, two more bags sat on the walker's seat.

Erin and Opa followed her, several bags looped over their arms. After one more trip, Erin had the rest of it inside. She helped them put everything away, then kissed them goodbye, with orders to call if they needed anything.

Once back in her SUV, she pulled her phone from her purse. She would text Cody and let him know she was on her way home. When she swiped the screen, she'd already missed a text from him. It was simple, an address, then CC. Probably short for *Cape Coral*.

But it was the three numbers that followed that put a knot of dread in her gut.

He'd ended the text with 911.

She checked the time stamp with her heart in her throat. More than fifteen minutes had passed since he'd sent the text.

With shaking fingers, she pulled up the keypad, ready to relay what she had to Dispatch. She had no idea what was significant about that location or what might be happening there.

But one thing she knew. Cody was in trouble.

God, please let someone get there in time.

* * *

Cody drove through the Friday lunchtime traffic, one hand on the wheel. The other was wrapped around his phone, currently pressed to his ear.

It was his business phone, the number that was on all his advertising and the one his customers used to reach him. It was Candy Hutchinson who'd called him this time, a sweet middle-aged lady, not the pushy type at all. But she'd phoned twenty minutes ago, pleading with him to come over so they could discuss some changes. And it had to be today. Now.

He'd promised to come right away, but every time he'd tried to end the call, she'd come up with something else, her tone even more urgent.

She was acting so out of character, he'd asked her if everything was all right. The assurances she'd given him weren't convincing at all. Something was off. So with his other hand, he'd grabbed his personal phone to send a quick text to Erin, then headed out. At the first red light, he pulled up the same text and forwarded it to Bobby.

He was walking into a trap, and he knew it. Someone was forcing Candy Hutchinson to make the call, trying to draw him out. Erin would have a fit. But what choice did he have? If he didn't cooperate, things could go badly for Candy.

The light ahead turned yellow, and he braked to a stop, again reaching for his personal phone. His neighbor Jack was another one who knew about the case. He'd be able to decipher his obscure text and call for help.

Cody held his thumb against the message, then selected Forward as Candy continued to babble. Now to select Jack's name from his contacts. Several seconds of silence passed before he realized Candy had asked him a question.

"I'm sorry. What was that?"

"I was asking about tile, the difference between porcelain, ceramic and marble. Do you recommend one over another?"

He touched Jack's name and pressed Send. A horn sounded behind him. Multitasking had never been his strong suit.

He returned the phone to the cup holder and surged forward, engine revving. Where were the cops when he needed them? For the past twenty minutes, he'd hoped to draw the attention of law enforcement by breaking a few traffic laws. If successful, rather than tipping off whoever was with Candy, he'd keep driving and likely have a tail three or four cruisers long by the time he rolled into the Hutchinsons' drive.

But he hadn't seen a single cop. And now the house was only three blocks away. He moved into the left turn lane and waited for the light to change. Had anyone gotten his text? He picked up the phone. Erin hadn't responded. Neither had Bobby or Jack.

Meanwhile, Candy continued to ramble. "Bill and I aren't in agreement on what we want. He wants to change the whole color scheme, materials and everything."

Cody dropped his personal phone back into the cup holder. He couldn't count on anyone seeing his message. Bobby and Jack were both at work, and Erin was en route from LaBelle. He needed to call 911.

But the killer was listening. Cody was sure. And the man was forcing Candy to keep him on the line so he couldn't call for help. Now time was running out.

"I'm about two minutes away. Let me go, and I'll be pulling in shortly."

"No, please don't hang up." Panic laced her tone. "This whole situation has me so upset."

The light changed, and Cody accelerated into the turn. How had his attacker linked the Hutchinsons to him? He and Leroy had gone by there a week and a half ago, but Erin had made sure they didn't pick up a tail. And since Leroy had driven, Cody had kept a constant eye on the traffic behind them, too.

It wasn't from raiding his home office, either. The Hutchinson job was the only one in progress, and he'd brought the file to Erin's when he'd collected the rest of his belongings.

As he moved down the Hutchinsons' street, his chest tightened. He should see emergency lights by now. But there was nothing.

He pulled into the drive and killed the engine. At every window, the blinds were drawn. The sight set off even more alarms.

Candy loved natural light. She'd told him so. The first thing she did every morning was open all the blinds in the front part of the house. He'd never seen any of them drawn other than the ones at the bedroom windows.

When he reached for the driver door, his gaze swept across the yard and settled on one of his signs— Another quality project by Elbourne Construction. His heart dropped. It hadn't been there when the three of them had visited previously. Bill must've removed it to mow and then put it back.

His signs were free advertising. This one was advertising he didn't want. Why hadn't he thought of it before? He'd made it easy for the killer to get to him.

He opened the driver door. "Candy, I'm here, so I'm hanging up now."

Maybe he could dial 911 before getting out of his truck, mumble a quick call for help and drop the phone into his pocket.

There was a slight pause before she responded. "Wait. Can you come in first?"

He hesitated. This was his last opportunity. No, he wouldn't put Candy in even greater danger. He picked up his personal phone, dialed 911, then dropped it back into the cup holder. Now that he'd arrived at his destination, they could trace his phone's location. Maybe the dispatcher would send help, even without him asking for it. He'd just have to stay alive until it arrived.

He stepped from the truck. A high-pitched whine sounded in the distance, definitely sirens. But that didn't mean they were for him.

He closed the truck door, listening as they drew closer. The vertical blinds at one of the living room windows parted, and something appeared in the opening. Cylindrical, such a dark shade of gray it was almost black.

The barrel of a pistol.

He dived sideways as a shot rang out, then rolled toward an oak tree. As he stood, a second shot sent splinters of bark spraying outward. He turned sideways and pressed his shoulder to the tree, hoping his body didn't overlap the medium-size trunk.

The sirens were so loud now, they set his teeth on edge. But he'd never heard anything so beautiful. Two police cars pulled into the drive, a third stopping at the edge of the road. The sirens died. A crash sounded from inside. Then another shot.

No, not Candy.

The first two officers jumped out, weapons drawn.

Cody remained behind the tree. "There's a gunman in the house."

The front door opened, and four weapons swung in that direction. A second later Candy Hutchinson burst through as if she'd been shot out of a cannon.

"Hands in the air."

The command didn't register. She kept running, casting frantic glances back at the house.

Cody held up a hand. "She's the owner."

Her head swiveled in his direction, and relief flooded her features. She ran to him, plowing into him so hard she almost knocked him down.

"I'm so sorry." She threw her arms around his neck. "He said if I didn't get you over here, he was going to kill me."

Before he could respond, she spun to face the police. "He ran out the back. Blond hair, shoulder length. Mid to late thirties. Blue jeans and a yellow T-shirt with a fish on it, a Guy Harvey. A blue baseball cap, too."

The officers in the first two cars had already disappeared around the side of the house. One of the officers in front relayed the description over his radio. The other approached Candy.

"What happened?"

"The mail lady had just come. I walked to the box, and when I came back, a man jumped out of the bushes and forced his way in before I could get the door locked."

"Had you ever seen him before?"

"Never. He told me to get Cody over here."

The officer looked in his direction. "You're Cody?"

Cody nodded and brought the officer up to speed on

everything that had happened. When Cody finished, he frowned. "He traced me to the Hutchinsons' through my sign, which was a pretty stupid oversight."

Candy continued. "Whatever the guy wanted with Cody, I'm sure it wasn't good. When he started shooting, I figured he wasn't going to leave either of us alive. I didn't have anything to lose, so I grabbed the vase from the table and brought it down over his head as hard as I could."

Cody's jaw dropped. That was the crash he'd heard. He didn't know Candy had it in her.

Candy pursed her lips. "His head was bleeding, and he was stumbling, but he was still on his feet. So I swung the brass lamp like a baseball bat, knocked the gun out of his hand and ran for the front door. By then, you guys had pulled into the drive, so he picked up the gun and ran toward the back."

If the officer was surprised at the spunk of this five-foot-two-inch lady, he didn't show it, just continued to take notes. "Can you describe the suspect, other than the clothing and hair?"

"Eight or nine inches taller than I am, somewhat stocky build. His face…" She looked at Cody and both officers, then frowned, apparently not finding what she was looking for.

"His face was a little longer than yours." She nodded at the younger officer. "And he had a beard and mustache."

"Do you think you could work with our artist to do a composite?"

"You betcha. He's had a gun pointed at me for the past half hour. I don't think I'll ever forget his face."

Cody gave her a wry smile. She made a much better

witness than he did. Of course, she saw the guy for more than a second or two and wasn't drugged at the time.

He gasped and grabbed Candy's arm. "You and Bill have to get away from here." The killer had been relentless in trying to track him down so he couldn't identify him, and Candy had now seen his face.

The older officer nodded. "He's right. Do you have somewhere you can go until we catch this guy?"

"We have family. I need to call my husband. Can I do that now?"

"Sure."

A familiar SUV screeched to a halt in the street, and Erin jumped out. "I've been blowing up your phone for the past fifteen minutes. Why didn't you answer?" She hollered the words, her tone accusatory.

He bit back a defensive response. Erin's concern often came across as anger. The more worried she was, the angrier she appeared. It was one of her quirks. He could live with it.

He could even deal with her walls, because they seemed to be slowly crumbling. Her sharing with him what had happened in that remote cabin so many years ago was proof of that. But if they ever decided to move beyond friendship, she'd have to commit to a serious long-term relationship, and he'd have to risk someone walking away yet again. Neither scenario was likely in this lifetime.

He tapped his pocket. The phone was there. But that was his business cell. His personal one was sitting in the cup holder in his truck. He retrieved it and swiped the screen. There were numerous texts and missed calls from Erin, along with a missed call from Jack and a text from Bobby. Among the three of them, they'd probably kept Dispatch busy.

Cody turned back around to face Erin. But she wasn't watching him. Instead, she stood in profile, mouth agape. "Why did you put that up?"

"I put it up when I started the job, before the hurricane."

She planted her hands on her hips. "That sign was not here when we stopped last week. I would've noticed and told you to get rid of it."

"Bill took it down to mow and put it back up when he finished. But we were already gone."

Gradually, some of the panic fled her features, and she gave him a slow nod. Maybe she understood. But Erin wasn't the only one who had a hard time forgiving herself. He'd always been his worst critic, and he wasn't about to let himself off the hook that easily. His transgressions were piling up.

Convincing Pops to leave his home and come to Florida instead of making the move back home himself.

Not checking on Pops sooner and forcing him to leave well ahead of the storm.

Now carelessly leaving a sign in his customers' yard, leading a killer to their door.

Just one more mistake on an unending list.

NINE

Cody poured a cup of coffee, then doctored it with cream and sugar. The kitchen was as in need of work as it had been two days ago. The ugly harvest-gold appliances were still there. So were the green laminate countertops and the worn-out cabinets. After the excitement at the Hutchinsons' place, the remodeling had been put on hold until Monday.

He'd gotten about half of the items transferred from the cupboards to the plastic shelves before receiving the call from Candy. He'd take care of the rest tonight and be ready to start the demo in the morning.

Right now the house was quiet. Erin had left for a morning run with her neighbor and taken Alcee with her. She'd invited him to join them, but he'd refused. His sore body wouldn't handle forty minutes of pounding the pavement. Besides, he didn't want to crash Erin's girl time. He was upending her life enough.

He headed into the living room with his coffee. He'd promised Erin pancakes for breakfast, but if he wanted to serve them hot off the griddle, he'd have to wait thirty minutes to start them. In the meantime, he'd see if early

Sunday morning programming offered anything interesting.

He sat on the couch and reached for the remote. It was sitting on the end table next to a Bible and the same book he'd noticed on Erin's nightstand. Bypassing the remote, he picked up the book and thumbed through it. Each of the pages had a date, but apparently, Erin wasn't following the recommended schedule, because her bookmark was inserted at the page marked March 7. He removed the bookmark, curious what she'd be reading that day.

The first sentence intrigued him. *Let Me help you through this day.* Given that the name of the book was *Jesus Calling,* he was probably supposed to read the words as if Jesus had spoken them. Was that what Erin did, relied on Jesus to help her get through the day? That didn't sound like her. If any woman could take care of herself, it was Erin.

While the first sentence caught his attention, the next two grabbed him by the throat. One said the challenges he was facing were too much to handle alone, and the next acknowledged the helplessness he felt in the events he was facing.

Yeah, he was feeling helpless. Who wouldn't in his circumstances? Driven from his home, the target of a foe who was always a step ahead of him. But he was dealing with it. He didn't need a crutch.

Without bothering to look up the scripture references at the bottom of each page, he moved through two more days, grumbling about those the same way he had the first. At the jiggle of the doorknob, he looked up with a gasp. The lock turned, the front door swung open and Alcee trotted into the room.

Cody grabbed the bookmark from the couch and

stuffed it back between the pages. As he spun to return the book to its place, the corner hit the edge of the table. The book fell from his hand, hitting the hardwood floor with a thud. Erin stepped through the doorway, phone pressed to her ear. What was she doing back already?

He watched her gaze go from him to her book lying on the floor. Her brows lifted almost imperceptibly, but there wasn't any anger or annoyance. Probably because she was focused on her phone conversation.

He put the book back on the end table and hurried to the kitchen, Alcee following. Erin was such a private person. If she thought he was snooping through her things while she was away, she'd throw him out on the street. He measured some flour into a bowl and added the other dry ingredients. Maybe if he had breakfast ready for her when she finished her call, she'd go easy on him.

As he beat in the eggs and oil, Erin's voice drifted to him from the living room. That phone call was probably the reason she'd returned early from her run. Judging from her side of the conversation, there'd been some new developments in the case. One of her cases, anyway. He sometimes forgot his wasn't Lee County's only case.

While he worked, Alcee sat on the floor at his feet, occasionally pressing her side into his leg. She wasn't asking for anything. Erin had fed her before they'd left for their run, and since the dog hadn't been in that long, there was no way she had to go out. Now she just seemed to be guarding him against anything threatening. Though nothing dangerous was going to slither through the air vents or penetrate the glass behind the closed vertical blinds, it was a nice thought.

By the time Erin joined him in the kitchen, six pancakes sat on the electric griddle, undersides working their way to a golden brown. He cast her a glance over one shoulder. "News?"

"Yeah. Jordan McIntyre's girlfriend reported him missing this morning."

Cody's jaw dropped. Pops's neighbor to the right. "Maybe he witnessed something after all."

"That's an angle we're considering."

Cody slid the rubber spatula under the edge of one of the pancakes and peeked beneath. Perfect. After he'd flipped them all, he retrieved plates and glasses from the temporary shelving in the dining room.

Erin poured two glasses of orange juice and brought them to the table. "The residents in both houses said they evacuated before the storm. But maybe McIntyre learned something after the fact, and the killer is making sure he won't go to law enforcement with it."

She sat and drizzled some maple syrup over her pancakes. "His girlfriend was just about hysterical when she made the report. She insisted he didn't have any trips planned, or he'd have told her. They usually hang out at Dixie Roadhouse on Saturday nights, and he never showed to pick her up."

Cody waited while she bowed her head. Grace before meals was one of Erin's new habits, along with church attendance. And reading books like *Jesus Calling*.

She opened her eyes and cut into her pancakes. "It doesn't look good."

"Is his vehicle gone?"

She shook her head. "The Tacoma's still sitting in the drive, so it looks like he disappeared from his house. We're there now, searching for clues. I told Danny to keep me posted." She took a long swig of her orange juice. "McIntyre seemed like a pretty nice guy. I'm hoping we don't find a body."

Cody frowned. "Knowing this guy's history with explosives, you might get your wish, just not in the way you hope."

The creep was determined to eliminate anyone who could identify him. At least Bill and Candy were gone. They'd cleared out before the sun set and headed to her sister's place in South Georgia. They didn't have to be told twice. The ordeal was probably going to leave Candy with some nightmares.

Cody's insides twisted. It was his fault. If he'd thought to remove his sign, the killer would never have connected him to the Hutchinsons. Fortunately, since this was his only job still in progress, there weren't any other signs out there.

He pushed the thought aside. He had other mistakes to atone for. "Sorry for messing with your things. I didn't mean to pry." Or maybe he did. If satisfying one's curiosity could be considered prying.

Her pancake-laden fork stopped halfway to her mouth. "Messing with my things?"

"Your book. I was planning to watch some TV while you were out. But instead of getting the remote, I picked up your book."

She gave him a relaxed smile. "It's not a diary. If I had a problem with you looking at it, I would've stashed it somewhere in my room. You're welcome to read it anytime."

She put the bite in her mouth and chewed slowly. "I've found it helpful. So often, what I'm reading is just what I need at the time."

"I sort of figured that out."

"Several of the passages talk about trust. That doesn't come easy for me. Actually, it's a major struggle. Trusting God, trusting others. Even trusting myself."

He grinned. "I figured that out, too."

One side of her mouth lifted. "If you're reading *Jesus Calling*, you should know my Bible isn't off-limits, either."

"Now, that's pushing it."

When they'd finished breakfast, he took their empty plates to the sink. "I'll do these while you get ready for church."

"I'm not going."

He lifted his brows. Missing church without a good reason didn't seem like something Erin would do. "You're not staying home on account of me, are you?"

She shrugged, then followed him into the kitchen. When she started rinsing the plate he'd just washed, he frowned at her. The last thing he wanted was to keep her out of church. "Go ahead and go. Alcee won't let me out of her sight. When Candy called, I had to sneak out through the mother-in-law suite."

Her features drew into a scowl. "Sending that 911 text to me was smart, but you should never have left my house."

"And let Candy Hutchinson pay the price for something she had nothing to do with? I don't operate that way."

Her expression relaxed. "I know you don't."

The respect and admiration in her eyes sent a shot of warmth through his chest. What she thought of him mattered.

"But if you'd like to attend church, I promise I'll stay

put. I'm in good hands. Alcee seems to understand she's been charged with protecting me."

Erin shrugged. "I've got another two days of vacation. I figured I'd spend them with you." She grinned. "Besides, I don't feel like doing my hair and makeup."

Church or not, the hair and makeup weren't requirements. She looked great just like she was. Well, if she went to church, the yoga pants and T-shirt would have to go. But otherwise…

That long-ago summer in Punta Gorda, he'd seen her just one way—dressed in a tank, shorts and flip-flops, hair pulled into a ponytail, face clean and makeup free.

And he'd been completely smitten.

Now there were walls that hadn't been there before, and that carefree abandon had disappeared, but everything that had attracted him before was still there. If he wasn't careful, he was going to be right back in the same situation—hopelessly in love with a woman who wasn't willing to be anything more than a friend.

Was Erin fighting the same feelings he was? Did she feel the same draw, that longing for something deeper than friendship? If so, she kept it well hidden behind those walls she'd erected.

She finished placing the rinsed dishes in the rack. "My church livestreams its services. I figured we could watch from here."

Great. He wasn't leaving the house, but he was going to be stuck sitting through a church service. Oh, well, he could think of worse things than sitting next to Erin, a dog stretched across their legs.

Once they were finished with the dishes, Erin led him into the living room. "We've got thirty minutes till service time. What do you say we catch some news?"

She picked up the remote. A meteorologist stood in front of a map of the Gulf, pointing toward a large cone over the southern part of the state.

Cody sank onto the couch. "Are you kidding me? Three weeks after the last one?"

Erin smiled. "You weren't in Florida in the summer of 2004."

He narrowed his eyes. "You only told me about Charley."

"Charley's the one my grandparents and I went through. But two more hit the state from the other side. The three paths crossed within miles of each other in the middle of the state. Three major hurricanes within a six-week period." She shrugged. "So it's happened before."

Cody shook his head. "I guess I've had it easy. Until this season, we haven't had any bad ones since I've been here."

"We'll keep an eye on it. I've got hurricane shutters in the shed. They're easy to install. For the last storm, I put them up and took them down by myself." She frowned. "What about your place? If this thing's going to hit us, it won't be safe for you to go over there and do any kind of hurricane prep."

"I've got the electric rolling shutters. The remote is in my desk drawer. I could send my neighbor Jack in to do it."

"Better to have someone from the department do it. If the creep sees your neighbor go in, he'll know you've been in touch and might try to use him to get to you."

After letting Alcee out and back in again, Erin settled on the couch to watch her church service. Cody couldn't think of any way out of it without being a jerk, so he sat next to her.

It wasn't what he'd expected. Of course, he had only one experience to draw from. Years ago he'd visited a friend's church, a huge building in Chicago with vaulted ceilings, stained-glass windows and an organ with pipes spanning the height and width of the front loft.

He couldn't speak for his grandfather's church. Pops had invited him more than once. Cody had come up with an excuse every time. If he'd just given in, it would've meant so much to Pops. One more cause for regret.

He shut down the thoughts and focused on the television screen. Erin's church occupied what could have been a store at one time. Instead of a choir with its matching robes, three musicians and three singers stood in a row across the front platform, a drummer in the center. The songs weren't what he'd expected, either. Erin's church obviously didn't hold to the preconceived notion that music wasn't sacred unless written at least a hundred years ago.

But it was the sermon that caught him the most off guard. If he didn't know better, he'd think Erin had relayed the details of their conversation the other night to the preacher. Just like that devotional book. He was experiencing too much of that today.

When the message was over, one sentence stuck in his mind as if spelled out in neon. "You contribute nothing to your salvation except the sin that made it necessary." The pastor had attributed the quote to Jonathan Edwards, probably some famous preacher or something.

Whoever originally said it, the words disturbed him. He'd always felt religion was a crutch. He'd never been critical of those who needed it, but he didn't consider himself in that camp.

After the closing song, Erin killed the power on the remote. "What did you think?"

"It wasn't what I expected."

"In a good or bad way?"

"Neither. Just different."

"How did you like Pastor Mike?"

He lifted a brow. "Other than I think he's got your house bugged?"

Erin grinned. "No bugs. Not even any covert phone calls. But that's how God works. I can't tell you how many times I've felt like the preacher was talking directly to me."

He pursed his lips. "I'm not convinced. I mean, the concept of sin sounds a little antiquated, don't you think?"

"Depends on how you look at it. Granted, it's been around since Eve took the first bite of the fruit. But man hasn't changed much."

"I just don't see where all that's necessary."

"So you think you're perfect."

"No." Far from it. He'd made plenty of screwups. But they'd never been with intent to harm someone else, at least not since he was a troubled teen. "In the whole scheme of things, I think I'm all right. There are people a lot worse."

"It's not a scale, you know. Not in the way you're thinking. There's a standard, but it's not Hitler or even the guy next door."

He frowned. He'd had enough conversations with Erin to know what standard she was referring to. Jesus Christ was perfect, which made Cody's attempts at being good enough pretty hopeless.

He pushed himself up from the couch. "What do you

say we fix ourselves some lunch? Then we'll get the rest of the cabinets emptied."

By ten o'clock that night, they'd moved all the dishes and food stuff and relocated the refrigerator. They'd even made time for a long walk with Alcee in the ball park, since Erin's morning run had been cut short, and enjoyed a couple of movies.

Now they were both in their respective beds, and Alcee was on patrol, lying outside his door for short spurts, then padding down the hall to keep an eye on Erin.

The thoughts he'd kept at bay since the church service ended rushed back in. He'd shrugged off Erin's arguments. But lying alone in the dark, he couldn't dismiss them so easily.

The problem was, he'd spent most of his life trying to be good enough. If he'd been good enough, his mother would've loved him enough to stay.

If he'd been good enough, Erin would've finished college and come back to him.

If he'd been good enough, his ex-wife wouldn't have run off to find fulfillment with someone else.

He'd failed on all fronts. But maybe he didn't have to be good enough. Because someone else was. If he truly believed that, he wouldn't find the concept of Christianity to be so restrictive.

Instead, he'd find it freeing.

Erin opened the sliding glass door, and Alcee shot into the backyard. As Erin and Cody followed, the dog danced in front of them, dark eyes darting between Erin's face and her hands.

Usually, a trip out back meant playtime, especially if it happened right after she arrived home from her shift.

"Not tonight, girl."

She glanced at Cody. Beyond him, the sun sat perched against the treetops. "I've got the panels standing against the wall inside the shed."

Sunday and Monday there'd been little change in the storm's projected path. Most models showed it traveling due east across the southern tip of the state.

This morning that had started to change. By lunchtime, the huge mass of wind and rain was moving more northeast than east. Although another eastern turn was expected, no one agreed on when that would happen.

She slid the key into the shed's lock. Alcee still watched her, but her excitement had dwindled. Once this was over, Erin would give her some extra playtime.

She led Cody inside. "I know we're supposed to get just the northern edge of this, but I'd rather be safe than sorry."

He raised both hands. "You won't get any argument from me. After my recent experiences, I'm in support of any precautions you want to take."

"Good."

This one made her uneasy. It was as if something ominous was waiting to pounce the instant they let down their guards. Maybe the images of the emergency personnel pulling Cody's grandfather's unconscious form from the rubble were still too fresh in her mind. Or maybe it was knowing she was responsible for Cody's safety. Or maybe it was the combination of the storm and everything else that had been going on.

Whatever the reason, she was uneasy enough to go to the trouble of reinstalling the shutters she'd removed after the last storm, even if it meant finishing in the dark via flashlight. Cody's home was already secured. Joe, aka Bobby, had gone in with Cody's key and lowered all of the shutters.

Mimi and Opa were safe, too. LaBelle was forty-five minutes inland from Fort Myers, but they'd gone to stay with some friends in Altamonte Springs, well north of the storm's projected path.

Erin grasped three of the fourteen-inch-wide metal panels and headed for the open door.

Cody followed her out with his own panels. "What about the hardware?"

"The bolts stay in the lower track, and I leave the wing nuts screwed onto them. So this is it."

Soon they had a good stack of panels leaning against the front of the house. After removing the wing nuts, Cody picked up a panel and slid it into the H-track over the first window, then secured it onto the bolts at the bottom.

He glanced at the western sky. All except the top edge of the sun had disappeared, and streaks of orange and pink stained the horizon. "I think we're going to be finishing this project via flashlight."

"You're right. But by daylight we'll probably be getting outer bands. I'd rather work in the dark than the rain." And she'd rather work with Cody than alone. Being alone had never bothered her. It beat spending her life tethered to someone who didn't make her happy. There was a third option—finding love with Mr. Right in one of those relationships that ended in happily-ever-after.

Except hers never did. So that left her with options one and two. Option one won, hands down.

But Cody's nearness over the past two weeks had her rethinking the appeal of being alone. There was something comfortable about having someone to cook and clean alongside her, someone to talk with and share the events of her day. Someone to hold her and chase away the remnants of a nightmare.

Someone to…love? No, she wouldn't go that far. She cared for him, always had. At one time she'd loved him. Things were different then. There'd been no need for protective barriers, because neither of them had had their ideals crushed and their souls bruised.

Erin removed the rest of the nuts and then frowned as Cody picked up another panel. "Are you sure you don't want me to lift those?"

"Broken bones heal in six weeks. Since I just passed three, I'm halfway there. Besides, these aren't that heavy. Not like using plywood."

Erin let him continue while she secured each panel with the wing nuts. "We had an interesting development in the McIntyre disappearance. Not sure if it means anything, but several of the guys that frequent Dixie said he showed up there alone the night before he disappeared and was trying to borrow money."

"Did anyone loan him the money?"

"Not that we know of. They claimed they didn't have the kind of money he was looking for. We're not talking beer money. We're talking several thousand dollars."

"Interesting."

Yeah, it was. They'd looked into his finances, and though he didn't have large sums of money in the bank, there weren't past-due loans or any debt, for that matter, other than his vehicle loan. And that was current. His girlfriend told investigators the same thing.

Cody frowned. "Maybe he borrowed money from some bad dudes, and they're calling in the loan. He might have disappeared on his own to keep from ending up in concrete boots at the bottom of Charlotte Harbor."

She nodded. Financial problems provided motive. Were the man's problems serious enough to prompt him to take down the apartment building to speed up the purchase of his property? Just how desperate was Jordan McIntyre?

As dusk gave way to darkness, they finished the front of the house, and Erin went in to retrieve a flashlight.

"Come on, girl. Let's go inside." The dog wouldn't run off. Even if she did, a simple command would bring her right back. But she and Cody had enough to do without the distraction of keeping up with Alcee.

They'd just finished the side when her cell phone rang. She pulled it out of her pocket and checked the screen, intending to let it go to voice mail. Instead, she frowned at a familiar number. "I've got to take this. It's my supervisor."

As she listened, Cody watched. She finished the call and pocketed the phone.

"I have to go in. McIntyre's girlfriend stopped by his place and surprised someone when she opened the front door. Her car's lights hadn't shut off yet. A guy ran out of the house, knocked her down and took off on foot. When he crossed through her headlight beams, she got a good look at him. Medium height and build, shoulder-length blond hair and a beard."

Cody's eyebrows dipped toward his nose. "What does our guy want with McIntyre?"

"I don't know." She handed him the wing nuts she held. "I'm sorry. I have to leave you."

"No problem. I'll finish this."

"Are you sure?"

"I'm positive. All we've got left is three windows in the back and what's on the other side. When I'm working inside the fence, Alcee can keep me company."

"The minute you're finished, get in the house and lock the doors."

He gave her a salute. "Yes, ma'am."

A few minutes later she was in her vehicle headed toward the station. As she turned onto Cleveland and left her neighborhood behind, her thoughts churned.

How were McIntyre and the guy who'd attacked Cody linked? Had McIntyre learned something? If so, he would have shared it with the police. Unless he was using it to blackmail someone.

McIntyre's girlfriend had lots of reasons for concern. There were too many scary scenarios. Whether a killer thought McIntyre knew more than he did, or McIntyre had stumbled onto knowledge about Cody's grandfather's murder, his life was in danger. And if he was stupid enough to get involved with loan sharks or attempt blackmail, that compounded the danger a hundredfold.

And now he'd disappeared.

Whatever the threat, things weren't likely to end well for Jordan McIntyre.

Cody lay in bed, eyes struggling to take in the minuscule amount of light that seeped into his room from Erin's at the end of the hall. She was home. He'd heard her come in, then gone right back to sleep.

Now he was wide-awake, an underlying tension flowing through his body. The moonlight that usually filtered in around the edges of the mini blinds wasn't there. With the hurricane shutters in place, darkness swallowed the window against the far wall.

Maybe Erin's practice of sleeping with night-lights wasn't a bad idea. Three was a little overkill, but one would've been nice. Because tonight something about the darkness disturbed him. It was making him feel... unsettled.

A whine intruded on the silence, followed by the click of claws against the hardwood floor. Alcee padded past his room toward Erin's, emitting another whine. What had the dog been doing in the living room, and what had her upset? Maybe his uneasiness didn't stem from the darkness.

Cody threw the covers aside and sprang to his feet, retrieving his phone with a quick sideways swipe. Whatever was going on, he needed to alert Erin.

It wasn't necessary. When he burst into her room, she was already sitting up. Alcee stood and put a paw in Erin's lap as Erin swung her silk-clad legs over the side of the bed. "What's going on?"

He shook his head. "I don't know. Alcee just came from the living room. I think she might have heard something."

Alcee turned from the bed and left the room, her repeated backward glances telling them to come with her. Erin snatched both her phone and her weapon from the nightstand and took off after the dog.

As Cody followed them into the living room, the uneasiness that had plagued him when he'd awoken bore down on him. With hurricane shutters covering every window, they were cut off from the world.

That could be good or bad. The killer couldn't see them, even though Erin had turned on the hall light.

But the shutters also kept them in the dark, ignorant of whatever threats lurked outside.

They'd just reached the living room when the dog erupted into frenzied barking, her eyes focused on the locked front door.

Erin raised her weapon. "Someone's out there. Call 911."

The next moment, the crack of splintering wood punctuated the sharp barks. The metal head of a sledgehammer appeared through a jagged hole, then withdrew to strike again.

Alcee went nuts, charging back and forth in front of the door. Though Erin shouted at her to stand down and move away, none of the commands seemed to register. This scenario probably hadn't been a part of her training.

Erin grabbed the dog's collar with her free hand and pushed her in Cody's direction. "Quick! Get into the hall, and take Alcee with you."

"Come, Alcee." He moved away from the door, tugging the dog with him. "It's okay, girl."

By the time he reached the hall, four more hammer blows had opened a two-by-two hole in the heavy wooden door. With the locks undisturbed, the alarm hadn't been triggered yet.

Cody punched the three numbers into his phone and waited for the dispatcher. The killer had found him. With a few more strikes, he'd be inside the house.

Erin was ready. She stood next to him at the end of the hall, ready to shoot whoever came through the opening.

When the dispatcher answered, Cody relayed the situation, his words tumbling over one another. The woman said she was dispatching police immediately.

"Please hurry. He's almost inside."

Cody clamped down on his lower lip. For the past several seconds everything had been quiet. They could escape through the back door, but running out blind didn't seem like a good idea. Had the assailant heard his 911 call and given up? Or was he waiting somewhere outside?

Cody had his answer right away. An object protruded through the opening, small and cylindrical. Like the barrel of a pistol or rifle. His heart leaped into his throat, and he jerked Alcee farther into the hall.

But something was off. The barrel had looked like a hard plastic. Why bring a toy gun? He peered around the corner in time to see a liquid stream arch through the opening. Several followed it, the angle shifting with each one to encompass the entire room. Erin fired three shots, but no grunts or shrieks indicated that any of them had found their target.

Within moments the stench of gasoline assaulted Cody's nostrils. Panic spiraled through him. The assailant planned to burn them alive inside the house. But even with the windows and sliding glass door covered, there were two other ways out.

He shouted one more command into the phone. "Send the fire department, too. He's soaking the living room with gasoline."

Cody slid the phone into the pocket of his gym shorts and grabbed Erin by the arm. "Come on." She'd want to stand her ground and protect her house. He understood. But it wasn't worth their lives. "We can escape out the back."

She gave a sharp nod. "Come, Alcee."

They'd just reached the back door when fire crackled behind them. Cody spun. A knotted bundle of cloth lay in the middle of the living room floor, engulfed in flames. Another missile followed, landing three or four feet away. Mini walls of fire erupted, flaming paths following the trails of gas. Within seconds the fire was moving across the living room rug.

He twisted the doorknob lock and threw the dead bolt while Erin grabbed the extinguisher from its holder two feet away. She pulled the pin and aimed a stream of foam at the base of the flames. The fire retreated as she swept left to right, then back again. Alcee stood at the door, her barking rapid and piercing. The alarm sounded, adding its shrill screech to the chaos.

Before Erin could make her third sweep, the stream sputtered and went out. She shook the extinguisher, then pressed the discharge lever again, eyes wide and panic filled. "It's empty."

"Don't worry about it." He pulled her toward the door. "We've got to get out of here."

He twisted the knob, but when he leaned into the door, it didn't budge. He gave it a harder shove. It still held fast.

When he looked back at Erin, the flames were moving forward with a vengeance, as if angry at her attempts to extinguish them. "The door's stuck."

Erin's eyes widened, and Alcee barked louder. They had to get out. Cody steeled himself for what he'd have to do. In spite of his broken ribs, he had a good seventy pounds on Erin.

He leaned back, then slammed his left shoulder into the door. The impact jarred his whole body, sending a bolt of pain through his right side. The door moved a half inch.

It wasn't stuck. Someone had wedged something against it. He cast another glance over his shoulder.

Behind Erin, most of the living room was engulfed in flames. They danced across the couch and licked at the curtains. A haze hung in the air, and smoke rolled toward them.

He gave the door another try, with no better result than before. Perspiration soaked through his T-shirt, as much from fear and desperation as the wall of heat pressing into him. His nostrils burned, and his eyes watered. He inhaled, and his throat closed up midway through, inducing a coughing fit. After he recovered, he took several breaths through his damp T-shirt.

When he looked at Erin, she was filtering the smoky air through the neckline of her silk pajama top. Her eyes reflected his own desperation.

He attacked the door with renewed vigor, then shook his head. He couldn't do it. The only thing he'd accomplished was giving his body a beating. He looked frantically around him. The front door wasn't an option. Neither was the door to the mother-in-law suite. Reaching either one would involve a sprint through an inferno.

Desperation pressed down on him. "Is there any other way out? A pet door, anything?"

He knew the answer before he asked the question. He'd already looked the entire house over in preparation for the renovations. There was no other way out. Except...

Hope tumbled through him. "The attic." He'd noticed the framed opening in the hallway. "Do you know if the gable ends are vented?"

Her eyes widened, and a smile curved her lips. "Yes, they are." She grabbed his hand and pulled him toward the living room. "If we can get to the gable over my bedroom, we can kick out the grate and drop to the ground."

The flames had almost reached the dining room. The heat was intense, and he struggled to hold his eyes open against the stinging black smoke. Would his idea even work? The roof wasn't that steeply pitched. Erin was small enough to fit through the trusses, but he didn't know about himself. Then there was the challenge of climbing a wooden fold-down ladder carrying a full-grown German shepherd. In his current condition, he wasn't sure he could do it.

Erin scurried along the edge of the living room, back pressed against the wall, and Cody followed. Alcee held back, whining, flames reflected in her dark eyes.

"Come on, girl." Erin clapped her hands. "You can do it."

While Erin coaxed the dog, Cody reached up to pull the hinged panel down. He'd just finished unfolding the ladder and planting its end against the hardwood floor when Alcee shot around him and bounded up the wooden steps.

At his silent question, Erin smiled. "Ladders were part of her SAR training."

Erin made her way upward while a furry white face watched from above. She was barefoot. So was he. But moments taken to get dressed and retrieve shoes could cost them their lives.

Finally, it was Cody's turn. He released his shirt and held his breath. When he poked his head into the attic space, it was illuminated. A beam of light came from the back of Erin's cell phone.

He squatted on the step and reached below him. "I'm closing this back up. It'll help keep smoke out and buy us some extra time."

The hinges creaked as he folded the two bottom sections of the ladder against one another. His ribs again protested the abuse. He ignored the pain. He'd have time to recover later.

If they survived the night.

The access door creaked shut, and he looked around. Trusses lined up ahead of him, braces at uniform angles, held in place by metal fasteners. It would be a tight fit, but he was pretty sure he could make it, if there wasn't an air handler or anything obstructing his path.

Erin sent Alcee ahead, then began to make her way toward the end of the house. Cody followed, careful to keep his weight on the trusses. If Alcee stepped between them, onto the back of the drywall, the ceiling would hold her. Not so for him and Erin.

God, please help get us out of here. Would God even hear him? He was a pretty decent guy. He'd even watched a church service Sunday. But according to Erin, that wasn't what it took.

It wouldn't hurt, though, to add his prayers to the ones Erin was no doubt sending up.

Even though things didn't look half as hopeless as they had a few minutes earlier, they were still light-years away from being safe.

TEN

Erin made her way from truss to truss in a modified duck walk, the wood bruising the balls of her bare feet. As long as she kept her head down, she could pass through without having to lie down. She held her phone clutched in one hand, the beam from the flashlight app illuminating the way ahead of her. With her other hand, she moved her weapon forward, laying it between the next two trusses.

She should have grabbed the holster, but when she'd charged into the living room, ready to defend them, she hadn't anticipated having to crawl through the attic.

Alcee's training had prepared her well, and she'd navigated each two-foot span without a problem. Now she was waiting for them at the gable end. Beyond her, moonlight slanted through the rectangular vent in horizontal slivers.

Cody didn't have it as easy as her or her dog. He had to crawl from one truss to the next. Twice, Erin stopped to check on him, aiming the beam behind her. Though he was probably trying to hide it, she didn't miss his grimace of pain. Both times he told her to keep moving and not let him slow her and Alcee down.

He was right. Ominous creaks and groans vibrated through the wood beneath them. At any time the living room roof could collapse, sending heat, smoke and fire blasting through the attic space where they were. *God, please help us make it out of here.*

If anything happened to Cody or her dog, she'd never forgive herself. She should have replaced the fire extinguisher as soon as she moved in. She was going to, just hadn't gotten around to it yet. It hadn't been critical. The needle had still been in the green, a hairsbreadth away from the line separating it from the red *recharge* area, more than sufficient to extinguish a small kitchen fire or other minor mishap. She hadn't considered anything like this.

She stopped next to Alcee and ran a hand down her back. The dog's usual reward was a game of tug-of-war with her rope toy. Not this time. The toy was lying on the dining room table, where Cody had left it yesterday after playing with her.

The flames would've reached it by now. The whole table was likely ablaze, along with her new kitchen cabinets and everything she'd accumulated over the years. A wave of despair washed over her, so sudden and powerful it stole her breath.

She squared her shoulders. Her sole focus needed to be on getting Cody and Alcee to safety. She shone the light behind her. Cody was making progress but still had a good ten feet to go.

"Can you push out the grate?" His voice sounded strained.

She pressed against the metal. It felt solid, likely attached to the plywood with multiple screws. "I can't push it, but I can probably kick it out."

She squatted on her left leg and braced a shoulder against one of the trusses. After two hard kicks with her right foot, the grate dangled from one screw. She twisted it loose and tossed it to the ground. The opening was large enough to squeeze through, even for Cody. But escape would involve a ten-foot drop to the ground with no protection for their bare feet.

She turned off the light and scanned the area, weapon raised. The night was clear, the outer bands they expected still hours away. Moonlight spilled over the landscape. The hedge of sea grapes bordering her yard provided a good hiding place. She and Cody would be easy targets for someone waiting with a rifle.

But the killer wouldn't be expecting them to exit from the attic. He might even be gone, sure they'd be unable to escape. She listened for approaching emergency vehicles. What was taking so long?

She moved to the side and turned to Cody. "Squeeze through the opening, feet first."

"No way." His tone was adamant. "I'm not escaping until I know you're safe."

She heaved a sigh. They were losing precious seconds arguing. "I'm covering you. At the first sign of attack, I'll shoot." In all her years in law enforcement, she'd never had to kill anyone. But if it came to that, she'd do it without hesitation.

She pushed him toward the opening. "As soon as you're on the ground, I'll tell Alcee to jump. I need you to catch her. I don't know that I can handle sixty-five pounds falling through the air."

Cody stared her down for another second or two, eyes hard and jaw tight. Jumping to safety while she was still in danger clearly went against every protective instinct he possessed.

She gave him another nudge. "Don't worry. Alcee will be right behind you. And I'll be behind her."

The emotions skittering across his face collided in his eyes. The air between them was heavy with tension. Suddenly, he grabbed her by the shoulders. Before she knew what was coming, he pressed his mouth to hers in a hard, desperate kiss. Warmth exploded inside her, searing her mind and stealing the strength from her limbs.

All too soon he pulled away, waiting another second to release her. If he hadn't given her that moment to recover, she'd have fallen between the trusses in an undignified blob. The warmth inside was gone, replaced by longing so intense it was painful.

She struggled to set her world back on its axis while Cody backed into the opening. Lifting her weapon, she kept watch through the small spaces over his shoulders. He'd just put one foot through when a voice came from somewhere outside.

"Don't go any farther, or I'll shoot."

She stiffened at the voice with its heavy Northeast accent, the same Cody had described the day of his rescue. He jerked away from the opening, and Erin peered around the edge of the wall.

Everything was still. She fixed her gaze on the hedge, straining to see something. There was no hint of movement, no variations in texture or color amid the large rounded leaves.

"The police are already onto you." The confidence she injected into her tone masked the fear coursing through her. "Cody isn't the only witness. The woman you held at gunpoint for a half hour gave the police a pretty detailed description."

There was McIntyre, too. Chances were good he'd seen something, and the killer knew it.

"You already have one murder to answer for."

Well, two. Each day that passed, McIntyre was less likely to be found alive.

A distant wail traveled on the quiet night air. Behind her, Cody spoke in hushed tones. She cast a glance over her shoulder. He held his phone pressed to his ear.

"Send the police to the north side of the house." Urgency filled his tone, in spite of the softness of his words. "We're in the attic, and there's a shooter on the ground."

The emergency vehicles grew closer.

"Hear that?" Erin projected the words through the opening while Cody's soft conversation with Dispatch continued. "The police are on their way. Give it up. If you turn yourself in now, you've got a chance of getting off. You didn't mean to kill anyone. The courts will take that into account."

"The building was supposed to be empty."

She jerked her gaze in the direction of the voice. He was definitely behind the hedge. If she wasn't too far off on the angle, he was at about eleven o'clock. She needed to try to keep him talking. "I know. They'll understand that."

"No, they won't. Murder is murder. Cody saw me, and it's just a matter of time until he figures it out."

Figures it out? What was he talking about?

Before she had a chance to ponder further, there was a large crash, and the house shivered. Moments later a blast of heat and smoke whooshed past them and out the opening in the gable. A section of roof had caved in.

She cast a panicked glance over her shoulder. The flames had reached the attic and were charging toward them.

"Go, now!" She gave Cody another push. "Stay low so I've got a clear shot."

The sirens were closer now. She could hear them over the roar of the fire. But help wouldn't arrive in time. The flames were advancing too quickly.

Cody lay facedown and shimmied backward while Erin held her position beside him in a deep squat. She peered out the top left-hand corner of the opening, right arm extended, weapon clutched in that hand. How would she be able to hit anything in such an awkward position?

Smoke billowed around her, stinging her eyes and searing her throat. She waved a hand in front of her face, but more rolled in to obstruct her view.

God, help me do what I must to protect Cody and Alcee.

Cody squeezed into the opening, legs dangling down the outside wall. As he pushed his torso through, Erin repositioned herself to steady her aim with her left hand. For a fraction of a second, Cody hung suspended. Then he released his grip to fall to the ground. The same moment, the hedge moved. The crack of a gunshot followed, the simultaneous muzzle flash vivid in the darkness.

Erin fired three rounds. A cry came from the hedge—half grunt, half muffled shriek.

"Cody!" She'd wounded the shooter. But had he hit Cody?

"I'm okay."

Her breath came out in a rush. The emergency vehicles were closer now, their high-pitched wails filling the night. Tears streamed down her face, and several deep coughs stole her air. When she cast a glance over her shoulder, flames licked at the wood less than ten feet behind her.

"I'm sending Alcee down."

She wiped away her tears, made worse by the coughing fit, then again fixed her gaze on the hedge. Cody straightened and stepped a couple of feet away from the house, arms extended upward. Without relaxing her aim, she commanded Alcee to go.

As Alcee jumped, another shot rang out, and Erin fired again. Cody released a grunt as the dog landed in his arms.

"I've got her. We're good."

The sirens were ear piercing now, coming from right in front of the house. They fell silent, and only the roar of the fire surrounded her.

She gave in to another coughing fit, then shouted down at Cody, her voice raspy. "You and Alcee get to safety." Safety would be out front, where officers were likely exiting their cruisers, weapons drawn.

She held her breath against the smoke streaming past her and prepared to back her body into the opening.

A crash shook the house, and everything around her shuddered. A blast of heat slammed into her, and a ball of fire shot toward her at light speed.

She spun to face the opening, curled into a squat and leaped into the smoke-filled darkness.

Cody lay in the grass on his back, Erin on top of him. For several long moments he couldn't breathe. Pain stabbed through his rib cage, and his lungs were paralyzed.

He'd put Alcee behind the air-conditioning unit to

shield her from the shooter's view. Then instead of obeying Erin's command to get to safety, he'd moved into position to help lower her to the ground.

His plans hadn't gone as he'd hoped. A series of cracks had shaken the house, and flames had shot twenty feet into the sky over where the living room roof had been. Instead of dropping gently to the ground, she'd jumped, and he'd tried to catch her.

Alcee bounded toward where they lay. After sniffing his face, she turned her attention to Erin and nudged her shoulder with her nose.

Erin rolled off him and tried to pull him to his feet. "Come on. Let's get to safety."

He nodded, unable to do anything else. The shots had stopped as soon as the police pulled up in front. Two officers had already disappeared behind the hedge to pursue the suspect on foot.

Finally, the vise around Cody's chest released. He sucked in a constricted breath, then followed it with several painful coughs.

Erin cast a nervous glance toward the hedge. "Can you walk?"

"I think so." Or maybe he was being overly optimistic.

He fought his way upright and stumbled with her into the front yard, Alcee following. The streetlamp near her property line spilled its light over them. More emergency vehicles approached, their sirens growing louder. Probably fire and ambulance.

Deep, painful coughs overtook him. He stood bent at the waist, hands on his knees. Erin was having the same struggle. They'd both inhaled too much smoke.

When she recovered, she wiped her eyes. "Are you okay? I wasn't sure back there."

He nodded. "You just knocked the breath out of me."

"Thanks for breaking my fall. But I told you to get to safety, not stand there waiting to be shot at again."

Cody patted the dog's hip. "I hid Alcee behind the AC unit so she wouldn't be shot, but I told you before. I wouldn't escape until I knew you were safe."

The scolding left her eyes, and an uncharacteristic tenderness moved in. That kiss he'd given her in the attic was a mistake. It was clear now that they were both safely on the ground. But that didn't stop him from wanting to do it again.

A fire truck arrived, an ambulance not far behind it. One firefighter rushed toward them while the other unwound the hose to attach to the hydrant in front of the house next door.

"Is everyone out?"

"Yes. She and I are it." And Alcee. If the attack had happened a few days earlier, Opa and Mimi would've been there. The outcome might have been different with two older people in tow. Erin would say they owed that detail to the hand of God. So would Bobby. Cody wasn't sure. But just in case, he whispered his own prayer of thanks.

Two paramedics approached. Erin made it halfway through an inhalation before a cough took over again. Knowing Erin, she'd downplay her injuries. Cody wouldn't let her.

"She needs to be treated for smoke inhalation."

Erin lifted a hand. "I'll be all right."

Her voice was several pitches lower than usual, deep and raspy. His was, too.

"You inhaled a lot of smoke." He turned to the paramedics. "She was the last one out of the house."

As soon as the words left his mouth, he winced. He shouldn't have escaped first, no matter how adamant she'd been.

One of the paramedics put a hand on his shoulder. "Let's get you both checked out."

Cody let him lead them to the ambulance, where they both sat on the back. Erin's condition seemed worse than his, but he was having trouble drawing a full breath. Whether from the smoke, the broken ribs or Erin body-slamming him, he wasn't sure.

A second ambulance arrived, its siren falling silent. A short distance away the hedge rustled, and Cody tensed. But there was no threat. Two police officers stepped into the yard, a struggling man between them. One officer carried a rifle in his free hand, a cloth wrapping the barrel where he held it.

A blond wig sat cockeyed on the suspect's head, skewed a good forty-five degrees to the left. Curls tumbled past his shoulder on that side, the same curls they'd seen at the hospital. Was the beard fake, too?

Cody squinted at the man's clothes in the streetlamp's glow and the light cast by the semicircle moon. A large wet spot marked the right shoulder of the T-shirt, making the dark fabric even darker. Blood. Erin had hit him. He'd heard the man cry out. That shot had likely saved their lives. With a bullet in his shoulder, the man's next shots had gone wild.

The man turned, and the wig slipped another forty-five degrees before falling to the ground.

Erin gasped. "Jordan McIntyre? Why?"

He didn't respond. Cody didn't expect him to. But he

hoped they'd eventually have some answers. It wouldn't bring Pops back or make up for everything he'd been through, but it might bring some closure.

While the paramedics worked on him and Erin, Alcee sat and watched, dark eyes alert. Other emergency personnel treated McIntyre, and firefighters continued to shoot powerful streams of water onto the flames. Soon, they'd have the fire put out. Maybe part of the mother-in-law apartment and Erin's bedroom and bathroom would be salvageable. He didn't hold out hope for anything else.

He looked over at Erin as a blood pressure cuff tightened on her arm. "I'm sorry about your house."

She gave him a sad smile. "We're safe, and that's what matters. Things can be replaced. People can't."

How well he knew that. He released a sigh. "It's over."

Erin glanced at the other ambulance. "I didn't see that coming. McIntyre grew up in Florida. The Northeast accent he used was as fake as the hair and beard." She took a rapid, shallow breath. "But it was him in every attack. And who his girlfriend surprised at his house last night."

Cody gave her a wry smile. "You wondered what connection there was between the blond guy and McIntyre. There's your answer."

A bathrobe-clad woman stepped off the porch next door and approached. "Are you guys okay?"

Erin nodded. "We're okay, but they're taking us to the hospital to check us out. And I'm worried about Alcee. I'm sure she inhaled as much smoke as we did."

"No problem. I'll get dressed and take her to the emergency clinic."

"Thank you. Have them call me for my credit card information."

The woman dropped to one knee. "Come here, girl."

Alcee went right to her. Cody had met the woman previously. According to Erin, she'd cared for the dog before he and Erin's grandparents moved in. The neighbor headed back to her house with Alcee in tow, removing an excuse Erin would've used for not getting checked out.

At the paramedic's request, Cody opened his mouth for him to look at his throat. Erin was undergoing the same assessments, and judging from the comments he overheard, the man wasn't happy with what he was seeing. Something about soot in airway passages, red and irritated eyes and rapid breathing.

The paramedic tending Erin stepped back. "We're hooking *you* up to oxygen right away, but we need to take you both in for observation. You might think you're okay now, but things can worsen in a hurry as swelling and mucus increase. Breathing isn't something to play around with."

Cody nodded. "Take her. I'll follow."

Erin nailed him with a stern glare. "Oh, no, you don't. If I'm going to the hospital, you are, too."

He held up both hands in surrender. "I'm going, just not in an ambulance. When this is over, we're going to need a ride home."

"I've got friends. Coworkers, too. Any number of them will be willing to pick us up."

"No need for that. I'm perfectly capable of driving." He wanted to be able to get out of there as soon as the doctor released him. He hated hospitals, at least when he was the patient.

She narrowed her eyes. "If I find out you bailed, I'll hunt you down and bring you in myself. In handcuffs, if I have to."

"Yes, ma'am. I'll be right behind the ambulance and

won't leave until I get a clean bill of health. Now get on that gurney and let them get some oxygen in you."

"When did you get so bossy?"

He left the question unanswered. The fire was out, and the firemen were putting away their equipment. Wisps of smoke rose from a collapsed and smoldering center, capped by the two ends still standing.

An investigator would likely make contact with Erin tomorrow. She'd also need to report the incident to her insurance company. Then would come all the work of filing a claim, obtaining estimates and getting her home rebuilt.

But the first priority was taking care of her medical needs. His, too. Because if he skipped getting checked out, she'd do just what she threatened.

Soon, everything would go back to normal. He'd return home, and there'd be no reason for him and Erin to have contact beyond what they wanted. He didn't know what Erin wanted, but he knew his own desires. In a perfect world, he'd keep Erin by his side forever.

But it wasn't a perfect world. It was a world where plans changed on a whim and hearts got so badly broken they never fully healed.

The first time Erin left him, he'd been devastated. If he gave his heart to her and she walked away a second time, it would destroy him.

It was a risk he wasn't willing to take.

The television broadcast its morning programming into an otherwise silent room. Erin lay in the bed, staring out the tall, narrow window, a small hose feeding oxygen into her nose.

Over the past few hours the rain had come and gone.

The storm did make that projected eastward turn, so the Fort Myers area had been spared the worst. She was one of a handful of people in her neighborhood who'd boarded windows to protect their homes. Then she'd lost hers to a fire.

She picked up her phone from the bedside table. No missed calls or texts. Cody had texted her at seven o'clock. After being kept awake by a nasty cough for several hours, she'd finally fallen into a fitful sleep and hadn't woken up for the notification. Her return text at eight fifteen had gone unanswered so far. Now it was almost ten.

She'd already called her insurance company and, between coughing fits, told the representative what had happened. They'd promised to send an adjuster to survey the damage later that day.

She'd also taken a call from a panicked Courtney, who'd thought she might have heard sirens over the sounds of her white noise machine but had missed the other commotion. Courtney hadn't seen the condition of the house until she'd left for work that morning.

The familiar tickle in Erin's throat started again, and she leaned forward as more deep coughs overtook her body. When the spell passed, she plopped back against the bed. Her chest hurt and her abdominal muscles felt as if she'd completed a couple hundred sit-ups.

Her head was killing her, too. Whether from the smoke she'd inhaled or all the coughing she'd done, she wasn't sure. The mucus was forming faster than she could get rid of it. Her hopes of being discharged today were growing dimmer by the hour.

She shifted her gaze back to the window. Maybe she should try calling Cody. No, if his night had gone like hers, he was probably sleeping. She was just bored; no reason to disturb his rest.

Okay, maybe it was more than boredom. She was restless, confused. They were at a crossroads, and she had no idea where she stood.

Over the past few weeks they'd fallen into an easy camaraderie. She'd hoped that could continue, that they'd maintain a friendship. She'd been sure that was all she wanted.

Then he'd kissed her. Just thinking about it sent her pulse into overdrive. That kiss had to have meant something. Or maybe it had just been an impulsive response to emotional stress, the uncertainty of not knowing whether they'd survive the night.

Footsteps sounded outside her room. She turned away from the window, expecting a nurse. Instead, Cody approached wearing a warm smile and a pair of shorts and T-shirt she'd never seen before. A plastic bag dangled from one hand. In his other hand, he held two more bags.

Her stomach did a backflip. Then she narrowed her eyes. "Why aren't you in a hospital gown?"

He'd texted her to see how she was doing. He hadn't mentioned anything about his own treatment. If he'd reneged on his promise to get checked out, she was going to flog him.

"I've been discharged. I was asleep when you texted me back, didn't wake up till the doctor came in. He said he was releasing me later this morning, so I figured I'd come in person and surprise you instead of sending a text." He pulled a pair of sneakers from one of the bags and plopped them on the floor.

"You've got my tennis shoes."

"Yeah." He pulled the chair up beside the bed. "After

they loaded you in the ambulance, I asked the firemen if I could grab my keys and wallet and shoes since I was driving myself to the hospital. The fire was completely out at that point, and anything that was going to fall had already fallen. But they still wouldn't let me go inside. Rather than leaving me stranded, though, one offered to get what I needed. While he was at it, I asked him if he could grab some shoes for you, too."

"Thanks."

"There's more. Bobby called right after the doctor left. When I told him what had happened, he asked if there was anything he could do. I asked him to swing by Walmart and pick us each up a change of clothes." He pulled a T-shirt and some exercise pants out of the second bag. "I hope I got your size close. At least spandex is pretty forgiving."

She held the items up. "It looks like you did pretty well."

"I have one more surprise for you." He reached into the last bag and pulled out her devotional book.

Her mouth dropped. "But how…?" The book had been in the living room. There was no way it survived the fire.

"I sent Bobby on one other errand. I asked him to go by the Christian bookstore and pick up two copies of *Jesus Calling*."

"Two?"

"One for each of us. Since I'm going home, it'll be a little hard for us to share."

Erin couldn't stop the grin that spread across her face. "And the Bible?"

"I haven't gotten one yet. But I did find a free app for my phone. Bobby said I should start in the Book of John."

"Courtney said the same thing. Good advice." She paused. "So what brought this about?"

"I had trouble sleeping last night. I couldn't stop thinking about how close I came to dying. That kept going through my mind, along with bits of your pastor's message and our conversation afterward, as well as some of the things I've been reading in your book. I finally told God that my life is a mess, but if He wants it, it's His."

She reached out and squeezed his hand. "You won't regret it." She certainly hadn't.

He sat back in the chair. "When are they releasing you?"

"Not today. I'm still coughing up a lot of junk. They're doing another chest X-ray this afternoon, making sure no delayed lung injury shows up."

His brows drew together over eyes filled with concern. "Are you having shortness of breath?"

"A little. That's another thing they're concerned about."

"When they do let you out, you're welcome to stay with me until your house is livable again." He gave her a crooked smile. "I'll get to return some of that Southern hospitality."

"Thanks for the offer, but Courtney beat you to it."

"Already?"

"I got a call from her right after I talked to the insurance company. She was leaving for work, saw my car still sitting in the drive and the house half destroyed." She gave him a wry smile. "It took me a while to calm her down."

Two soft raps sounded on the doorjamb, and Erin looked past Cody to where a Lee County detective stood just inside the room.

"Jeff, come on in."

He approached, shaking his head and making clucking sounds of disapproval. "You're back on duty one day after a four-day vacation, and now this. You'll do anything to finagle more time off."

She laughed. As she made introductions, Cody stood and offered the detective his chair, taking the one farther away. Erin filled Jeff in on what had happened inside the house from the time Cody showed up in her bedroom doorway until she'd leaped from the attic.

Jeff released a whistle. "Scary."

Yeah. It would probably give her fodder for some pretty serious nightmares. Not that she didn't have enough already.

But they hadn't come last night. Her cough hadn't allowed her to get into REM sleep. Once life got back to normal, she'd be adding fire and the thought of being burned alive to the other terrors that tormented her sleep.

Or maybe, if she truly trusted God for the healing she craved, she'd defeat all of them.

Jeff intertwined his fingers over his abdomen. "We finally got the toxicology report back, not that it matters at this point. The soup was positive for arsenic."

Though Erin had expected as much, the news was still jarring. She shook her head. "I still can't believe Jordan McIntyre was the one behind all of this. I'm usually a good judge of character. I don't suppose anyone has gotten him to talk."

"That's another reason I stopped by, other than to check on you. Those background checks we did turned up some interesting things."

"What kind of things?"

"He did a short stint in the military and was dishonorably discharged fifteen years ago."

"What was his assignment?"

"He worked on a demolition crew."

She raised her brows. "As in blowing things up?"

He nodded. "That was part of it. Since his discharge, he's done a variety of construction-type jobs."

"That fits with what he told me."

"Part of it. Your report says he came from Wisconsin."

"That's what he told me."

"He did come from Wisconsin…by way of New York and New Jersey."

She frowned. "Why didn't he mention those states? Were his stays there brief?"

"A total of almost six years. While in the Northeast, he worked for three different demolition companies. Apparently, when he left, he took some souvenirs."

Her eyes widened. "No wonder he didn't mention New York and New Jersey."

He nodded. "It was safe to tell you about Wisconsin, because he held carpentry jobs there. Demolition companies in his work history would've raised too many red flags."

"What about the Camry? McIntyre drives a red Tacoma, and that's the only vehicle titled to him. We checked."

"He got the Camry a while back, never transferred the tag. He rents warehouse storage space in Cape Coral where he keeps it stashed."

Erin shook her head. "I still don't understand why he did it. He had a good job, no money problems." Or so they'd thought until learning he'd hit his friends up for money.

"There's where you're wrong. Once we told him everything we'd learned, he came clean with the rest of it. Turns out he has a gambling problem and got in over his head. He'd been stringing the guys along for a few months. They finally threatened a slow and painful death if he didn't pay up."

Erin nodded. The last of their questions had been answered. After saying his goodbyes and wishing Erin well, Jeff left the room.

Cody took the chair he'd vacated. "It's hard to believe it's finally over."

"I know."

Ever since escaping the house, she'd been waiting for that sense of relief to settle in. It was there, but too many other emotions overshadowed it.

Now that the danger was over, Cody would return to his own home. As friends, they'd occasionally get together. But with no real excuse to see each other, those times would grow further and further apart, until they lost touch completely. She'd had more than one friendship disintegrate that way. Sometimes she regretted not having a social-media presence. It at least kept people loosely connected.

Somehow, she'd make sure she didn't lose contact with Cody. He'd become an important part of her life and she wasn't ready to let him go.

Who was she kidding? What she felt went way deeper than that. She didn't just care for him. She'd fallen in love with him. Judging from everything he'd poured into that kiss, he had to be feeling at least some of what she was.

"I'll be heading home today, getting back to doing estimates and meeting with customers without a babysitter." His words cut across her thoughts, so practical and unemotional compared to the path hers had taken. "I'd leave you your spare key, but if you're going to have me do the repair work, you might want me to hang on to it."

"That would be a good idea."

"Would you like me to pick up Alcee and take her home with me till you get out of here?"

"That would be great."

Their interactions had become stiff. What was he feeling? She had to know.

"You kissed me in the attic."

His gaze dipped to the floor. "I'm sorry. I didn't mean it. I was afraid we weren't going to make it out of there alive." He met her eyes. "It won't happen again."

"No problem." She forced the words past a lump in her throat.

The kiss had meant nothing. It was just what she'd thought but hoped against—an impulsive reaction in an emotional moment.

At one time he'd been ready to commit to forever. She'd wanted the freedom to experience life. Over the past twelve years she'd learned adulthood wasn't all it was cracked up to be. Neither was freedom.

She'd removed the rose-colored glasses and found what she really wanted had been right in front of her.

But that window of opportunity had closed.

ELEVEN

Cody strolled next to Erin, the Punta Gorda Harbor-walk stretching before them. Peace River lay to their left, reflecting a blue sky dotted by a handful of clouds. A light breeze negated the September heat and humidity.

Erin smiled up at him. "Thank you for dinner." They'd left Hurricane Charley's Raw Bar and Grill a few minutes ago and would soon cross under the south-bound Tamiami Trail bridge. "Alcee says thanks, too. She's gotten spoiled with all this fine dining."

"No problem." He gave Erin a smile of his own. "I owe you at least two more thank-you-for-saving-my-life dinners. Or is it three? It's happened so many times, I've lost count."

A week had passed since Erin had been released from the hospital. They'd kept her a day and a half longer than they had him. Now they were both back at work. He didn't know about her workload, but between finishing the Hutchinson addition and continuing to provide esti-mates, he'd been slammed. They'd talked but had seen each other only once.

Sunday morning he'd surprised her by sliding into the pew next to her. He'd gotten to meet Pastor Mike in person, along with several of the other church members. Now he had a new activity in his schedule—weekly church attendance. He hoped it would be with Erin. If not, he'd try Pops's church. If Pops could see him now, he'd be smiling.

A box truck roared closer as they stepped into the shade of the overpass. Cody waited for it to move by, his smile fading. "I'm afraid I owe you guys more than a few dinners. You lost your house because of me." He frowned. "But now that it's over, I'll get my debt paid eventually."

She gave him a little push. "There's no debt. None of it was your fault. But I'm sure if Alcee could talk, she'd tell you to keep the dinners coming."

He grinned. "I'm sure she would."

Even though he hadn't seen much of Erin, she'd never left his thoughts. He missed her, more than he ever imagined he would. Two nights ago he'd clicked on the TV, hoping to dispel his loneliness with some evening sitcoms, and found they made a poor substitute for the nearness of one amazing woman and her dog.

So yesterday he'd come to a decision, made a trip to the Punta Gorda Post Office, then called Erin to set up today's outing. Now he needed to work up the courage to continue with his plan.

The Harborwalk made a couple of bends, and the northbound Tamiami Trail bridge stood in front of them. Soon, they'd be back at Laishley Park, where he'd left his truck.

And where he'd hidden a key.

His stomach rolled over, and his palms grew moist. When it came to reading women, he wasn't always the brightest bulb in the pack. Erin had brought up the kiss he'd given her the night of the fire, and he'd been sure a reprimand was coming, at least an explanation of why she thought it was a mistake. So he'd beaten her to it, rushing ahead to assure her the kiss had meant nothing when it had shaken his world.

But she hadn't looked relieved. Instead, he'd seen disappointment in her eyes, noticed how her face had fallen, the almost imperceptible way her shoulders had curled forward. He'd hurt her.

Now he was going to take those words back. Maybe. What if he'd read her wrong? What if he'd seen relief instead of disappointment? It wouldn't be the first time he'd been clueless about a woman's thoughts and feelings.

Erin cast him a sideways glance. "Are you in a hurry to get home?"

"No. Why?"

She shrugged. "I was thinking about watching the sunset."

"Sure."

A lot of eagerness came through in his tone. He didn't care. All evening he'd tried to read her mannerisms, to search out meaning behind her words, anything that might hint at where he stood with her. She'd given him nothing. How had he expected anything else? He'd kissed her, then told her it meant nothing.

But now she wanted to spend more time with him doing something nostalgic. How many times had they enjoyed the sunset from one of the park benches overlooking the water while Pops fished nearby? It had to be a good sign, right?

When they took a seat a few minutes later, Alcee plopped down at their feet. The first streaks of orange

already stained the western sky, the bridge in the fore-
ground. As the sun sank lower, Cody lifted his arm to
let it rest on the back of the bench.

Erin didn't lean into him, but she didn't stiffen or
pull away, either. Another good sign. Or maybe he was
grasping at straws.

She released a soft sigh. "I love the sunsets here."

"Me, too."

There was something special about watching the sun
set over water. But what had always made the Laishley
Park sunsets special was sharing them with Erin.

He bent his arm to encircle her shoulders. Now she
did lean into him, and he gave her a squeeze.

Okay. This was it. He was going to do it.

The colors deepened, and the sun disappeared into
the horizon. Behind them, palm fronds rustled in the
gentle breeze, and distant voices drifted to them. Dusk
settled in.

Cody rose and held out a hand. "Let's walk."

She grinned up at him. "The two-mile hike we took
earlier wasn't enough for you?"

Yeah, they'd covered a good percentage of the two-
and-a-half-mile Harborwalk, heading toward the Village Fish Market on its southwest end, then stopping by
Hurricane Charley's on their way back.

"We've got one quick visit to make."

She put her hand in his, and he helped her to her feet,
ignoring the raised eyebrow and head tilt. When he intertwined his fingers with hers, she didn't seem to mind.

They continued hand in hand, past streetlamps and
another bench before the sidewalk veered right. Soon
they stood in front of the Hurricane Charley memorial
with its sundial and two palm trees.

"This is where we're going?" She looked up at him. There was a lot of curiosity in her gaze. But something else, too. Anticipation? Excitement?

"Have you ever checked the palm fronds?"

"Should I have?"

"Maybe."

She narrowed her eyes. "What did you do?"

"Something I should have done eight years ago." If he'd held out for Erin, he could have saved himself some grief.

"If you had, I wouldn't have seen it. I've only been here a year, and when I arrived, I didn't look."

He understood. She hadn't been ready then. But had anything changed? What made him think she was any more ready for commitment now than she'd been then?

What he'd done was dumb. She'd seemed disappointed when he'd said the kiss didn't mean anything. She'd even let him put his arm around her and hold her hand. But that was a far cry from committing to forever.

If only he could take her home and retrieve the key later. But it was too late. He'd already opened his big mouth.

He'd poured out his heart in that letter. Once she read what he wrote, their friendship would become uncomfortable. Actually, simple friendship had become impossible somewhere between fearing he was going to lose her in the fire and realizing he'd once again fallen in love with her. And that was why he'd written the letter. He'd always been an all-or-nothing kind of guy.

She stepped onto the platform next to the bent-over palm and stretched, raising herself onto her toes. After sliding her fingers into a few of the recesses between the bases of the metal fronds, she eyed him with a frown.

"There'd better not be any spiders in here. Whose idea was this, anyway?"

"Yours."

"Oh, yeah."

Moments later she stepped down, arm raised in triumph, the key clutched in her hand. His own had grown clammy. His pulse had taken on an erratic rhythm, and the food he'd eaten had congealed into a doughy lump.

He swallowed hard. "I'll wait here."

That was the arrangement. One would leave the note; the other would digest it in privacy and decide how and whether to respond.

Of course, if her answer wasn't what he'd hoped it would be, the ride back to Fort Myers would be really uncomfortable. He hadn't thought that part through.

She handed him Alcee's leash. She wouldn't need his truck. The post office was at the edge of the park. "I'll be back." She bounded away from him at a half jog.

Some of his tension dissipated. Maybe he wasn't making a mistake. Erin had to have an idea of what was in his letter. If she had no desire for a romantic relationship, there would be some stiffness in her step.

He moved up the sidewalk and strolled the length of the parking lot, Alcee trotting beside him. Then he turned and did it again. Three times, and Erin still hadn't appeared.

That was good, right? That meant she was thinking about it rather than giving him a firm, reactive *no*.

He changed direction once again. No, it wasn't good. The fact she had to think about it at all meant she wasn't ready. And the longer she thought about it, the more reasons she'd come up with for why a romantic relationship was a bad idea.

He'd jumped the gun. He should've waited, given her more time to get used to the idea of allowing what they had to progress beyond friendship. Now he'd blown it.

He dropped to one knee and cupped the dog's face between his hands.

"Oh, Alcee, what have I done?"

Erin leaned against the brick facade of the post office, a single sheet of paper clutched in one sweaty hand. Her heart pounded, and she was having a hard time drawing in a full breath.

Cody had done it. He'd gotten a post office box and written a letter. And she was on the verge of a full-blown panic attack.

She had to give him an answer. She could tell him she needed more time. He'd give it to her. But that wouldn't be fair to Cody. She knew herself. The decision would hang over her like a piece of nasty unfinished business, the dread building, making it impossible to ever say yes. *God, please show me what to do. Whatever decision I make, please let it be the right one.*

She reached for her phone. Her purse was in Cody's truck, tucked under the passenger seat, but she'd slipped her phone into her back pocket. It was a good thing, because she really needed to talk to Courtney. Courtney would know how to talk her off the ledge.

No. She slid her phone back into her pocket. She couldn't call a friend when she was out on a date with Cody.

She pushed herself away from the wall and started to pace. Yes, she could. Even *Who Wants to Be a Millionaire* allowed phone-a-friend. She could actually see some correlation between her situation and the popular game show. The stakes were astronomical. She could be blissfully happy with her all-time true love, or she could crash and burn, like all the other times.

She pulled up Courtney's number in her contacts and pressed the call icon. Courtney was her sounding board. More than that, she was her lifeline. Actually, wasn't that what they called the helpers on the game show?

When her friend answered, Erin skipped the greeting. "You gotta help me. I think I'm going to hyperventilate."

"Slow down and take some deep breaths." For the next several moments Courtney did exactly that, sending the sounds of heavy, controlled breathing through the phone. Erin closed her eyes and joined her friend.

"Now, tell me what's going on."

Erin took a final deep breath. "It's Cody."

"Is he all right?" Courtney's tone held a note of alarm. "I thought the case was over."

"It is." She lowered her voice. "He wrote the letter."

"What does it say?"

She held the piece of paper under the glow emanating from the overhead lighting. Somehow, reading the words aloud seemed like being untrue to Cody. But she couldn't do this alone. She cleared her throat.

"'Erin, I'm better at building things than composing poetic words, but I'm going to give it my best shot. I was reminded recently that God works in mysterious ways. Our paths didn't cross by accident. I believe God used circumstances to bring us together.'"

"See, what did I tell you?"

Erin smiled at the interruption, which was exactly what she'd expected to hear from Courtney. "'When I left Chicago for a warmer climate, I chose here, hoping you'd found your way back, too, or would eventually.

Everything I felt for you so long ago was still there. Now it consumes me. I love you and want you to be a part of my life forever.'"

She lowered the page. There was more, language that was typical Cody—concern and understanding for everything she'd been through, the desire to be there for her. He'd ended by begging her to let down her guard and trust him with her heart. But it was the last sentence she'd read to Courtney that had her thoughts spinning and panic coursing through her. Cody loved her and wanted her to be a part of his life forever.

Courtney was silent for several moments. "And you're having trouble making a decision."

"Of course I'm having trouble with the decision. Forever is a long time."

"You love him, right?"

"I never said that."

"You don't have to. You talk about him every time we run, and there's emotion behind every word."

Yeah, she loved him. She'd been fighting it almost from the moment they'd pulled him out of the rubble. She began to pace again, and her gaze fell on one of the windows. Inside, the box Cody had rented was wide-open, the key still in the lock. She walked back through the glass door.

Courtney didn't force her to answer the first question before she moved on to the second. "Are there any red flags?"

"None yet. But I'm good at missing those until it's too late."

"From the times I've talked to Cody and everything you've told me about him, I'm not sensing any land mines." A sigh came through the phone. "Life is filled with uncertainty. Sometimes you have to be willing to take some risks to get the rewards."

Erin closed the box and pocketed the key. She didn't like risks, especially when it came to her heart. She was sure Cody was everything she believed him to be. But what if she was wrong? It wouldn't be the first time. Or even the second or third.

Worse yet, what if she committed to him, made promises, then found she couldn't follow through? She knew what her leaving had done to him the first time. If she did it again, how long would it take him to pick up the pieces? She couldn't do that to someone as sweet and selfless as Cody.

"Have you prayed about it?" Courtney's tone was sympathetic.

"Yes. But before tonight my prayers were to help me guard my heart and not be hurt again." Out loud, the words had a selfish ring. She turned around to face the bank of boxes, letting her head rest against one of them. "I can't bring myself to say no, though. I don't know if I can commit to what he's asking for, but I'm afraid that if I walk away again, I won't get another chance. And I believe that's something I'd regret for the rest of my life."

"It sounds like you might have just made your decision."

The tightness in her chest fled, coming out in a relaxed smile. Yes, she'd made her decision. She would risk anything to love and be loved by Cody. Even her heart.

She thanked Courtney and ended the call. When she turned toward the door, two figures stood at the bank of windows. Her heart fluttered as Cody walked through the front door leading Alcee. His eyes were filled with hesitation. When she held out her hand, the hesitation turned to hope.

"I'm sorry I had to think about this so long."

One side of his mouth lifted. "You had me worried. I think I wore down the asphalt with my pacing."

"I'll admit, I had to phone a friend. I hope you don't mind."

"That depends on what you and your friend came up with."

She pulled her hand free and wrapped both arms around his neck, still clutching his letter. "I think you'll be happy with my answer."

His concern dissolved in a broad smile as his arms circled her waist. The joy in his eyes confirmed she was making the right decision.

"I'll be honest." She drew in a deep breath. "The thought of making a commitment like this scares me silly. All my adult life, I've been so determined to not end up where my mom is, having to get my dad's permission for everything she wants to do. So I always tried to keep my relationships casual. Sometimes that worked. Sometimes it didn't. But after ten years of dealing with losers and users, I'd decided I was through. From here on out, it was going to be just me and Alcee."

He gave her a crooked smile. "Alcee *is* pretty good company. She's not a bad conversationalist, either."

Erin grinned. "She's a better companion than a lot of men I've met."

"I hope you're not including me in that group."

"You're the exception to the rule." She once again grew serious. "As much as the idea of commitment scares me, the thought of living the rest of my life without you is unbearable. I love you, Cody, and I'm so glad you didn't give up on me."

He tightened his embrace. "I love you, too. Now that there's not a burning building ready to collapse around us, can we try that kiss again?"

She grinned. "I think that's a great idea."

He dipped his head, and she met him halfway, rising up on her toes. When his lips met hers, her eyes fluttered shut, and she relaxed into him. This time there was no fear or desperation. Just an all-consuming sense of contentment. This was where she belonged.

At Alcee's bark, he pulled away. "I think she's being protective."

"No, she's being jealous. Neither of us is paying attention to her."

She cupped the dog's face in her hands and scratched her cheeks. "You're spoiled. You know that?"

When she straightened, he drew her into his embrace again. The fluorescents above them bathed their stark surroundings in harsh white light. Not the dreamiest setting. But anywhere with Cody was romantic.

She laid her head against his chest. "This is a big step for me, but I recognize what you had to go through to get to this point. Letting down your guard enough to trust that I won't walk away like your mother and your wife couldn't have been easy. I decided if you're willing to face your fears, then I could find the courage to face mine."

"I'm glad you did." He moved his hand up her back and entwined his fingers in her hair. "So does this mean you'll marry me?"

"No."

His arms fell, and he stepped back, brows drawn together. "Why not?"

"Because you haven't asked."

Relief spilled out in laughter. "I can remedy that." He took both of her hands and dropped to one knee. "Erin Jeffries, will you marry me?"

"If you give me a little time to get used to the idea, yes."

He rose, wrapped her in a sideways hug and led her toward the door. "You can have all the time you need."

When they reached the parking lot, he opened the back passenger door of his truck. Alcee hopped in and stretched across the seat.

Erin nodded in her direction. "That's our ring bearer there."

"Absolutely. From what I've seen, she'll have no problem learning how to walk down an aisle carrying a silk pillow."

Cody opened her door, and she climbed in, shaking her head.

"What?"

"I can't believe you asked me to marry you in a post office lobby."

"Hey, this all started with you digging me out of rubble."

She slid both arms around his neck. "I guess we don't do anything normally."

"You never have." He leaned in to kiss her on the tip of the nose. "And I love you for it."

* * * * *

LOVE INSPIRED

Stories to uplift and inspire

Fall in love with Love Inspired—
inspirational and uplifting stories of faith
and hope. Find strength and comfort in
the bonds of friendship and community.
Revel in the warmth of possibility and the
promise of new beginnings.

Sign up for the Love Inspired newsletter
at **LoveInspired.com** to be the first
to find out about upcoming titles,
special promotions and exclusive content.

CONNECT WITH US AT:

f Facebook.com/LoveInspiredBooks

🐦 Twitter.com/LoveInspiredBks

IF YOU ENJOYED THIS BOOK
WE THINK YOU WILL ALSO LOVE

LOVE INSPIRED SUSPENSE
INSPIRATIONAL ROMANCE

Courage. Danger. Faith.

Find strength and determination in stories
of faith and love in the face of danger.

6 NEW BOOKS AVAILABLE EVERY MONTH!

"Marshal Nelson? Colt? Wait up!"

He turned to find Morganne jogging toward him. "Do you need something?" He stopped and faced her. "I can help board up your broken window."

"Where are you going?"

"I need to check in with my boss and talk to the witness who claimed to see Winston. I need to hit the road."

"Give me a few minutes to change and I'll be ready to go."

He blinked and tipped the brim of his cowboy hat up to see her face more clearly. He met her gaze head-on. "I'm sorry, but you really don't have any jurisdiction in this matter. You're a local cop, Morganne, and this is a federal case."

"You have jurisdiction, and I can help." Her wide eyes beseeched him. "Come on, Colt. If Blaine's the one who shot at my house, it's only fair to allow me the opportunity to assist in finding him."

"What if this attack was the result of something else?" He wasn't entirely convinced the shooter was Blaine. "I'm sure there are other bad guys you've helped put away."

She shrugged. "None as dangerous as Blaine. You and I both know you're here in Jackson because Blaine was sighted in the area. And there is a possibility he came to exact his revenge."

He couldn't deny it. And he'd already considered asking for her help, as she knew Blaine Winston the best of anyone.

If the shooter was Winston, there was always the possibility the guy would return to make another attempt to kill Morganne.

She'd be safer with him. She might be a trained law enforcement officer, but he didn't like the idea of Winston getting hold of her a second time.

Apprehending a known serial killer before he harmed anyone else was the most important thing.

And if Morganne could help even in the smallest way, Colt refused to pass on the opportunity.

He only hoped he didn't live to regret it.

Don't miss
Fugitive Hunt *by Laura Scott wherever*
Love Inspired Suspense books and ebooks are sold.

LoveInspired.com